D0721010

Praise for the Whisper Horse Novels

"Like slipping into a warm bath, Herkness eases readers into her story. She's spot on when it comes to tugging at the heartstrings, and the vibrant setting of the West Virginia mountains is perfect for characters who will haunt readers long after the last page is turned. Animal lovers will especially be delighted." —*RT Book Reviews*, 4 stars for *Take Me Home*

"Her extensive background in poetry lends a symmetrical, lyrical quality to her prose." —*West Virginia South* on *Take Me Home*

"The small-town vibe and endearing characters keep the pages turning as their struggles and strengths evolve throughout the book. Fans of horses will enjoy this sensitive take on horse whispering as well as the bonds that can form between horse and rider. The romance is compelling, with a couple whose realistic problems and vices keep it firmly grounded in the real world." —*RT Book Reviews*, 4 stars for *Country Roads*

"A charming—and hot!—tale of falling in love for all the right reasons, *Country Roads* should be on your must-read list!" —Mariah Stewart, *New York Times* bestselling author

The Place
I Belong

A WHISPER HORSE NOVEL

*We all need a place
to belong.*

Nancy Hunkness

Also by Nancy Herkness

A Bridge to Love

Shower of Stars

Music of the Night

Other Whisper Horse Novels

Take Me Home

Country Roads

The Place I Belong

A WHISPER HORSE NOVEL

NANCY HERKNESS

Montlake
Romance

The characters and events portrayed in this book are fictitious. Any similarity to real persons, living or dead, is coincidental and not intended by the author.

Text copyright © 2014 Nancy Herkness
All rights reserved.

No part of this book may be reproduced, or stored in a retrieval system, or transmitted in any form or by any means, electronic, mechanical, photocopying, recording, or otherwise, without express written permission of the publisher.

Published by Montlake Romance, Seattle

www.apub.com

ISBN-13: 9781477823002
ISBN-10: 147782300X

Cover design by Laura Klynstra

Library of Congress Control Number: 2014900303

Printed in the United States of America

To my brilliant critique partners:
Miriam Allenson, Catherine Greenfeder,
and Lisa Verge Higgins.
You know when to praise
and when to raise the bar.

Chapter 1

"*W*E HAVE AN EMERGENCY PATIENT. GUNSHOT WOUND," the receptionist said, sticking her head into Hannah's office.

Jumping up from her new desk, Hannah yanked her long, blond hair back into a tight ponytail. She grabbed her wrinkled lab coat from the chair where she'd tossed it ten minutes before, barely catching the stethoscope that slipped out of the pocket. "How bad?" she asked, starting for the door.

"The dog limped in under his own steam, but there's a lot of blood on the floor," Estelle said. "A German Shepherd named Trace."

Relief loosened the knot of concern in Hannah's chest. If the dog was walking, the wound shouldn't be too severe. "Ask Heidi to prep for surgery, just in case," she said as she strode down the hallway, her sneakers silent on the blue tile floor.

"Got it. He's in Room 4. His owner's Adam Bosch." Estelle continued on toward the back of the hospital where the veterinary technicians were working.

Hannah tried to remember where she'd heard that name before as she eased open the examining room door. For a moment she saw nothing but what seemed like a deep shadow in the center of the brightly lit room. Then the man raised his head and she fell into eyes so dark it was difficult to find the brown in them. She realized he was bent over a large, black dog lying on the examining table. Because his hair and the dog's were nearly identical in color, and Adam Bosch wore a black shirt, the two had merged into one lightless shape. "Hello, Mr. Bosch. I'm Dr. Linden."

"Where's Dr. Tim?" Adam asked, the slashes of his brows drawing down into a frown.

"Out of town," Hannah said, moving to the dog. She'd been at the veterinary hospital for only two months, so people were still surprised not to find Dr. Tim Arbuckle there. He'd hired her because he wanted to travel the world with his art dealer wife, and Hannah had been grateful to get the job. "I understand Trace may have been shot."

Adam gave a curt nod. "I found him lying on the back porch with blood on his fur and the floor. The only thing I could think of was a hunter mistook him for a bear and shot at him." The tendons in Adam's neck stood out. He was obviously struggling to keep his fear for his dog's life under control. Hannah was a sucker for someone who genuinely cared about their animal, and she found herself warming to the man.

As she reached toward Trace, his owner straightened, although he kept his hands on the Shepherd's head and flank. Hannah noticed several scars on his fingers. "Careful. He's not friendly to strangers," Adam said.

"I think I can handle him." Hannah bent to examine the dog, stroking him soothingly as she probed for injuries under the blood-matted fur on his right side. "Hello, Trace. What a handsome fellow you are!"

Her compliment was not an idle one; the German Shepherd had to weigh over a hundred pounds, with a fit, muscular body and a healthy sheen to his coat. Mr. Bosch took good care of his pet, another point in his favor. She explored around the wound on Trace's right shoulder, and the dog whimpered but offered no resistance. She watched his ears, felt the tension in his body, listened to his breathing, and checked his position on the table. Absorbing all the clues Trace was giving her, she relaxed. The dog was not communicating serious pain or injury.

"It looks like a bullet wound to me," Adam said.

She studied the raw, bloody slash marring Trace's beautiful coat and decided the man was probably right. "I hate hunting season," she murmured.

"So do I."

The vehemence in his voice made her glance up at him. Once she got past the hypnotic depths of his eyes, she saw the anguish etching lines around his mouth. "It's just a graze," she said, her sympathy fully engaged. "No internal organs were hit. It didn't even reach the muscle."

"I checked him over and couldn't find anything else wrong," he said, tension still holding his broad shoulders rigid.

"Let me clean and bandage this, and I'll get a vet tech to help turn him over so I can check his left side," she said, opening drawers to gather her supplies. "However, I don't think we'll find anything else. He's not showing any signs of significant distress."

"No need for a vet tech," Adam said. "It's better if I handle Trace."

"He's a big dog," Hannah said, eyeing the bulk of the Shepherd as she shaved the hair away from the wound.

"He didn't react well to the vet tech on his last visit. Only Dr. Tim could handle him. And now you."

"If I can't manage to touch a patient, I'm not a very competent vet," she said with a smile, hoping a little self-deprecation would relax him. Of course, the Chicago media had portrayed her as both heartless and inept. She shoved the thought away as she finished trimming around the wound before swabbing it and applying a sterile pad. Trace flinched but lay still. She scratched behind his ear. "What a good boy you are!"

She slid her hands under the dog and traced along ribs and bones to make sure turning him wouldn't do any damage. He exhibited no symptoms of further tenderness or injury, even thumping his tail on the table when she gave him a little tickle along his tummy.

"Incredible," his owner muttered.

Hannah believed in giving her patients a little pleasure to offset their pain. Evidently, the black-browed Mr. Bosch disapproved.

"Nothing seems broken, so let's turn him," she said briskly.

As the two of them gently rolled the dog over, their heads came within a few inches of each other and an intriguing aroma of spices filled her nostrils. She was nearly overcome by a desire to bury her nose in Adam's thick, dark hair to inhale more. She jerked her head away, locking her attention on the dog.

A thorough examination of Trace's left side showed no fresh trauma, but she could feel ridges of what seemed to be scar tissue beneath his fur. She frowned as she traced them with her fingertips.

"What is it?" Adam asked, his voice tight with worry.

"Has Trace been injured before?" Because he had come in as an emergency case, she hadn't checked the dog's history.

"He tangled with a bear a few years ago. Dr. Tim saved his life."

"Ah, that explains the scars." Hannah lifted her head to take her first real look at Adam, discovering he had an aquiline nose, a marked cleft in his chin, and a noticeable five o'clock shadow. Her experience with her ex-fiancé had taught her not to trust good-looking men, but she couldn't repress a little shiver of appreciation. And he cared about his dog. "There's nothing to worry about. The wound should heal fine. I'll show you how to clean and dress it, and I'll want to see him again next week to make sure there's no infection."

She'd never before seen a person literally sag in relief, but Adam Bosch seemed to be held upright only by his palms braced on the examining table. "Thank you," he breathed. "I'd never forgive myself if he'd been seriously injured again."

"Let's get him to sit up so I can put a bandage on him to hold the gauze in place."

He pushed up from the table, the muscles in his forearms flexing under the shift in weight. "Sit." The note of authority in Adam's voice sent another zing of surprise through her. He sounded like a man accustomed to being obeyed. Trace came to a sitting position instantly. "Good dog," Adam said, as the dog kept his gaze on his master, ears alert and upright.

"He's well-trained," Hannah said, winding a bright-green bandage around the dog's chest and front legs.

"I claim no credit. As a former police dog, he's used to taking orders," Adam said.

Hannah made the mistake of glancing up from her task and was ensnared by the charm of his smile. It emphasized the full curve of his lower lip while giving the corners of his eyes appealing crinkles. He was a shockingly attractive man. She jerked her gaze back to her patient, who sat like a statue on the table as she wrapped him in fabric. "You are such a sweetheart," she said, unable to resist rubbing her cheek against Trace's gleaming head as she scratched under his chin. He gave her a wet doggy kiss.

"Unbelievable," Adam said.

Annoyed at his repeated comments on her bedside manner, Hannah gave him a cool look. "Do you have a problem with my treatment of your dog?"

He leaned back in surprise. "Absolutely not. Why?"

"You keep muttering things under your breath."

"Trace is generally a one-man dog but with you he acts like a marshmallow."

"Mmm." Hannah didn't want to admit she took pleasure in his comment. "You really shouldn't let him outside in the woods until hunting season is over."

His finely sculpted nostrils flared with anger. "I didn't."

"Oh, sorry." She felt a twinge of regret at accusing him unjustly. "He escaped?" A dog as well-trained as this one wouldn't generally bolt, but every creature had its quirks.

"My son let him out." Adam winced as though he hadn't meant to say that. The rueful smile he gave her was forced. "He's thirteen and not as well trained as Trace."

"Oh, teenagers." Hannah gave him an understanding grimace. She had cousins near that age so she was familiar with the challenges of dealing with them. "They're tough."

"You seem to know something about them," he said, the smile vanishing into a sharp focus on her face. "Do you have children?"

"Good heavens, no. I have teenaged cousins. Their mother complains a lot." She adjusted a fold of the bandage to lie flat.

"Do the cousins have pets?" he asked.

"A Labrador and a couple of guinea pigs," she answered absently. Taking a final turn around Trace's chest, she tucked the end of the bandage neatly under itself and tugged at it to check its security.

"Do you have any ideas on how to teach a teenager the responsibilities of dog ownership?"

"I'm no expert, but maybe if you show him Trace's wound when you change the bandage, he'll understand the consequences of being careless." She went to the computer and began typing in notes on the dog's condition.

"I think he did it deliberately."

Shock made her spin around to face him. "Are you sure? Kids aren't generally malicious that way. Most of them like dogs."

Adam scraped his fingers through his hair. "His action was aimed at me." He took two short steps away, his gaze on the floor, before he pivoted to look at her with those fathomless, dark eyes. "I don't want Trace injured because my son and I are having issues."

Hannah hesitated, her sympathy reluctantly engaged. "He could join the 4-H Club and raise his own lamb or calf. That would impress on him the responsibilities of having an animal."

Adam's expression brightened. "Maybe Matt could volunteer here. Then he would see how much you care about the animals."

Having a young, untrained observer at the clinic could be problematic, Hannah thought, *but Estelle could probably handle the kid, since she was a former first-grade teacher.* As she opened her mouth to suggest it, Adam spoke again, a note of entreaty in his voice. "Would you talk to Matt?"

"*Me?*" Hannah was flabbergasted. "I'm a veterinarian, not a child psychologist."

"That's why you would be the best teacher." His eyes bored into hers. "You can make him understand animals are living beings. That Trace isn't a pawn to be used to strike at me."

"But I don't know how to talk to teenagers any more than you do." The man must be at his wit's end. Uncomfortable, Hannah turned back to the computer.

She heard footsteps and felt a light touch on her shoulder, making her look around. Adam stood close.

"Show him." His tone combined pleading and persuasion. "Let him see you working with the animals people bring in. Let him see how the owners feel about their pets."

Dragging a surly teenager through a day at the office sounded like her worst nightmare.

He must have seen refusal in her expression because he gave her a smile of such seductive power she nearly gasped. "Just for one day," he said. "I'll repay your kindness with dinner for you and a companion at my restaurant, The Aerie, anytime you want to come. As my guests. Please."

The sudden switch to practiced charm made her flash back to her first meeting with Ward. He'd wooed her with the same smiling persistence, making her believe in the Cinderella story of a charismatic, powerful man falling for a shy, unglamorous veterinarian. Then he'd crushed her. She wanted Adam Bosch to go away so she could shove her ex-fiancé back into the dungeon she'd built for him in her memory. "I'm sorry," she said gently. "I'm not the right person for this job."

With a gesture of acceptance, Adam turned back to his dog.

Guilt washed over her as she saw Trace's tail move on the table when he caught his master's gaze on him. How could she let this sweet, gorgeous dog be further endangered by teenage rebellion? She twisted her stethoscope between her fingers. "Okay, I'll do it, if you think it will keep Trace safe," she said. "I assume your son goes to school?"

Adam nodded, hope lighting his face.

"Tomorrow's Saturday, so you can drop him off here at eight and pick him up at four."

If she had found his smile dazzling before, it now stunned her with its intensity because it reached deep into his eyes. "You are a lifesaver, Dr. Linden. You will have a bottle of the finest wine in my cellar with your meal."

"I'm doing this for Trace, not for dinner," she said, knowing she sounded ungracious. At least now she understood why his name was familiar. The Aerie was famous well beyond the borders of Sanctuary.

Unbothered by her churlishness, he chuckled in a smooth baritone. "I hope you'll change your mind after you taste my food." He offered his hand and she put hers in it, feeling the strength of his grip. "I'll provide lunch for you and your staff tomorrow to prove my mettle," he said.

She pulled her hand free and moved to the opposite side of the examining table. "Sounds great. Now let me show you how to treat Trace's wound."

Hannah had just finished up the notes on Trace when Estelle walked into her office. "I've locked the front door and forwarded the phone to the answering service," the older woman said.

"Do you have a minute to sit down?" Hannah asked, waving to the two comfortable new armchairs in front of her handsome teak desk. The furniture, which she'd ordered at Tim's insistence, had arrived two days before. She had to admit it was nice not to have a mismatched set of his castoffs anymore.

Hannah came around the desk and sat in the other chair, wishing she could emulate the elegance of the silver-haired receptionist. While Estelle wore ladylike black pumps with her stylish lavender pantsuit, Hannah had on her standard office attire of khaki slacks, green polo shirt, and running shoes—the same thing her boss usually wore in the office. That thought made her smile inwardly. Tim was a foot and a half taller and weighed at least a hundred and fifty pounds more than she did. They didn't much resemble each other except in their concern for their patients. "I got myself into something I don't know how to get out of."

Estelle's gaze sharpened. "I'll see if I can help." She perched on the edge of one chair, back straight, ankles crossed. "Mr. Bosch invited you to dinner and you accepted?"

It had become something of a joke around the veterinary hospital that the town of Sanctuary had decided Hannah needed a boyfriend. For the past month, they had equipped the single males of the town with various creatures in more or less need of medical attention and sent them in when Hannah was working. She had a soft heart, even when it came to humans, so turning them down wasn't easy for her. Estelle had taken to telling her whether her next patient's owner was married or single, so she could prepare herself.

"I wish it were that simple."

"That's a shame, because he owns The Aerie. It's the fancy restaurant on top of Two Creek Mountain. People come in by helicopter to eat there."

Hannah had come to Sanctuary, West Virginia, to escape "fancy" so she wasn't tempted.

Estelle shocked her by adding, "He's quite handsome too."

"But he has a son!" Hannah exclaimed.

Estelle nodded. "Matt. His mother drowned about four months ago, leaving the boy to Adam's custody."

Hannah rocked back in her chair. "His mother just died? This is worse than I thought." That meant Adam was dealing with the death of his wife on top of his son's intractability. No wonder he was grasping at straws when it came to his child. "Is that why Adam was wearing black? He's in mourning for his wife?"

"Oh, they weren't married, dear," Estelle said. "The boy's last name is McNally. His mother was Irish. He'd never been to Sanctuary before she died."

Now Adam appeared to be a cold-hearted charmer who seduced women with his handsome face and silver tongue and left them to face the consequences alone. It reminded her of Ward's desertion. Hannah pulled her thoughts up abruptly. After what she had been through in Chicago, she should know better than to judge someone without knowing all the facts of the situation. Still it was hard not to think less of him, knowing he had avoided any parental duties until he had no choice in the matter. It explained his problems with his son.

Now she was convinced he needed a therapist, not a veterinarian, to deal with them. She considered her own dilemma, which had gone from bad to worse with this news. Her heart hurt for everyone involved. "According to Adam, his son deliberately let Trace outside, even though he knew it was hunting season. Adam wants Matt to understand that animals have feelings and significance, so he asked me to let the kid shadow me. Tomorrow." Hannah rubbed her palms over her thighs as the idea of having a grief-stricken, thirteen-year-old boy by her side for an entire day made her break out in a cold sweat. She didn't want to add to the poor kid's problems.

"And I thought it was just Dr. Tim everyone told their troubles to while he was taking care of their animals," Estelle said, shaking her head. "That's more than I've heard of Adam Bosch admitting to anyone before. He usually keeps himself to himself."

"I know I agreed to take the kid tomorrow, but do you think I could put him off until Tim gets back?" Hannah pleaded as panic set in. "Wouldn't it be better for the boy to have a male bonding experience?"

"Dr. Tim won't be back for ten days, which leaves the dog in danger a long time."

Hannah slumped in defeat. "How did I get myself talked into this?"

"Well, he's a very charming man. Not to mention those smoldering good looks."

"I liked him better when he was genuinely upset over his dog than when he turned on the charm." She was bothered by the fizz of awareness she'd felt. She should know better. "It seemed fake." Ward had done the same thing, using his charisma like a weapon, turning it off and on at will.

"I suppose it *might* be a skill he uses professionally," Estelle allowed, her lips pursed. "He caters to some very demanding, high-powered customers so perhaps he's cultivated it beyond what's natural to him, but I find him well-mannered and pleasant."

"Hmm." Hannah didn't want to discuss Adam any longer because the topic kept conjuring up comparisons with her ex. "Do you know anything more about Matt? If I can't avoid my day with him, I might as well prepare myself."

"Nothing of significance, but I still have friends in the school system so I'll make inquiries and pass any information along first thing in the morning." Before her retirement Estelle had taught virtually everyone—and often their children as well—in the town of Sanctuary.

"Anything you can find out would be appreciated," Hannah said. She grimaced. "Sorry you had to stay late for all this drama."

"My husband knows when to put the casserole in, and it won't hurt him any to set the table himself every now and then." Estelle stood and walked to the door, where she hesitated. "If Adam Bosch offered to cook for me, I'd take him up on it," she said before she walked out of the office.

"I'll see how lunch is first," Hannah muttered. She hadn't mentioned the bribe of dinner at The Aerie to Estelle because she didn't have anyone to take there. She had no intention of raising the hopes of any of the town's bachelors by inviting one of them, and it seemed pathetic to go by herself. She knew The Aerie's style because she'd attended political fundraisers with Ward at places like it; it was one of those restaurants where a meal stretched to three hours and involved a different wine with each course. You needed a companion—preferably one you liked a great deal—for that kind of dinner.

Now she had to do some fast research on thirteen-year-old boys. She glanced at her stainless-steel wristwatch. There was time to make a call before she headed home to feed her dogs and cats. Hannah's aunt Carolyn had teenaged sons; she should have some helpful hints. She slid her cell phone out of her pocket and dialed.

"Hannah! When are you coming down here to visit? We missed seeing you this summer!" Carolyn said, her Texas twang belting through the receiver.

Hannah winced. Last summer she'd been mired in the scandal that had ended her engagement and her veterinary career in Chicago. "I just started a new job, so I won't have a vacation for a while."

"What about Thanksgiving? They can't work you the whole weekend."

"I'm on duty the day before and the day after," Hannah said. She would be happy to work the holiday itself, but Tim closed the practice, and his wife, Claire, insisted she join them for Thanksgiving dinner. "I called to ask your advice."

"I love giving advice. Who is he?"

"Matt McNally."

"Nice name. Tell me all about him." Carolyn's voice quivered with excitement.

"He's thirteen."

"Thirteen?! Honey, I know you got burned by Ward but you shouldn't go around cradle-robbing."

"Funny," Hannah said, but her lips twitched into a smile. Carolyn could always cheer her up. "Listen, I promised to let this kid follow me around at work all day tomorrow so he won't let his father's dog outside during hunting season. His father wants it to be a sort of object lesson in the importance of animals. So I need to know what to do with the kid."

"First, let's go back to his father. Is he married or divorced and would you kick him out of bed?"

"He's single now. I don't know about his marital history other than that. As for the other question, I wouldn't let him *in* my bed. He's got that slick, smiling kind of charm that reminds me of Ward." She found herself not wanting to share the more tragic parts of Adam and Matt's story; it seemed too much like gossiping.

"Not every charming man is a snake like your ex, you know," Carolyn said. "Unless he's also a politician."

"No, this one owns a very fancy restaurant up on a mountain."

"Are you talking about The Aerie?"

"How did you know?"

"Because it's world famous, honey child, and we keep up with things like that in Texas. Besides, I know you work in Sanctuary, West Virginia, and that's where The Aerie is." The fervor was back in Carolyn's voice. "Adam Bosch is the owner and he's a hunk and a half. They profiled him as one of the great restaurateurs on television a couple of years ago. I've been begging Kevin to take me there ever since."

"You two can have my bribe then. For taking the kid on, I get a dinner for two *gratis*. It's all yours."

"Tempting, but I have a better idea. You go with the chef himself. After all, I'm happily married."

"You won't be for long if you keep calling chefs 'hunks and a half'," Hannah observed. "Forget about the father. Help me out with the son. What do I do with him?"

"Well, let's see, he's going to hate you for ruining his Saturday, so he'll be disagreeable and uncooperative. Probably monosyllabic. I suggest you handle him like you would a particularly difficult cat."

Relief flooded Hannah. She understood cats. "I can do that. Thank you."

"I told you I'm good at advice. And now I'm going to give you some about Matt's father. You should buy yourself some black lace—"

"Sorry, I have to go. Someone just came in and all the dogs are barking. Talk to you soon!" Hannah punched the disconnect button and grinned as Carolyn's number showed up on her incoming calls screen after a few seconds. She dropped the ringing phone in her pocket as she left her office. She couldn't wait to get home to the uncomplicated affection of her three dogs and two cats.

"Stay!" Adam commanded as he opened the back of his SUV to find Trace standing in the nest of blood-stained blankets with an eager look on his face. He wanted to ease the dog out of the car so as not to reopen the wound. "Let me give you a hand, boy." He put his arms under Trace's belly before bracing himself to lift a hundred-plus pounds of dog and gently lower him to the river stones paving his driveway. "Heel."

Trace took up position beside Adam's left thigh and fixed his gaze on his master, awaiting the next command. Relief that his dog was all right overwhelmed Adam, and he knelt in front of the big black Shepherd, scratching him in all his favorite spots.

He'd bought Trace when he moved to his isolated home in Sanctuary, thinking the fearsome-looking creature would deter any would-be burglars. Much to his surprise, the dog had become devoted to him, and Trace's unwavering, nonjudgmental love had worked its way into the darker corners of Adam's soul, dispelling some of the bleakness he could no longer drown with alcohol.

"Thank God I didn't lose you," he said, burying his face in the dog's thick ruff.

As he absorbed the comfort of Trace's presence, Adam felt guilty about his initial abruptness toward Dr. Linden. He'd been so taken aback to encounter a pretty blonde who appeared to be about eighteen years old, rather than the confidence-inspiring bulk of Dr. Tim, that his manners had deserted him. Yes, he'd been upset about Trace, but that was no excuse for his behavior.

He could keep his cool in a kitchen serving eighty demanding customers a nine-course meal. Certainly, one female veterinarian shouldn't be more than he could manage.

In his own defense, Dr. Linden hadn't been especially cordial. However, when she focused on Trace, the concern on her face had quelled his irritation at her brusque manner toward him. It wasn't treatment he was accustomed to, and he had to laugh at himself for being offended. "I'm getting swelled up with my own self-importance," he said, ruffling Trace's fur.

What had fascinated him were her strange moments of stillness, when she had simply stared at Trace. He had the sense the woman and the dog were communicating on some level he couldn't access. It was eerie but comforting. When Dr. Linden said the dog wasn't seriously injured, he had believed her.

Then all common sense had deserted him when he insisted the veterinarian allow Matt to spend the day with her. He put that down to sheer desperation. He had no idea how to handle the son he'd never heard of until four months ago, a son who didn't want him as a father. Not that Adam blamed the boy for that.

However, until the private investigator he'd hired could find some other relative who might be a more capable parent, the two of them were forced to live with each other. He made every allowance for the boy's grief and tried to draw him out about his mother's death, even offering to find a trained grief counselor for him to talk with. That suggestion had been met with such blazing hostility he'd avoided the subject of Matt's mother ever since.

All he asked was that his son follow the bare minimum of guidelines necessary for civilized behavior, but that appeared to be as impossible as cooking a perfect soufflé over a campfire. The boy's room was a pigsty, but Adam had decided to cede that territory to Matt, simply closing the door when he couldn't bear the chaos or the odor wafting from it. Only Sarah Duckworth, the live-in housekeeper he'd hired when Matt arrived, could bring temporary order to the chaos when she ventured in once a week.

Endangering Trace's life was a whole different level of rebellion, though, one Adam would not tolerate. If he didn't get satisfactory results from Matt's day with Dr. Linden, he would be forced to take stronger measures. Steeling himself, he rose to his feet and walked up the wide shallow steps to his front door with Trace by his side. Pushing open the door, he grimaced as the blare of rap music assaulted his ears. Trace whimpered and laid his ears flat back on his head.

Adam strode across the living room to the media room, the most self-indulgent addition to the house he'd built on Two Creek Mountain. The lights were off, and a movie that appeared to involve nothing but four-letter words and car crashes was flashing across the wall-wide screen. Matt was sprawled in one of the forest-green plush chairs, his ratty red high-tops resting on the back of the seat in front of him, a bowl of popcorn spilling over into the chair beside him.

Adam hit the lights and the kill switch on the projection system at the same time.

A loud sigh emanated from his son's prone form.

"Matt."

His son didn't move. "What?"

"I'd like you to look at Trace."

Another loud sigh. Matt slowly lowered his feet and twisted around in his seat.

Adam considered forcing the boy to stand up and come to him but decided that was a battle he didn't want to fight. He signaled Trace to accompany him to his son's chair.

He stopped in front of the chair and regarded the child in it. It still gave him a shock to see those brilliant blue eyes in a face that otherwise was almost identical to his own when he was young. Although the attorney had offered a DNA test, Adam hadn't needed it once he saw the boy. Matt's face still held the roundness of pre-puberty, but the features were all Adam's.

"Trace was shot," Adam said, knowing the bright-green bandages made the wound appear more severe than it really was but wanting to impress Matt with the consequences of his actions. He was reassured when he saw Matt shift his gaze to the dog and flinch just enough so Adam caught it.

"The stupid dog wanted to go out," Matt said.

"Trace doesn't know he's endangering his life by going outside. You do."

Matt shrugged.

Adam released Trace from his side. The big dog lay down, putting his head on his paws with a whiff of a sigh. "Matt, I need to know you won't let Trace out again without a leash until hunting season is over."

"Fine. I won't."

"Thank you." Adam leaned his hip against the back of the chair in front of his son. "I've arranged an outing for you tomorrow."

Matt just stared at him, those blue eyes compelling in their vividness.

"You're going to spend the day with the veterinarian who treated Trace. You need to appreciate that animals are living beings who feel pain, just like a person."

"I've got better things to do."

"I'm afraid you'll have to postpone them. This is not negotiable." Especially since he'd already coerced Hannah into agreeing to it.

Matt hurled himself out of his chair and stalked out of the room, muttering. Adam picked out the words "asshole," "jerk," and "wanker," before his son's voice faded out of earshot.

He collapsed onto a chair and dropped his head into his hands. He was going to have to make one heck of a lunch for Dr. Linden.

Chapter 2

"MR. BOSCH AND MATT ARE HERE." ESTELLE'S VOICE came through the intercom.

Panic fluttered in Hannah's chest as she closed the last of the patient records she'd been reading prior to her appointments, noting which animals were best kept away from an inexperienced teenager.

She slipped on her white coat and headed for the supply room where Sonya Woods was working. She'd briefed the veterinary technician on her temporary babysitting responsibilities already. Sticking her head in the door, she said, "You're on."

Sonya closed the cabinet door and "tsked" as she fell into step beside Hannah. "You didn't flinch in the face of Slasher, the half-wolf, half-pit bull, but you're terrified by a thirteen-year-old boy?"

"I'm not a kid person."

"Kids are a lot like pets. They just want to be loved."

"But they aren't cute and furry," Hannah said and opened the door to the reception area, waving Sonya through.

Adam Bosch stood in the middle of the room, his hand on the shoulder of a boy who clearly carried his genes. Except for the kid's bright blue eyes. Hannah shifted her gaze back and forth between the two, noting the similarities and differences. Matt McNally was going to be a heartbreaker when he lost the last traces of childhood roundness.

Adam had hit heartbreaker and gone beyond. His fathomless gaze and sensual mouth tugged at some primitive place deep inside her. At least he wasn't pouring on the charm. A furrow between his black eyebrows indicated tension, and his free hand was clenched in a fist beside his thigh. The corners of his mouth turned upward, but the crinkles at the corners of his eyes were absent, so she didn't believe the smile was real.

"Dr. Linden, this is my son, Matt. Matt, Dr. Linden."

Hannah pasted on a nervous smile before she walked over to put out her hand. "Nice to meet you."

Without hesitation, Matt shook it. "Nice to meet you too, Dr. Linden."

Surprise and relief chased each other across Adam's face, and she saw him give his son's shoulder an approving squeeze before he released it.

Hannah waved Sonya forward and introduced her. Matt's eyes widened and a beet-red blush crept up his cheeks as Sonya shook hands with him. The vet tech had a long black braid, huge brown eyes, and a smile that brought grown men to their knees.

Hannah allowed herself a little smirk of triumph at her spot-on calculation of the effect the gorgeous vet tech would have on a thirteen-year-old boy. She glanced at Adam to check his reaction and was disconcerted to find his gaze on her rather than the dazzling Sonya. She raised her eyebrows at him.

A dimple appeared in his cheek. "What time shall I bring lunch and for how many?" he asked.

Hannah was thrown off balance. "You mean you don't just have take-out boxes we can stick in the refrigerator?"

His dimple disappeared into a mock frown. "I don't fix the sort of lunch that can sit around for several hours. I'll be delivering it fresh from the kitchen."

"Oh. I guess for five of us. The thing is lunchtime has to be flexible. If you come at noon, we might still be tied up."

"I'll adjust." He reached out and took her hand between both of his. "Thank you for doing this."

The warmth and strength of his hands wrapped around hers drew her eyes downward. His skin appeared very tan in contrast to her pale wrist and once again she noted the crisscrossing lines of scars.

"An occupational hazard," he said, somehow guessing her thoughts. "I play with knives."

She tugged her hand out from between his and held it up to show him the three parallel welts across the back of it. "Ditto, except I play with lion cubs."

"So not every animal succumbs to your charm like Trace?"

"Dogs are easy."

He nodded toward his son who was smiling shyly at Sonya. "So are boys, given the right incentive." The humor in his voice couldn't quite conceal a touch of wistfulness.

"You only have seven more years before he grows out of being a teenager," Hannah said, allowing herself to enjoy the banter just a bit.

His expression of horror was only half-pretense. "I'll be locked in a padded cell long before then. Happily."

The fact that she wanted him to take her hand again made Hannah pivot away sharply. "All right, let's give Matt the grand tour before the patients come pouring in."

Adam stepped back. "I'll be here at noon."

She nodded and watched him walk out the door, his stride long and relaxed. Only now did she notice he was dressed entirely in black again. She shrugged at the eccentricity and joined Matt. "Sonya, why don't you show him a couple of the operating rooms and whatever else he might be interested in before you bring him to my office?" She lowered her gaze a few inches to meet Matt's. "We'll go over the patients I'm going to see before lunch so you'll know what I'm dealing with."

"Yes, ma'am," Matt said.

At least the boy had nice manners.

"This is Matt. He's observing today," Hannah said to her fourth pet owner of the day.

"Nice to meet you, ma'am," the boy said to Mrs. Lewis before he plunked himself down on the rolling stool Hannah used when she was sitting at the computer.

Hannah kept up a running commentary of what she was checking for on Mrs. Lewis's calico cat, Binky. She slipped her stethoscope into her ears, just as Mrs. Lewis gave her a smile and jerked her head slightly in Matt's direction.

Hannah glanced sideways without moving her head and caught him staring down at his smartphone as he tapped on the screen. Bringing her eyes back to her client, she mouthed, "Teenagers."

Mrs. Lewis nodded with a glint of mischief in her eyes. "I guess Binky's brain tumor is going to turn him bright purple."

Hannah stifled a spurt of laughter, but Matt didn't even twitch.

"Yup, those giant lice are about eating the poor cat alive," Mrs. Lewis said.

Hannah grinned as she reached for a prepped hypodermic. "Guess we'll have to give him a vaccination to prevent magenta-spotted-if-you're-happy-and-you-know-it disease."

No response from Matt.

"This is his rabies vaccination," Hannah said with a resigned sigh. She had a ten-minute break right after Binky, so she was going to be forced to have a chat with Matt about paying attention, a prospect that made her stomach clench.

"Good luck," Mrs. Lewis said as Hannah helped her get Binky back into his carrier.

Hannah closed the door behind Mrs. Lewis and turned back to the boy. His cell phone was no longer visible. She gave him credit for good timing.

"Who's the next patient?" Matt asked, a mask of polite interest on his face.

Hannah leaned back against the examining table and crossed her arms. "Who was the last patient?"

For a moment he looked like a deer in headlights. Then he gave her a smile that brought out a dimple exactly where his father's was. "A cat."

"Well, you got that right. What color was the cat?"

"Black?"

"Nice try. What game are you playing on your phone?"

The boy's smile turned into defiance. "I wasn't playing a game. I was texting the friend I was supposed to be hanging out with before my father made me come here."

"Ah." Now what was she supposed to say? Adam had forced his son to give up his Saturday for this visit, so Matt's resentment didn't surprise her. "Look, your relationship with your father is your own business. However, when you drag a helpless dog into your battle, it's not okay. That's why you're here."

She was relieved to see a flash of guilt in his expression before the defiance hardened again. "You call Trace helpless? He could kill you," Matt said. "He was a police dog."

"He's helpless against a gun. When Trace is running through the woods, a hunter can't tell the difference between him and a bear."

"So you think it's okay to kill bears?"

Hannah recognized the attempt at diversion. "That's not the issue. Trace is a domesticated animal. He trusts people; the bear knows to run away. How would you have felt if your father had found Trace's dead body on the back porch?"

Matt wouldn't meet her eyes. "Bad. I didn't mean for him to get hurt." He shrugged. "I thought my father was just making another stupid rule I had to follow."

Every angle of his body spoke of loss and yearning, like a calf separated from its mother. Hannah had to keep her hands firmly tucked under her arms to fight off the urge to hug him. She was sure he'd be horrified if she did. She remembered Adam's desperation and thought she'd throw in a plug for him. "Maybe you're being unfair to your father. Maybe he's only making rules to keep you and Trace safe."

"Yeah, making the bed is a safety issue." Sarcasm dripped from Matt's voice.

"Well, you could strangle on your messy sheets. Or trip over them if they're dragging on the floor. Maybe suffocate under a pillow."

He shot her a glare of loathing.

"Lighten up," she said. "I was joking."

He hunched a shoulder.

"So have you paid any attention to what I've been doing all morning?" she asked.

"The first dog was a mutt named Ninja and it had hot spots. You gave it oral corticosteroids and Panalog." Now he met her eyes in a challenge. "The second patient was a Persian cat with a sinus infection. Its name was Tartufo, which is the wrong nationality for that breed."

"Not 'it.' The dog and the cat were both male so you refer to them as 'he.' These are living creatures with feelings just like yours. They can't articulate them in language but they feel them all the same." Still, she was impressed with his memory.

"I get it," he said. "All creatures great and small. The Lord God made them all."

The kid was quoting a hymn? Her surprise must have shown in her face because Matt gave her a wry grimace that reminded her of his father and said, "My mom and I went to Mass every Sunday."

He had mentioned his mother. That seemed like a good sign in their relationship. *Whoa, girl!* The kid would go home at the end of the day, and she expected never to see him again. So, no relationship. "Okay, so we have another couple of hours before your dad brings lunch. Here's my offer: you pay attention to the next two appointments because they're the most interesting. Then you can sit in my office and play games or text or whatever on your phone until 11:40. After that, you're with me again."

"That's a good deal," Matt said, his expression lighting up with relief. "Thank you, ma'am."

"Lose the 'ma'am.' I'm not fooled by the pretty manners," Hannah said, but she gave him a wink. "Keep the phone stowed out of sight or you'll lose office privileges."

Matt nodded, and his blue eyes crinkled at the corners, like Adam's. Now that his surly façade had crumbled, he had his father's charm without the years of polish. It must come naturally with the Bosch genes.

"Geez, what animal gets a needle that big?" Matt asked, watching as Hannah packed syringes into a carrying case for their farm patient visits.

"Cows. Horses. Hogs. It's all calculated by weight." Hannah latched the case. "You'll see this afternoon."

"What do you mean?" Matt eyed her with sudden disfavor just when she'd been congratulating herself on how well she was handling him.

"We're doing large-animal calls after lunch. Country vets handle all shapes and sizes. You have something against cows?"

He shook his head but the blank façade was back in place.

"You knew this was an all-day visit, right?" she probed.

"Yeah." He glanced away. "I just wasn't expecting to tramp around in manure."

She glanced down at his faded red high-tops. "I don't think it'll hurt your footwear any."

He shrugged. Before she could figure out what his latest problem was, Estelle came to the door of the supply room. "Mr. Bosch is here with quite a feast. He's setting it up in Dr. Tim's office at the conference table."

Hannah's stomach growled at the thought of food, and Matt shot her a scowl as though she'd betrayed him somehow. "What?" she asked.

"Nothing." He shoved away from the counter he'd been lounging against and plunged his hands into his jeans pockets. "My father's good at bribing people with food."

"Last I heard that wasn't illegal," Hannah said.

Matt managed a very creditable sneer. "At least you can't drink his fancy wine since you have to work after lunch." He stalked out of the supply room, leaving Estelle to give Hannah a questioning look.

Hannah lifted her hands palm out in a "don't ask me" gesture. "I wonder if he knows where he's going," she said, joining Estelle outside the door.

Matt had been paying more attention than Hannah realized because he headed unerringly for Tim's office door. She was torn between amusement and pity when the boy stopped just outside it and rearranged his posture and his features to express total indifference.

"His father has his work cut out for him with that one," Estelle murmured.

"I don't get it. Why should he resent his father so much? Adam doesn't seem like a bad guy. He loves his dog." Hannah knew that wasn't always an accurate gauge of a person's worth, but if she'd used it to measure Ward, she wouldn't have fallen in love with him. Her ex had merely tolerated her pets after they'd moved in together.

Estelle shook her head. "There's a lot we don't know about their history. And the boy's mother just died. Grief often expresses itself in anger, especially in adolescents, as I learned in my teaching days. His father may just be the most convenient target."

They both fell silent as they walked through the door. Sonya and Lucy were already there, goggling at what had once been a battered conference table but now could pass for a photo from a gourmet food magazine. A deceptively simple arrangement of exotic flowers in shades of burgundy and peach blazed in the center of a white linen tablecloth. Square plates of white china were nestled between clean, modern cutlery and tall, slender, glass tumblers.

Over it all hovered the shadowy presence of Adam Bosch, his hands moving at lightning speed as he finished dealing out the flatware and straightening a napkin. The sleeves of his black shirt were rolled back to his elbow, so Hannah could see the flex of muscle and tendon beneath his olive skin.

"What have you done with Tim's office?" Hannah asked to distract herself from her sudden fixation on Adam's forearms.

He lifted his gaze to hers and smiled. This time it was genuine, not calculated, and it socked her in the gut. "Just a little stage setting so you can better enjoy the food," he said.

The scent of something appetizing and well-spiced swirled past Hannah's nostrils. "If the smell is anything to go by, we won't have a problem with that."

"Everyone please have a seat," Adam said, pulling out one of the rolling wooden chairs. Tim refused to upgrade to more comfortable seating because he said hard seats kept meetings short and people awake.

Hannah did a quick survey. "There are only five place settings."

"I'm the chef and your server," Adam said, nodding toward the insulated bags arrayed on Tim's big oak desk as he continued to hold the chair. "Mrs. Wilson?"

Estelle gave him a downright flirtatious thank you as she gracefully seated herself, and Adam moved her chair into place.

He moved to the next chair and slid it out. "Dr. Linden?"

She'd already washed her hands and shed her soiled lab coat, so Hannah had no excuse not to approach Adam Bosch. She walked slowly though, trying to tamp down her disquieting reaction to him. Nearing the chair, she couldn't stop herself from taking note of the strong texture of his hair as it swept back from his face to curl over his collar. Up close his eyes revealed themselves as a rich, cognac brown rather than black. She forced herself to turn her back on him so she could sink onto the chair. His breath stirred the hairs that had fallen out of her ponytail and onto the nape of her neck. A delicious shiver slithered down her spine as he rolled her to the perfect distance from the table.

The other two ladies waited for him to seat them as well. Not that Hannah could blame them. Somehow his attention made her feel elegant and beautiful. Matt, of course, slouched into his chair with a hostile glare at his father.

Adam picked up a glass pitcher and poured what he said was iced tea into their glasses. Her first sip told her it was nothing like any iced tea she had tasted before. This version held flavors of caramel, cinnamon, and amaretto. She drank half the glass in one swooning gulp.

He wore a gratified smile as he refilled her glass. Surprise nipped at her when she realized her appreciation gave him pleasure. With his success and reputation, she would have thought amateur admiration wouldn't mean much to him.

She glanced across the table, catching Matt staring down at his lap, undoubtedly at his cell phone. Not wanting him to get in trouble with his father, she said the first thing she could think of to draw him into the conversation. "Matt, what was the joke Mr. Cahill's parrot told you? I missed the punch line."

The boy started and tried to cover up his inattention by grabbing his glass and taking a swig. "Um, it was kind of inappropriate."

"Knowing Bernie Cahill, that doesn't surprise me," Sonya said. "Go ahead, Matt. We can handle it."

Color washed up Matt's cheeks, and Hannah came to his rescue. "That's okay. I can never remember jokes anyway." She worried about just how inappropriate the parrot's joke had been.

"I heard a good one last week," Lucy said. "A fellow was driving along a country road and spotted an exotic bird flying overhead. The creature was black, with a huge red-and-gold beak. 'Hey, look! A toucan!' he yelled. 'Toucan nothin',' said his passenger. 'It's a crow with its beak stuck in a McDonald's fries carton.'"

Relief made Hannah laugh out loud and she threw Lucy a grateful glance just as a plate of exquisitely arranged greenery appeared in front of her. Adam was breezing around the table with plates of salad balanced all the way up his arm. He plucked them off and served them one at a time with his free hand. It was an amazing feat of coordination and concentration, yet he accomplished it with smiling ease before he stepped back so say, "Kale-apple salad with pancetta and maple vinaigrette. The kale is from our greenhouse, picked this morning. The apples are the last from The Aerie's orchard. *Bon appétit!*"

He cast a quick glance over the table before moving back to Tim's desk. Hannah forgot about her salad as she watched him flip open several bags to unpack covered plates at high speed. He arranged them on the desk before he pulled storage containers from the bags and began to add to each plate's contents. His movements were fluid and economical; his concentration total.

"Oh my goodness, this is unbelievably delicious." Sonya's exclamation yanked Hannah's attention back to the table.

"I never thought I could like a salad this much," Lucy agreed, chewing with her eyes closed.

Hannah snatched her fork up and jabbed it through a slice of apple and a leaf of what she assumed was kale. She cast a surreptitious glance at Adam to find a smile playing around his lips as he continued his preparations. He was definitely not immune to their praise. That made her like him more, rather than less.

She put the bite of salad in her mouth and felt a burst of flavors on her tongue. Adam's minimalist description did not begin to encompass all that had gone into the dish.

"You seem surprised." His voice came from right beside her and held an undercurrent of amusement.

"It's, well, it's more than a salad. You've done something to it."

He nodded and the amusement showed in his eyes. "That's a good way of describing most gourmet cooking."

"I'm sure you've heard this before but it's extraordinary," Hannah said as she lifted another forkful to her lips.

"I've also heard it's extraordinarily awful," he said with a wry smile.

"I can't imagine that," Estelle said, dabbing the corner of her mouth with her linen napkin. "Not only would it be untrue, it would be rude to say such a thing."

"Ah, but food critics aren't being rude, they are being discerning," Adam said.

"Saving our less-developed palates from the assault of terrible dishes like this one." Hannah pointed at the plate with her fork.

Adam's voice held mock sorrow. "You sound like one of them. That's not a wig you're wearing to disguise your true identity as a secret diner, is it?"

Her hand went up to her sloppy ponytail, and suddenly she wished she had taken the time to remove the elastic and brush out her hair. She noticed Sonya had done so, her long, dark hair falling in glossy waves around her shoulders. "If I were going incognito, I'd come up with a better-looking wig than this one."

He shook his head. "It's beautiful, like corn silk."

She slanted a peek up at him, thinking it was some sort of chef joke, but he was assessing her hair with focused seriousness. When she brought her gaze back to her dining companions, Sonya gave her an encouraging nod and Estelle raised her eyebrows with a prim little smile.

"You can assault my palate again if you have another one of these," Sonya said, chasing the last leaf around her plate with determination.

Adam turned to whisk the empty plate from in front of the vet tech. "I see it's time for the next course."

Relief and regret washed through Hannah as she quickly finished her salad. Adam's attention was becoming too addictive; she didn't want to feel so pleased by his description of her hair. It had sounded sincere, but so had Ward's compliments and she'd found out how little they meant. When Adam cleared her plate, she deliberately kept her eyes averted from his hands.

"Dr. Linden, how does Mr. Cahill's parrot decide what to say?" Matt's question was a godsend.

"Well, when it comes to telling jokes, I think Mr. Cahill cues him, either verbally or with a gesture. Otherwise I think Pappy responds to the words and body language of the people around him. If he says something and you react in a way Pappy likes, he'll repeat that in a similar situation."

"So you don't think he knows what he's saying?" Matt seemed disappointed.

"Not really, no," Hannah said. "His brain hasn't developed in that way."

"Do you think dolphins can understand human language?"

"There've been some interesting studies that seem to indicate they could learn at least some, but I don't know enough about their brains to be sure. Why?"

"It would be cool if we could talk to them," Matt said.

"Sometimes I think we should try to learn *their* language instead," Adam said, startling her. She thought he was busy with the food, but his son's voice seemed to have drawn him back to the table. "Their experiences and perceptions would be fascinating."

"They just use a bunch of clicks and squeaks," Matt scoffed. "We'd never be able to figure that out."

"So you think we're dumber than dolphins?" Hannah interjected to keep Adam from becoming a target.

"Maybe." Matt slumped back in his chair and went silent again. Adam waited a moment, his eyes on his son, before he turned back to the food on the desk.

Hannah wondered what had caused Matt's sudden burst of conversation. She was glad he wanted to join in, but his topic seemed oddly arbitrary. "What would you ask a dolphin if you spoke the same language?"

Matt shrugged. "I dunno."

"I'd ask them if they could talk to whales," Lucy said.

"I'd warn them to stay away from fishing nets," Estelle commented.

Matt sat up. "If they're so smart, you'd think they would have figured that out by now."

Hannah saw Adam's movements slow as he listened to the conversation. This time he did not attempt to join in.

"Maybe they just swim too fast to avoid them," Hannah said.

"But they use echolocation," Matt said. "They should be able to hear where they are."

"I guess nets are hard to spot with sonar," Sonya said.

Plates appeared in front of the diners as Adam did his smooth tango around the table again. He finished and stepped back. "Brook trout over apple-parsnip puree with an apricot Grenobloise. My local supplier delivered the trout five minutes before I grilled it."

The fragrance wafting up from the steaming dish in front of her made Hannah groan with appreciation. "Who needs to eat? I'm just going to sit here and inhale."

Adam wore his practiced smile, but his attention was on Matt. His son's opinion was the one he cared about. Hannah took up her own fork and flaked off a bite of trout as she surreptitiously watched the two Bosch males. The smile moved all the way up into Adam's eyes when Matt seized his fork and shoveled up a mouthful of fish and parsnips.

The rest of the meal passed smoothly, with a dessert of chocolate pots de crème bringing moans of ecstasy from all but one of the diners. Matt made no comment, but Hannah noticed he swirled his finger around the empty bowl and licked it when he thought no one was watching.

As everyone rose amidst a general surge of gratitude for the spectacular meal, Adam leaned down beside Hannah and murmured, "May I speak with you alone for just a minute?"

She nodded and signaled Sonya to take Matt out of the room with her. The door closed behind them and Adam turned to her, his smile vanishing like snow in June. "I know you're busy so I'll just ask. How is Matt doing?"

"Fine," Hannah said, putting conviction in her voice. "He's a smart young man. He gets the message. He seems genuinely sorry Trace was injured."

"You don't think it was deliberate?"

"Definitely not. It was pure carelessness that he covered up with bravado."

She could see the tension in Adam's posture ease. "You seem to know humans as well as you know animals."

The gross inaccuracy of that made Hannah shake her head emphatically. "I'm a vet for a reason. People lie. Animals don't."

Surprise flashed across his face before speculation took its place. "One of the less impressive attributes of higher intelligence."

How had he found that crack in her carefully maintained professional façade? Irritated with herself for revealing too much, she checked her watch. "Matt and I have to get going on my farm rounds. Thanks for a delicious lunch."

"I'll take Matt home with me," Adam said. "I've imposed on you enough already. If I hadn't been at the end of my rope, I never would have asked you to do this."

Relief swept through her. Matt had been unenthusiastic about visiting the large animals, and now she didn't have to drag him along with her on her farm rounds. Then she remembered his admission of guilt over Trace. She'd breached his defenses for a minute there.

Some impulse of charity made her say, "He might prefer to go with you, but I'd like to find out more about his interest in dolphins."

He scanned her face with a questioning gaze. "You must be trying for sainthood. Thank you."

His comment shocked a short laugh out of her. Maybe she did have a yen for martyrdom, considering her recent personal and professional history. Except people didn't usually bring it out in her. Just Matt with his air of a half-wild dog, wanting to trust someone but afraid of having his trust betrayed.

Hannah started toward the door.

"Dr. Linden, I'd like to ask another favor."

Dismay zinged through her as she stopped.

"Would you have dinner with me Monday and tell me what you learn about Matt and the dolphins? It might help me talk to him."

What was he up to with the dinner invitation? His refusal to take no for an answer was causing flashbacks to her ex again. Ward had kept asking her out until she finally accepted.

No, this was different. She'd seen how Adam watched Matt at lunch. He wanted so badly to connect with his son that he was bribing her with food to give him any tools he could use. The charmer routine was just a way to cover his desperation.

"You don't have to feed me," she said. "I'll meet you at Moonshine on my way home from work. You can buy me a glass of wine." That would keep their meeting short, as the wine bar didn't serve meals. She didn't want to get drawn any farther into Adam's situation than she already was.

"Feeding people is what I do," he said, "but they have some excellent cheese at Moonshine. Five o'clock?"

She nodded, knowing she was crazy to think he seemed disappointed when she turned down dinner. The same thought prompted her to say, "I'll drop Matt off at your house when I'm done with my farm visits. We'll be driving around in the truck anyway so it's no trouble."

"Do you need directions?"

She snorted. "Everyone knows where The Aerie is. The hard part is getting reservations."

He laughed before he turned serious. "For you there will always be a table."

His dark eyes were locked on her, and she felt wrapped in the sensuousness of black velvet against her bare skin. The sensation was so vivid she had to give her head a tiny shake to bring herself back to the reality of standing in Tim's office in her polo shirt and khakis. "See you later," she said and fled.

❖

Adam stowed the dishes in the insulated bags without conscious thought. He was contemplating the enigma of Dr. Hannah Linden. There was a kindness in her that extended beyond the animals she cared so deeply for. Yet she didn't seem to warm up to him. He wasn't offended, just puzzled. His job required the ability to make his customers feel as though they were the center of his attention, and he'd gotten good at it. Most people enjoyed it, yet Dr. Linden kept backing away.

Maybe he'd scared her with his anguish over Trace and his desperation over Matt. He'd twisted her arm into mentoring a surly boy, so perhaps it wasn't surprising she wanted nothing further to do with him.

Although when he'd offered her the perfect out for the afternoon, she'd rejected it. She actually wanted to spend more time with his son.

"What does that say about me that she prefers Matt's company to mine?" he muttered, zipping up a bag.

Despite that, he wanted to comb his fingers through her straight, corn-silk, blond hair, an impulse he had squelch every time he bent down to serve her a dish. He wondered if her blue eyes would widen in shock or flutter closed in pleasure. He'd only had a few glimpses of her standing without her lab coat, but it looked as though there were some interesting curves there. Maybe it was because he was a chef that he liked women whose figures showed a certain appetite.

He shook his head. Given her reaction to him, he shouldn't bother to speculate on her body. Although he would see her again Monday.

He piled the bags into a big plastic carrier and hefted it in both hands.

He would just have to be more charming at their next meeting.

Chapter 3

*H*ANNAH DROVE THROUGH THE GATES MARKING THE road to Healing Springs Stables, Sharon Sydenstricker's world-class breeding and training facility and horse rescue center. Sharon spent all the money she made from her high-paying clients on the horses she saved from bad situations. "Have you been here before?" Hannah asked.

Matt shook his head.

"Ms. Sydenstricker is an Olympic gold medalist." Boys liked athletes, didn't they?

"Cool." His voice was devoid of enthusiasm.

Hannah had tried at least six different topics, including dolphins, and Matt had refused to participate in any conversation. She pulled the truck over to the side of the road and slammed on the brakes, making Matt brace his hand on the dashboard and swing his gaze around to her. "What the–?" he said.

"Enough with the silent treatment," Hannah said, twisting around in her seat and crossing her arms.

He dropped his gaze. "What are you talking about?"

"I'm tired of getting one-syllable answers from you. It's rude and annoying."

"I'm sorry, ma'am." He put the tiniest bit of emphasis on the last word, and Hannah felt an unwelcome admiration for his slyness. He was using good manners in a way she had specifically asked him not to.

"Two points for the inverse courtesy," she said, raising a finger to mark the score in the air. "Now lose the attitude or I'll tell Sharon you love to muck out stalls."

He sighed. "It's not an attitude. I don't like farm animals."

"Because why?"

"I dunno. They're big."

"Did you grow up in a city?" Hannah had no idea where he'd come from before he'd landed with Adam.

"I guess so."

She cast a weary glance at the roof of the truck. "Does that mean yes or no?"

"I lived in a bunch of places," he said, giving her a sullen scowl. "A couple were cities."

She gave up, deciding it was too much trouble to drag the information out of him. "Dolphins are big too," she said, reverting to his original complaint about farm animals. "People don't realize that because they've never been in the water with them."

"I have," Matt said abruptly.

Progress. "Where?" She kept her tone lukewarm. Too much enthusiasm might scare him off the topic.

"Disney World."

Back to short answers. She tried a more open-ended question. "What did you think?"

He shrugged. "They were bigger than I expected. And strong. You could tell even though we didn't swim with them."

Hannah noted the "we" and wondered if he'd been with his mother. "So what did you do with them?"

"We stood on a platform in the water and they swam up to us." He turned toward her, his left leg bent at the knee and flat on the seat. "The trainer would signal and the dolphins would let us hug them or they'd roll over so we could scratch their bellies. They'd even open their mouths so you could touch their tongue and their teeth. I was pretty nervous but my mom got into it."

Hannah wasn't sure how to keep him talking so she just told the truth. "That's an amazing experience. I'd like to try it myself."

"The hugging part is when I realized how big they are. The dolphin came right up and kind of put his chin on my shoulder. My arms went about half way around him and I could feel his tail moving to keep himself in position." Matt curved his arms as though the dolphin was in them, and all his surliness dropped away. His blue eyes were alight with remembered excitement. "That's when I realized how strong he was."

"So that's how you got interested in dolphins?"

He let his arms fall onto his lap. "Yeah. We were supposed to go back there when I was old enough to swim with them." A shadow passed over his face, and he turned to look straight ahead through the windshield.

Hannah tried to bring the animation back. "How old were you then?"

"I forget."

She'd lost him. She could see it in the stiff set of his shoulders; he had closed down on the memory, maybe because it reminded him his mother wouldn't be taking him to Disney World again. "Hey, you'll get back there for that swim," she said, unable to resist reaching out to give him a brief comforting touch on his arm.

He didn't acknowledge the contact but he didn't jerk away, either.

"Maybe you could just think of horses as dolphins on land. With hooves," she said, putting the truck in gear and pulling back onto the road.

"Sure. Thanks." His tone was sarcastic but not hostile, so Hannah figured she'd done all right.

She spent the few minutes it took to reach the barns explaining what vaccinations she would be giving the horses and why. Matt nodded occasionally but made no comment.

Parking the truck in the gravel lot, she jumped out and walked around to the back. Matt surprised her by following. "Want me to carry one?" he asked, as she flipped down the tailgate and reached for the cases she'd packed at the clinic.

"That'd be great," Hannah said, handing him the smaller case. His mother had raised the kid right.

He slouched along beside her as they walked through the barn toward Sharon Sydenstricker's office. The place was bustling with stable hands leading glossy horses of all colors and sizes in and out of stalls. One young man passed with a wheelbarrow loaded with bags of feed, and Hannah inhaled the sweet, thick scent of molasses-infused grain. The hollow clomp of hooves, the musical jingle of metal buckles, and the occasional throaty whicker or irritated squeal of a horse brought back memories of her summer internship at a rural veterinary practice during vet school. She'd considered specializing in racehorse medicine because she'd enjoyed that summer but decided it was more practical to go for small domestic animals. It meant she could live in a city, which seemed desirable at the time.

That had led her to Chicago and Ward. *She should have stuck to the Thoroughbreds.* She turned her attention back to the boy just as a large black stallion was led past them. Matt veered sharply away from the horse and bumped into her, making her stagger.

"Sorry," he said, keeping a wary eye on the big creature's muscular haunches as the groom walked him away. "That one looked kind of mean."

"And you wouldn't want to get your foot under one of those hooves," Hannah agreed. "That would grind a few bones."

Matt gave her a look of gratitude. He must have been expecting her to scoff at his nervousness.

"Here we are," Hannah said as they walked up to a human-sized door at the end of the barn. She walked inside the office to find the stable's owner hunched in front of a computer screen, scowling.

"Thank the lord you're here, doc," Sharon said, spinning her desk chair around and leaping to her feet. "I can't abide bookkeeping."

"Sharon, meet Matt McNally. He's my assistant today." Hannah stifled a smile as Matt gaped at the six-foot tall horsewoman with her flyaway mop of flaming red hair. Every inch of Sharon Sydenstricker was in shape under the polo shirt and riding britches she wore. When she stepped around the desk to shake Matt's hand, there was no mistaking the fluid motion indicating an elite-level athlete.

"Nice to meet you," Sharon said.

"Nice to meet you too, Ms. Sydenstricker," he said. Hannah felt an absurd spurt of pride at his manners.

Sharon gave her an I'm-impressed-and-surprised look before she said, "So Dr. Tim left you to do the heavy lifting while he's off gallivanting in some foreign country? Lordy, I can't keep track of where he and Claire are going next."

"It's lucky for me he wanted to gallivant," Hannah pointed out. "Otherwise he wouldn't have hired me."

"Didn't you come from some big city?" Sharon asked with casual friendliness as she led the way into the barn. "Sanctuary must seem real different."

"In the best possible way," Hannah said fervently. *No political rallies, no charity galas, no reporters manufacturing scandals, and no Ward Miller to stomp on her heart.*

"So Matt, where'd you live before you came here?" Sharon asked, clearly wanting to include him in the conversation.

Hannah held her breath.

"California," he said, surprising her with his immediate response.

"That's a trip and a half," Sharon said. "I go out there a lot to pick up racehorses no one wants anymore. Some of 'em make great jumpers."

"What do you do with the rest of them?" Matt asked.

Sharon shrugged. "Give 'em a place to live." She stopped in front of a stall. "Here's your first victim, doc."

The nameplate on the stall's half door read: Don Diego's Favorite Son.

"We call him Sonny," Sharon said.

Remembering the boy's fear of big animals, Hannah said, "Matt, maybe you should wait out here, just in case Sonny doesn't like having so many people in his stall."

"Nah, he's a good horse," Sharon said. "He won't give you any trouble."

Hannah saw the boy swallow hard and tried to think how to rescue him. "You know, I left my tablet in the pickup. Tim likes me to keep notes on the animals I see so I really need it. Would you mind getting it for me, Matt? You can help with the next horse."

"No problem, Dr. Linden," he said, practically singing at the reprieve. "I'll be right back."

As soon as he was out of earshot, Hannah lowered her voice, "He's afraid of horses."

"What in tarnation is he doing here then?" Sharon asked, amusement and exasperation in her face.

"It's a long story," Hannah said, walking in the stall to find a handsome bay gelding with black points gazing at her, his eyes bright with affable curiosity. "Sonny, my boy, how are you feeling today? We're just going to give you a quick check up and a vaccination. Nothing to worry about."

As Hannah ran her hands over the bay's body, probing for any sign of discomfort, Sharon said, "He's Adam Bosch's boy, right?"

"Yup," Hannah grunted, leaning over to pick up Sonny's hoof. It had been awhile since she'd dealt with an animal this large. She really needed to work out more.

"Poor kid, he's had a tough time of it." Sharon shook her head. "Having his mother drown and all. Rumor has it Matt had never met his father until the mother died."

Hannah straightened. "That's heart-breaking. How could someone not want to meet their own child?" Even if she didn't trust Adam's polished façade, he still didn't seem like the sort of man who would abandon a woman who was pregnant with his child. Maybe he was more like Ward than she thought. She was pretty sure her ex-fiancé would have claimed not to know how reproduction worked if he'd gotten another woman pregnant during his election campaign. And he would have convinced the media it was true.

"Adam has his own problems," Sharon said with a shrug. "Maybe he didn't want to involve Matt in them."

Hannah's interest in Adam got the better of her and she glanced out over the door of the stall to make sure Matt wasn't approaching. "What kind of problems?"

Sharon tucked her hands into her breeches pockets. "Well, maybe I'd better let the man tell you himself. That way you can form your own opinion."

Consumed by curiosity, Hannah made a mental note to ask Estelle about Adam's issues. Then she went back to examining Sonny, loving the feel of the big, solid bones under his smooth coat and the warmth of his body in the enclosed stall. She'd forgotten how solid and reassuring the presence of a horse could be.

She finished Sonny's checkup and gave him his shot, making sure to reward him with a horse treat for being such a good patient. She was feeling more confident about her large-animal skills now.

As she and Sharon walked out of the stall, Matt pushed himself off the wall where he'd been leaning. "I didn't want to interrupt you," he said, holding out the tablet.

"I appreciate that," Hannah said, although she knew he was just making an excuse not to come into the stall. She made a show of tapping in some notes on Sonny so Matt's pride wouldn't take a hit.

Sharon strode down to another stall and turned. "This mare's a bit touchy, so it's best Matt not come in with us. She might get spooked." She rubbed a finger against her chin. "You know if you want to go out back, there's a few benches by the riding ring. You can hang out until we're done."

"Yes, ma'am." Matt practically bolted for the back door of the barn.

"You're a good person," Hannah said to Sharon. "He would've died rather than admit he's scared."

Three more checkups completed her roster of patients at Healing Springs Stables. "Let's go find your assistant," Sharon said, after Hannah closed up her bag.

They strolled outside, where the slanting sunshine seemed to set the nearest mountains ablaze in scarlets and golds. Hannah stopped a moment to absorb the beauty of the undulating ridges rolling away into the distance, the brilliant colors fading to cool blue on the furthest slopes. The nearer view offered white fences and horses scattered over rolling grass. She spotted Matt standing beside a paddock, staring between the fence rails.

"Matt, we're done here," she called, expecting him to greet her announcement with enthusiasm. Instead, he looked at her and then back into the paddock before he waved her over.

She exchanged a glance with Sharon, and they joined him by the fence.

Matt pointed toward one corner of the enclosed field. "I think there's something wrong with that little horse over there."

Hannah peered in the direction he was gesturing. She saw a chestnut pony, his coat dull and rough, with a wild puff of a flaxen mane and tail. He was standing away from all the other horses in the field, his head drooping and one back hoof propped on tiptoe. "He may just be napping," she said. "Horses often sleep standing up."

Matt shook his head. "Nah, he's awake. Another little horse came over to him and he tried to bite him."

"That's Satchmo," Sharon said. "His stall buddy down in Florida died, so he's grieving. I brought him up here about a month ago, and he's been down in the dumps ever since. I'm getting kind of worried about him."

Hannah scanned Satchmo from head to tail, trying to pick up clues as to what was wrong. "Why don't I take a look at him?"

"I'd be real grateful for that," Sharon said, heading for the gate.

"Can I come too?" Matt asked, as Hannah followed. Her surprise must have been obvious because he shrugged and said, "He's small."

Hannah nodded and waved him through the open gate. "Tell me Satchmo's history," she said to Sharon as they walked toward the sad-looking pony.

"He was the stall buddy for Jazzman." Sharon turned to Matt. "Some racehorses need company to keep them calm, so their trainers find them a friend. Sometimes it's a dog or a goat. Seabiscuit had a monkey. In Jazzman's case, it was a pony."

Hannah recognized the name of the racehorse. "He was supposed to win the Triple Crown."

"Until he developed acute laminitis, and they had to put him down," Sharon said. "Such a tragedy. That horse could run."

"So they killed Satchmo's stall buddy?" Matt asked.

"I'm sure they tried everything they could to treat Jazzman's laminitis," Hannah said, feeling sympathy for the unknown vet who'd administered the final injection, "but it's horribly painful when it becomes acute, so it was a mercy to the horse to euthanize him." She decided not to point out that Jazzman was extremely valuable and therefore putting him down would have been a last resort for financial reasons, if nothing else. She hated being so cynical, but hard experience had taught her the realities of life among the rich, especially when it came to their animals.

"Man, that's rough," the boy said, stopping ten feet from the pony and eyeing him warily.

"Come on up and hold him for me," Hannah said. His unexpected interest in the pony seemed like progress, so she wanted to encourage it.

He hung back. "He's got big teeth."

"I'll show you how to hold his halter so he can't bite you," Hannah said. Satchmo finally turned to gaze at the three humans discussing him. His ears drooped toward the ground, giving him an air of listlessness. The pony didn't look like he cared enough to snap at anyone, but Matt said he had, so she approached with caution. "Hey, Satchmo. How's it going, fella?"

He offered no resistance when she slipped her fingers under the cheek strap of his halter and gripped it firmly. She ran her free hand over his neck, feeling the coarseness of his coat. It contrasted sharply with the glossy good health that shone in most of Sharon's horses.

"He eats just enough to keep body and soul together," Sharon said, "but he's lost weight since he got here. Dr. Tim gave me some high-calorie supplements and vitamins to keep him from wasting away."

Hannah kept hold of the halter with one hand, stretching sideways to probe along the pony's back and ribcage with the other.

"I'll take him," Matt said from behind her as she came to the end of her reach. She was wondering why Sharon didn't volunteer to help before she realized the horsewoman knew what she was doing when it came to people too.

"Great. Stand here beside his head so he can see you easily. Now take the cheek strap of his halter with your right hand." Hannah said. "If he seems restless or uncomfortable when I touch him in a certain place, let me know. And you can stroke his nose to keep him calm, if you want." She hoped she hadn't pushed Matt too much with the last instruction.

The boy stepped up beside Satchmo's head, moving gingerly. The pony flicked an ear but didn't offer to bite him as Matt took the leather of the halter. The boy stood very still as though afraid any movement would set off an attack from Satchmo's big, square teeth.

"Relax," Hannah said, giving Matt's shoulder a friendly squeeze. "He's not much bigger than a dolphin."

Matt gave her a nervous smile, but his stance remained rigid. As she went back to feeling the pony's belly, she worried she might hit a sensitive spot and provoke Satchmo to nip at Matt. A quick glance sideways reassured her as she saw Sharon join Matt by the pony's head. Now Hannah could focus on what was ailing the sad little creature. After giving Satchmo a thorough examination, she stood back to look at him, taking in all the visual cues again.

"I think you're right, Sharon," she said at last. "I can't find anything physically wrong with him, so it must be an emotional issue."

"That's why I've got him in the field with other horses," Sharon said. "I was hoping he'd find a new friend."

Hannah noticed that Matt was carefully running his palm down Satchmo's nose so she kept talking. "I notice you have a good variety of friends for him to choose from. Thoroughbreds, quarter horses, another pony."

"That's the one he tried to bite," Matt said, switching hands on the halter so he could stroke down Satchmo's neck. The pony blew out a loud breath and leaned into the boy, making him stagger slightly. Matt looked up at Hannah, his eyes wide. "Does that mean he likes being petted?"

"Yup, he wants more. Try scratching behind his ears."

The boy's face lit up and he reached for the base of the pony's left ear. Satchmo lifted his head and brought it down to rest on top of Matt's shoulder, his eyelids half-closed. "He likes me," Matt said, shifting his ministrations to the other ear.

Hannah looked at Sharon, who was grinning from ear to ear as she watched the interaction between the boy and the pony. "I haven't seen Satchmo look this happy since he walked out of the horse trailer that brought him here," Sharon said. "You've got a gift, young 'un."

"Really?" Matt said, giving the pony's neck a long stroke. "You think I do?"

"I reckon so. You'd be doing me a big favor if you'd come out to visit Satchmo regular-like. Maybe you could even take a ride to exercise him."

Matt seemed to have forgotten all about his fear of the pony's teeth as he alternated between ears. Sharon's last comment brought his fingers to a halt. "I don't know how to ride."

"No problem," Sharon said. "I'm a decent teacher."

Hannah coughed at the understatement.

Matt's expression went from excited trepidation to flat disappointment. "I don't have a way to get here and I can't afford to pay you."

"I'm sure your dad could help with both those things," Hannah said. She was certain Adam would be thrilled to have his son involved with something so worthwhile for both him and the pony.

"Nah," Matt said, dropping his hand and releasing Satchmo's halter. "He's busy with the restaurant in the afternoons. And he's not big on spending money."

Hannah was stunned. The Aerie was beyond successful; the whole town knew Adam Bosch was a wealthy man because of it. Did he really withhold money from his son? She shook her head and glanced at Sharon. The other woman stood with her hands on her hips, frowning. "You're the one who's doing me a favor," Sharon said, "so I'm not looking for money."

Hannah surprised herself by saying, "I can give you a ride after I get off work. Maybe not every day, but we can work something out. We have to talk with your father first to make sure it's all right with him."

Now she was having second thoughts about how thrilled Adam would be over this new development. She looked at the drooping little pony and remembered the signs of life he'd shown when Matt touched him. She'd just have to convince the chef this was a good thing for his son too.

She glanced at her watch and sucked in her breath. "We have to go. The Zicafooses' cows are waiting for us." She turned to Matt. His hands were shoved into his jeans pockets and he was staring down at the toes of his faded, red sneakers. He looked as miserable as the pony. "Do you want to hang out with Satchmo a little longer?" she asked, thinking fast to come up with a reason to let him linger. "I need to go over some medications with Sharon in her office."

"Nah, I'll go wait in the truck," he said, but she caught the longing glance he cast toward the pony.

The three of them left the paddock together and retrieved the veterinary cases from the stable. Matt veered off toward the parking lot while Hannah and Sharon walked toward the office to continue the pretense of needing to talk further. Sharon watched Matt disappear out of the barn before she said, "That boy has found his whisper horse."

"His what?"

"Well, I guess it would be his whisper pony. The one he can tell all his troubles to," Sharon said. "Everyone has a special horse—or pony—who will take on their burdens and help carry them. I reckon that boy has found his."

Hannah eyed the tall woman walking beside her. "Isn't Satchmo the one who needs help?"

"That was just his way of bringing the boy to him."

Hannah bit her lip. She'd heard rumors about Sharon's mystical theory regarding whisper horses but dismissed them in the face of the horsewoman's achievements and down-to-earth common sense.

"I know you don't believe anything I'm saying," Sharon said with unabated cordiality, "but you ask Dr. Tim when he gets back. He was a skeptic too."

"Tim has a whisper horse?" Hannah hoped she didn't sound too dubious.

"His wife Claire does. Willow. When Claire came down here to Sanctuary, she was hurting from a real ugly divorce. Willow was one of my rescues, so she had some healing to do too. As soon as Claire and Willow laid eyes on each other, they felt that bond." Sharon said it as though it was the most normal thing in the world. "Claire even brought her little niece down here to talk to her whisper horse. Truth is, if it hadn't been for Willow, Claire and Tim might not be married today. She brought them together."

Hannah was fascinated but unconvinced. "There's no question Satchmo touched something in Matt," she said. "He wouldn't go near any of the other animals you have here." Of course the pony was significantly smaller than the Thoroughbreds who made up the majority of Sharon's stable residents. The reason didn't matter. She was just glad to see Matt slough off the prickly façade he usually presented to the world.

"So how'd you end up with Matt as your shadow today?" Sharon said, continuing toward her office.

"His father asked me to give him an animal's-eye view of the world. They're having a little problem with Matt being careless about Adam's dog."

"Well, there's no one better qualified to do that than you," Sharon said. "I admit I was a little worried about a big-city vet joining a country practice, but Tim did a smart thing taking you on as a partner. You read horses as easily as a third-grade textbook."

The compliment was especially gratifying because of Sharon's expertise, and Hannah's confidence needed the boost. After the blow her career took in Chicago, she wasn't sure she'd ever practice veterinary medicine again. "I was lucky to get such a great position," she said with sincerity. Her former partners had given her the most minimal of references, fearing possible legal repercussions. Sometimes their lack of support hurt her almost as much as Ward's desertion.

"We're pretty lucky with the city slickers who settle here," Sharon said, stopping in front of her door. "You don't really have any medications to go over with me, do you?"

"You saw through my ploy," Hannah said, smiling.

"It was worth a try. The boy wanted to stay with Satchmo. I can't figure out why he made himself leave."

"Fear of loss?" Hannah suggested. "He's heading it off at the pass."

"Could be." Sharon put her hand on the doorknob. "You'd better get over to Zicafoose's. George is a cranky old codger."

"I appreciate the warning," Hannah said, taking off at a jog for the truck.

Hannah eased the truck onto the highway. "So did your sneakers get any manure on them?"

When she'd gotten behind the wheel, Matt had been wedged against the passenger door slouched over his cell phone, typing at high speed. He'd responded to her greeting and gone back to texting. Now his gaze shifted down to his feet as he lifted first one and then the other to check for dirt. "Maybe some."

"Just throw them in the washing machine when you get home."

He stared at his feet. "They won't come apart?"

She took a quick glance downward, noticing again how ratty the red high-tops were. "Well, if they do, you can just get a new pair."

She felt him shift on the seat. "My mother gave these to me."

She'd put her foot in it now. "I understand. Sentimental value."

"Sort of," he said. "I didn't like the red at first."

"I had a pair of red boots I loved." Hannah kept talking as relief surged through her that he hadn't clammed up. However, she heard the weight of regret in his voice. She suspected he had told his mother he didn't like the shoes and now he felt guilty about it. She knew she shouldn't allow herself to become further entangled in the situation, but her heart ached at the sadness wrapped around her young companion.

"What happened to your boots?" he asked.

She'd hurled them into a Goodwill bin in a Walmart parking lot right after Ward broke off their engagement. Along with all the other fancy clothes she'd bought to go to Ward's charity galas and political fundraisers and ribbon-cuttings. She knew she could never wear them without having his betrayal slice through her heart all over again. But darn, she missed those boots.

Out of the corner of her eye she saw Matt lean forward, craning his neck as he tried to look into her face, and she realized she hadn't answered his question. She could lie, but something about the boy's pain compelled her to be honest with him. "I donated them to charity."

"How come, if you liked them so much?"

"Because they reminded me of someone I didn't think much of anymore. Kind of the opposite of your sneakers."

He sat back. "That's cool."

"It is?"

"Yeah. But maybe you should buy some new boots. In a different color." There was a hint of humor in the boy's voice.

Hannah looked down at the lace-up tan Timberland boots she wore. She'd bought them when she moved to Sanctuary. This was only the second time she'd worn them, and their lack of use was glaringly obvious. "You have something against Timberlands?"

"You should scuff 'em up some and then they'll be okay."

"I'm getting fashion advice from a teenaged boy," Hannah said, giving him an exaggerated eye roll.

"Are you kidding?" he said. "That's the *best* person to get fashion advice from."

A smile tugged her lips upward. Matt was actually teasing her.

Maybe Sharon was right about that whisper pony.

Chapter 4

*M*ATT HAD GONE SILENT AS SOON AS SHE'D TURNED off the main road at the sign displaying the words "The Aerie" painted in a rich burgundy. No other information was necessary for a restaurant of its reputation. In a barely audible mutter, the boy had directed her past The Aerie, and down a drive lined with the dark, dense foliage of rhododendron bushes and evergreen trees. As they rounded a curve, the vegetation fell away and the drive widened to meet a broad apron of river stone. Adam's house was a graceful modern design similar to the restaurant, with great expanses of glass framed by substantial timbers stained a warm, blond hue. The glass looked like sheets of gold as it caught and reflected the late afternoon sun.

"Nice house," Hannah said, pulling up in front of the steps.

"It's okay," he allowed grudgingly.

Hannah swung open her door and hopped down from the high cab. As she walked around the truck's front end, Adam came through his front door.

Every thought in her brain evaporated as he jogged down the wide stone steps. He was dressed in a black suit cut to emphasize the very masculine proportion of his shoulders to his waist. A black shirt and tie and highly polished black leather shoes completed the elegantly funereal effect. She'd thought Ward had a sophisticated sense of fashion, but this man made her ex-fiancé look downright provincial.

When she realized her fingers were practically twitching with the desire to rumple the perfection of his hair as it waved back off his high forehead, she shoved her hands into the pockets of her khakis and tried to re-engage her brain.

"Dad?" Matt sounded as shocked as she felt. "I thought you'd be at the restaurant."

"I wanted to hear how—" Adam began, but Matt stalked past him up the steps and through the front door, slamming it behind him. His father turned to watch his son, flinching at the bang.

Hannah stood feeling helpless while Adam turned his palms outward in what she was sure was an unconscious gesture of baffled defeat. He dropped his hands before he turned back to her. "I hope he didn't slam any doors in your face," he said, a rueful smile not concealing the pain she read in his expression.

"Teenagers only treat their parents badly," she said. "He and I got along fine."

His head tilted back as he sent a look of relief skyward. "I've been asking myself all day how I could foist Matt on a virtual stranger, and the only answer is sheer desperation. My apologies for imposing on you."

"Really, Matt was great." She hesitated as she realized the difficulties of explaining the concept of a whisper horse to him without sounding like a lunatic. She needed to emphasize the positive impact of the bond between Matt and Satchmo, but it would be hard to describe it rationally. "I need to discuss something with you."

"I'd like nothing more than to talk at length about how the day went, but I'm already late for work." His smile conveyed every shade of regret from simple courtesy to the implication that he found her company so irresistible it was a struggle for him to withdraw from it. She'd seen that kind of smile before. It was one she had no faith in.

"I'm sorry. I forgot it was Saturday. You must be incredibly busy."

"My staff is excellent, but it sets a bad example if the boss shows up too late." His shrug was smoothly self-deprecating. "I hate to ask you this when you've been working all day, but would the walk between here and The Aerie give us enough time to at least begin our discussion?"

It wasn't wise to put herself in close proximity to this man who could reduce her to a state of mind-blanking enthrallment by simply wearing a suit, but she wanted to work out arrangements for Matt to visit Satchmo. "I can manage a few more steps."

When he offered her his arm, she looked at the pristine wool of his suit jacket and then down at her own attire. Mud-and-manure spattered khakis, filthy clod-hopping boots, and a barn jacket blanketed with horsehair met her eyes. And he wanted to play courtly escort?

She took a step away. A little distance was safer anyway.

"What is it?" he asked, looking perplexed as he stood with his arm held out and bent at the elbow.

"You're about to serve people expensive food, and I've been tromping through cowpies."

"You make a valid point." He lowered his arm and gestured for her to walk beside him as he started down a flagstone-paved path through the woods beside his house. "My customers undoubtedly would prefer I not bring, er, cowpies into the dining room."

She couldn't help liking the fact that he hadn't let her messiness affect his chivalrous impulse, but she pushed the thought aside to concentrate on her request for Matt. She decided not to mention whisper horses to Adam. He'd think she'd lost her mind. "I took Matt to Healing Springs Stables today, and he sort of bonded with a pony named Satchmo. The pony was the stall mate of a racehorse who was euthanized, and he's feeling lonely and not eating well. Horses are very social creatures."

She glanced sideways to gauge what Adam thought of her explanation but saw only polite interest, so she kept going. "Sharon Sydenstricker, the owner of the stables, says it would be doing her a favor if Matt would come out and spend some time with the pony. She'd even give him some riding lessons for free. I told her I could give Matt a lift out there a couple of days a week, but I need your permission."

Adam was frowning. Hannah wondered where she'd gone wrong.

"I can take him to the stable and pay for his lessons."

So that's why he was irritated. So much for the cheap dad reputation Matt was trying to spread around. "Don't you have to be at the restaurant in the afternoon?"

The frown wasn't dissipating. "He's my son. I'm responsible for his transportation."

"Look, I need to keep an eye on Satchmo anyway, so it's not a problem for me to take Matt."

"Thank you, but no." His tone said further argument was not an option.

Hannah shrugged. "It's your call, but I hope you'll let him go to the stable."

"Of course I will. I had no idea . . ." He ran the fingers of one hand through his hair, exactly the way she'd wanted to. "I thought he didn't like horses."

The back of The Aerie loomed through the trees. "He didn't until he met Satchmo. I'll tell you about it on Monday. You have to go." She gestured toward the restaurant.

He stopped and captured one of her hands, dirt and all, between his, looking down at her with those impenetrable eyes. "You don't realize what a gift you've given Matt . . . and me," he said, his palms radiating a heat that coursed all the way into her bones.

"Um, glad to do it," Hannah said, dropping her eyes to his chest, where she noticed his tie had a subtle, burgundy stripe in it. All the textures of silk, cotton, and wool made her want to press her palm against them, especially when she saw them rise and fall with his breathing. She knew she would be able to feel the warmth of his body through the fine fabrics.

She pulled her hand out from between his as quickly as she could without seeming rude. Or at least she hoped she didn't seem rude. "I've got to get back to the office." She turned without looking at him again and strode back down the path toward his house, wiping her hand on her grubby trousers. It didn't help. She could still feel the calluses and the strength of his fingers wrapped around hers.

Breaking out of the trees, she saw Matt slouched against the truck, his thumbs flying across his cell phone. She crunched on some fallen leaves and the boy looked up. "I'm glad you're still here," he said, dropping the phone into his hoodie's pocket.

She wished she could say the same. She looked longingly at the cab of the truck. "What's up?"

"I didn't say thank you," he said with a shrug. "Today was cool."

The urge to flee melted under this major compliment from a teenaged male. She reached out to give his shoulder a quick squeeze. "Yeah, it was. And your dad says you can visit Satchmo and take riding lessons."

His blue eyes went electric with anticipation. "Tomorrow?"

She shook her head. "We're working out the logistics on Monday. But he's pretty psyched you found a pony you like."

Some of the vividness faded from his expression. "Yeah, well, I just wanted to say thanks."

"Stop by the animal hospital anytime," Hannah said, surprising herself by meaning it.

"Okay," he said, giving her a fleeting smile. "See you."

He shoved off the truck and headed for the front door. Hannah crossed her arms and watched him go.

How in the heck had the two Bosches managed to work their way under her skin?

Adam walked through the side door of The Aerie, closing it softly behind him. He stood in the quiet hallway thinking about his conversation with Dr. Linden. She'd performed a miracle for him: getting Matt interested in something other than video games and violent movies. He wanted to cook a spectacular meal to thank her, yet she kept pushing him away when he tried to express his gratitude.

He shook his head in frustration. She'd enjoyed the food at lunch, so she wasn't one of those people who considered food mere fuel. And she'd claimed Matt wasn't a difficult companion.

By process of elimination, it had to be Adam himself she didn't care for. He should have known his superficial charm wouldn't fool her. She was accustomed to looking beneath the surface in her animal patients. Evidently she did the same with humans.

"Mr. Bosch!" Lucy Porterfield, one of his hostesses, stopped short as she saw him. "I didn't know you'd arrived."

"I'm late," he said, giving her an apologetic smile. He cast a dispassionate glance over the young woman standing in front of him. The slim, black, sheath dress fitted her with a tasteful seductiveness, its knee-length hem showing off her stocking-clad calves and classic, black, high-heeled pumps. Sun-streaked brown hair was piled into a loose bun on top of her head and her makeup was subtle. Pearl drops dangled from her earlobes. Her voice held just enough of the local mountain twang to charm his customers. He was exacting in his requirements for all his staff members, and the first face they saw was especially important. Lucy filled her role perfectly.

"Any new reservations I should know about?" he asked, falling into step beside her. He'd checked the evening's reservation list when he brought the dirty dishes from lunch back to the kitchen.

"No regulars," she said. "But we have a group of eight coming in by helicopter for a seven o'clock seating. I just managed to squeeze them in."

Patrons who came in by helicopter were valued by the staff because they were generally big tippers, so he understood her desire to accommodate the last-minute diners.

"All cleared with local air traffic control?" He was certain it would be; his staff was capable and well-trained. However, he'd learned it paid to double check on the issues that most affected his customers. Not being able to land on the restaurant's private helipad would definitely annoy them.

Lucy nodded. "I heard Rick on the phone with the airport about an hour ago."

"Well done," he said, putting his appreciation into his smile. He held open the door that led to the main dining room and waved her through in front of him. She headed for the front door while he strolled around the room surveying his dream-made-reality.

Adam was not admiring the huge sheets of glass framing vistas of gray-green mountains rolling away in the gathering dusk, nor the hand-wrought bronze chandeliers shedding a warm light over the gleaming crystal and silver. Instead he was checking to see if any table was missing its arrangement of burgundy calla lilies, crabapple berries, and chartreuse spider mums, if a single gold velvet-upholstered chair was set crooked, or a utilitarian serving tray had been left out on the floor. He checked water goblets for spots and smoothed the folds of a white linen napkin.

He nodded in approval when he saw Lucy adjust a flower arrangement as she passed one table; she'd convinced him to let her provide flowers for the restaurant in addition to her hostess duties, and her work was outstanding.

When members of his staff approached, he greeted each one with a smile and covertly inspected their black suits and burgundy shirts and ties, all of which he provided and had individually tailored. He took care to train his employees thoroughly, never asking them do a job they weren't fully prepared to do. However, he expected them to live up to the standards he set. Those who did were paid well and treated with respect; those who didn't were politely let go. After five years in Sanctuary, he had virtually no turnover in his personnel, seeing as jobs at The Aerie were coveted.

Once Adam made a complete sweep of the room and reviewed the table assignments with Lucy, he passed through the heavy mahogany doors into the kitchen. The transition from the serene elegance of the dining room to the brightly lit frenzy of the gleaming kitchen never ceased to enthrall him. This was his true home.

"Chef, we're still waiting for the lobster delivery," Bobby, his chef de cuisine, greeted him.

Adam swore under his breath and jerked his cell phone out of his pocket to punch in a speed-dial number.

"I'm turnin' into your parking lot right now," said the voice on the other end of the call. "Had a flat on the interstate."

"Sounds like you need a new truck," Adam said, pinching the bridge of his nose. This was the third late delivery in two weeks, all supposedly due to the truck's mechanical failures. He needed to find a new supplier for the fresh lobster he had trucked down from Maine.

"Pay my boss more for these danged crawdads and he'll buy one."

"Hmm," Adam said. "I'll send someone out to help you unload."

He ended the call. "Donnie, go hustle those lobsters in here." Gripping Bobby's shoulder, he said, "I'll make sure you don't have this problem again."

Bobby nodded and moved away, issuing a string of instructions to various underlings as he walked.

The urge to rip off his jacket and tie and seize a sauté skillet nearly overwhelmed Adam. Instead he closed his eyes and inhaled the scents swirling past his nostrils, parsing the ingredients by smell alone, a game he'd played with his mother in her kitchen when he was a child. It had turned out to be a useful skill. Satisfied that all the aromas fit somewhere into the menu he'd created for the evening, he opened his eyes and left the kitchen, walking down the hall to his office to research an alternate shellfish vendor.

Sitting down at his sleek walnut-and-brass desk, he reached for the computer mouse but changed his mind, instead unlocking the center desk drawer. Inside lay the rubber band-wrapped manila folder he'd been given by the social worker who'd been assigned to Matt's case. Adam had opened it exactly once before and slammed it shut again.

Now he took the thick, dog-eared folder out of the drawer and put it on his desk. He splayed his right hand on top of it, wondering why he felt drawn to it at this moment. Maybe it was because Hannah had given him new hope of connecting with his son. He slipped the rubber bands off and, taking a deep breath, flipped it open to find the same photograph that had sent pain ripping through his chest on first sight. Prepared for it now, he stared down at the little boy standing on a kitchen stool with a wooden spoon in one hand, a stainless steel mixing bowl in the other, and a huge grin on his face. He realized that previously he had seen both his son and himself in the photo; the pain was so piercing because it twisted together strands of guilt and regret from both his past and his present.

The boy in the kitchen had yanked him back to the afternoons he'd helped his mother in their kitchen, when she'd taught him the sniffing game, as she called it. Those were rare, happy times when his father was out of the house, either at work or, as he later learned, in a bar drinking away his paycheck. Either way, he and his mother were safe from the slashing criticism—and worse—his father ladled out, whether he was drunk or sober. They would experiment with ingredients to create dishes which his mother gave colorful names to. His favorite was a wildly inventive variation on macaroni and cheese she dubbed "Mac the Cheese Wizard." The memory was so vivid he could taste the combination of cheese, bacon, croutons, and pasta they had concocted.

He looked down at the picture again and felt the sear of loss at missing his son's childhood, of not being in that kitchen with him, sharing his passion with his child. He'd offered to let Matt work at The Aerie, thinking his son might enjoy the chance to cook and earn some money for it, but Matt had rejected the proposal as he did everything Adam suggested, with hostility and disgust.

It was only a small photograph, so Adam could see there were more under it, as well as a child's drawing on top of a stack of papers, but he couldn't get past the one picture. He closed the folder, gently this time, wincing at the agony washing through him.

How could he blame Maggie for not wanting him in Matt's life? When she'd known him, he'd been drinking heavily and calling it normal for a hardworking, young sous-chef. He'd drowned any thought that he might be following in his father's footsteps with another drink.

In fact, Matt had been conceived on a night when Adam had gone bar-hopping after work with some of the staff at the New York City restaurant where he'd landed his first real cooking job. Maggie was a waitress there, a young Irish girl come to the "golden shore" of Manhattan to make her fortune. They'd both gotten drunk and ended up in bed at his tiny, dingy apartment in Brooklyn.

When they woke up together the next morning, naked, hung over, and muzzy, she'd scrambled into her clothes and bolted. He'd tried to talk to her at the restaurant, but she just blushed scarlet and muttered she wasn't that kind of girl before she walked away. Three days later she quit. He never saw her again.

The truth was he had nearly forgotten about her until he got the phone call that threatened to rip apart his carefully constructed life in Sanctuary. The call informing him that he had a thirteen-year-old son.

He snapped the rubber bands around the folder and shoved it back into the drawer.

Chapter 5

I DON'T THINK ADAM BOSCH COULD MAKE A CHICKEN cordon bleu any better than this," Hannah said, putting down her fork and sitting back in the Victorian oak chair in the dining room of Julia Castillo and Paul Taggart's renovated train station house. Before she and Tim left for Europe, Claire Arbuckle had practically ordered Hannah to have dinner with Julia and Paul, saying she needed to get out and meet people in Sanctuary.

Hannah had nearly cancelled. After a day of dealing with Matt and his father, she had wanted to collapse onto her couch, warmed by a puffy quilt and her pets. However, she dragged herself into the shower, pulled her wet hair back in a French braid, and tossed on a blue silk blouse over a pair of gray pinstriped slacks. She'd even shoved her aching feet into black pumps with kitten heels.

Now she was glad she had come.

Julia was a notable artist with a disconcerting but refreshing disregard for polite niceties. Her husband, Paul, balanced her perfectly with his rational legal mind and occasional intervention. Sometimes, when they looked at each other in a way that reminded Hannah of what she'd lost when her fiancé walked away, she'd take a swallow of wine to dull the jab of pain.

Paul smiled and shook his head. "I'm pretty sure Adam hasn't made anything as basic as chicken cordon bleu since he was a teenager."

"Do you know him?" Hannah asked, fishing for information about the man who kept popping up in her thoughts.

"Yes, he's Jimmy's—" Julia clapped a hand over her mouth and looked at Paul, exchanging with her husband one of those unspoken communications Hannah envied. Paul nodded, but Julia shook her head as she took her hand away. "Maybe we shouldn't tell her. Not everyone understands."

Curiosity had Hannah by the throat. This must be the revelation Sharon had refused to make. She leaned into the table to demonstrate her interest.

"He doesn't try to hide it, and I admire his courage in putting it out there," Paul said.

Julia looked skeptical. "I think he's just a realist. He knows you can't keep a secret like that in a small town like Sanctuary. But you're right. He's open about it and he does a tremendous amount of good."

Hannah was trying to figure out what on earth they might be talking about when Julia turned back to her and said, "Adam's been a great help to Paul's brother, Jimmy. He's his Alcoholics Anonymous sponsor."

Shock made Hannah blurt out, "Doesn't that mean Adam is a former alcoholic?" He didn't seem at all what she expected of someone who was an addict. She thought of his clear, brown eyes and the lean body under the black clothing. There was none of the outward damage often left by alcoholism. Adam exuded health, strength, and self-possession.

"He's been sober for some years," Paul said, "which makes him an excellent mentor."

"Of course," Hannah said, embarrassed because she was afraid she'd insulted Paul's brother as well as his sponsor. "I just didn't . . . he doesn't seem . . ."

Julia rescued her. "I know what you mean. He's so smooth and in control all the time. It's hard to imagine him falling-down drunk."

Hannah tried to rejigger her assessment of Adam Bosch. His alcoholism could explain his seeming neglect of Matt in his son's younger years. It could take a terrible toll on a family.

"I'm surprised you've met him," Paul said. "He doesn't come down off that mountain much."

Hannah pulled her mind back to the conversation. "His dog was injured, so he brought him in to the hospital."

"Again?" Paul said. "Tim had to patch Trace together a few years ago. He lost a fight with a black bear."

"I felt the old scars. This time it was a gunshot wound." Hannah debated a minute. "Do you know Adam's son, Matt?"

"Not well," Paul said. "He's around my nephew's age, but he just came to live with Adam a few months ago. Why?"

"He shadowed me today to see what a vet does." Hannah decided it wasn't fair to Adam or Matt to reveal why. "He got interested in a pony named Satchmo at Sharon Sydenstricker's stable." She made a wry face. "Sharon says Satchmo's his whisper pony."

"A whisper pony," Julia said. "Why not?"

"You know about Sharon's whisper horse theory?"

"Remember that big, cranky black stallion at the stable?" Paul asked.

"Darkside," Hannah said with a nod.

"That's Julia's whisper horse."

Hannah swiveled around to stare at Julia. "But I thought whisper horses were supposed to be soothing and supportive."

Julia gave her a serene look. "It depends on what you need from your whisper horse." She reached over to touch Paul's hand. "Darkside helped me show Paul and my family I was stronger than they thought." She held up her left hand, where an unusual horseshoe-shaped ring glinted with a dark light. "Paul even had my engagement ring designed as a symbol of Darkside's importance in bringing us together."

"Er, I see. The ring is lovely," Hannah said, not sure how to deal with the artist's conviction. All these seemingly normal people believed in Sharon's whisper horse theory. It was beginning to make Hannah feel like *she* was the odd one. She understood that owning a pet could be therapeutic, but much as she loved them she didn't think animals could solve human problems, much less play matchmaker.

Paul took pity on her. "Are you ready for some apple pie?"

"Yes, please," she said, throwing him grateful look.

Julia stood and picked up her dishes, waving Hannah back into her seat when she started to follow suit. "I can manage to slice pie and scoop ice cream, despite my general lack of culinary talent." She gathered up all the dishes on a tray and carried it into the kitchen, leaving Hannah and Paul at the table.

He leaned back in his chair. "I hope you won't be offended, but Tim's told me something about the events that brought you here to Sanctuary, and I think I could help you out."

Hannah stiffened as the memories of her flight from Chicago scorched through her mind. She remembered Paul ran a prominent national legal organization that provided pro bono legal assistance to those who couldn't afford it, and her guard went up. Given his job, he would have to be well connected in the political world, and she suddenly wondered just how much of her story he already knew. "It wasn't really a legal issue," she said to deflect him.

"Senator Sawyer claimed you could have contacted him via cell phone before you made the decision about his children's dog. Tim says you tried every channel available to you and were blocked by his staff. That's slander," Paul said. "What was written about you on social media and in the local paper was libelous. Those are both legal issues."

"It's nice of you to offer, but I prefer to leave well enough alone. It's behind me now." Nothing could undo the damage of being abandoned and denounced by her ex-fiancé when the story blew up. Robert Sawyer had tremendous influence and Ward had high political aspirations, so she became a liability to him. She sometimes wondered if he'd ever been in love with her, or if she'd just been a useful accessory for photo ops.

Paul nodded but she could tell her answer didn't satisfy him. "Think about it. You might want to set the record straight so it doesn't affect your future if, say, you wanted to leave Sanctuary someday. Not that Tim wouldn't give you a glowing reference, of course."

Everything he said was true, especially about Tim's generosity. After all, he'd hired her in spite of her tarnished employment record. However, she didn't have the stomach to face either Ward or Sawyer again. That's why she was hidden away in the town of Sanctuary, protected by the Appalachian Mountains. Perhaps the ugliness wouldn't find her here. "I'll think about it, thanks," she lied.

Julia reappeared with the tray, this time laden with wedges of warm pie à la mode and cups of fragrant, fresh coffee. "Don't mind Paul. He can't help himself," she said, with an affectionate glance at her husband. "He's a crusader for truth and justice."

Paul shifted in his chair. "Nope. Just a lawyer."

His discomfort at his wife's description was disarming, but she was still uneasy. Paul must have sensed it because after dinner he walked her to her car. "Julia's got a point about my crusading," he said, his tone rueful. "Sometimes I don't know when to leave well enough alone."

"You're a good person to want to help," she said, trying to smooth over her lack of enthusiasm. "It's just that some things can't be fixed."

Chapter 6

O N MONDAY EVENING, HANNAH SLOTTED HER SUV INTO
a parking space twenty feet from Moonshine and felt
guilt wash over her for about the tenth time. It didn't matter
how often she reminded herself she hadn't known about Adam's
addiction, she was still horrified that she'd suggested meeting in
a wine bar to a recovering alcoholic. Even though Adam ran a
restaurant where they served all kinds of liquor, she wished she'd
chosen a spot not so completely devoted to the appreciation of
alcohol. Her impulse to keep their meeting short had led her into
this uncomfortable situation.

She dropped her forehead onto the steering wheel. She'd spent
far too much time thinking about Adam and Matt yesterday,
her one day off. Even today at the hospital, the man and the boy
had worked their way into her thoughts at odd moments.

Lifting her head to check her reflection in the rearview mir-
ror, she smoothed her hair behind her ears. She'd touched up her
makeup before she left the veterinary hospital and added a pair
of gold hoops to her earlobes. Annoyed with herself for getting
gussied up for Adam, she shoved open the door and nearly hit a
passing car. The other driver swerved and, in typical Sanctuary
fashion, gave a friendly wave.

It was hard to stay grumpy in this town.

She stalked up to Moonshine and through the beveled glass
door. The interior sported a bar and polished paneling in exotic

woods with brass-rimmed round tables and comfortable arm-chairs arranged on the plush green carpeting. A constellation of miscellaneous, vintage chandeliers threw a soft, cozy glow over the room. The back wall was glass, allowing patrons to view the racks in the climate-controlled wine storage. As she hesitated, Adam rose from a table by the front window. "Dr. Linden. So nice to see you again."

She lifted an eyebrow at his formality as she walked up to the table. "Mr. Bosch, a pleasure."

He held out his hand. "Hannah, then?"

She nodded, intent on bracing herself for the moment of contact since she knew what her reaction would be. It happened again, that fizz of awareness created by the heat of his skin against hers. She was glad when he released her hand and held the chair for her to sink into.

As he returned to his seat, she noticed a large goblet of clear liquid sat in front of him on the table and wondered if she should order water too. Or would that just make it even more awkward because he'd know she knew?

"This is one of my favorite places in town," he said, settling in his chair. "Their cheese selection might be almost as good as The Aerie's."

His casual statement seemed aimed at easing her discomfort, but how could he possibly know what she was thinking? "I'm not much of a connoisseur," she said.

His face lit up. "Then may I make some recommendations?"

"You're the expert. You can order everything." She was trying to focus on something other than how the open collar of his black shirt framed the strong column of his neck.

He raised his hand just a fraction and a waiter materialized at their table. "We're pouring four excellent wines by the glass this afternoon," the young man said before reeling off the names, vintages, *terroirs*, and adjectives describing flavors Hannah never could taste. She was about to ask Adam for his recommendation when her eyes fell on his glass of water and she flushed again. "Um, the first one," she said, having no idea what she had ordered.

"A wise choice," the waiter said. He produced two hand-lettered cards and handed them to Hannah and Adam. "Our cheese selection for the day."

Adam scanned the card, his face intent, almost to the point of frowning. "Do you have a Cahill's Farm cheddar tonight?" The waiter shook his head and leaned down to suggest an alternative. When Ward used to debate over wines with the sommelier, it was to show off. He'd once sent back a perfectly good bottle of wine when they were out with another couple, making Hannah cringe in embarrassment. However, as Adam discussed the various offerings with the waiter, his genuine passion for the cheese shone through.

"We'll have your recommendation, as well as the Garrotxa, the Taleggio, and the Ewe's Blue," Adam said. "And some chutneys as well."

"Chutneys?" Hannah gave her menu back to the waiter, wondering what color wine she'd ordered.

"They accent the cheeses with a little hint of fruit." Adam picked up his glass and took a sip. His shirt sleeves were rolled up to just below his elbows, baring curves of muscle in his forearms. Evidently stirring large pots of food made for a good workout.

"About Matt," Hannah said to distract herself from speculating on what the flex of those muscles would feel like under her fingers. "He seems genuinely sorry for what happened to Trace. He considered your warning about letting the dog out as just another arbitrary rule you decided to make. He didn't understand the real danger to Trace. So I don't think you need to worry about it occurring again."

Relief crossed Adam's face. "Thank you. Every time I see that bandage on Trace, I get a punch of guilt right in the chest."

"Sorry about that. Those bandages only come in neon colors, so you can't miss them."

His smile was brief and didn't make it to his eyes. "Tell me more about the pony Matt likes."

The waiter appeared with a graceful crystal wine glass and a bottle of white wine. With a flourish he set the glass on the table and poured a mouthful of wine into it. Hannah grabbed the glass, took a swallow of the wine, and nodded. "Great. Thanks." She waited while the waiter filled her glass with a generous serving before moving it aside so she could talk to Adam.

He watched with a little crease between his brows. "Are you sure the wine is to your liking?" he asked.

"It's fine. Why?"

He shook his head. She looked from Adam to her wine glass, reminding herself food and wine were his profession, and he probably felt she'd been too hasty in her tasting. She picked up the glass and tried to get the wine to swirl around in it to prove she was paying attention. A drop sloshed over the edge of the glass, so she gave up on that and took a sip, letting the wine roll over her tongue in a deliberate way. Much to her surprise, she noticed how crisp and dry the flavor was. "It's excellent," she said, after swallowing.

He relaxed into his chair. "The pony?"

Hannah debated how much to tell him about whisper horses. "Do you know Sharon Sydenstricker?"

"I've met her once or twice."

"Have you heard about her whisper horse theory?"

He rubbed his chin. "She makes horses better by whispering to them?"

"No, people get better by whispering to horses. Not only that." Hannah took a hurried drink of wine. "There is one particular whisper horse for each person."

His eyebrows rose over a skeptical smile. At least *he* appeared to share her opinion of Sharon's theory.

Hannah plowed onward. "Not that I believe this woo-woo stuff, but I know animals can have a therapeutic effect on people. And I think Satchmo might help Matt, as well as Matt helping Satchmo."

Adam shifted forward. "It sounds unusual, but I'm willing to try anything."

"Then you need to talk to Sharon about setting up a time for Matt to take riding lessons. He was very interested when she offered."

"I'll get in touch with Sharon first thing tomorrow." His gaze was steady on her face. "I was ready to give up, but you've given me a handhold."

"I just treated Matt like a grouchy cat."

He looked startled, then gave a chuckle that held the deep vibration of a kettledrum. "I can see how that might work."

The waiter arrived again, this time with an elegantly arrayed cheese board, a divided condiment dish containing the colorful chutneys, and a basket of bread. He identified the first cheese and started to describe it before interrupting himself. "Mr. Bosch, you know more about these than I do, so I'll let you handle it from here."

"May I?" Adam asked Hannah, picking up the cheese knife.

She nodded. Her attention was drawn to his hands again as he cut perfectly uniform slivers of cheese and laid them on the bread before topping each one with a different chutney.

"Mildest first," he said, placing one of his creations on the small plate in front of her. "The Garrotxa, a goat's milk cheese from Catalonia."

She picked up the bread and took a bite. The taste of sweet fruit, creamy cheese, and crusty bread made her moan in appreciation.

Her stomach rumbled loudly and he chuckled. "Hunger is the best sauce." He bit into his own slice, his white teeth flashing. She watched in fascination as he went still, his concentration clearly on the flavors bursting on his tongue.

He nodded and began to chew. "As good as I remembered," he said. Noticing her observation, he raised the remainder of the bread in a salute. "It's not an easy cheese to obtain, so I haven't tasted it in a while. So far no amount of persuasion or bribery has convinced Brenda to give me the name of her supplier."

"Brenda?"

"The owner here," Adam said.

"What do you bribe her with?"

"The names of *my* suppliers, of course," he said, his smooth façade slipping back into place as he gave her one of his practiced smiles. "I've also tried chocolate."

"That would work on me." She bit into the other half of the bread and cheese.

"I'll keep that in mind." His voice had slid into a seductive purr, and she nearly choked. He put the next selection on her plate. "The Taleggio, from near Lombardy in Italy. It's a washed-rind cheese made with cow's milk. I've paired it with the quince chutney."

He watched her as she sampled it.

"Mmm, delicious." She finished it off and licked one of her fingers before she noticed a flicker of hunger in his eyes, one that had nothing to do with food. She dropped her hand to wipe it on the napkin in her lap. "Aren't you going to eat yours?"

"I enjoy watching your reaction," he said.

What other kinds of reactions might he enjoy watching? She gave herself a mental smack to check her overheated imagination.

He moved the third cheese to her plate. "Quicke's cheddar, also from cow's milk with the mango peach chutney."

She waited until his hand was all the way back on his side of the table before she picked up the sample and took a prim bite.

She was hungry and the cheese was wonderful, so she wolfed down the rest. "That's my favorite so far."

"You like the bold cheeses then." He looked impressed. "Now try the Ewe's blue from New York State."

"What's the chutney?" she asked, catching the aroma as she lifted it to her mouth. "Apple something?"

He nodded. "Cranberry apple. It has to be strong to counterbalance the blue."

The flavors exploded in her mouth, the sharpness of the cheese making her eyes water slightly. She seized the wine glass and took a swig to wash it down. "Wow! That one's great."

"More?" he asked, his fingers hovering over the cheese board.

She nodded, still tasting the wallop of the blue cheese. He shifted all the previously constructed samples to her plate. "I've made a cheese clock for you," he said, looking up with a smile. "The mildest cheese is at six o'clock. Then work your way around clockwise to reach the Ewe's blue."

He shifted back to assemble combinations for himself. She waited to eat hers not so much from courtesy but because it was fascinating to watch the confident efficiency with which he handled the food and knife. He had the hands of a working man, the nails trimmed short, the scars visible against his slightly olive skin. Her imagination took off again, conjuring images of those hands on her skin. "Are all those old injuries from knives?" she asked to deflect her thoughts.

"Knives, graters, grills, oyster shells," he said, filling his own plate. "Cooking is a hazardous business."

"Being a vet has its perils too." Hannah glanced down at the parallel welts on her hand. "I have these and some tooth marks that will never fade away." Hannah began progressing around her plate.

"You've been bitten? I got the sense you could soothe any savage beast."

"They don't mean to hurt me. They're in pain and they lash out to protect themselves."

A shadow crossed his face and was gone. "You're very forgiving."

"Of animals." She savored the cheddar.

"Not of people?"

She hadn't meant to go down that road. Something about his feeding her created a false sense of intimacy. "People should know better," she said with a shrug.

He gave her a sharp look but didn't comment.

"How's Trace doing?" she asked as the silence lengthened.

The furrows between Adam's brows smoothed out. "I re-bandaged the wound this morning. There was no redness or swelling."

"Good to hear." She didn't know what else to say, so she made a show of drinking the last of her wine. The waiter materialized almost the minute she set down the empty glass, a bottle at the ready.

"May I pour another glass?" he asked.

Hannah already felt a little buzzy, probably from having only a few pieces of bread and cheese to absorb the alcohol, but she nodded just to give herself something to fiddle with.

"Would you bring us some more bread and some country pâté?" Adam asked before he looked back to her. "You seem hungry."

Since she had planned to toss a frozen pizza in the oven for dinner, she didn't argue with him. Pâté sounded a heck of a lot more appetizing.

"So, what brought you to Sanctuary?" he asked.

It was a perfectly normal, friendly question, but it always threw Hannah when someone asked it. The reasons she had come to Sanctuary were so wretched she preferred to shove them into the darkest recesses of her mind. Not that they stayed there all the time, but she was getting better and better at ignoring them. Except when she was asked.

She used her standard bland, false answer. "I wanted to get back to working with large animals and saw Tim's job posting."

"I noticed your degree is from the University of Pennsylvania."

Estelle had insisted on hanging her diploma in the waiting room. The receptionist said all that fancy lettering impressed the clients.

"Maybe I came here for the same reasons you did," Hannah said, deciding the best defense was a good offense.

Adam's eyes went opaque. "I doubt it."

Hannah wasn't sure whether to bless or curse the timing of the waiter as he placed another bread basket and a tray with a little loaf of pâté on the table. Adam picked up the knife and began slicing pâté, laying it on bread and piling tiny gherkins on top before he glanced up at her. "When would you like to come to The Aerie?"

"Er, I'm waiting for a special occasion," Hannah said.

"There's no need to wait. You can come again for the special occasion."

Hannah snagged one of the pâté tidbits and stuffed it in her mouth, chewing to give herself time to think. She swallowed. "Next month." She didn't pick a day, hoping the time would pass by and he would forget. She was sure he was too busy to notice whether she showed up for a free meal or not.

"Why don't you—" He stopped with a little shake of his head and nudged the serving tray toward her. "Have another."

As she enjoyed another morsel, she remembered the additional piece of information she wanted to share with Adam. "There's something else you might want to do with Matt."

He went still, his gaze fixed on her with the message that she had his full attention.

"Take him to Disney World to swim with dolphins," she said.

"Disney World?" His head jerked back a fraction of an inch. "Isn't he too old for that?"

Now that she had to explain her suggestion, she realized what a minefield she'd strayed into. Would mentioning Matt's mother upset Adam? She had no idea what the dynamic had been between the two parents and whether he would be mourning his dead lover too. "He went to Disney World with his mother and interacted with dolphins from a platform. She promised to take him back when he was old enough to swim with them. It means something to him."

He began twisting the stem of his glass with one hand. When he raised his eyes to hers, they were filled with regret. "I don't think he'd want to go with me."

She couldn't help herself; she reached across the small table and laid her palm over the back of his hand, willing comfort into her touch. "Ask him."

His gaze dropped to their hands and an odd smile tugged at the corner of his lips. She didn't know how to get herself out of this position, so she froze. His smile twisted before he said, "I suppose the worst he can do is say no."

He turned his hand under hers so their palms met and wrapped his fingers around hers. "No wonder Trace lets you touch him." He gave her hand a gentle squeeze and released it, reaching for the cheese knife.

She pulled her hand back and seized her glass, gulping the wine to wash away the flare of response his comment had evoked deep in her gut. Instead of dousing it, the wine spread the heat through her body.

Adam fell back on the only thing that seemed to relax the jumpy veterinarian: food. He arranged more cheese and pâté on her plate. It was something he did well. For some reason she seemed very resistant to the idea of coming to his restaurant. That pricked his pride.

It also left him feeling in her debt. She'd found out more about Matt in eight hours than he had in four months.

She plowed through a few more bites of bread and pâté, looking as though she might flee for the door at any moment if he spoke again, so he just gave her an encouraging smile.

She returned it briefly, tossing a few stray strands of that silky, flaxen hair behind her shoulder. The gold hoops gleaming in her earlobes drew his eye to the tender skin of her neck and he wondered what she would taste like there. She said something and he yanked his thoughts away from their inappropriate path. "I'm sorry," he said. "I missed that."

"I need to go home and let my dogs out," she repeated. "The dog walker had to do her afternoon visit early today. It's been an education eating with you though." She fumbled with her purse.

"This is my treat," he said, not sure whether to be insulted or amused. "You took the time to talk with me about my son."

"Well, if you're sure." She started to rise, looking nervous.

"I'm very sure," he said, coming to his feet and walking around the table to pull out her chair.

She stood and sidestepped away from him. "I guess I'll see you when you bring Trace in again. Thanks so much."

He started to hold his hand out to shake hers, but she was already walking toward the door.

Lowering his hand, he sank down into her chair, feeling the lingering warmth of her body heat and catching a faint tangy scent of citrus. He shook his head. It shouldn't surprise him that the one person who could talk to his son wanted to avoid him. That was the way his life with Matt seemed to go.

He reached for his water and took a swallow, thinking about the dolphins at Disney World. Matt's mother had drowned, something he imagined Hannah didn't know, so it seemed insensitive to offer to take his son swimming. On the other hand, maybe that was the best thing to do so Matt wouldn't associate the water with her death.

He let his head rest against the arm chair's high back. How was he supposed to know the right way to help a child deal with his mother's death?

He found himself eyeing Hannah's half-finished wine, practically tasting the crisp, cool vintage sliding down his throat, blurring the edges of his problems.

He picked up the glass and carried it to the bar, leaning over to pour it down the drain in the stainless steel sink.

Hannah took her mail out of the box and opened the front door of her house to be greeted by her animal family with wild enthusiasm. She knelt to let her dogs lick her and her cats rub against her. She'd started adopting them as soon as she'd bought her own condo in Chicago because she couldn't understand why people wanted to come home to an empty house when they could have this kind of welcome.

"Okay, guys," she said, pushing to her feet. "Let me sort through the mail and we'll take a quick walk before dinner." The "w" and "d" words sent the dogs into paroxysms of yelping excitement, while the cats leapt onto the back of the couch and looked down on the canine hysteria with disdain.

She waded through the fray, flipping through the flyers and catalogues until she came to a handwritten envelope with no return address and a Chicago postmark. Frowning, she put it down on the kitchen counter and dropped the other mail in the recycling. There was no one she wanted to communicate with in Chicago, so she considered adding it to the discarded catalogues.

Curiosity got the better of her and she ran her finger under the flap to open it.

Inside were two pieces of paper folded together, one a single sheet of lined paper torn out of a spiral notebook, the other a Xeroxed copy of the standard information form that was filled out for every patient brought into the practice. The note was short and signed by one of the vet techs who had worked in the Chicago clinic with her.

Dear Dr. Linden,

What happened to you was crappy. I found the admission form so you can prove that jerk didn't leave his cell phone number when he dropped off Sophie. Here's a copy, but I know where the original is. I can get it for you if you want it.

Sincerely,

Vicky Landers

Hannah flipped to the Xeroxed page, skimming down the sheet. There it was: the bold black mark where Robert Sawyer had slashed through the blank line for a cell phone number where he could be reached. This was the document she'd needed to prove she'd had no way to contact the dog's owner before she made her decision about Sophie. When the office staff had tried to locate it, it had mysteriously vanished. She collapsed onto a kitchen stool as she stared at the papers in her hands.

Paul Taggart's offer floated into her mind. Now that she had proof, was it worth trying to clear her name?

She laid the documents on the counter and stared off through the sliding glass doors that led to the big, fenced backyard of her rented house. It would feel so wonderful to be free of the shadow that hovered over her life. She tried to picture her moment of vindication, but the image of Sawyer admitting he had lied just wouldn't come into focus.

Would it stir up the local media again, or was the story old news by now? She didn't think she could face another barrage of ugly, confusing questions. When the drama was playing out she'd stopped patronizing her regular coffee shop because the local weekly newspaper was displayed right beside the cash register, and she couldn't avoid seeing the accusatory headlines.

Her breathing grew rapid and shallow while a fist of anxiety squeezed her throat.

That answered her question. If just thinking about the possibility made her react like this, she certainly didn't want to face it in reality.

She slipped off the stool and shoved the papers in her kitchen junk drawer.

She'd have to find a way to thank Vicky for her support and persistence. The vet techs had surprised her with their partisanship. Three of them, including Vicky, had offered to swear they had seen the information form with the cell phone number blank, even though they hadn't. She'd refused their offer, not wanting their perjury on her conscience along with everything else.

Her partners, on the other hand, had distanced themselves from her, claiming the office staff wouldn't have allowed the sick, elderly dog to be left without a valid contact number. They were protecting the practice in the public eye, but she would have appreciated a little private sympathy. They were afraid of the influence Robert Sawyer could wield. Just as Ward had been.

"I love you, but I don't think you're cut out to be a politician's wife," he'd said, trying to cast their broken engagement as a favor to *her*.

She knew now how stupid she'd been to believe someone like Ward had fallen in love with her, but his courtship had been both persuasive and determined. She was flattered when he asked her three times to accompany him to the most prestigious charity gala on the social calendar, saying he didn't want to go if she wasn't beside him. She'd felt like a princess, all dressed up in a stunning silver gown she'd shopped for with his stylish campaign manager. As they entered the ballroom, the orchestra was playing a waltz. Ward had swept her onto the nearly empty dance floor, his tall, tuxedo-clad body just brushing against hers, his light blue eyes fixed on her as though no one else mattered.

She'd been flustered when the waltz ended and a smattering of applause broke out. The people around them had been nothing but a blur to her, so she hadn't been aware they were watching.

Ward had known it, though.

He always recognized exactly how to get people to watch him, and she was simply one element of his strategy. They'd met at a fundraiser for an inner-city animal shelter where she offered free spay/neuter clinics. A reporter had singled her out for an interview, casting her as the good-hearted vet who donated her time and expertise to animals no one else cared about. Ward had stood beside the cameraman, watching the whole performance.

As soon as the reporter found a new victim, Ward sauntered up, introduced himself, and asked her to the charity gala for the first time. She was pretty sure he'd proposed because someone told him single male candidates weren't as electable as married ones.

When she was being brutally honest with herself, she could admit she'd fallen in love with him against her better judgment. Some small voice in the back of her mind kept whispering that he was the wrong man for her, but Ward had convinced her he was crazy about her. It had seemed impossible not to reciprocate that kind of devotion. Tears burned in her eyes and she drew in a shaky breath. Glancing down she discovered her knuckles had gone white with the grip she had on the edge of the counter. She released it and flexed her hands to stretch the strained muscles.

She was safe in Sanctuary, nestled in the protective folds of the mountains. Her past wouldn't catch up to her here.

Chapter 7

HE BOSS LADY'S IN THE INDOOR RIDING RING, GIVING a lesson," the stable hand told Hannah. "Go through the north barn and you'll run into it."

Hannah turned in the direction the young man pointed, hefting the heavy medical duffel bag she'd brought from the truck.

"Hey, you want a hand with that?" the young man asked.

"Thanks but I'm okay," she said, not wanting to take him away from his work. She hadn't expected the darn bag to be so heavy. Tim carried it like it weighed nothing. "That's because he's the size of a mountain with muscles to match," she muttered.

She'd come to examine Satchmo more thoroughly. After reading Tim's notes on the pony and refreshing her knowledge of equine anatomy, she'd thought of some more tests she wanted to run on the sad little fellow. He might be grieving but he also might be ill, and she wanted to rule that out. She had meant to call Sharon but her day had been frantic, so she had dashed out the door without warning the stable owner she was coming.

Half-dragging her burden, Hannah staggered through the swirl of activity inside and outside the barns until she found the entrance to the riding ring. She eased open the door and pulled her duffel bag through it. The change in sound level was both startling and soothing. The thick bed of sand and sawdust muffled the fall of hooves, while voices echoed once before sinking into its depths.

She dropped the duffel and rolled her shoulders as she surveyed the arena. Dust motes danced in the late afternoon sunshine slanting through huge windows that rose from shoulder-height up to the massive wooden rafters supporting the vaulted ceiling. She stood behind the fence that outlined the ring itself. To her left a set of wooden bleachers stepped up nearly to the roof. She sucked in her breath when she saw a black-clad figure sitting alone halfway up the risers, his attention riveted on the ring. His ensemble was casual today, consisting of oft-washed jeans, a polo shirt, and a scuffed leather jacket. Awareness sizzled through her, and she jerked her gaze back to the arena.

Several horses circled it, some with attendant instructors. In the far corner, she saw Sharon, her height and flaming red hair making her easy to spot, walking beside a pony and rider. As they came closer, she recognized Satchmo and Matt.

Her heart gave a little lift as she saw the boy smile and lean down to pat the scruffy pony on the shoulder. Although Satchmo wasn't exactly prancing around the ring, his ears showed a livelier tilt.

"Well, I'll be, it's Dr. Linden," Sharon said as the trio approached. "What brings you out this way again?"

"Satchmo," Hannah said, pointing to her bag. "I wanted to give him a more thorough going over." She nodded to Matt. "Hey, how's the riding going?"

"It's okay," he said, but his face was alive with excitement.

"He's got a way with Satchmo, no doubt about it," Sharon said, coming to a halt beside the fence.

Matt sat up straighter on the polished English saddle.

"I can see that," Hannah said. "Satchmo looks a lot happier than he did the last time I was here."

The boy ducked his head, but Hannah glimpsed the grin of pride he was trying to conceal.

Sharon glanced at a big clock hanging on the wall to her left. "I'll take them around one more time and then Satchmo's yours. I appreciate your concern, doc."

As they continued around the oval, Hannah heard footsteps, turning just as Adam leapt lightly down from the seating area. His dark hair and dark attire, combined with his smooth, athletic stride reminded her of a panther. A very hot panther.

Maybe that's why he always wore black: he knew it suited him. Or maybe it was merely a way to simplify his life. The burn of her curiosity was disconcerting; his fashion choices were none of her business.

His smile flashed white in the dimness and the cleft in his chin deepened. She imagined tracing her fingertips over it.

"Hannah, what a pleasure to see you," he said, reaching out to take her hand between both of his.

Now the heat and texture of his palms against her skin added to the haze of her reaction to him. "You didn't waste any time organizing Matt's riding lessons," she said, trying to ease her hand from between his without success.

"You threw me a lifeline and I grabbed it with both hands," he said, slanting his gaze downward to where their hands were still clasped with a glint of humor in his eyes.

He finally let go, and she tucked her hand into the pocket of her quilted brown barn jacket.

His gaze shifted to Sharon's tall figure. "Sharon fit Matt into her schedule because she's worried about Satchmo. Or so she told me." He looked back at Hannah. "I think she's worried about Matt too. She's taking a lot of time and trouble with him."

"It doesn't surprise me," Hannah said. "She's a rescuer."

"Like you."

"Me?" Startled, she shook her head. "I'm a doctor. That's different."

"A healer then," he said. "Of body and soul."

This conversation was making her squirm, but he'd given her an opening to move it in another direction. "So you believe animals have souls?" she asked.

"It wouldn't be much of a heaven if there were no animals in it so, yes, I think they have souls." He shrugged, an eloquent lift of his shoulders. "Hell would have no animals in it, just to make it even more hellish."

"You must have been raised in a very open-minded religion," Hannah said, reluctantly impressed. Even people who loved their pets didn't necessarily feel their spirits went on after death.

"My religion is food," he said.

It sounded like an answer he'd given often, but she believed him after seeing the way he treated the cheese at Moonshine. In fact, she was starting to believe most of what he said. The smooth charm seemed natural, not calculated.

A creak of leather announced the approach of Matt, his mount, and their instructor. "Do you have time for Matt to take Satchmo back to his stall? He can help Dr. Linden with him," Sharon said.

The boy tried not to look eager, but his gaze was fastened on his father as he waited for his answer.

"Of course," Adam said. He gave Sharon one of his oh-so-charming smiles. "We'll stay until you throw us out."

Sharon didn't seem to find his smile suspect, either. She winked and said, "Make yourself comfortable."

As Matt guided the pony to the gate, Adam jogged over and pushed it open to let them out. The boy swung off Satchmo, his knees sagging when his feet hit the ground. He straightened, and Hannah gave him credit for a quick recovery. Sharon showed him how to run the stirrups up the leathers so they wouldn't bang against Satchmo's side as he walked.

"Okay, take him back to his stall," she said.

Adam started to follow, but Sharon made a small gesture to hold him back.

"You go ahead, Matt," Sharon said. "I need to have a word with Sasha about how she's working JoJo." She nodded in the direction of the ring. "Just hang with Satchmo until we get there."

Matt rubbed a hand down his pants leg and swallowed. "Okay," he said, his voice quavering slightly. He resettled his grip on Satchmo's bridle and urged the pony forward again.

Hannah saw Adam ball his hands into fists as he watched his son lead the pony through the big door. "He'll be fine," she said. "Satchmo's more likely to fall asleep than to bolt on him."

Adam uncurled his fingers and flexed them as he turned back to her. "He seemed nervous."

"He can do it. He just needs to find that out," Sharon said. "You got a good kid there, Mr. Bosch. He'll be a fine horseman if he keeps up the riding."

Adam's face lit up at the praise of his son. "I appreciate your working him into your schedule at such short notice. And it's Adam, please."

"I got a soft spot for young 'uns who like horses, Adam," Sharon said, walking toward the door.

"Don't you have to talk to Sasha?" Hannah asked.

"Nah, that was just an excuse to let the boy build his confidence," Sharon said.

Hannah went back to where she'd dumped the duffel bag by the door. Before she'd done more than get a good grip on the handle, Adam was leaning down beside her. "Let me," he said, his hand brushing against hers as he grasped the canvas strap.

"Happy to," she said, releasing it instantly and jerking her hand away from the possibility of another searing touch. "That sucker weighs a ton."

He lifted it like it was a shopping bag filled with filmy lingerie. "I'm used to carrying fifty-pound bags of flour," he said with a wry look.

Hannah eyed him a moment. "Maybe you could get the X-ray machine out of the truck for me too," she said. She'd been debating whether to try dragging the gismo in; it was on wheels, but that didn't help much in the barn's thick pine bark footing.

"My pleasure," he said.

"It's the big, yellow, boxy thing marked 'X-ray'," she said, giving him a brief smile before she started toward Sharon.

"I might have figured that out." He fell into step beside her, his fluid stride unaffected by the burden he carried on his right side.

Hannah walked between Sharon and Adam, aware the whole way of the physical presence of the man beside her. She snuck quick exploratory glances at him, discovering he wore smooth black leather boots and a bold stainless-steel wristwatch. His hair waved with more abandon now than when he'd been dressed in his go-to-work suit, while the denim of his jeans traced the flex of his thighs as he walked.

Sharon stopped outside the stall, unlatching the door and waving Hannah through. Matt stood beside the pony, saying something low in his ear. He looked up. "Hey, Dr. Linden. Do you really think Satchmo seems better? I wasn't sure I should even ride him, but Ms. Sydenstricker said it would do him good if we kept it to a walk."

Hannah saw the anxiety in the boy's eyes. "Exercise is good for ponies. They need it to help their digestion. Besides, if Sharon says it, it's true. She knows everything there is to know about horses."

His expression eased until his father walked in. Matt turned his face back to the pony.

"You looked great on Satchmo," Adam said. "Sharon says you'll be a fine horseman."

Matt hunched one shoulder. "I just started."

"But it's a good start," Adam said before he turned to Hannah. "Where would you like your bag?"

"Over in the corner," Hannah said, pointing. "Let's get Satchmo's tack off."

"I can take care of that," Sharon said, coming through the door.

"I'll get the X-ray machine," Adam said, stepping aside for Sharon and then striding out before Hannah could say anything. The unhappy set of his shoulders sent a pang of guilt through her. Why did Matt have to make it so obvious he preferred her company to his father's?

Sharon and Matt soon had the pony's saddle and bridle off and his halter buckled on. Then Sharon took the tack and left with a promise to return with a grooming kit for Matt to brush down Satchmo.

"So what do you think's wrong with him?" Matt asked as he stood holding the lead line attached to the pony's halter.

"I don't know," Hannah said, troubled that she didn't have a better answer. After moving around the horse to compare his muscle tone on different sides, she used her pen to flick alongside his spine, watching for a normal skin twitch.

She took the lead line from Matt and tugged gently. Satchmo let her turn his head to the left and then to the right without noticeable concern. "Good. His neck's not bothering him."

"Okay, take his lead line again." She walked behind the pony and grabbed his pale-blond tail. "Walk him forward a step," she said and pulled Satchmo's tail hard sideways. He staggered slightly. "Hmm, a balance issue there."

That was the first sign she'd seen that his problem might be something other than emotional.

"What does that mean?" Matt asked, looking worried.

"It might mean something is affecting his nervous system. If so, we can find it," Hannah reassured him. "Or he might just be a klutz."

That got a brief smile from the boy, who stroked the pony's reddish-brown neck. "He wasn't klutzy when I rode him."

"A good rider actually helps his mount stay balanced," Hannah said, remembering her own riding lessons.

"Really?" Matt's smile was genuine this time.

"Here's the kit," Sharon said, swinging a plastic tack box filled with various brushes, curry combs, and other grooming equipment over the stall door. "Remember what I showed you before we saddled him up? Just brush the same places, with some extra attention to where the saddle and girth were. He'll like that."

Matt took the caddy and set it down on the straw bedding under Satchmo's hanging water bucket.

Adam looked over the half-door. "I've got the X-ray machine."

"Bring it in," Hannah said, giving Satchmo a nudge to move him out of the way. She liked the fact that Matt continued to smooth his hand over the pony's neck and shoulders. Satchmo didn't look especially bothered by the commotion, but Matt's soothing might be partially responsible for that.

Adam half-carried, half-shoved the bright-yellow wheeled chest into the stall. He dusted his palms on the back of his jeans. "This thing wallows rather than rolls."

"It's not well-designed for cross-country travel," Hannah said with an apologetic look. She knelt to flip open the latches and began assembling the pieces of the machine.

Adam squatted down beside her. "What can I do to help?"

She hesitated a moment, not sure she wanted to work so closely with his distracting presence. She could think of no polite reason to refuse, so she handed him the stand for the scanner. "If you could set this up . . ."

He took it and stood, turning it over in his hands several times. "My father used to work on antique cars in his spare time. After a couple of attempts to teach me where the carburetor was, he gave up." He managed to pry out one of the legs. "I'm better with pans."

"Don't feel bad," she said, taking the stand and flipping open the other legs before she set it on the straw. "I can't make a soufflé."

She heard a snort of laughter from Matt. Adam's head swiveled toward his son before he turned back to Hannah with a somber smile. "Give me clear instructions, and I'll do the heavy lifting."

"Deal." With his assistance, she assembled the machine swiftly. "Okay, Matt, keep Satchmo as still as you can while I scan this over him."

Tim bought only the best equipment for his practice, so the X-ray machine was digital, allowing her to examine the images as she took them. The boy and the pony showed remarkable patience as she had them shift positions to improve the pictures. She didn't see any noticeable abnormalities, although she'd go over the X-rays again at the office. Blowing out a frustrated breath, she almost wished there'd been something wrong that she could diagnose and treat.

"All done. Satchmo deserves a good brushing for being such a cooperative patient," she said, running her hand along the pony's back before moving to his head to scratch behind his ears. He huffed out a long sigh that made Matt chortle.

"I know," Hannah said. "Doctors are such a pain." She caught the ache of longing in Adam's eyes as he watched the by-play between her and his son.

"Did you see anything bad?" the boy asked.

Hannah shook her head. "No tumors, no obstructions, no spinal damage. I'm going to draw some blood while you're grooming him to see what else I can rule out."

"So he might be sad about his stall buddy," Matt said. "That could be all that's wrong with him."

"It could be," she agreed. However, she didn't want to take the chance that it was something she should be treating medically.

She unhooked the scanner from its stand. Adam disassembled the rest of the machine, proving he was a quick study, while she stowed the parts back in the chest. "I'll wheel that back to the truck when you're ready to leave," he said.

It took only a few more minutes to draw Satchmo's blood. As she packed the vials away in their hard case in the duffel bag, Matt cast a glance at her and cleared his throat. "I thought . . . maybe . . . well, could you text me if you find out anything? I'll give you my cell number." His voice shook slightly, and Hannah realized he was expecting the worst.

"Sure thing," she said, pulling out her phone to type in the number he gave her. "It may take a couple of days to get results but whatever I find out, I'll tell you right away." She met the boy's eyes straight on. "Don't make yourself crazy worrying. We'll figure out how to make Satchmo feel better."

As she stooped to pick up the duffel, the bag was whisked out from under her fingers. "I'll put it on top of the X-ray machine," Adam said.

"But—"

Clearly torn between parental concern and chivalry, he held up his hand to stop her objection before he turned to his son. "Matt, will you be okay here while I help Dr. Linden?"

Matt cast him a look of disgust. "Sharon trusted me to lead Satchmo back here."

"How about I stay here until you get back?" Hannah said. It was safer for her peace of mind not to spend any more time than necessary with Adam.

He gave her a perplexed look, as though he suspected she was avoiding him.

Matt nodded and went back to brushing Satchmo, while Hannah held the stall door open to let Adam wrestle the X-ray machine out into the barn's wide central passageway. When they emerged, Sharon broke off the conversation she was having with a groom and came over. "Is Matt in there with Satchmo?"

"He's still brushing him," Adam said. "I'll be right back."

"I'll stay here while you lug that mini-school bus back to Doc's truck," Sharon said, strolling over to the stall door.

"Well . . . okay," Hannah said, wishing Sharon weren't so darned accommodating. Sticking her head back in the stall, Hannah said, "Matt, Sharon's here, so I'll be in touch with you as soon as I know anything."

She jogged along the central corridor to find Adam had hauled the X-ray chest, burdened with the extra weight of the duffel, halfway through the barn. Catching up with him, she noticed the pull of the black leather over his shoulders as he strained to move the machine through the thick pine bark. He bent to adjust a wheel, making his jeans tighten across his muscular butt and thighs. She found herself cursing the chest's awful design for giving her such an eyeful.

"I'll help," she said, getting on the other side and pushing so she didn't have to resist the temptation to gawk at him.

"What did they think you would be rolling this over? Paved roads?"

"Tim ordered larger wheels, but they haven't arrived yet," she said.

Once they got the chest out onto the relatively smooth gravel parking area, Adam said, "I can handle it from here." Hannah stepped back and let him go. He slid the duffel bag carefully onto the front seat and walked back to hoist the chest into the truck. She was struck by the easy grace with which he moved, like one of Sharon's Thoroughbreds.

She joined him just as he slammed the tailgate closed. "Thanks," she said. "I was going to co-opt one of Sharon's stable hands to deal with that."

When he turned, she noticed his chest rising and falling, his breathing accelerated from his exertions. And suddenly she was aware of him on a different level, one that was primitive and physical. The feeling curled low into her belly and made her eyelids grow heavy as her gaze focused on his mouth, its sensual lower lip edged by that dusting of dark stubble. She found herself imagining what his shadow beard would feel like against her skin.

His breathing grew louder, and she lifted her eyes to find him staring down at her with an intentness that matched her own. For a long, still moment, she let herself drink in the velvet darkness of his eyes and the scent of spices that drifted across the small space between them. With a faint creak of his leather jacket, he lifted a hand to catch the loose strand of her hair blowing across her face and smooth it behind her ear.

The slight brush of his fingers against the shell of her ear sent a shiver racing through her body.

For a moment they simply looked at each other, whatever it was between them vibrating in the air.

He lowered his hand. When he spoke, his voice was hoarse. "You've been so good to Matt."

She felt like he had changed the subject, even though they hadn't exchanged a word after she'd thanked him. She shrugged and shoved her hands in the pockets of her jacket. "He's helping Satchmo."

He stared at his boots in silence before looking back up. "I plan to buy Satchmo, so send the bill for today's visit to me."

She shook her head and he frowned. "I came on my own today," she explained. "Sharon didn't ask me to, so there's no charge."

"You used expensive medical equipment and spent a lot of time on the pony. You should be paid."

"If we get Satchmo right, that's payment enough." She scuffed her toe in the gravel. "That's a nice thing to do, buying the pony for Matt."

"There isn't a lot I can do for my son, so I'm glad to have this."

Sadness seeped through her. It must be tough to have his child reject him so completely. "I'd better tear Matt away so Sharon can get on with her day," he said. Instead of turning away, as she expected, his gaze stayed on her face while he seemed to debate some question with himself. "Hannah, I . . . thank you." He leaned forward to lightly touch his lips to hers, the stubble barely grazing her skin.

That briefest brush of his mouth against hers sent her nervous system into overload. She felt herself begin to lean into the kiss just as he pulled back and wheeled away toward the barn.

She stood there, watching his back, while his touch seemed to repeat itself all over her body.

She turned and bolted into the truck, slamming the door to shatter whatever had just passed between them.

Adam walked into the barn as though he knew exactly where he was going. The moment he stepped out of the sunlight and into the shadowy interior, he dodged into an empty stall and leaned his forehead against the rough wood of the partition.

What the hell did he think he was doing? He'd found someone who could actually communicate with Matt and he was going to screw it up by adding personal complications. He smacked his palm against the wall.

For a moment he'd forgotten about everything except the pale silk of Hannah's hair, the cold-heightened pink of her cheeks, and the certainty that kissing her would be the best thing he'd felt in a long time.

It had to be her kindness toward Matt and Satchmo that made him lose his bearings. Watching her sensitive hands as they glided over the pony's body in search of unseen problems, he'd found himself wishing it were his body she was touching with such gentle inquiry. He felt a stirring in his gut as the image of Hannah skimming her fingers down his bare chest washed through his mind.

He pounded the wall harder.

Chapter 8

$\mathcal{A}$FTER SCANNING THE INTAKE SHEET ON THE DOOR, Hannah walked into the examining room to meet her sixth patient of the day. A squat, gray-haired woman wearing a paisley housecoat stood beside the examination table, on which a plastic cat case rested.

"Good morning, Mrs. Shanks. I'm Dr. Linden. I understand Willie is having trouble with hair balls?"

"Where's Dr. Tim?" the elderly woman asked, grabbing the handle of the cat case.

"He's out of town," Hannah said with a smile, going to the sink to wash her hands. "I'm his new partner."

"I'll just wait until he gets back," the woman said, swinging the cat case off the table.

Startled, Hannah looked up. "He's not returning until Monday, and it sounds like Willie needs treatment now."

"Then I'll take him to the vet over to Humphries." Mrs. Shanks maneuvered the cat carrier through the door and was gone before Hannah could dry her hands.

She was concerned about the cat's health, so she followed the woman down the hallway to the door into the reception area. Mrs. Shanks was in a hurry, and the door swung shut in Hannah's face. As she reached for the knob, she heard the woman say, "Estelle Wilson, I'm not having that woman vet work on my Willie. How could you think such a thing?"

So Mrs. Shanks was sexist. Hannah could handle that. She started to turn the knob, when the woman continued. "I hear she killed a dog in Chicago without the owner's permission. I'm going to Dr. Lawson in Humphries." Her voice grew louder. "And everyone in this waiting room should too."

Hannah let go of the knob and walked blindly into the first empty examining room she saw, closing the door and bracing herself on the counter.

Her past had found her even here in Sanctuary, a place she had been certain was far enough away and isolated enough that no one but her boss would have heard her story. Since Tim knew what had happened and had still hired her, she hoped that even those who were aware of it wouldn't care about what happened in a distant city.

Mrs. Shanks's words yanked her back six months to the horrible days in Chicago when patient after patient cancelled appointments with her. Or worse, they kept their appointments so they could tell her in no uncertain terms what they thought of her actions before they whisked their pets out the door, just like Mrs. Shanks.

She braced herself on the Formica countertop, her head hanging as she sucked in deep breaths to ease her anxiety. She'd done the right thing back in Chicago. Why was its shadow falling on her here?

She wondered how many people in the waiting room outside had followed the woman's advice and walked out. Her throat closed up and she struggled to swallow. She couldn't go through this again. And she couldn't do this to Tim.

The door opened and she jerked upright, turning away from whoever was entering and wrenching on the faucets to pretend she was scrubbing her hands.

"Oh, sorry, Dr. Linden," she heard Sonya say. "I'll go to another room."

She was heaving a sigh of relief when a familiar voice said, "Wait, I'd like to talk with Dr. Linden."

Adam must have glimpsed her over Sonya's shoulder. She just hoped he hadn't seen her moment of weakness on the counter.

"Um, we'll meet her in Room Four," Sonya said. "This one hasn't been prepped yet."

Hannah sagged against the sink, her hands still soapy, as she mentally blessed the vet tech for giving her time to compose herself. She quickly rinsed and splashed cold water on her face. Refastening her ponytail, she straightened her stethoscope, and after taking another breath, walked out the door and down the hall to Room Four.

She stopped in front of the closed door to grab the intake sheet out of the plastic holder before pasting a smile on her face. Twisting the knob, she walked in, saying, "Good morning, Adam. Hey, Trace." Keeping her gaze on the big black dog, she went straight to him to scratch behind his ears and get a couple of slurps from his long pink tongue.

She finally worked up the nerve to glance at Adam. He stood on the other side of the table with his arms crossed and concern written on his face. "What's wrong?" he asked.

She shook her head and turned back to the dog, tugging at the end of the bandage wrapped around his chest. "How's Trace been?"

"I saw you in the other room. Talk to me."

Her eyes began to burn with tears, and she had to blink hard. "You're here to see me as your dog's veterinarian."

He came around the table and gripped her shoulders, forcing her to face him. "What was the woman in the reception area talking about?"

She shrugged out of his grasp. "Something that happened in the past. It just caught me off guard."

He muttered a curse under his breath. "No one left the waiting room after the woman made her announcement. Not one person."

"They wouldn't dare with Estelle glaring at them," Hannah said. She reached for Trace's bandage again.

Adam caught her hand and held it. "Tell me what I can do to help."

"Nothing. It's over." She tried to pull her hand away, but his grip was unrelenting.

"It's not over if that woman is talking about it." He lifted his other hand to tip her chin up so she couldn't escape his gaze. "You've helped me with Matt. Let me return the favor."

There was so much kindness and caring in his eyes the tears threatened again. "You can't help me. I euthanized a dog without informing the family who owned it." She waited for Adam to look shocked or horrified.

"Knowing you, I have no doubt it was necessary," he said.

Some dam inside her collapsed, and the story came spilling out. "Sophie was the sweetest old golden retriever you'd ever meet. The staff loved her. But, like so many goldens, she developed cancer. I'd been treating her for a month, trying to slow the cancer's progress, but it was spreading everywhere. All I could do was give her pain meds to keep her comfortable."

She leaned back against the counter, needing the anchor of something solid to keep her from being swept away into her past. "At Sophie's last appointment, I told Mrs. Sawyer that Sophie's pain was increasing, and I wouldn't be able to control it much longer. As hard as it was to contemplate, she needed to consider euthanizing Sophie."

Adam nodded, his attention centered on her.

Hannah wrapped her fingers around the edge of the counter as the scene grew more vivid in her mind. "I was flabbergasted when she said her family was about to leave for a two-week vacation, and she didn't want to distress the children by putting their dog to sleep. I tried to make her understand that the dog her children loved so much would be in excruciating pain long before their vacation was over, but she wouldn't even consider it." She looked at Adam. "I didn't want to upset her children, but Sophie was going to die, no matter what I did. I thought Mrs. Sawyer would want to spare her a slow, agonizing death." Hannah shook her head, remembering her disbelief at the woman's callousness toward the dog. It struck her that Adam had a child he might protect in the same way, and she bit her lip as she cast him a sideways glance.

He made a gesture of repudiation. "You know how I feel about children understanding the responsibilities of owning a pet. I love Matt, but I wouldn't allow Trace to suffer for the sake of a vacation." After seeing him with Trace, she should have known how he would respond.

"So they went on their family trip," Adam prompted.

"I agreed to board Sophie because I wanted to make sure she got the best possible care." She shoved away from the counter to pace around the small room. Trace lay down with his head on his paws, his ears swiveling to follow her. "Robert Sawyer brought Sophie in, probably because his wife was afraid to face me. I tried to reason with him, but he brushed me off as though I were an annoying insect." Anger stiffened her spine as she remembered the man's dismissal of her pleas on Sophie's behalf. "I was so furious, I sent him out to the receptionist to fill out the form for boarding Sophie. She told me later that he refused to leave a cell phone number where we could contact him while he was away. He didn't want his vacation disturbed."

"Bastard," Adam muttered under his breath.

"Yes!" She'd gotten more worked up than she realized. Pivoting on her heel, she walked back to where Trace lay on the table, stroking his sleek head to calm herself. "I did my best for Sophie. During the day, we put her bed in my office, so I could monitor her constantly. Whenever the staff members had free time, they'd go in and sit with her. She always greeted us with a wag of her tail and a lick on the hand." She buried her fingers in Trace's thick fur, drawing comfort from his warmth. "After two days, she couldn't walk, so we had to carry her in and out. Even then, she'd wag her tail when she saw us. I dosed her with all the pain meds I could, but the third day, I gave her the lightest of strokes on her head and she whimpered. When one of the vet techs tried to take the soiled blanket out from under her, Sophie growled." Hannah felt the tears spill down her cheeks as she remembered. "No one had ever heard Sophie growl before, so I knew the meds weren't working anymore."

She swiped the tears off her face with the sleeve of her lab coat. "I gave her sleeping pills, hoping that would give her a rest from the pain. Her eyelids would close for a few seconds, but then she would wake up with a moan. She'd gotten so thin her bones showed through her coat, which was long and thick. All the vet techs begged me to put an end to her suffering."

She remembered the moment her conscience told her she couldn't allow the sweet, faithful golden retriever to suffer any longer. She'd grabbed the intake form and gone to the phone herself, dialing the Sawyer's home phone and then the office phone. Neither the housekeeper nor the administrative assistant would give her a way to contact the family, saying they had strict orders not to bother them on their vacation. The Sawyers' staff was either very loyal or very intimidated. No amount of pleading would budge them.

"I tried to reach the family, but once it became clear I wouldn't be able to, I wasn't going to wait any longer. I got two vet techs to witness the injection." She swallowed a sob. "I held her in my arms as she died, telling her what a great girl she was and how much she was loved, so much that her family didn't want to let her go."

"I don't understand why you were blamed." His hands were clenched in fists by his thighs.

She pulled a paper towel out of the nearby holder and swiped it over her cheeks. "The father was Senator Robert Sawyer. He didn't want to look bad in front of his children, so he lied to them about leaving a cell phone number."

"But you had the intake form."

"That's the thing. It disappeared." She thought of the Xeroxed copy stashed away in her kitchen drawer. "I'd used it to make all the phone calls, and I couldn't swear I'd put it back in the proper file . . . or in any file. I wasn't that concerned about the paperwork at the time."

"So Sawyer was a liar and a jerk. That shouldn't drive you out of Chicago. Unless he sued." Adam's dark eyebrows slashed down with his frown.

"Worse. One of his kids talked about it on Twitter," Hannah said. "The local weekly gossip sheet got hold of it, so the senator was forced to either stand by his story or admit he lied to his children. Guess which he chose?"

Adam paced a step away and back. "So he ruined your career in order to preserve his image."

She shrugged. "He's an important man who just wanted to have a pleasant time away with his family. I'm a heartless quack who doesn't care about his children's tender feelings." She knew she sounded bitter, but she had no tolerance for the sense of privilege that valued an undisturbed vacation more than easing an animal's profound pain.

Of course, she wasn't going to tell Adam that her then-fiancé had jumped right on the bandwagon with Senator Sawyer as soon as he saw which way the wind was blowing. Being on the senator's good side was more important to an up-and-coming politician than supporting his future wife. She stifled a gasp as the shock of Ward's defection ripped through her all over again.

She'd underestimated Adam's powers of observation because he said, "There's something more to the story."

She shook her head. "It's just residual anger." She yanked out another paper towel and blew her nose. "Your poor dog has been so patient. It's his turn now."

She could see Adam forming another question, so she turned to Trace and unwound the bandage to forestall any further discussion. "The wound is healing beautifully," she said, putting another pad in place and winding a fresh length of elastic around it. "I don't think it will even leave a scar."

Adam ran a hand over Trace's glossy head. "You hear that, boy, no scars to scare off the ladies. You owe Dr. Linden for that." He stroked Trace's flank before he looked up at her. "I owe you too. On the way home after Matt's riding lesson, he talked to me about Satchmo. It's the first real conversation I've had with him."

"Animals have a way of opening people up," Hannah said, leaning forward to let Trace give her a wet kiss.

Adam sent her a slanting smile. "*You* have a way of opening people up."

"Didn't I just spill my guts to *you*?" she said ruefully, as she pushed the button to lower the examination table to floor level.

"I caught you at a bad moment."

Embarrassed by her meltdown, she moved to the computer terminal to start typing notes on Trace's condition.

She felt his nearness before he touched her, cupping her shoulders lightly. "Come to The Aerie for dinner," he said by her ear.

Her fingers went still on the keyboard as she felt his breath stir her hair. She closed her eyes and fought the urge to lean back against him. She could imagine his arms coming around her so she was enveloped by his strength and the delicious, spicy scent he carried.

For a minute she thought he was asking her on a date, and the prospect sent her heartbeat into overdrive. Then she realized she was fooling herself the same way she had with Ward.

The sexy, famous chef didn't want to spend the evening with his veterinarian. Supermodels and movie stars were probably more his type.

He was only repeating his previous offer of a free dinner at his restaurant. She forced her eyes open and started typing as though he hadn't set every one of her nerve endings dancing. "You need a date for a dinner like that, and I haven't been in town long enough to have one. So I'll take a rain check for now."

He continued to hold her. "Come on Tuesday. It's my day off, so I'll keep you company."

She wanted to move away from him, but he had her trapped between the counter and his body. There was no graceful way to extricate herself unless he released her. She saved Trace's computer record and laid her hands on either side of the keyboard. "You don't want to go to the restaurant on your day off."

He laughed and let go. She scooted sideways before she turned around. He stood about two feet away, his thumbs tucked into the pockets of his black jeans.

"I'm at the restaurant every day," he said. "I just don't supervise on Tuesdays. It's good to give the staff a day on their own. Let them stretch their wings. I'll pick you up at 6:30."

She opened her mouth to refuse.

He raised a hand to stop her. "Food is what I'm good at. Let me do this."

"I haven't got anything to wear," she said, grasping at straws.

"A clean lab coat meets the dress code," he said with a glint of a smile.

She managed a smile in return. "I guess I can swing that."

He picked up the end of Trace's leash and stood jiggling it for a moment. "There has to be a way to clear your name," he said. "I have political connections because of the restaurant. I can—"

She shook her head. "I appreciate the offer, but I don't want to stir it all up again. Tim will come back Monday, and Mrs. Shanks will let him treat Willie. I just didn't expect the story to follow me here."

"For what it's worth," he said, reaching out to gently squeeze her shoulder, "I believe you made the right decision."

She touched the back of his hand. The feel of his skin turned the comfort to something deeper and hotter. "It's worth a lot."

He let his hand drop from her shoulder, and led the dog out the door.

As she slipped the intake form into Trace's medical folder, she felt a curious sense of lightness.

Adam pulled into a parking space in front of Paul Taggart's law office and unbuckled the re-bandaged Trace from his seat harness. Coming around to the passenger door, he signaled the dog out of the car. "Paul says you can come in."

Trace fell in beside him as he jogged up the front steps of the gingerbread-trimmed Victorian house Paul worked in. It was too frou-frou for Adam's minimalist taste, but much of Sanctuary was built before the Civil War and the residents liked their historic curlicues.

Paul stood and came around his big, oak desk as his receptionist ushered Adam and the dog into the office. The lawyer bent and gave Trace a scratch under the chin. "Have a seat," he said, waving to the sofa under the window and dropping into an armchair. "What can I do you for?"

Adam sat and Trace lay down at his feet, his head on his paws, his ears pointed up. "Do you know the new veterinarian who works with Tim? Hannah Linden?"

Paul looked surprised. "Sure do. She had dinner with Julia and me a couple of nights ago. Nice lady."

"She and Matt get along well," Adam said, groping for a way to bring up a matter that was not, in fact, his concern. "She's gotten him interested in horseback riding."

"That's a positive step."

"She told me a story today," Adam said. "About why she left Chicago and came here. Has Tim mentioned anything about it?"

Paul nodded. "He thinks she got railroaded."

"I'd like to help her straighten things out. What can we do?"

Now Paul shook his head. "I offered to look into it, and she turned me down." He scanned Adam's face. "She turned you down too."

Adam shifted on the cushions. "She did the right thing, and it ruined her career. Someone should go to bat for her."

Paul gave him a questioning look. "And you're that person?"

"I owe her for what she's done for Matt."

"It's tough to start anything without Hannah's participation. We'd need to track down the people who were working in her office at the time of the incident and get their statements and any documentation they might have."

"She said the admission form disappeared right after she euthanized the dog. Conveniently, for Senator Sawyer's story."

"Yeah, I heard that, which makes it even more difficult to prove libel." Paul shook his head. "You know, maybe she's right. Maybe it's better to let it alone. She's doing fine in the practice with Tim."

"Not anymore. This morning she got blindsided by an old grouch named Bertha Shanks who announced to everyone sitting in the hospital's reception room that Hannah killed a dog without its owner's permission."

Paul looked disgusted, then thoughtful. He sat forward. "We'd have to keep our investigation behind the scenes. And whatever information we collect, we share with the doc before making a move."

"That's fair. So you'll do it?"

Paul nodded and scooped up a legal pad from the table.

Adam reached down to touch Trace's bandage. "I'm not a poster child for facing up to the past," he said, "but I want to help Hannah lay hers to rest."

Chapter 9

AS SHE DROVE HER PICKUP TRUCK SLOWLY BETWEEN the pristine, white fencing that lined the road to Healing Springs Stables, Hannah admitted she'd been fooling herself about outrunning the scandal in Chicago. She'd thought Tim was the only person in Sanctuary who knew or had any reason to care about her past. Now it turned out Julia and Paul had known about it from the beginning. Even Mrs. Shanks had found out somehow—and broadcast it to the entire reception room. Then Hannah herself had told Adam.

There was no chance it would remain a secret now. She smacked her hand on the steering wheel in frustration. She could face the consequences to herself, now that she was forewarned, but she didn't want it to affect Tim's practice. She'd have to monitor how many appointments were made and cancelled for the next few days. If she saw a decline in one and an increase in the other, she'd resign. What she would do after that she refused to consider.

Her decision made, Hannah stepped on the accelerator. She was still concerned about Satchmo's health. It wasn't that she didn't believe a pony could be grief-stricken over the loss of his stall mate. However, something about him seemed off to her. She looked forward to consulting with Tim when he returned from his trip. In the meantime, she decided to run a couple of more tests. Satchmo's balance issue suggested a neurological disease, in which case, the sooner she started treating the pony, the more likely he was to recover fully.

Arriving in the stable parking lot, she swung the truck around to park beside the sleekest automobile she'd ever seen. Careful not to bang her door into the dark gray paint, she jumped down from the truck's cab and walked a circuit around the car, admiring its beautiful curves and elegant, wood-accented interior. She wasn't a car fanatic, preferring usefulness to aesthetics, but she could appreciate a work of art when she saw one.

"Like it?"

She jerked around to see Adam standing a few feet away with his hands in his trouser pockets and an inquiring look on his face. He was sporting a tailored black suit, shirt, and tie nearly identical to the ones he'd worn Saturday afternoon, and his hair was tamed into dark, gleaming waves.

"What?" she asked.

"Do you like the Maserati?" he asked, strolling forward.

"It's yours?" She couldn't put a coherent thought together when he looked like that.

He nodded as he came to stand beside her. "An indulgence for driving the curves of these mountain roads."

"But it's not black." She clapped her hand over her mouth in dismay.

He frowned. "Why would you—?" Then he glanced down at his clothes and said, "I see."

"You have a black dog too," Hannah said to explain herself.

He looked torn between irritation and amusement. Fortunately, the latter won out and self-mockery lit his face. "So you think I consider Trace a fashion accessory?"

"I know you love him, but you do seem to like black." She waved a hand in a gesture of futile defense as she gave him a wry smile. "Some people choose dogs that look like themselves."

"My affectations have caught up with me," he said. "I started wearing black years ago and it's become a reflex."

"Did you have a reason, or was it just because you lived in New York City?" Hannah asked, daring to tease him.

He skimmed a finger against her cheek. Her breath hitched at the tiny contact between them. "Both," he said. "I'll tell you about it at dinner on Tuesday."

"Are you bringing the Maserati?"

"If it persuades you to come."

"I already said I'd come."

"Yes, but I could see the excuses forming in your brain," he said. Casting a glance at his watch, he grimaced. "I have to go. Matt's in there with Satchmo."

"I'll give him a ride home."

He shook his head. "Thanks, but my housekeeper is picking him up in a couple of hours. You've got other things to do."

The little blip of disappointment surprised her. She wanted the chance to talk with Matt. Now she'd have to get him alone in the barn.

Adam opened the door and folded himself into the exquisite car, giving her a wave as he brought the engine purring to life. As he pulled out of the parking lot, she stood in a daze staring at his taillights as they disappeared down the drive.

He moved like a panther and his car sounded like a tiger. No wonder she found him fascinating.

Hannah walked up to the railing of the indoor arena and spotted Sharon immediately. The horsewoman stood in the middle of the ring watching Matt work Satchmo on a longe line. Surprised that Matt wasn't riding the pony, Hannah waited while Sharon adjusted Matt's grip on the long whip used to signal the pony as he circled the boy at the end of the thirty-foot line.

Sharon said something to the boy before she strode across to Hannah, her boots kicking up spurts of fine dust from the ring's thick bed of sand and sawdust.

"You're teaching Matt to longe?" Hannah said.

"That what I told him," Sharon said, her expression grim. "I didn't want him to ride Satchmo. The pony's not moving right today."

"Lame or stiff?"

"Off-balance," Sharon said. "Come and take a look. Just don't mention it to the boy."

From Sharon's description and her own research, Hannah knew that Sharon feared Satchmo had equine protozoal myeloencephalits, a parasite that attacked the horse's central nervous system. Depending on how long Satchmo had been infected, there might be permanent damage.

Anxiety squeezed her chest as she jogged along beside Sharon's long-legged stride.

"Stop here and watch him," Sharon said, halting outside the circle Satchmo was inscribing.

Hannah waved to Matt, who grinned and nodded a greeting as both his hands were occupied. Then she turned her attention to the chestnut pony walking obediently around his young master. For a few moments she didn't see anything wrong. Then she caught it: Satchmo stepped slightly outward with his hind foot. He adjusted for his misstep almost imperceptibly, but it was there. The shift was so subtle she would have missed it if Sharon hadn't cued her to watch for something. It was one of the telltale signs of EPM.

"You have an amazing eye," she said to the tall woman beside her.

"Hon, I've been around horses since I was knee high to a grasshopper. I can practically hear 'em thinking."

Hannah caught several more tiny but awkward movements as the pony circled. She nodded. "I need to do a spinal tap." She really wished Tim were here; she hadn't done a spinal tap on a horse since her summer internship during vet school.

"His blood test didn't show anything?" Sharon asked.

"It showed what half of all equine blood tests show. He's been exposed to the EPM parasite. I could start treating him without the spinal tap, but if it's not EPM we'd be wasting valuable time and money."

Sharon heaved a sigh. "I guess you'd better get your needle, Doc. And put it on my bill."

"But I thought—" Hannah stopped. It was none of her business who paid for Satchmo's treatment. For all she knew Adam had changed his mind about buying the pony for Matt. She'd let Tim sort that out. Sharon looked at her. "Never mind," Hannah said hastily.

"Matt, let's get Satchmo back to his stall so Doc Linden can suck out some more of his body fluids," Sharon called before she murmured to Hannah, "If Satch has EPM, he needs rest, not exercise. Have you got your bag of tricks with you?"

"In the truck," Hannah said, watching the pony's ears tip forward in anticipation as Matt began to walk toward him, coiling up the longe line as he went. When Matt reached Satchmo, the pony butted his head against the boy's chest, rubbing it up and down and making Matt stagger backwards. Satchmo followed him and did it again, and Hannah realized it was a familiar game they were playing.

Maybe she should call in another vet with more large-animal experience to do the tap. In theory she knew where the lumbosacral cistern was, but in practice she was—well, out of practice. She could practically hear Mrs. Shanks's voice announcing that she'd crippled Matt McNally's pony. Her palms began to sweat and she rubbed them against her khaki slacks.

She'd done spinal taps on kittens; the spinal column of a pony was huge by comparison, giving her a larger, easier target. She swiped her hands one more time and turned toward the gate, saying to Sharon, "I'll meet you in his stall. Ask Matt to stay. He can keep Satchmo calm while I do the procedure."

Hannah jogged out to the truck and grabbed the animal hospital's computer tablet, swiping away at the screen to get to the detailed description of executing a spinal tap on a conscious horse. As she skimmed through the instructions and diagrams, memories from vet school bubbled to the surface and she nodded to herself.

Going to the back of the truck, she rummaged through the large-animal kit she kept stowed in case of emergency calls. Everything she needed was there, including the Styrofoam packaging to send the samples to the lab.

"I wish Adam were here to carry this," she grumbled, dragging the heavy bag out of the truck bed.

She staggered into the barn, where a stable hand took the duffel from her despite her protests. "You need your strength for fixing horses," he said, hefting it over his shoulder.

This was one of the reasons she didn't want to resign from Sanctuary Animal Hospital. People valued her profession here in a way they didn't in Chicago. In many cases, the animals she treated were an important part of their livelihood. Not just the cows and sheep and horses, but the working dogs and even the barn cats who kept down the rodent population. It was a different relationship between the animals and their owners, one in which the animal was respected as more than just a companion.

The man brought her bag into Satchmo's stall and waved off her thanks. She found an anxious-looking Matt standing beside the pony while Sharon slipped a halter over Satchmo's head.

She went over to the boy. "Hey, don't look so worried. This is just a test. No big deal."

"I thought you said you hadn't found anything wrong with him," Matt said, stroking the pony's neck.

"There's only so much you can tell from the usual blood tests," Hannah said, resting her hand on Satchmo's back. "If there's something medically wrong with him and we don't treat it, he could get really sick. But if I find it now, before it gets worse, we'll be able to cure him." She crossed her fingers behind her back. If the pony had EPM, the nerve damage could have been done already.

"I've got a stock if you want to use it," Sharon said, fastening a chain lead to Satchmo's halter and winding it across his nose. The chain kept the horse's attention on his nose and gave the person holding the halter a little extra control.

Hannah looked at the placid pony and the worried boy and shook her head. "I trust you and Matt to keep him still." Putting the pony in a stock—a sort of cage to confine him—would upset both Satchmo and Matt. "I'll take a stool, though. And ice to pack the fluid in until I get back to the clinic."

While Sharon sent a groom off to fetch a stool and ice, Hannah set up a portable table, snapped on a pair of sterile rubber gloves, and laid out her supplies, including two eight-inch needles that made Matt's eyes go wide. "They look scary," Hannah said, "but horses are bigger than humans."

When everything was arranged to her satisfaction, Hannah went over to Matt. "So here's what's going to happen. I'm going to give Satch here a local anesthetic on his rump. Once he's numb, I'm going to insert the big needle into what's called his lumbosacral cistern and draw out some cerebrospinal fluid. I'll send that off to the lab for testing. That's it. Nothing more to it."

Matt gave her a nervous smile.

"The thing is I need Satchmo to stay still while I'm inserting the needle and extracting the fluid." She didn't mention that any movement could injure the pony's spine. "Sharon knows exactly how to hold him, but you'll make it easier for everyone, including Satch, if you keep his attention on you. Got it?"

The boy swallowed and nodded.

"I'll let you know when it's time," Hannah said.

She returned to the table and began prepping the injection site before she administered the local anesthetic. Satchmo flicked his tail once and then stood still, his head resting against Matt's chest while the boy rubbed behind his ears.

Once she was sure the anesthetic had taken effect, she stripped off the old gloves and put on a clean pair. She was taking every precaution to make this go smoothly. She picked up one of the giant needles and climbed up on the stool.

"Okay, I need you to keep him still until I say I'm done," she said, turning to check on her helpers. Sharon shifted her grip on the lead chain to just under the pony's chin and nodded. "You ready, Matt?" Hannah asked.

"Yes, ma'am," Matt said, his voice holding only a slight quaver.

Hannah rested the tip of the needle on the spot she had marked and pushed. As the needle found its mark, she felt a lessening of resistance. The tension in her shoulders eased, but her relief was short-lived. Satchmo suddenly tucked his tail down between his hind legs. Was that a signal that the pony was going to try to move or lash out with his back hooves?

Hannah held her breath and took a quick look toward Satchmo's head. Sharon stood with her feet braced wide, ready to counteract any movement. Matt's face was pale and his eyes were resolutely turned away from the huge needle, but he murmured to the pony in a low, soothing voice as he continued to scratch behind his ears.

After a few seconds passed and Satchmo continued to stand quietly, Hannah let out her breath and removed the trocar from the needle, beginning the process of collecting the spinal fluid.

When she had enough, she carefully withdrew the needle and stepped down from the stool. "Okay, it's all over. I just have to put a stitch in to close the opening."

She finished by packing the fluid in the Styrofoam transport chest surrounded by ice.

"Satchmo, you are a model patient," she said, coming up to his head to join Matt in giving him a good rub. "I've never had a horse stand that still for a spinal tap." She squeezed the boy's shoulder. "You and Sharon are great assistants."

"Ms. Sydenstricker was the one holding him," Matt said, his voice still a little shaky. He rested his forehead against Satchmo's.

"I didn't need to do a thing," Sharon said. "You had him practically tranquilized, young man."

Hannah went back to stowing away her supplies in the medical bag. She kept an eye on the pony to see if he was showing any sign of discomfort. When she finished, she looked at Sharon. "Would you take Satch on a circuit of the stall?"

"Is something wrong?" Matt asked, stepping away from Satchmo's head so Sharon could turn the pony.

"Nah," Sharon said, urging Satchmo into a walk. "Just standard operating procedure after a spinal tap."

As the pony plodded around his stall without any noticeable change in his gait, Hannah nodded.

Matt's face lit up in a grin. "He's okay, right?"

"He looks good," Hannah said.

"Keep him company while I help the doc with her bag," Sharon said, handing the lead line to Matt.

She picked up one handle while Hannah hefted the other. As soon as they were out of earshot of the stall, Sharon said, "How long until you'll know?"

"I'm going to overnight it to a lab in Kentucky where they collect data on EPM, so they know what they're doing. I'll tell them to put a rush on it."

"That boy needs that pony," Sharon said.

"I'll do everything I can to get Satchmo healthy."

"I know that, Doc. You're one of the good guys."

Would Sharon say that if she knew about what happened in Chicago? The horsewoman cared about her horses, but she was a businesswoman too. Or maybe she already knew, like half the people in Sanctuary. "Where was Satchmo before he came here?" Hannah asked.

"At the racing stable in Florida with Jazzman. They're careful there, so I figure he picked up the parasite in transit. Dirty water. Contaminated feed. Something like that."

"Poor little fellow to have such bad luck," Hannah said.

"I won't be using that horse transporter again," Sharon said.

"How did you come to own Satch?" They'd arrived at the truck and together slung the bag into the back.

"Lost horses just find me," Sharon said with a shrug. "Once Jazzman died, the stable owner had no use for Satchmo, so he was going to sell him for dog food. One of the grooms was fond of Satch and got hold of me."

"Sounds to me like *you're* one of the good guys," Hannah said.

"If Satch hadn't come here, Matt wouldn't have found his whisper horse."

Hannah nodded. She wasn't going to argue with this woman who knew more about horses than she ever would. "Have you got a whisper horse for me?" she asked, only partly in jest.

Sharon grinned. "If you're lookin' for one." She held out her hand. "Nice job on the spinal tap, Doc. It went as smooth as silk."

Hannah shook her hand, wincing slightly at the strength of Sharon's grip. "It's been awhile."

"Like riding a bicycle, I guess," Sharon said before she started back toward the barn.

As soon as Sharon was out of sight, Hannah slumped against the truck, her knees suddenly unwilling to hold her upright without assistance. She braced her hands on her thighs and took a few deep breaths. If she hadn't been so worried about Satchmo, she would have waited for Tim to come back because it wasn't at all like riding a bicycle.

A couple of more breaths and she straightened and climbed into the truck's cab. As she turned the key, she muttered, "You know, maybe a whisper horse isn't such a bad idea."

Chapter 10

*A*DAM FELL INTO THE BIG, LEATHER CHAIR BEHIND his desk at the restaurant and stripped off his tie. He'd expected an easy night, but a group of businessmen had flown in from Atlanta at the last minute, growing more and more demanding as they emptied several bottles of wine. He'd eventually switched all of their wait staff to men because one guest persisted in grabbing the waitresses and making lewd comments. As the group was leaving, Adam spoke with its host and explained that the offensive diner would not be welcome back. He didn't tolerate abuse of his staff, no matter how much money his patrons spent.

He tossed the tie onto the desk, jogging the mouse of his computer so the sleeping screen came to life.

A glance at the new emails in his inbox made him sit forward when he saw the name of one sender: William Gaspari, the private investigator he'd hired to find someone from Maggie's family who might be a better parent to Matt than he could be.

His stomach clenched as he clicked open the email.

Dear Mr. Bosch,

I've located a first cousin to Margaret McNally who appears to be a possibility. Attached is the background information. Call me at your convenience to discuss how to proceed.

Regards,
William Gaspari

He waited for the lift of relief. Instead his stomach seemed to turn itself inside out.

It wasn't that Matt had become more open after finding his whisper pony. His son still shut him out ninety-nine percent of the time. But that one conversation in the car—when Matt hadn't been able to contain his excitement about Satchmo—had given Adam a glimpse of what might have been.

Adam reached into his pocket for the key to his desk, unlocking the center drawer. Pulling out the dog-eared manila folder the social worker had handed him four months ago, he slipped off the rubber bands and squared it on the desktop. He took a deep breath and flipped it open. There was the photo of Matt in the kitchen, the one that had stopped Adam from continuing before.

He moved it aside.

Beneath it was a souvenir photograph of a younger Matt engulfed by a yellow life preserver standing in blue water with a dolphin's nose touching his face. His expression held both excitement and fear. Adam's throat tightened. Maggie had not had much money in the bank when she died, so she must have scrimped and saved to take her child on this trip.

The next photo was the same pose, but in this one Maggie was being kissed by the dolphin. Adam studied her image. The vivid red curls piled on top of her head, with damp tendrils clinging to her neck and cheeks, were the same as when she'd been twenty-two. Her freckled face was sunburned and thinner, but the sheer joy radiating from her smile lit it with beauty.

Would he have recognized her if he'd run into her in the crowd at Disney World? He shook his head and shifted his gaze to stare at the black rectangle of the window. Those years of working in New York were an alcohol-hazed blur, and his memories of anything but the kitchen itself were fragmentary. When he'd gotten the apprenticeship with the world-famous chef Conrad Faust, he'd burned his bridges with his parents and jumped on a bus to the city, sure his name would be tripping off the lips of influential foodies in no time.

Instead he'd been plunged into hell. Conrad managed by fear: fear of verbal humiliation; fear of physical abuse; fear of being fired. Adam was used to the first two from the years of living with his father, but he couldn't stomach the thought of crawling back to his parents because he'd been sacked.

One evening, Conrad had walked out of his office, scanned the kitchen, and walked straight to Adam's station. Without tasting the fiddlehead ferns Adam was sautéing, the chef had picked up the pan and hurled it onto the floor, splashing burning hot butter and oil up to Adam's knees. Then he launched into a brutal tirade about Adam's lack of talent, work ethic, and breeding. Adam stood with his head bowed, feeling the blisters rising on his legs as the hot butter soaked through his houndstooth-check cooking trousers. At the end, he said what he had to say in order to keep his job: "Yes, chef."

Conrad stalked back into his office and slammed the door, while Adam sagged against the countertop. One of the sous-chefs handed him a flask of vodka. Having sworn not to follow his father's path to destruction, Adam started to hand it back. Then he looked at the perfectly sautéed vegetables Conrad had hurled onto the floor. If he lost this job, Adam had nothing. He unscrewed the top of the flask, filled his mouth with the cheap liquor, and threw back his head to swallow it in one gulp. The vodka burned down his throat and spread through his gut, blunting the razor-edge of his fear. He bought a flask of his own the next day.

He learned to ration his drinking while he worked, balancing on the edge between being drunk enough to tolerate the terror of Conrad's unpredictability, but not so drunk he couldn't function in the controlled chaos of the kitchen. He climbed up the hierarchy by working twice as hard as anyone else and flattering Conrad's senior sous-chefs into teaching him their secrets. After work, he went out with anyone willing and drank himself into oblivion. Maggie had made the mistake of joining him for one of those alcohol-soaked expeditions.

That night had changed her life forever. And now his.

He went back to the photos, riffling through the stiff school portraits, the group shots of tee-shirt clad soccer and baseball teams, the snapshots of Matt on a bicycle with training wheels. There was Matt beside a dinosaur skeleton in a museum, Matt on the beach at various ages, Matt grinning as he held up a chess trophy. One of the last photos was of Maggie in a hospital bed, holding a swaddled newborn, her face radiant with love. Next were the hospital portraits of the infant Matt, his hands hidden in mitts, his eyes sleepy, his head already covered with a dark fuzz of hair.

The gut-twisting regret walloped Adam, and he shoved the pictures away. He hadn't been present for the birth of his child. Maggie had suffered through the agony and awe of that miracle alone. Anger and a sense of loss slashed through him, but he knew he had only himself to blame.

Looking down again, he discovered Matt's art work next in the pile: hand-drawn Mother's Day cards, Valentine's Day cards, Christmas cards, and various other crayoned masterpieces. The common theme was how much the child loved his mother. A fist closed around Adam's heart, squeezing at the enormity of Matt's loss when Maggie died.

He moved the drawings aside to reveal an unsealed, gray business envelope with his first name written on it. Inside were magazine clippings and internet printouts tracing Adam's career in the restaurant business. Had she shown these to Matt, telling him this was his father? Matt had never let on about such a conversation, so it seemed unlikely. Why had she bothered to collect these if she wasn't going to share her child with him? He thumbed through them to find they included several articles about The Aerie and its success.

So she knew he had money, yet she'd never approached him for the financial help he gladly would have given.

He picked up the gray envelope to stuff the clippings back inside and felt something thick lodged in the bottom. Turning it upside down, he shook it hard. A smaller envelope fell facedown onto his desk. The flap was sealed, so he flipped it over. The front was blank.

Adam stared down at it. There was something ominous about its lack of address.

He steeled himself and tore open the envelope with a single twist of his wrist. Inside were a couple of handwritten sheets of notebook paper, the writing Maggie's. Unfolding the top sheet, he felt a nearly physical blow in his chest.

The letter was to him.

Dear Adam,

I'll never mail this to you, so you'll never read it and you probably shouldn't, but sometimes I feel so alone I need someone to talk to. Since you're Matt's father, I ought to be able to talk to you.

You might want to know why I didn't tell you I was pregnant. I came close a few times, but it just didn't seem right to upend your life because I was stupid and careless. You were so young and beautiful—beautiful as sin, my mother would say—and so driven. I knew you would be a great chef or a great something one day. If the drink didn't ruin you.

He felt a hot sear of anger at being cut out of his son's life without being given any choice.

That's the real reason I kept it from you. We Irish know too much about liquor, so I worried about how you were damaging yourself. About how you might hurt me and our child even. Not that there was an ounce of malice in you, but the drink makes people do things they wouldn't otherwise. I couldn't have borne to watch you destroy yourself and us.

The anger died as abruptly as it had flared to life, leaving cold, dry ashes in his gut. He couldn't argue with Maggie's reasons.

So, as frightened as I was, I didn't tell you. Instead I told my mother and father back in Dublin. A mistake. I thought they would support my decision not to end the pregnancy, good Catholics that they claimed to be. Instead they condemned me because I wasn't married and wanted me to put Matt up for adoption. I told them they were unchristian, which didn't help my case. So there I was, an unwed mother in a foreign country with no health insurance and no one to hold my hand through labor.

But you know, there are good people in the world, and God helped me find them. Someday I hope to repay them. Dr. Nagy, who did my pregnancy checkups for free and found a midwife to deliver Matt at home so I wouldn't have to pay for a hospital room. Mr. Grossman, the pharmacist who finagled a way to get me neonatal vitamins for next to nothing. Kathy Arnold, at my job, who put me on the company's health insurance plan six months early so Matt could have well-baby care. My neighbors, Josephine and Manuela, who clipped all the coupons they could find and gave them to me; if there was a deal on baby care products, they tracked it down. Betty Gallagher, at the Goodwill down the block, who let me trade in old baby clothes for new ones, free of charge. Oh, I could go on, but these kindnesses are what kept me from despair.

And the thought of you. I knew if I truly needed help I could go to you.

He put the paper down and scrubbed his hands over his face to wipe away the unfamiliar burn of tears in his eyes. His life then had been all about cooking and drinking, while Maggie had struggled to buy diapers. And she had found the thought of him a comfort. A groan, welling up from low in his ribcage, tore from him.

He forced himself to read on.

But for all the times I wake up in the night in a cold sweat of terror at the thought of my responsibilities, you gave me the greatest gift I've ever received. Matt is the light of my life, the center of my universe, the proof that love is the most powerful force in the world. I didn't understand love until I held Matt in my arms that first time, and the way I feel about him has grown stronger and more glorious every day.

I hope someday I find the courage to tell you about our son. I hope you will want to meet him because he is the most amazing person.

For now, I thank you every day for him.

Fondest regards,

Maggie

The paper rattled in his hands. He dropped it and pressed his spread fingers against the wood of the desk to stop their shaking. Maggie had thanked him for getting her pregnant. Thanked him. He deserved curses and he got gratitude.

She considered Matt a gift, one she had involuntarily passed on to him. Now he was trying to give that gift away. Because he didn't deserve it.

He pushed down harder on the desk as the craving for a drink grabbed him by the throat. He could almost feel the fire of one of the fine brandies in The Aerie's cellar as it spread through his body, washing away the guilt and the corrosive sense of unworthiness. If ever there was a time he could justify breaking his AA vows, this was it.

He used his hands to lever himself to his feet and stood with his head bowed, leaning on the solid wood under his palms. He held himself very still, trying to quell the battle raging inside him.

He could feel himself losing the fight, surrendering to the need for oblivion.

He closed his eyes, trying one last time to find an anchor to hold onto, and Hannah's image formed in his mind.

He didn't think; he just reached for his cell phone and found her contact information, hoping the number she'd given him was one she'd answer even at midnight.

Chapter 11

*H*ANNAH REACHED ACROSS GINGER, ONE OF HER rescue dogs, who was curled up on the covers beside her, grabbing the cell phone vibrating and chiming on her bedside table. She'd crawled into bed early, wrung out from the stress of doing Satchmo's spinal tap. Since Tim was away she was on emergency call 24/7, so she'd left the phone's ringer on full volume.

She cleared her throat and hit "answer." "Hello, this is Dr. Linden."

"Hannah! You're there." It was Adam's voice, but distorted.

She shoved herself up to a sitting position. "Adam? What's wrong? Did Trace get out again?"

"It's not Trace." There was a long pause, and she was trying to clear her sleep-fogged brain to ask another question when he said, "I have to get away from here. I'd like to see you."

"At the office?" She was confused.

"Wherever you are now."

"Well, I'm at home, so I guess you could come here."

"Thank you." She heard him exhale as if he'd been holding his breath. "Where do you live?"

She gave him her address. He muttered "thank you" again and disconnected so fast she didn't have time to ask anything further.

She frowned down at the phone, trying to remember exactly what he'd said. Something about he had to get out of there. Had he had a fight with Matt? She shook her head. The boy would be asleep by now. Since Adam spent even his days off at the restaurant, it couldn't be that he was tired of work. Unless something had gone terribly wrong at The Aerie. But why would he want to talk to her about that?

Giving up on her useless speculations, she threw back the covers, earning her a disgruntled stare from Ginger, who retreated to the foot of the bed. It would probably take Adam about twenty minutes to get down from his mountain lair, assuming that's where he was. Dragging on a pair of jeans and a pale-blue, long-sleeved tee shirt, she shifted into speed clean-up mode.

She'd whipped the dog quilts off the sofa and chairs, scrubbed out the dirty pasta pot, and hurled all the chew toys into a floor basket before she remembered to run a brush through her hair and twist it into a loose bun at the back of her head with a plastic clip.

The doorbell rang and the dogs set up their usual chorus of greeting. Hannah put them in a sit-stay, smoothed down her shirt, and opened the door.

Adam stood on the front porch, his hair picking up glints from the yellow bulb of the porch sconce. The light was too dim to see much other than his usual color scheme of a black leather jacket over black trousers. "Come in," she said.

He hesitated. "I shouldn't be bothering you."

She swung the door open wide. "You wouldn't have called if it wasn't important."

When he stepped into the illuminated foyer she nearly gasped. The lines around his mouth were etched so sharply he seemed to be in physical pain. The leather jacket had been thrown on over what she recognized as his work suit, minus the tie. His hair looked as though he had repeatedly worried it with his fingers.

"Let me get you some tea," she said, closing the door behind him.

He shrugged out of his outer jacket with a travesty of a smile. "Tea sounds great."

She hung his coat in the closet by the door and led the way into the kitchen, releasing the dogs from their "stay." "Herbal or Earl Grey? Those are my only offerings."

He shoved his hands in his trouser pockets and leaned against the doorframe. "Earl Grey, thanks."

Three dogs filed past him and took up stations around Hannah, hoping a treat was in store.

"May I be introduced?" Adam said, squatting and offering the back of his hand for sniffing.

"Pardon my lack of manners. Ginger, Annabelle, and Floyd," Hannah said, smiling when the dogs abandoned her for the intriguing stranger who knew all the best places to scratch. As she boiled water and dropped teabags into mugs, she snuck glances at her unexpected guest, happy to note the tension in his jaw easing. Dogs had that effect on people.

"They're all rescues?" Adam asked, rubbing Floyd's exposed tummy.

"Why do you think that?"

He switched to stroking Annabelle's long, multicolored coat and lifted his gaze to Hannah's. "Because that's what you do."

His eyes were haunted and intense, making Hannah shift uncomfortably. "Mm, yes, Anabelle is a purebred collie with epilepsy. Her owner couldn't afford the meds. Floyd is pure street mutt. One of our vet techs found him lying on the sidewalk near her apartment in Chicago with multiple fractures. Probably got hit by a car. Ginger, well, she adopted me. She lived in my neighborhood, and when her original owner moved, he left her behind. So she followed me home."

She poured the boiling water into the mugs. "Sugar? Honey? Lemon juice?" She remembered he was used to gourmet beverages. "The juice is from a bottle, though."

"Black," he said, straightening to take the mug from her. He wrapped his big hands around the handmade pottery, making it look as though the thick crockery had shrunk.

She picked up her own tea and waved toward the living room. "I'll turn on the fire." She was embarrassed that the fireplace was one of those gas imposters which required only the flick of a switch to ignite. It was like her lemon juice—convenient but not real.

She hit the switch and settled on the couch, joined immediately by Ginger and Floyd while Annabelle laid herself elegantly at Hannah's feet. The two cats had fled at the sound of the doorbell, but now Blanche strolled into the room and began rubbing against Adam's ankles, leaving a trail of white cat hair on his expensive trousers.

"Oh heavens, Blanche, stop!" Hannah exclaimed, plunking her mug down on the coffee table and starting to rise.

"I like cats," Adam said, waving her back and settling into one of the armchairs before he leaned forward to scratch under the cat's chin.

"Yes, but your suit will have Blanche hairs woven into it for the rest of your life."

"When you wear black, you have to be prepared for that."

Again she wanted to ask why he always wore the same dark color, but decided this was not the time.

"I owe you an explanation," he said, cradling his mug in his hands, while Blanche stalked off in a huff at the withdrawal of his attention.

"You said you needed to get away from something."

"Myself," he said. "A hard thing to do." He sat back in the chair and blew out a breath. "I didn't know I had a son until Matt's mother died four months ago. And now I hate that I missed all those years I could have known him."

"That seems like a normal reaction." Hannah was out of her depth here.

He looked straight at her. "I have no right to feel that way."

"Oh." Way out of her depth. She took a gulp of hot tea, scalding her tongue.

"I'm an alcoholic. Adam's mother knew that and decided to keep him away from me."

"But I thought . . . don't you sponsor, er, people at AA?" Hannah wasn't sure she was supposed to know about Paul's brother being mentored by Adam.

He propelled himself out of his chair and paced over to the weak flicker of the gas fire, staring into it for a long moment before he turned back to her. "I've been sober for nine years, but I will always be an alcoholic. It's not something you can be cured of."

"But you control it," she said. "Isn't that all you can ask of yourself?"

"Tonight I saw a photo of Matt as a newborn, and I was overwhelmed by a gaping sense of loss. You know what I wanted to do with that?" His mug rattled as he set it down on the mantel. "I wanted to flood it with liquor."

She understood. He'd needed to get away from the craving. He'd reached out to her for help because he couldn't fight it alone.

When she looked at him, she saw not a world-famous chef but a creature in pain. Suffering was something she couldn't bear, whether it was a dog, a horse, or a man.

She put her mug down and stood up, quickly crossing the room to wrap her arms around him. "I'm sorry," she said.

For a moment, he stood motionless, and she wondered if she'd done the wrong thing. Then his arms came around her shoulders, moving her in against the solid wall of his body.

She let out a relieved sigh. When she drew in the next breath, it came laden with his distinctive aroma of spices and warm male. No words came to her so she did what she would do with a distraught patient. She slid her palms up and down his back in long, soothing strokes.

His grip on her tightened.

She was pressed so closely against him she was having trouble filling her lungs. But she didn't want to pull away for fear he would think she was withdrawing her comfort. She closed her eyes and listened to his heart thump against her ear, taking small sips of air.

"Hannah." His voice was low.

It wasn't a question, but she answered it anyway. "Yes?"

He shifted, putting one finger under her chin so he could tip her face up to meet his gaze.

What she saw made her gasp for an entirely different reason. His eyelids were half-closed, and his eyes were intent on her lips. His touch slid from her chin and along her jawline until his fingers tangled in the hair clipped at the nape of her neck.

He stopped and waited, looking at her with an intensity that set off flares of heat deep inside her. She felt his hand at the back of her head, and the clip clattered onto the hearth while her hair spilled down her back. He combed his fingers through it, sending delicious shivers dancing over her scalp and down her spine.

Still he gazed down at her, the space between them snapping with a strange, unexpected awareness.

Nervousness caught in her throat as she realized he was waiting for her to decide. She froze, balanced between her yearning to feel his big, calloused hands against her skin and her fear of losing herself to another man who might be using her. She searched his face, finding suffering even as his eyes glittered with the fever of arousal.

He was beautiful and troubled and in pain. She rose onto her tiptoes and brought her mouth against his.

There was no hesitation from him this time. He angled her head back farther so he could drag his mouth from her lips to her throat and back again. Breathing no longer seemed important as his other arm came around her like an iron band, locking her against him from thigh to shoulder, her breasts crushed against his chest. Between kisses, he murmured her name like an incantation, as though it could ward off the demons clawing at him.

She kneaded the fine cotton stretched across his back, trying to hold on as he sent waves of sensation shuddering through her. It wasn't enough. She yanked at his shirt, pulling the tail free so she could slide her hands up under it against his bare skin. His hands might be calloused and crisscrossed with welts but his back was pure satin. She skimmed her palms up to the muscles of his shoulders before tracing back down along his spine.

His murmur turned to a low groan of pleasure as he released her lips and arched back into her touch. A sense of power swept through her and she slipped her hands around his ribcage and up over his chest, savoring the springy texture of his hair and the hard points of his nipples.

When she dragged her hands back downward toward his waist, he seized her wrists and pulled her hands out from under his shirt. "Where's your bedroom?"

"Down the hall," she said, nodding toward the open arch opposite the sofa.

Before she realized his intention, he had scooped her up in his arms and started across the living room. Startled, she grabbed his shoulders. "Wait . . . what?"

Without breaking stride, he looked down at her. "Having second thoughts?"

"No, I just figured I could walk."

"I don't want to let you go long enough for that," he said, turning sideways to get through the doorway without banging her head or feet against the frame.

She snagged the edge of the door and slammed it in the face of her three dogs.

He strode over to her unmade bed, lowering her onto the rumpled sheets and following her down. She splayed her hands on his chest as she looked up into the face of a man she barely knew. It was a beautiful face, the velvet brown eyes incandescent with desire, the angle of jaw and cheekbone strong and sharp, the curve of lips sensual but completely male. She wanted to graze her fingertips over the dark stubble in the cleft of his chin and smooth away the lines drawn around his mouth.

None of that seduced her, though. It was his need that swamped her good sense. Just as she wondered if she should reconsider, he shifted position so his thigh drove between hers, making contact with the sensitized spot between her legs. Arousal sent her arching upward in mind-blurring response.

"Yes," he said, wrapping his hands around her hips and tilting them so he could press his thigh against her again.

She nearly came from just the friction.

Releasing her hips, he snagged the hem of her tee shirt with his thumbs and pulled upward. She wondered what bra she'd thrown on in her haste to get dressed. Her concern evaporated as he hauled her shirt up over her breasts and his gaze sharpened to a fascinated hunger.

"So perfect," he murmured before he slid his hands under her back and unhooked the bra, yanking it and her shirt up over her head and flinging the tangle of fabrics away. He cupped her breasts in his hands and bent his head to take one of her nipples in his mouth. Lightning arced directly down to the already blazing heat between her legs.

"Adam!" She ground against his thigh.

He lifted his head and wrenched the zipper of her jeans open, shifting to pull both the denim and her cotton panties down to her knees before he slipped one hand between her thighs. They both moaned at the same time as he slid one finger inside her and then withdrew it.

"Yes," he breathed, levering himself up from the bed to slip her jeans off before he unfastened the sleek, silver buckle of his belt and tugged down his own zipper. She gave an inward sigh of relief when he reached around to his back pocket and produced a foil envelope. Her attraction to him had been so swift and unlikely, she'd been caught unprepared.

He had the condom rolled onto his erection and was kneeling on the bed again before she could decide where she should be. He came down over her, using his knees to wedge hers apart. The craving inside her intensified with the sense of being opened to him. Then he buried himself inside her in one swift, sure movement, and she nearly cried out at the delicious fullness.

He withdrew and drove into her again, his eyes closed, his neck muscles taut as he braced his forearms on either side of her. She felt the fine fabric of his trousers brushing against the inside of her thighs, piling sensation on sensation.

He levered himself higher so he could thrust faster and harder, the angle making his shirt rub back and forth over the tips of her nipples. The friction sent sparks of heat streaking down into the tension coiling tighter and tighter in her belly.

She grabbed his shoulders and met his next thrust with a roll of her hips, the collision setting off her release in a blast of searing pleasure. She dug her fingers into his muscles and bowed up from the bed as he rode her orgasm into his own, throwing his head back and shouting her name while he pumped inside her.

He stayed poised over her as they drifted down from their explosive joining, dropping his forehead onto her bare shoulder so the ends of his hair tickled her cheek. His weight still held her thighs open, adding a lingering eroticism to the last ripples of her climax. His breathing quieted and he slid out of her, pushing himself up and off the bed in slow, deliberate movements.

Noticing he was still almost fully clothed, she rolled to her side and wrapped a corner of the sheet around her torso as he disposed of the condom.

He came back to the bed and sat down beside her, smoothing a hand along the covered curve of her hip. "I preferred you without this," he said, tugging lightly at the sheet.

She grabbed the fabric as it started to slip. "Seems to me the clothing quotient is a little one-sided." She swept her gaze over his intact ensemble, a tiny shiver running through her at how dark he looked against the pastel sheets and quilt.

He slid his hand up to her shoulder so she could feel the texture of his palm against her bare skin. His thumb traced back and forth along her collarbone, sending shimmers of heat waltzing over her body. "I'd like to stay," he said.

He was giving her the choice of whether to take this further. She looked up into his face, which was half-shadowed, half-illuminated by the bedside lamp. The tension was gone from his jaw and the desperation in his eyes had been replaced by a slow-burning intensity. "If you take your clothes off, I'll consider it."

"Fair enough," he said, an undertone of amusement in his voice. Without hesitation, he began to unbutton his shirt.

She propped herself up on her elbow to get a better view as the black fabric fell open to reveal the sculpted chest she'd only felt before. He flicked open the buttons of his cuffs and shrugged out of the shirt, undressing with a matter-of-factness that was neither coy nor self-conscious.

Standing up, he stripped off his trousers and briefs, and she let her gaze drift down the angles and planes of his body. She especially liked the long line of muscle that curved down the front of his thighs. She scanned upward until she met his eyes, which were glinting with heat and humor. "What are you waiting for?" she asked.

"You to finish the X-ray," he said, joining her on the bed. "It was scorching."

"I was only going skin deep," she said, burying her fingers in the strong waves of his hair as he crouched over her. "I'm shallow that way."

"I plan to go much deeper than that," he said, lowering his lips to hers for a short kiss. "But not yet. First, I want to savor you. If you're ready."

The scuff of his bare skin against her thighs and breasts was already setting off curls of heat inside her. "Oh, I'm more than ready," she said, trying to pull his mouth back down to hers.

Instead he slid downward, kissing a path between her breasts and over her stomach until he brushed his lips against the most sensitive place on her body. The light contact was like a match touching a fuse as arousal spiraled through her. "Oh, yes, Adam, there!" she moaned.

He wrapped his hands around her knees and tugged her toward the edge of the bed. Slipping off the mattress to kneel on the floor, he lifted and spread her legs so they were draped over his shoulders.

She felt a flush of shyness rise up her neck and cheeks as he looked at her. "I want to taste you," he said.

Of course he did. He was a chef. As he waited for her permission, he ran his palm over her stomach to brush between her legs again, sliding against her with his finger and changing her flush of embarrassment to a tide of yearning.

"Yes," she breathed, her hips undulating with his touch. "Yes, taste me." And then her eyelids slammed closed as the first exquisite lap of his tongue sent pure ecstasy pouring through her.

They both moaned at the same time and he murmured something indistinguishable against her, the puff of his breath magnifying the sensation. "What?" she panted.

He lifted his head. "You taste like caviar."

She vaguely remembered going to a restaurant with Ward that had caviar on the menu with a price so exorbitant she hadn't bothered to read further. Then the memory of her ex-fiancé vaporized as Adam put his mouth between her thighs once again, sliding first one and then two fingers inside her as he drove her closer and closer to another orgasm.

As his fingers and tongue sent her teetering to the edge, she reached down to pull his head away from her. "With you," she said.

His face was glazed with the mindlessness of desire and he gave his head a little shake, like a wet dog, before he reached for his trousers. She heard the rip of foil, and then he shifted her legs off his shoulders so he could surge up over her, settling himself between her thighs.

She gasped as his cock rubbed against her. She bent her knees and tilted her hips in invitation, but he lowered his mouth to hers for a long, exploratory kiss. Even as she met his tongue with hers, the hot emptiness inside her craved filling. She pulled her mouth away and tilted her hips against him again. "I want you inside me," she said, her lips nearly brushing against his as she spoke.

He stroked her temples with his thumbs. "I don't want this to end," he said, his voice rough.

"There's always dessert," she said. "And coffee."

"Not coffee," he said. "The finest, most complex Cognac, meant to be sipped and lingered over for hours." Flexing his hips, he glided inside her, stoking and appeasing her arousal all at once.

Her head fell back, her eyelids closed, and she breathed, "Oh, yes!"

The satisfaction of him moving within her, the spicy scent of his heated skin swirling around her, the anchoring press of his weight, and the sound of his voice as he told her how luscious she was enveloped her in a mind-bending kaleidoscope of bliss. She felt the build of her orgasm as a point of white heat, concentrating every molecule of pleasure into its intense center. His rhythm increased and she felt the heat contract even further, until he thrust hard and her climax blasted through her.

She tried to stop her scream, but it was wrenched from her by muscles bursting with exquisite release. He drove deep one more time and went utterly still for a split second before his back bowed upward and he exhaled a long, harsh groan. She felt the hard pulsing of his climax, and then he sagged downward in a hot rush of expelled breath. Where his chest crushed her breasts his heart pounded, matching the thump of her own.

They lay that way as their breath and pulses slowed. When he slipped out of her and rolled away to strip off the condom, she curled into a ball, trying to retain the sensory memory of him.

"Cold?" he asked, pulling the quilt out from under her and slipping in beside her.

"No, just missing you," she said, snuggling into his warmth.

"Here I am." Even though she couldn't see his face, she could hear the smile in his voice.

She stretched out full length against him, tangling her legs with his to feel the muscles of his thighs and calves against the softness of her skin. He skimmed his palm down her back to her bottom.

"Mmm," he murmured. "Like a perfectly ripe peach. Makes me want to nibble on it."

"No biting," she said drowsily. "I get enough of that from my patients."

She felt the huff of his laugh as he gave her a squeeze that pulled her even closer against him. He nuzzled against the top of her head. "You are delicious."

Coming from a chef, she figured that was a higher compliment than telling her she was beautiful.

Chapter 12

ATCHMO WAS IN TROUBLE. JUST AS HANNAH TOOK the first bite of her sandwich, Sharon had called to say she could coax the pony to his feet for a few minutes but then the little animal would lie down again.

Hannah slipped through the door of the pony's stall to find Sharon looking at Satchmo with a worried crease between her brows. The horsewoman's expression lightened as she turned to Hannah. "Thanks for coming so quickly, Doc. He's been like this since Lynnie came in this morning. Any results from the spinal tap?"

Hannah shook her head. "I won't have any until tomorrow." Zipping open her duffel, she pulled out her stethoscope and knelt in the straw beside Satchmo. She was relieved that he was not stretched out full length but lay with his legs curled under him and his chin resting lightly on the straw, his eyelids half-closed. He hadn't given up yet.

"Hey, Satch, what's going on with you?" She ran her hands over him, looking for signs of discomfort. The pony's pale lashes didn't flicker. In fact, he sighed as though he enjoyed her touch. "You are the sweetest little fellow," Hannah said.

"Ain't that the truth!" Sharon agreed. "Every hand in the barn has been by to see him this morning. He's got something that makes you want to be around him."

"I guess that's why he was Jazzman's stall buddy," Hannah said, putting her stethoscope against the pony's chest.

Once again she could find nothing overtly wrong with Satchmo. She took off the stethoscope and let her hands rest on his shoulder and barrel, feeling the slight roughness of his coat and the rise and fall of his breath, as his warmth seeped into her palms. She couldn't let this lovable pony just slip away without a fight.

She shifted to sit cross-legged beside his head, stroking down his forehead to his velvety nose, his whiskers prickling against her hand. "Talk to me, Satch," she murmured. "Give me a clue."

The pony's eyes came fully open and his ears turned toward her. He whickered into her hand.

"You speak pony, Doc?" Sharon asked. "Cause I think he was trying to tell you something."

Hannah closed her eyes for a moment and let all the images of the pony and her examinations flow through her mind. There was only one real possibility.

She shoved to her feet. "I'm going to treat him for EPM. Starting now."

Sharon frowned. "With what drugs? There's no fully effective treatment for EPM that I ever heard of."

Hannah rummaged around in the duffel bag. "I talked to the vet at the research lab yesterday. There's an experimental drug combination they've been having some luck with." She found the containers she'd pulled from Tim's shelves earlier, just in case. Thank goodness her boss kept an unusually well-stocked pharmacy, so she didn't have to wait for any of the medications.

She gave Sharon instructions on dosage and frequency, adding, "I'm including an immune system stimulant and an anti-inflammatory as well."

"You sure you don't want to wait for the test results?" Sharon asked, her arms crossed.

Yes, Hannah wanted to wait, but her instincts told her not to. The longer the parasites were in Satchmo's body, the more likely they would cause irreversible damage. She didn't want the little fellow to limp or stagger or ache for the rest of his life. Especially since Matt cared so much for his whisper pony. "We don't have the luxury of time," she said, tilting her chin up to look the taller woman in the eye. "It's EPM. I'm sure of it." She injected a confidence she didn't feel into her statement.

"You're the doc," Sharon said, holding Hannah's gaze for a long moment before she bent to give the pony a pat. "Okay, Satch, we're going to get you cured."

"He shouldn't be worked," Hannah said, packing up her supplies. "Just let him rest as long as he wants to. I'd get him up about once every two hours and make sure he drinks. Keep up the nutritional supplement Tim prescribed since he's not eating much."

Sharon took one handle of the medical bag and fell into step beside Hannah as she headed out for the truck. "Matt's coming after school to see Satch," Sharon said. "Do I need to call his father and cancel that?"

Hannah stumbled slightly at the mention of Adam. She'd managed to shove the prospect of talking to him out of her mind while she was working. The magnitude of what she'd done last night flooded through her, making it hard to focus on Sharon's question. Instead of answering it, she asked a different one that had been bothering her. "Did Adam talk with you about buying Satchmo?"

"Yeah, but I don't sell sick animals to my clients." Sharon helped Hannah stow the bag in the truck. "Even if they can afford the medical treatment better than I can."

Hannah's admiration for the horsewoman rose another notch. Sharon's decency gave her a dose of gumption. "I'll call Adam and explain the situation," Hannah said. "He can decide if he wants Matt to see Satchmo in this condition."

Sharon shoved her hands in her breeches pockets. "Hey, Doc, I didn't mean to question your judgment back there."

Hannah felt a niggle of doubt creeping in again, but she quashed it. Part of the art of being a veterinarian was giving the animals' owners confidence in her ability to diagnose the problem. "It's a tough disease to pinpoint without the test results, but everything I've seen adds up to EPM."

Sharon nodded and her stance relaxed.

Hannah opened the truck door and climbed in. "I'll stop in again on my way home from work."

"I guess you'll be glad when Dr. Tim comes home so you can have some time off," Sharon said.

Mrs. Shanks's voice echoed in Hannah's ears. *Where's Dr. Tim? I'll just wait until he gets back.* She gave the horsewoman a wan smile. "Yeah, it'll be nice."

Sharon swung the truck door closed and gave it a friendly slap in farewell before she turned back to the barn.

Hannah slumped in the seat, feeling the weight of her decision lying heavy on her. Maybe she should have waited for Tim. Or for the test results.

"No! No more second-guessing!" She slammed the seat with her fist, making the half-eaten sandwich sitting there pop into the air. "I'm a darned good vet and I know it's the right thing to do."

She started to turn the key in the ignition and then remembered her promise to call Adam. She crossed her arms on the steering wheel and dropped her forehead against them with a moan. Her little spurt of courage had deserted her.

It was impossible to decide what to say to Adam about their encounter last night because her feelings were so tangled and conflicting she had no idea where to start. He was a terrific lover, and her body still fizzed with excitement at the memories. However, relief had washed through her when he'd kissed her awake at five a.m. to say he had to get home before Matt woke up. Her qualms about having to face Adam in the morning over the breakfast table spoke volumes about how little she knew the man. He was an enigma with troubles so serious she couldn't begin to fathom them.

The trick would be to keep the conversation about Matt and Satchmo. Avoidance. It was something she'd become adept at with Ward.

She swiped over Adam's cell number and beat a tattoo on the steering wheel with her other hand as she listened to it ring.

"Hannah." His voice was low and intimate. "I was going to call you later. I'd like to come by after the restaurant closes."

"Er, that's not why I'm calling." She rolled her eyes at her own gaucheness, but she didn't know how to answer him. "It's about Satchmo. His condition has worsened, and I've started treating him for EPM. Equine protozoal myeloencephalitis. It's a parasite that attacks the central nervous system, and it's tough to diagnose or completely cure."

Adam muttered a curse. "Matt's planning to spend most of the weekend at the stable. Should I keep him away?"

"Only you can decide that. However, Satchmo's not in pain. He's just lying down and staying down. I suppose he could die while Matt's there, which would be traumatic, but I don't think that will happen." She took a breath. "On the other hand, Satchmo responds to Matt. It might actually be beneficial to the pony to have your son there. But it's your call."

He blew out a breath. "The kid has the worst luck when he loves someone."

"It doesn't seem fair," Hannah agreed. "But I'm going to do my utmost to pull Satchmo through this."

"I don't know what to do," he said.

Hannah considered her own recent experience with kids and animals. "It seems like it's better to let children know what's going on with the animals they love. If Satchmo dies and Matt isn't there, it might be even more upsetting for him. Maybe you should give him the choice."

"Is that what a good father does?" he asked. "Leaves it up to the child?"

She hesitated before she said, "I think maybe a good father *does* leave it up to his child. As long as you assure him that you'll support any choice he makes."

"Of course I'll support him." Adam's voice lost its snap as he added, "I'm not cut out for this. And you don't deserve to bear the brunt of it. Last night was—"

"Something we should talk about later," Hannah said, going into avoidance mode again. "You mentioned coming by?" By then she hoped to have some plan in mind.

"It will be late."

She hesitated at the thought of another short night's sleep. Without Tim she had a busy Saturday ahead of her. "No problem."

"I'll bring caviar."

His last word sent heat surging through her body. *What had she gotten herself into?*

Adam parked the Maserati in an empty space a half-block from the junior high school. He was fifteen minutes early for pick-up but he couldn't sit still. Jumping out of the car, he paced down the sidewalk away from the square brick school building, scouring his brain for the right words to break the news about Satchmo to Matt and then offer him a graceful way to avoid the pain of watching the pony slide into death.

It didn't help that flashbacks of his night with Hannah kept intruding. Even though he knew she had offered him the comfort of her body out of sympathy, he had lost himself in her responsiveness, the craving for alcohol vanquished by the unexpected explosion of their coming together.

Why the hell hadn't he called his AA sponsor? What had possessed him to involve Hannah?

It was because she was his lifeline to Matt. After reading Maggie's letter, he'd needed to feel that connection with his son, so he'd turned to Hannah.

He shook his head. It was more than that. She was the light to his shadow. He wanted to bask in her healing warmth. Now he was going to screw things up between Matt and Hannah by tangling his own desires with their relationship.

He yanked his hands out of his pockets and shoved them through his hair, trying to force himself to think clearly.

It was Friday, one of the two busiest days at The Aerie, and he hadn't done anything more than glance at the reservations list. As of an hour ago, the lamb delivery hadn't arrived and they were down to the last bottle of Le Montrachet, one of their finest French white Burgundies.

"How do single mothers do it?" he muttered, pivoting on his heel and walking back toward the car. He leaned against the sleek fender, arms folded, and sank his chin to his chest as he returned to his first concern: Matt and Satchmo.

The kid couldn't catch a break.

It was Adam's fault. He selfishly wanted to keep his son with him when he wasn't fit to be a father. As soon as he got back to the restaurant, he would tell his investigator to do a full background check on the McNallys. He owed it to Matt to find him someone who could handle things like dying ponies the way a competent parent should.

The clanging of a bell jerked him upright. He straightened away from the car and scanned the mass of kids pouring through the flung-open metal doors. Spotting Matt's dark hair and green hoodie, he lifted a hand to catch his attention. His son's expression went from laughter to surliness in a split second as Matt nodded curtly in acknowledgment of his father's presence. Adam felt a jab of pain lance through his chest. He wasn't going to make Matt's mood any better.

"Did you have to bring this car?" Matt said, walking past his father to open the passenger door and fling his backpack into the back seat. "It's like you're showing off."

Adam knew better than to apologize. Matt would have objected no matter which car he had driven. "I needed to get here fast."

"Because you were running late as usual," Matt said, slamming the passenger door closed in Adam's face.

Temper sparked at Matt's rudeness, but Adam took a breath and walked with a measured step around the car's hood. He opened the door and slid into the driver's seat, wrapping his fingers around the steering wheel before he turned to look at his son.

Matt's gaze was glued to his phone, his thumbs flying across the touch screen. Adam waited.

"Why are we sitting here?" Matt lifted his head to glare at his father. "I'm supposed to be at the stable."

"Dr. Linden called. Satchmo's taken a turn for the worse."

The hostility in Matt's blue eyes was swamped by a heartbreaking panic. "He's not dying, is he?" the boy whispered.

"She's doing everything she can to prevent that," Adam said, not wanting to lie to his son.

Matt turned away to stare out the side window. He swallowed hard and his breath sounded ragged. Adam reached across to lay his hand on Matt's shoulder. "You don't have to go see him in this condition."

His son whipped around, shrugging off Adam's hand. The glare was back, heightened by the tears he was trying hard not to shed. "Did Dr. Linden say I couldn't?"

"No. In fact—"

"Then I'm going." Matt shifted in his seat so he was looking through the windshield. Adam punched on the ignition as he watched Matt blink repeatedly.

Putting the car in gear, Adam finished saying what he wanted his son to know. "Dr. Linden said it might help Satchmo if you were there."

He felt the bitterness of Matt's antagonism as his son snapped, "Why didn't you tell me that?"

"You didn't give me a chance."

Tension wound through the silence as Adam guided the car through the side streets to the highway.

"Dr. Linden really thinks I can help?" Matt asked, his voice husky.

"That's what she said, but she didn't want to put any pressure on you."

Matt sucked in a breath but said nothing.

"She's a highly skilled veterinarian," Adam said. "She'll do everything she can for Satchmo."

"I know," Matt said. His voice broke on a swallowed sob and Adam felt his heart twist. Not caring if he was rejected again, he took one hand off the steering wheel and gripped Matt's thin shoulder.

"I'm sorry," he said.

"This sucks," Matt said so softly Adam barely caught his words.

"Yes, it does." Adam gave Matt's shoulder a squeeze and brought his hand back to the wheel as the road bent into a hairpin turn. "It really sucks."

Chapter 13

AT FIVE THIRTY, HANNAH UNLATCHED THE DOOR TO Satchmo's stall and stopped in her tracks, her breath catching in her throat. The pony was stretched out flat on the straw bedding, his head resting in the cradle of Matt's crossed legs while the boy stroked down Satch's neck. Matt's gaze came up and a look of relief spread over his face. "Dr. Linden!"

A shadow stirred in the corner of the stall, materializing into Adam as he stood up, brushing straw off his black jeans. "We're glad to see you. Satchmo seems to be getting weaker," he said in a low voice.

The hope on Matt's face dimmed.

Hannah knelt by the pony. "It's good that you're here," she said to Matt. "He'll want to get well for you." Putting her stethoscope in her ears, she checked Satchmo's heartbeat and breathing. Neither was strong. She ran her hands over the pony's body and legs, watching for reactions that didn't come.

"He's not in pain," she said, sitting back on her heels. "So that's the good news."

"Sharon says she's been giving him all the medications you prescribed," Adam offered.

She glanced up to see his gaze straying back to his son, who was now bent over Satchmo, murmuring something in the pony's ear. The distress Adam felt on Matt's behalf was clear in the tightness of his jaw.

"How long has he been lying down flat like this?" Hannah asked.

"He did it right after we got here," Matt said. "I knew it was a bad sign."

"About three-thirty, so for the last two hours," Adam clarified, rubbing his hand over his jaw. As she watched his movement, a memory of that hand cupping her breast flashed through her mind, flushing her cheeks.

He must have read something of her thoughts in her expression because his gaze went hot and soft. Awareness rippled through her, making her fingers curl inward. Their eyes met and she saw the flicker of desire in his. She sucked in a breath.

Matt's voice snapped her out of the trance Adam had drawn her into. "I sat down beside him and he rolled over and stretched out like this."

"Maybe he just wanted to rest his head in your lap as a way to make contact," Hannah said. "I'm going to go see Sharon about getting Satchmo some treats." She skimmed her fingers over the back of Adam's hand in a brief, silent communication, her fingertips glancing across the raised scars.

"We'll be here," Adam said, the tightness in his jaw returning as he looked at Matt.

Hannah was halfway to Sharon's office when the horsewoman strode through the barn's big door. "Hey, Doc, I heard you were here. How's Satch?"

Hannah shook her head, and Sharon's face fell.

"Can I raid your feed room to see if I can mix up something to tempt Satchmo's appetite?" Hannah asked.

"Take anything you think will work," Sharon said, leading her to the green-painted door and fitting a key into the lock. "The door locks itself when you pull it shut, so I'll let you have my key in case you need to come back. We don't want the critters getting into something they shouldn't."

Hannah stepped into the fragrant room filled with bags, wooden bins, and various plastic containers, all labeled in neat, square handwriting. Oats, corn, barley, molasses, dried vegetables and grasses, soybean meal, bran, vitamins, and various already concocted pellets were on offer. She swung open the refrigerator door to find carrots, apples, probiotics, and high-protein liquids.

"These horses eat better than I do," she muttered, pulling out several containers and tossing the ingredients into a shallow, stainless-steel bowl she found on a shelf. She scooped out various grains and stirred everything around before she leaned down to sniff at her creation. "Maybe Satchmo has a sweet tooth." She added some molasses and rolled the mixture into bite-sized balls before heading back toward the pony's stall.

Adam waylaid her before she reached it, pushing away from the wall he'd been leaning against to take her elbow. He guided her back toward the feed room and into an empty stall well away from Satchmo's. As soon as they were inside, he released her and closed the door before turning. "Is Satchmo dying?" His voice was raw.

"Not if I can help it," she said, clutching the bowl against her stomach.

"But it's possible."

"If the EPM is advanced, it's possible. But I won't let him go without doing everything in my power to prevent it."

"I know," he said, as he ran his fingers through his hair.

She longed to offer him reassurance, but she couldn't lie to him after the searing intimacy of the night before. Instead she reached up with one hand to smooth down the worst of his tousled hair, savoring the satin slide of it beneath her palm until she forced herself to step away from temptation.

One corner of his mouth turned up as he dragged his palms over his hair in an unsuccessful attempt to neaten it further.

"My first boss used to yell at me for sticking my fingers in my hair when I was under pressure. It's a bad habit for a chef."

"It seems he didn't break your habit," she said, gripping the bowl to keep her hands away from him.

"He did," he said, the half-smile winking out. "When I'm cooking." He looked down at the horse food. "Is that something medicinal for Satchmo?"

"Medicinal? No, it's meant to tempt him to eat."

Adam picked up one of the balls and brought it to his nose, grimacing slightly as he inhaled. He broke off a piece and rubbed it between his fingers, testing the texture, before he let the crumbled bits fall into the straw bedding. "Hmm."

"What does that mean?" Hannah picked up one of the lopsided balls and took a whiff. It didn't smell as tantalizing as it had in the feed room.

"If you tell me what ingredients to put in it, I'll see if I can make it more . . . enticing." He took the bowl from her.

"You're going to cook for a horse?" The thought reminded her it was late on Friday afternoon and he had a restaurant to run. "Don't you need to be at work?" she asked, tugging on the bowl to take it back.

He held onto it. "My staff can handle it." His words were confident, but he didn't meet her eyes.

"I'm planning to stay with Satchmo," she said. "I'll keep an eye on Matt too."

He snapped his gaze to hers. "My son is not going through this without me."

She let go of the bowl. "You know, Matt's got better luck with his father than you like to think."

He raised his eyebrows at her in disagreement but made no comment. She scrabbled in her jacket pocket for the feed-room key and held it out to him. "You can put anything in it that's natural. No vitamins and no protein supplements because Sharon has given those to him already."

He wrapped his fingers around her extended hand and pulled her into him, releasing her to slip his free arm around her waist. "Thank you for last night. For being here today. For a generosity I don't deserve." He spoke in a low, husky voice that seemed to vibrate in her bones.

"You keep saying you don't deserve things," she said, leaning back slightly to see his face. "I think you deserve more than most."

His grip on her tightened and a spasm of denial twisted his mouth. "I have a lot to atone for first." He kissed her forehead and let her go.

She wanted to protest the loss. The solid weight of his arm felt so good resting on her hips, while the warmth of his body beat back the chill of the barn. But she knew it was better not to allow herself to enjoy it. Her feelings about him were so confused she had no idea where to go with them.

He used the bowl to wave her through the stall door. "This will be a real test of my mettle as a chef," he said, glancing down at its contents.

"I'll explain to Satchmo just how expensive his meal would be if he had to pay for it."

Adam bit off a laugh and headed for the feed room. Hannah slipped her hands into her pockets and watched him stride away, the dark color of his clothes creating the illusion that he was vanishing in the twilight interior of the barn.

She shook herself, trying to slough off the residual effect of his touch before she walked over to Satchmo's stall.

"Any change?" she asked as she closed the stall door behind her.

Matt shook his head, misery written all over his face. With one hand he kept up a rhythmic stroking down the pony's neck, while his other hand cradled Satchmo's head.

Hannah pulled out her stethoscope again, more to give Matt some reassurance that she was paying attention than anything else. Satch's vital signs were unimproved. She sighed and folded the scope back into her pocket. "Your dad's fixing something delicious to tempt Satchmo to eat. He didn't think much of my feeble efforts at horse cuisine."

"What does he know about horses' tastes?" Matt scoffed. "He cooks for people."

"I guess it's the same principle," Hannah said, settling herself into a more comfortable position on the straw beside the pony. "It should look good, smell good, and taste good. Do you think your father will actually taste it?" She wrinkled her nose at the thought.

That got a snort of laughter from Matt, and Satchmo's leg twitched. The boy looked at Hannah hopefully. "He moved!"

"I guess he thinks your dad eating horse food is funny too."

"Maybe we should talk normally instead of being quiet," Matt said.

"Not a bad idea. A little liveliness might cheer Satch up. You go first."

Matt thought for a moment before he asked, "What sort of stuff goes into horse food?"

"All kinds of natural things. Oats, barley, molasses, dried grasses, apples, carrots."

"You hear that, Satch?" Matt said, bending over to speak into the pony's ear. "Your favorite munchies. Mmm." He smacked his lips for emphasis.

"You sound like a mother trying to get her baby to eat." Hannah was amused.

Matt grinned. "Yeah, but it must work because mothers all do the same thing."

His smile made her blink because it looked so much like Adam's, with the dimple and the crinkle at the corners of the eyes. The cleft in Matt's chin was softened by traces of youthful chubbiness but it would stand out like his father's soon. She realized Matt didn't smile much, which is why it still surprised her when she saw the startling resemblance.

The stall door creaked open and Matt's face went blank as Adam slipped in with the bowl in the crook of his arm. "I tweaked Dr. Linden's recipe somewhat, so let's see what Satchmo thinks." He walked over to Matt and set the bowl down beside him in the straw. "He's more likely to take it from you than anyone else."

The boy threw his father an unreadable glance before he reached into the bowl and drew out a perfectly formed ball flecked with bright-orange bits of carrot and golden apple chunks.

"That looks good enough for me to eat," Hannah said, stretching out her arm to snag a treat ball. She brought it to her nose and looked up at Adam. "Definitely more appetizing."

Matt held his about six inches from his nose and took a cautious sniff. Surprise registered on his face as he brought it up close and inhaled again. "It smells like trail mix," he said. "Really good trail mix."

Adam's expression was a study in relief and pleasure. When Matt pinched off a bit and stuck it on the end of his tongue, he looked even more gratified, laughing out loud when his son spit it out in disgust. "It's not meant for human taste buds."

"I almost tasted it myself," Hannah admitted, waving the fragrant morsel under her nose again. "However, I learned my lesson about pet food after sampling my cat's Tuna Delight. It smelled like I could make a sandwich out of it but it tasted like sawdust."

"Eww, you ate cat food?" Matt said, still picking bits of alfalfa off his tongue.

"You ate hay," Hannah pointed out.

"You don't want to know what I've eaten," Adam said, squatting down between Hannah and Matt.

"Chocolate-covered bugs?" Hannah guessed.

"Perfectly normal and delicious," Adam said. "I was thinking of burnt goat head with the teeth included. And corn smut."

"Gross," Matt grimaced. "What's corn smut?"

"It's a fungus that deforms corn kernels and turns them purple, but it makes a great sauce or soup flavoring," Adam said.

"Gross squared," Matt responded. "I've had snails."

"What'd you think?" his father asked, his face alight with interest.

"Too chewy but not bad."

Hannah could see Matt begin to withdraw, almost as though he realized he was having a civil conversation with his father and that was a bad thing in the boy's mind. She leapt in to save Adam from a rebuff. "Well, I've chowed down on duck tongues," she said.

The two Bosches gave her nearly identical looks of disbelief. "Why?" Matt asked.

"It was a dare," Hannah said. "A friend and I were visiting New York City and they had them in a Chinese restaurant."

"Well?" Adam prompted.

"Let's just say I never ate another one."

"Smart move," Matt said. He rolled the horse treat around on his palm. "Should we make Satchmo sit up before I try to feed him this?"

Hannah looked at the pony as she debated. He was lying on his side with his front legs stretched out straight and his back legs slightly folded. His belly rose and fell with his breathing, and other than an occasional flick of an ear he appeared to be asleep.

"Considering how you and I reacted to the smell of the horse treat, I think you should hold it near his nose and let him get a good whiff of it. If he shows interest, we'll work on getting his head up."

Matt nodded and waved the horse treat in front of Satchmo's velvety nose a few times.

"Crumble it up in your hand," Adam said. "That will release more of the scent."

His son dug his fingers into the ball, breaking it apart so that Hannah could smell the fragrance from where she sat. He held it to the pony's nostrils.

It seemed as though nothing moved for a long moment before Satchmo's eyelid popped open, his pale lashes accentuating the liquid darkness of his eye.

"That's it, Satch," Matt said, swirling the bits of treat around in his palm. "Yummy stuff."

The pony fumbled against the boy's hand with his lips before his long pink tongue snaked out to lick the food up.

"He likes it," Matt said, lifting a face aglow with happiness.

"Your father makes a mean horse treat," she said, wanting credit to go where it was due.

Matt grabbed another treat from the bowl and smashed it in his slobber-slicked palm. "Here, Satch, have another one."

Hannah snuck a look at Adam to find the lines of tension around his mouth smooth away as he watched his son feed the pony.

When Matt reached for a third treat, Satchmo tucked his front legs under him and rolled up so he could get his nose directly into the bowl.

"Yessss!" Matt gave a fist pump.

As the pony munched on the gourmet treats, Matt stretched his legs out with a sigh of release. "I was getting kind of cramped," he said, flexing his feet in the ratty red high-tops. He watched Satchmo in silence before turning to his father. "I guess you know how to make good-tasting food for pretty much anyone."

"Anything I can do to help Satchmo get better," Adam said. "I'll make him more if Dr. Linden says it's okay."

"Let's see if he'll drink some water first." Hannah stood and walked to the water bucket hanging in the corner of the stall. She started to unhook it, only to have Adam's hand close around the handle and lift it away from her.

"Shall I put it on the straw in front of him?" he asked.

She nodded and watched him carry the brimming bucket and ease it down beside the now empty feed bowl without spilling a drop.

"Wash it down with this, Satch," Adam said. "Vintage well water straight from the hose."

The pony sniffed at the bucket and turned his head away.

"Can you make water taste better?" Hannah asked, looking at Adam with a wry smile.

He stood looking down at the bucket with his hands shoved in the back pockets of his jeans. "Hmm," he said finally. "Let me go back to the feed room and work on it."

"I was kidding," Hannah said.

"He needs fluids, right?" Adam said, picking up the bucket.

"Yes, but I can get them into him intravenously, if necessary."

"I might as well give it a try," he said. "All he can do is reject it."

Hannah saw Adam check on Matt with a quick, sideways glance before he walked out of the stall.

Matt stood up and rolled his shoulders. "It's good that Satch ate, isn't it?" he asked, a note of hope in his voice.

"Very good." Hannah watched the pony, who was now drowsing with his nose touching the straw.

"It's cool the horse treats worked," Matt said, his hands in his back pockets in an unconscious echo of his father's stance.

"I have to get your dad's recipe," Hannah said. "For other finicky equine eaters."

"I'm pretty sure his recipes are secret. So other chefs can't copy them."

Surprised by Matt's knowledge of his father's profession, Hannah saw an opening that she thought was worth taking. "So you understand that your father just put his world-class talent at the disposal of a sick pony?"

"Yeah." Matt kept his gaze on Satchmo.

"And you realize he's leaving his internationally famous restaurant in the hands of his staff on a Friday night to stay here?"

Matt glanced at her for a split second before he nodded.

"So I'd say he's putting you first in his life."

The boy's blue eyes were focused on her now. She saw a storm of conflicting emotions swirling there. Hope, fear, denial, and that bone-deep sadness that tore at her heart.

"For now," he said in a low voice. He dropped his gaze back to Satchmo. "I heard him talking on the phone. He's trying to find someone from my mother's family to adopt me."

Chapter 14

ANNAH JERKED AWAKE. SHE BLINKED AS SHE MADE out the rough beams supporting the barn's roof in the near darkness above her, reminding her of where she was. After a dinner of take-out sandwiches, Sharon had rounded up sleeping bags for the three of them when they refused to leave Satchmo's stall. As Hannah rubbed her hands over her face, she heard the harsh rasping of the pony's breath. That must have been what yanked her out of her uneasy sleep.

Adam's low voice came from her right. "I was about to wake you. He just started breathing like that."

She turned her head to find Adam propped up against the wall, his long legs extended in front of him and crossed at the ankles. Exhaustion made his handsome face look gaunt.

Matt's revelation socked her in the gut again. She couldn't reconcile this man who was camped out in a stable beside an ailing pony with the person Matt claimed wanted to give his son away. Remembering her own encounter with the injustice of slander, she decided not to condemn Adam before he'd had a chance to tell his side of the story. "Have you slept?" she asked.

He shook his head. "I'm used to late hours." He stood and leaned down to offer his hand.

She unzipped the sleeping bag and put her fingers in his, feeling his strength as he pulled her to her feet without visible effort. "Maybe he's just in an awkward position," she said, trying to ease his worry. She turned her watch to catch the low light slanting in from the corridor. It showed 3:20 a.m., right in the darkest hours of the night when all living beings seemed to loosen their hold on life.

She walked quietly to the pony so as not to rouse Matt, who was wrapped in a sleeping bag beside Satchmo. Shortly after they'd eaten, the pony had put his head down and stretched out on his side again. He still lay in much the same way.

Hooking her stethoscope in her ears, she moved it over Satchmo, listening to his heart and lungs, where the rasp was magnified, and to the faint gurgling of his digestive system. She put the scope away with a sigh before pulling his lips open and pressing a fingertip against his gums to test the capillary refill rate. The pony whiffled a little but didn't move.

She'd been hopeful when Satch had consumed Adam's gourmet offerings, but the little creature was drifting away from them again. She glanced up at Adam, trying to keep the dismay from showing in her expression.

He squatted beside her. "Is there anything else we can do for him?" he asked softly, tracing a long arc down Satchmo's flank with the palm of his hand.

She sat back on her heels and blew out a breath of frustration. Letting her gaze wander around the quiet, dimly lit stall, she noted the rise and fall of Satchmo's belly, Matt's cheek resting on his out flung arm, and finally the marks on the back of Adam's hand as he continued to stroke the pony's rough, reddish coat. She closed her eyes and inhaled the scent of horse, straw, and Adam's faint spiciness—which was now reminiscent of a feed room rather than a kitchen. That brought a tiny smile to her lips.

Everything was peaceful and serene. Her eyes flew open. She pulled the elastic band out of her sagging ponytail, gathered all the loose strands tightly at the back of her head, and wound the elastic back on with a snap. "We're making it too easy for him."

"What do you mean?"

"Matt had the right idea earlier. We're going to give Satchmo all the stimulus we can manage. Matt, wake up." She reached for the sleeping boy, but Adam caught her wrist to stop her. Startled, she looked at him to find a fierce protectiveness burning in his face.

"What if this doesn't work and Satchmo dies? Matt shouldn't have to watch that," Adam said, still holding her wrist.

"It won't work without Matt. He's the only one who can pull Satch back from the edge." She sat back on her heels.

Adam released her, his gaze resting on his son as the ugly grating of Satchmo's breathing filled the stall. After a long moment of stillness, Hannah sighed in relief when Adam leaned over and gently shook Matt's shoulder. "Matt, Satch needs you."

"Wha—?" Matt half-opened his eyes before burrowing down into the sleeping bag.

Adam shook him again. "Wake up. You need to talk to Satch."

Matt flopped onto his back, and squinted up at his father. "Satch? Is he okay?"

"No, he's fading. We need you to make him hang on."

As Matt dragged himself onto his elbows, Hannah began shaking Satchmo. "Hey, buddy, wake up! We're going to get you on your feet."

Other than pivoting one ear backward, the pony ignored her.

"I thought he was supposed to rest," Matt said. Even as he spoke, he started to tickle Satchmo's nose whiskers.

"Yeah, but that isn't working," Hannah said. "We're going to give him a reason to stick around." She looked at Matt. "And that reason is you. Talk to him."

The boy swallowed and scratched his head. "Um, Satch, you got to get up. The doctor says so."

Hannah stood and walked around to stand by the pony's back. Waving Adam around to join her, she knelt and slid her hands as far under Satchmo as she could get them. "We're going to persuade him to sit upright," she said, while Adam knelt beside her and matched her position. She felt the brush of his shoulder against hers as an almost electric shock, but pushed the sensation to the back of her mind to get to work on the pony. "Matt, grab his halter and pull his head up while we roll him. Now."

"C'mon, Satch," Hannah nearly shouted as she levered her shoulder against the pony's back. "Up you go!"

Adam grunted, and she felt the weight of the pony shift. Matt was tugging Satchmo's head up. "That's it, Satch," the boy said. "Get up! I need you to stay alive."

She heard the sharp intake of Adam's breath at Matt's last sentence. Adam must have heaved harder, because Satchmo's dead weight came off her arms as the pony tucked his legs in and sat up.

"Okay!" Hannah said, dusting her palms on her jeans. "Now we have to get him on his feet."

Adam eyed the pony. "How much does he weigh?"

"About six hundred pounds, I'd guess," Hannah said. "Don't worry. He's going to get up by himself. With a little encouragement."

She got to her feet, while Adam surged up beside her. "What sort of encouragement did you have in mind?" he asked.

"Matt and I are going to pull. And you're going to push," Hannah said, grabbing the lead line that hung by the door. Matt released the pony's halter and scrambled to his feet.

"By push I assume you mean from the rear," Adam said with a dry undertone. He knelt at Satchmo's rump and worked his hands beneath the pony.

"At least he can't kick you when he's lying down," Hannah said, giving him full marks for not hesitating to position himself there.

"Now you've given me something else to worry about," Adam said, but she noticed him shifting closer to the pony to improve his leverage.

Hannah clipped the lead line to one side of Satchmo's halter and threaded it under his chin and through the other side. "Matt, I want you on his right with your hands on his halter so you can pull too. But mostly I want you talking in Satch's ear, convincing him he's needed here."

Matt looked panicky. "I don't know how to do that."

"Is Satchmo important to you?" Hannah asked.

Matt nodded.

"Put that in your voice. The words don't matter but he'll hear the emotion."

She cast a quick glance at Adam, who was wearing an expression combining disbelief with something that might be admiration. Turning back to the pony, she wound the end of the lead line around her left hand and leaned down to grip it up close to the halter with her right. Matt bent down on the opposite side of Satchmo's head, wrapping his fingers around the cheek strap of the pony's halter.

"Everyone ready?" Grunts of assent came from her assistants. "Matt, you start talking while I count to three. On three we start encouraging."

"Okay, Satch," Matt said. "You've had your rest. You have to get up now."

"One," Hannah said.

"I need you to get better, Satch," Matt said, a pleading note in his voice. "So we can be friends."

"Two."

"We need time together, Satch." Matt's voice was wavering. "If you don't get better we won't have that."

"Three!" Hannah threw her weight against the lead line as Matt tugged at the halter. She could hear Adam muttering, "C'mon, Satchmo. Get the heck up!"

The lead line bit into the skin on Hannah's hands as she strained against the pony's dead weight. Matt's feet were braced and his arms were straight out as he put his whole body into the task.

"Satchmo," the boy yelled, his voice a cry of anguish. "Please don't die!"

Hannah felt the pressure on her hands lessen slightly and she took up the slack. "He's moving," she said. "Keep it up!"

A muffled groan of effort came from Adam, still crouched behind the pony. Satchmo scrambled to his feet.

"He's up!" Matt said, his face lit with joy. "We got him up!"

"I think your father did most of the work," Hannah said, as Adam put his hands on his thighs and bent over, sucking in a long breath. He shook his head and gulped in more air.

She handed the lead line to Matt. "Now we have to keep him up."

"How?" Matt asked, looking at the rope in his hand as though it were a snake.

"By taking him for a walk in the barn. You're going to keep talking to him and let him see the other horses. He's used to having a companion, so he should find that comforting."

"But he tried to bite the one who came up to him in the paddock," Matt said.

"That was before he met you. You've been a good influence on him."

"That's cool," the boy said, looking pleased.

Hannah unlatched the door. "Go ahead. When you get tired, bring him back and I'll take over."

As Matt led Satchmo past, she gave the pony's rump a pat before she put her back against the wall and slid down to the straw to put her head in her hands. Now that the crisis was temporarily past, the weight of her near-failure crashed down on her like a ton of bricks.

Adam was sitting on the straw beside her in an instant. "Are you all right?" he asked. She felt the comfort of his hand on her shoulder.

"I nearly lost him," she said into her hands.

Adam wrapped his arm around her and pulled her against his side. She felt his breath stir her hair as he said, "You've worked a miracle. Sharon told me how difficult it is to diagnose and treat EPM."

"I still don't know if it's EPM. If it is, I really shouldn't have Satchmo up and walking around." She thought of all the research she'd done on the sickness. None of her sources recommended forcing the horse to stay on its feet. She dropped her hands onto her lap and allowed herself to lean into the warmth and solidity of the man beside her.

"When I prepare a cut of beef, I adjust the temperature, the cooking time, and the seasoning based on what my instinct says about the specific piece of meat. That's what makes me good at my job," Adam said. "You're just as good at yours. You read your patient and decide what will work best for him."

"Except I don't plan to eat Satchmo."

She felt the tension leave Adam's body as he shifted and snugged her closer against him. She couldn't stop herself from slipping her arms under his leather jacket and wrapping them around his waist.

"Hannah," he murmured, his voice resonant with the same awareness stirring in her.

She felt the press of his lips on top of her head. Flashes of their previous night together sparked in her mind, and she lifted her head to him. All the fear and anxiety of the night needed an outlet and she found it in kissing him, tilting her head so she could lose herself in the textures of his mouth.

She welcomed the bloom of mindless sexual arousal down low in her belly; it blotted out her questions about the man who had brought it to life. For now, there was just the enveloping, molasses-laden scent of Adam, the feel of his warm, strong hands touching her through the cotton of her shirt, the hot slide of his lips down the sensitive line of her jaw, the shelter of his hard, muscular body. She fell into it, letting him wipe everything else from her mind.

The sound of Matt's voice made them jerk apart at the same time. As they scrambled to untangle themselves, he continued to talk to the pony. "Let's go to the other end of the barn, Satch. See what's going on down there. The horses up here are deadheads."

Hannah sprawled back onto the straw with her hand over her mouth to stifle the hysterical laugh trying to work itself free. Adam prowled over to her on his hands and knees. "Close call," he said, hovering above her, his face half in shadow.

She moved her hand. "Sorry. I didn't expect to get so intense."

"No complaints here." He bent his arms so he could touch his lips to hers for a lingering kiss that made her want to arch up into him. Rocking back on his heels, he seized both her hands to pull her upright.

"Time to make some more horse treats," he said.

Hannah took hold of the lapels of his jacket. "Satchmo could still die."

He covered her hands with his. "With you and Matt on his side, Satchmo will live to be a hundred."

Chapter 15

As the pale morning sunlight filtered through the window, Adam knelt in the straw by his sleeping son and gave him a light shake. "Matt, time to wake up."

The barn had come to life around 6:00 a.m., with the racket of clanging buckets, banging stall doors, and stable hands talking to their charges. Both Adam and Hannah had roused from the doze they'd fallen into once it was clear Satchmo was going to make it to morning. Sharon had come by to find out how the night had gone. It took the combined persuasions of both of them to convince Hannah to go home and grab an hour's sleep before she had to get to the office. And Matt had slept through it all.

Now the boy's eyelids fluttered open. He looked confused and then frightened. "Is Satchmo okay?" he asked, turning his head to look past his father.

Adam shifted so Matt could see the pony standing in the corner, one back hoof cocked up on its tip. "Dr. Linden checked him over just before she left and said he's making progress."

"Dr. Linden left?" His son's dismay was obvious.

"She had to go to work," Adam said. "Satchmo's not her only patient. She wouldn't have left if she thought he was in danger."

"I guess," Matt said, wiggling out of the sleeping bag to stand up. He walked to Satchmo and ran his hand down the pony's neck, murmuring something Adam couldn't hear. Satchmo's ears swiveled forward and he opened his deep, brown eyes. Matt looked at his father. "He seems better."

Adam joined his son. "I think we can leave him in Ms. Sydenstricker's care while we go home to clean up and get some sleep."

Matt shook his head. "I'm not leaving him until Dr. Linden says he's okay."

"If you rest up now, you can come back tonight," Adam said. "That's when he needs you the most."

His son looked torn. Adam reached out and plucked a piece of straw from Matt's disheveled hair. "There are a lot of people here who know more about horses than either of us. We can trust Satchmo to them for a few hours."

Matt continued to stroke the pony's neck. When he spoke, his voice was choked with unshed tears. "Something might happen while we're gone."

The stall door slid open and Sharon walked in. "Nothing's going to happen." She came over to scratch Satchmo behind the ears. The pony heaved a sigh of pleasure. When Sharon dropped her hand, Satchmo butted his face against Matt's chest. "See? He's back to his old, demanding self," Sharon said.

That got a shaky smile from Matt. The boy put his forehead against the pony's and said, "Okay, buddy, I gotta go for a while, but I'll be back. And you'd better be here."

Adam placed his hand on Matt's shoulder and turned him toward the door. "Let's get out of Ms. Sydenstricker's way." Stopping at the door, he looked back at Sharon. "I left a batch of Satch treats in a plastic container in the feed room. The recipe is taped to them."

"I'll keep it confidential in case you decide to go into the horse-treat business."

Adam smiled. It felt good after the high drama of their night. "I'll leave that to you and Matt. It's not my demographic."

His son gave a little snort that Adam chose to interpret as amusement. While they walked down the barn's central corridor, he racked his brain for a way to keep the conversation going. "Maybe you could call it 'Satchmo's Horse Treats' since he taste-tested them," he ventured.

"Yeah, maybe," Matt said. He thrust his hands into his jeans pockets as he slouched along beside his father. "We could put a picture of him on the label."

Adam felt a flash of satisfaction that his son had volunteered a suggestion. "Good idea. Marketers say people respond to faces."

Matt grunted and lapsed into silence as they walked toward the Maserati. Adam tried to conjure up the pleasure he usually got from the windswept lines of the sports car but today it didn't work. All he could think about was how close his son had come to losing someone important to him. And the danger wasn't over.

He brought the big engine to life and put it into gear as Matt buckled his seatbelt. The truth was Adam had thought Satchmo was a goner when his breathing started to rasp in that painful way. He now knew why they called it a death rattle. He'd prayed the horrible sound wouldn't rouse Matt from his sleep. The dread of his son waking up only to watch the pony die had gripped Adam's throat so tightly he could barely breathe.

He had seen the same helpless anguish in Hannah's face as she stared down at the boy and the pony, their backs pressed together. And then she'd yanked Satchmo back from the edge of death.

"Dr. Linden is awesome." Matt's voice pulled Adam out of his grim thoughts.

"I was thinking how awesome you were too. Not many people would sleep in a stall with a sick horse."

He glanced over to see Matt fiddling with the zipper on his jacket. "You did too," Matt muttered.

"I slept in a stall with my son."

"You made Satch the food that got him to eat. And juiced up his water to make it taste good." Matt's voice was still low.

"All I did was help you and Dr. Linden."

"You left The Aerie on a Friday night."

Adam threw a quick look sideways to find Matt's gaze on him.

"Thanks for staying," Matt said.

Adam wanted to assure Matt he would always stay, but he remembered the email from the private investigator and all the reasons he'd hired him. "You're welcome."

Matt went quiet again, but this time the atmosphere held no charge of anger. By the time they arrived at the house, Matt's head was tilted against the car window at such an awkward angle Adam figured he had to be dead asleep. When Adam turned the engine off, Matt jerked awake, looking sheepish as he wiped a trickle of drool from his chin.

"I don't know about you but I'm headed for the shower," Adam said.

"Oh man, yeah." Matt pushed the door open and staggered slightly as he got out. Adam caught up with him as his house-keeper, Sarah Duckworth, opened the door to let Trace out.

The dog raced up to Adam and dropped to a sit, his body quivering with the suppressed urge to leap on his master. Adam gave him the release signal, and Trace let loose all his enthusiasm, barking and dancing around both man and boy. When Adam knelt, Trace barreled into him, licking his face and hands as he tried to pet the frantic dog. "I'm glad to see you too, boy," he said, sinking his hands into the Shepherd's ruff and massaging it beneath the bandage.

Matt stood watching, his hands dangling empty by his sides. Catching a glimpse of his son's face, Adam thought he read yearning on it. Maybe Matt needed a puppy as well as a whisper pony.

Trace's enthusiasm quieted enough so Adam could stand. Waiting until Matt had turned back toward the house, Adam gave the dog a signal to go to the boy. Trace pushed his head under one of Matt's hands, and the boy's reaction mingled surprise and delight. He mimicked his father in dropping to his knees so he could give the dog an energetic ear scratch. "Does this feel good, Trace?" Matt asked.

The housekeeper joined them in the driveway, shaking her head. "That dog sensed you were here at least five minutes before you pulled up. I guess that fancy car engine sounds different because he paid no mind to all the other cars and trucks going to the restaurant."

"Those huge ears are like radio antennae," Adam said, enjoying his son's newfound pleasure in the dog. Satchmo seemed to have brought out the latent animal lover in Matt.

The boy rose and headed for the house with Trace by his side.

"Why don't you take a few hours off?" Adam said to Sarah. "He'll sack out, and I'm going to head to The Aerie after I clean up. You can come back about nine or so."

The housekeeper nodded. "That's mighty generous of you, but tell me how the pony is."

Adam blew out a breath. "Well, it was touch and go for a while there, but between Dr. Linden and Matt, they got Satchmo on his feet and on the mend."

"I don't care what that gossip Bertha Shanks says, Dr. Linden is a darned good vet," Sarah said. "She saved the life of my neighbor's parakeet. I figure anyone who can fix a little bitty bird like that can get a pony well."

"Dr. Linden did the right thing in Chicago," Adam said. "She just got tangled up in politics that had nothing to do with her medical expertise."

"I knew it!" the housekeeper said, putting her hands on her hips. "That old Shanks biddy can't tell whether she's punched or bored." She tsked and bade Adam good-bye.

Lured by the prospect of a shower, he jogged into the house. Trace joined him as he walked down the hallway toward his bedroom. He could hear the water running in Matt's bathroom as he passed. Once in his own bathroom, he kicked off his shoes and left his clothes in a heap of straw-laden, sleep-wrinkled black. Turning the shower jets on full, he stepped into the steamy glass enclosure with a groan of pleasure.

The hot water pounding on his tired muscles sent his mind in the direction of Hannah, not as a veterinarian but as a woman he'd made love to. Amidst all the night's drama, he had sensed a subtle withdrawal in Hannah. Yes, she had wound herself into his arms in the aftermath of pulling Satchmo from the verge of death, but she had been holding him at arm's length before that.

He frowned as the water sluiced over his bare skin, washing away the scent of horse feed that clung to him. Maybe Hannah had simply realized he was a bad bet. He couldn't say she was wrong about that.

Yet he kept thinking of the Beluga caviar he'd stocked in the refrigerator. He wanted to feed it to her, naked in bed, and watch her reaction to the explosion of flavor on her tongue. Then he would taste her and feel her writhe in the cage of his hands. His body tightened at the thought and he let it, giving into the surge of pure sensuality washing through him.

What he thought and did in the privacy of his shower was no one's business but his own.

Adam fastened the last button on his black shirt and shoved it into the waistband of his black jeans. Trace had vanished while

Adam was showering, so he went in search of the dog. As he passed Matt's bedroom, he took a quick look through the half-open door. To his surprise Trace lay beside the bed on which Matt was flopped belly down in sweatpants and a T-shirt, his fingers buried in the dog's thick, glossy fur. It was unusual for Trace to leave Adam, but maybe he sensed the loneliness in the boy.

Matt's face was lax with sleep, making him look more vulnerable. Adam's fingers twitched with the desire to smooth back a strand of wet hair that was stuck to his son's cheek.

He raised his hand to grip the doorframe, and tried to remember what he had wanted from a parent in his childhood. Maybe that would guide him toward how to handle his relationship with his son. The overwhelming answer Adam came up with was a father who didn't hit his mother.

Instead, Matt had no mother. And no father really. Maggie had not given him the chance, but he wondered what kind of father he would have been to Matt. Ambition had burned in him with scorching intensity. If the demands of parenthood had thwarted that, would Adam have become the bitter, angry alcoholic his father was?

He rested his forehead against the back of his hand. Even at his most drunken, he couldn't imagine himself lifting his hand to a woman or a child. But he knew there were other ways to abuse a loved one. Words could inflict equally painful and lasting damage.

He must have made a sound because Trace lifted his head, making Matt stir in his sleep. Not wanting to disturb his exhausted son, Adam shoved away from the wall and headed for the front door.

Locking it behind him, Adam strode along the tree-shrouded path that led to The Aerie. As he walked into the kitchen, the slam of a heavy freezer door, the scent of freshly chopped basil, and the clatter of a pan against a cast-iron burner made him close his eyes in appreciation.

"Chef! The butternut squash is unusable," Bobby said. "And Delores called in sick again so we're short a line cook."

As he pulled out his cell phone to find a substitute for both vegetables and personnel, a sense of ease sank deep into Adam's bones.

Here was a world where he was in control.

Chapter 16

THE LOUD BUZZING OF HANNAH'S ALARM YANKED her out of a sleep so deep she felt drugged. She hit the "dismiss" button and flipped on the light beside her bed. The digital numerals read 12:20 a.m., which meant Adam was picking her up in forty minutes. It was like having a relationship with a vampire.

She sat up and scrubbed her palms over her face.

After her Saturday afternoon appointments were over, she, Adam, and Matt had met in Satchmo's stall. She'd told them about the inconclusive test results she had received from the lab that morning, but since Satchmo was standing up and eating, the Bosches discounted her concern about an accurate diagnosis.

Hannah was happy the pony's condition seemed to have improved, but she hated treating him when she still wasn't sure what she was trying to cure. However, she told Sharon to keep up the EPM medications and Adam's gourmet horse food, projecting an image of confidence she didn't feel. It would be a relief when Tim was back in the office on Monday and she could consult with him.

It had taken some persuasion to convince Matt he didn't need to sleep with Satchmo again. When Sharon offered to move the pony to the foaling shed where there was a video camera the night groom would keep an eye on, the boy reluctantly agreed to go home. Hannah had assured Matt her phone would be on all night because she was on call.

The truth was she had let Satchmo come too close to dying, and guilt gnawed at her.

Adam had left Matt with the pony while he walked Hannah to her truck. That's when he'd talked her into this late-night date.

She extricated herself from her slumbering dogs and stood up to stretch.

If she'd pleaded exhaustion, he would have accepted her refusal, but the heat in his eyes and the husky timbre of his voice had conjured memories that melted her resolve as though it were a stick of butter in a saucepan. "I'm already thinking in food metaphors," she muttered.

Matt's statement about his father's plans to send him away haunted her almost as much as Satchmo's brush with death. It simply didn't fit with the Adam who had abandoned his restaurant on a busy Friday night to nurse a sick pony.

Hurrying into the bathroom, she took a fast shower, blew her hair dry, and rummaged around until she found a pale-blue lace bra with matching panties. She'd bought them right before the crap hit the fan in Chicago and never worn them, since Ward had dumped her shortly thereafter.

Unfortunately, she had no idea what to put on over the lingerie. As she stood staring into her unhelpful closet, Anabelle padded over to join her.

Smoothing her palm over the collie's narrow, elegant head, Hannah looked down. "You always look perfectly dressed, you lucky girl." With her other hand, she riffled through the various articles of unsatisfactory clothing hanging on the rod. "I guess it's going to be jeans, a silk blouse, and a blazer. And maybe a shopping trip next week."

After dressing, she twisted her hair up into a loose bun and pulled some strands down to frame her face. Sapphire studs sparkled on her earlobes in an attempt to dress up the outfit. She looked down at her bare feet and decided heels were called for. She had one pair of black stilettos, so that would be it.

After glancing at her watch, she shooed the dogs off the bed, pulled the comforter up over the rumpled sheets, and grabbed her purse and black wool blazer.

Just as she flicked on the hall light, the throaty rumble of a high-powered engine broke the dead-of-night stillness. Grabbing her keys, she slipped out the front door as Adam's Maserati eased into her driveway.

The driver's door opened and he emerged, coming around the car to take her by the shoulders and graze her lips with his. "Mmm," he said before raising his head to take one of the tendrils by her ear between his fingers and lift it to his nostrils. "Grapefruit and something floral. Magnolia? And a hint of cedar, I think."

"Now you're deconstructing my shampoo?" Hannah was trying to ignore the exquisite shivers racing over her scalp as he wound her hair around his finger.

"Scent is important to the palate," Adam said. He tilted her head sideways and bent to inhale beside her earlobe before he put his mouth against the side of her neck and kissed her there. "Texture is also crucial."

The feel of his lips made her eyes flutter closed as she gave in to the sensuality he so skillfully evoked. He gathered her in closer, his arms snaking around her back and her waist. She curled her fingers into the lapels of his leather jacket to give herself an anchor as he slid his mouth down to the base of her throat. Each time his lips touched her skin, heat and pleasure sparked and rippled through her body in widening circles that fed the tension building low in her gut.

"Delicious," he murmured against her.

"Mmmhmm," she agreed.

He huffed out a chuckle, his breath sending warmth tingling across her skin in contrast to the chill night air. He lifted his head and the porch light made his eyes shimmer like an expensive liqueur, tantalizing and opaque. "Time to try out the Maserati," he said, taking her hand and leading her to the low, curving car.

Hannah buckled into the leather seat, the richness of the car's interior cradling her as though she were priceless, like a Fabergé egg. Adam slid into the driver's seat beside her and set the engine purring. His hands moved over the polished wood of the steering wheel in a gesture that came close to a caress. She was beginning to understand the man was a sensualist in more than just food. The fabrics he wore, the car he drove, the scent of her shampoo—all fed his senses. Which made her wonder again about his monochromatic attire.

"You said you'd tell me why you always wear black," Hannah said, as he steered the car onto the street.

"Did I?"

"A couple of days ago. When I was surprised your Maserati wasn't black. So is there a reason other than it makes you look dark and enigmatic?"

He slid her a half-smile in the pale glow of the dashboard's illumination before he responded. "That's a good one."

"But not the real one."

He shook his head. "My first boss was a famous chef who was also a monster. Conrad Faust." Adam's voice took on a hard edge as he said the man's name. "He had a thing about wearing a spotless white chef's jacket. If someone splashed sauce on it or brushed against it with a dirty pan, he reamed them out and went back to his office to change it. The man was a chef and he couldn't stand to have food touch him." He seemed to realize he had revealed more than he'd intended because he shrugged. "Since I hated everything about him, I did the diametric opposite and wore black."

"In your personal life too," Hannah pointed out.

"Until I ran my own kitchen, I had to wear whatever color jacket the head chef chose, so my statement had to start in my personal life."

"The bad guy wore white, so the good guy had to wear black," she mused.

"Don't give me credit for being a good guy. Black suited my mood."

"I thought you loved your job."

"Faust came close to killing my passion." His voice dropped low as he continued, "That's when I started drinking."

"No wonder you hate him."

He shook his head. "Not for that. That's my own weakness. I hate him for ruining so many aspiring chefs before they'd even begun. He took pleasure in ripping apart the young people who came to learn from him."

"Some people think that's a good management style."

"He was a destroyer, pure and simple."

"Where is he now?" She hoped Faust's restaurant had failed, so he'd gotten a dose of his own medicine.

"Dead."

"You didn't kill him, did you?" she asked after a moment of silence.

He gave a short bark of laughter. "Only in my fantasies. He had a heart attack about five years after I moved on. Keeled over on a table where he was schmoozing with a couple of customers."

"I guess they got their meal comped."

He gave her another sideways glance. "You keep surprising me."

"Is that a good thing?" Hannah couldn't tell from his tone.

"It's what I strive for in my cooking. A layering of flavors that reveals itself in unexpected ways."

"So I'm like gourmet food?" she said, cherishing the ultimate compliment from a connoisseur of haute cuisine.

"Your base is sweet, but there's a tartness that's both startling and refreshing."

His words, spoken in that deep, seductive voice, vibrated inside her. Ward had liked only the sweet; the nurturing healer who added warmth to his political image. "Lemon sherbet, that's me," she said.

"Much more complex than that," he said, swinging the car in a wide circle. She wanted to find out what food he thought she resembled, but he brought the car to a stop and killed the engine.

She looked out her window to see the soaring glass facade of The Aerie. Adam came around to open her door, offering his hand to help her out of the low sports car. She shivered as his powerful fingers closed around hers and pulled her upwards with a strength that made her feel fragile and feminine. She'd never before thought it would be an enjoyable sensation, but his dark sensuality reached into some primitive place within her.

"Welcome to The Aerie," he said, tucking her hand into his elbow and leading her through the double doors into a large entrance foyer. Paved with stone and tile, it was lit by a giant chandelier of sculpted steel and glass.

"Your kingdom," she said, noticing the proud angle of his head as his glance swept over the silent dining room. The tables were set for the next day's patrons, the glasses and silverware gleaming against the white linen tablecloths that seemed to float like ghosts in the low light of the wall sconces.

He guided her between the tables while she craned her neck to take in the soaring ceiling of wooden trusses and the giant plate-glass windows giving a view of a star-spattered sky over the dark hulks of the mountains. A glow of golden light to one side showed the location of downtown Sanctuary. "Sunsets must be amazing from here," she breathed.

"My architect told me the view would be too much competition for the food, but I believe all the senses should be nourished by a truly fine restaurant. And I'm not afraid of competition," he said, stopping in front of a closed door made of wood set with gleaming brass panels. "Would you mind waiting here? I need a moment to get the room ready."

"It'll give me time to gawk some more," Hannah said. "I've heard so much about this place."

"But it's sleeping right now. You have to see it when it's alive with people and aromas and the sounds of food being savored." He brought her hand to his lips, just brushing the back of it so she felt the heat and texture of his skin before he let her go. It sent a tremor of delight through her body before he swung the door open and vanished into the darkness beyond.

She scanned the room, admiring the way low half-walls of exotic wood created havens of privacy around small groups of tables. The floor stepped down in terraces as it approached the huge windows so virtually every diner in the room could have a view of the mountain ranges rolling away into the distance. At this late hour, the sky was the real spectacle. The cold November air was so crystalline she felt as though she could count every star in the Milky Way.

His food must be incredible if he wasn't worried about competing with this.

"Too bad the moon has set," Adam said, coming up behind her. "It turns the tops of the mountains silver."

"The stars are enough," she said. "It looks like someone spilled diamonds all over the skirt of a black velvet dress." She turned to see his gaze fixed on the view, his eyes as dark as the sky. "Do you ever look out the windows when you're working?"

He shook his head. "There's no time."

"At least you appreciate it after hours."

He held out his hand to her. "Come with me for a different view."

She put her hand in his, feeling his fingers close around hers with a carefully controlled strength. He tugged her forward to the door and threw it open.

"Oh my goodness!" she breathed.

A set of stone steps led downward in a graceful curve. On each step stood a flickering white pillar candle casting a warm glow onto the pale stone walls.

"These lead to the wine cellar," Adam explained, putting his hand against the small of her back and guiding her onto the first step. "Of course, this is the decorative entrance. The sommelier uses the back stairs."

Hannah followed the gentle spiral downward, admiring the embossed, silver urns set in niches along the wall. "It's like walking from the twenty-first century into a medieval castle."

"You're in the ballpark. The steps are from a fifteenth-century French chapel that was being torn down to make way for an apartment building."

"Who uses this?"

"Private parties who want a different atmosphere or who like being surrounded by wine."

The bottom of the staircase opened out into a hallway paved with the same stones. Carved wooden benches with red velvet cushions stood at intervals along the walls, interspersed with standing brass candleholders. "Are those the pews from the chapel?" Hannah asked.

"Yes, and so are the candelabras."

She traced her finger over a carving of a flower on the nearest bench. "You can feel the age of these. It's a wonderful contrast to the modernity of upstairs."

He steered her toward a set of heavy, dark doors farther down the hall, stepping around her to push them open.

The room in front of her glowed gold with the light of dozens of candles. They lined a ledge along one wall, stood on tall floor stands arranged around a circular table, and lit an arrangement of bronze calla lilies and bittersweet on the table. A fire burned in a large, stone fireplace, making the rich blues and maroons of the thick Oriental rug come alive with moving light. Behind a wall of glass to her right, rack upon rack of cradled bottles extended away into the darkness.

When she looked back at him, his eyes held the reflection of the candle flames.

"It's beautiful," she said. And achingly romantic, but she wasn't going to voice that thought. Perhaps he considered it nothing more than a worthy setting for his gourmet food. After all, he hadn't strewn rose petals all over the floor.

He drew her to the table and pulled out a chair for her. Then he reached into a silver ice bucket and pulled out a champagne bottle. She watched the deft movements of his hands as he removed the wire basket and twisted the cork out with a subdued pop, losing not a drop of the sparkling liquid. She caught a glimpse of the distinctive Dom Perignon label. It was the champagne Ward had ordered the night he proposed to her. The candles seemed to dim but not the irksome memory, and she grabbed the intricately folded linen napkin from beside her decorative charger to shake it open with a snap.

Adam looked up from pouring the champagne into the slim, crystal flute at her place.

"Sorry," she said, draping the linen over her lap. Adam wasn't trying to impress her. He genuinely loved the taste of the things he served. She shoved Ward back into his cage and smiled.

Adam filled her glass before picking up a carafe of water to pour in his own flute. Lifting it, he saluted her in a toast. "To the brilliant veterinarian who saved Matt's whisper horse." He took a swallow.

Hannah shifted in her seat. "I don't want to be gloomy, but Satchmo has a way to go before he's out of the woods."

Adam sat down and shook his head. "You wouldn't be here if you thought he was in any danger."

It was true. The pony was still weak, and it remained to be seen if there was permanent neurological damage of any kind, but together the three of them had convinced Satchmo to fight back against the disease. "I didn't do it alone. You and Matt contributed just as much."

"We were only the foot soldiers. You were the five-star general."

She picked up her own glass. "Let's drink to the foot soldiers," she said, reaching over to clink it against his.

The dry, elegant fizz of the champagne made her close her eyes as it slid over her tongue and down her throat. She wasn't going to let the memory of Ward ruin a good drink.

She opened her eyes to find Adam lounging back in his chair, watching her. He'd taken off his leather jacket to reveal a black shirt, open at the neck. The candlelight turned his skin to shimmering gold, and even the waves of his dark hair caught glints of the warm light. Longing tightened her throat. She took a gulp of champagne to wash it away.

A faint look of dismay crossed his face, and she knew he was inwardly cringing at her lack of appreciation for a fine wine. She took a more sedate sip and was rewarded with a nod of approval.

He sat forward and reached for the handle on top of a silver dome, removing it with the flourish of a magician. A graceful, silver-footed dish stood in the middle of the tray. Its bowl was packed with crushed ice around a cut-crystal dish of silvery gray caviar. "Beluga," he said.

Her gaze met his, and she blushed at the memory of their first discussion of caviar. The flames reflected in his eyes seemed to flare hotter. "I've been saving it for you," he said, his voice low.

Now the images of their night together whirled through her mind, and she felt the longing turn to something stronger.

He reached for the mother-of-pearl spoon sitting on the tray and picked up a triangle of exquisitely thin toast with no crust, spooning a little hill of the shining, round eggs onto it.

Leaning forward, he offered the toast to her. She looked at his hand with its crisscrossing scars.

In a moment of daring, she shifted forward in her chair, opening her mouth instead of taking his offering in her hand. She heard the intake of his breath before he brought the food to her lips. She closed her eyes and felt him place it on her tongue. Closing her mouth, she bit into the roe, feeling the explosion of briny flavor against her palate. "Mmm," she said, rolling it on her tongue. "Mmm." She chewed and swallowed before opening her eyes. "Amazing!"

His hand was still stretched across the table, and his gaze was fixed on her face. She didn't move as he slowly raised his fingers to trace down the side of her cheek and along her jaw line before he brushed them over her lips. "Hannah," he murmured.

"Yes," she said, his voice and touch sending ropes of heat spiraling down between her legs.

He shoved out of his chair and strode around the table to come up behind her. She started to rise but he put his hands on her shoulders to hold her in place. "Wait," he said, sliding his hands under the collar of her blazer and pushing it down her arms, his thumbs caressing the silk of her blouse as the jacket slipped downward. His mouth was on the side of her neck, just below her earlobe, his lips slightly chilled from the cold water he'd drunk. They warmed quickly as she tilted her head to let him move more freely over her skin. Waves of sensation radiated downward, making her nipples harden.

He must have seen her reaction through the thin fabric because he brought his hands down from her shoulders to cup her breasts. "Oh, yes," she said as the pressure of his palms sent arousal streaking through her. She grabbed the arms of her chair and pushed into his touch.

Then it wasn't enough to have him touch her through her blouse and she let go of the chair to rip the buttons out.

His mouth opened against her neck and she felt the flick of his tongue. Then he pushed his fingers underneath the lace of her bra to roll her nipples, and she arched up out of the chair on a gasp of mindless pleasure. He pulled one hand loose from her bra to move it down between her legs, rubbing against the denim of her jeans.

"Adam," she said, the three points of his touch spreading pleasure and yearning through her body like a wildfire.

He opened the front catch of her bra and bent over her shoulder to bring his lips to her bared nipple. His mouth was hot and wet, and the swirl of his tongue against her skin brought her up from the chair again as he sent need coiling tighter and tighter inside her.

She reveled in his stroking until she felt an orgasm rising. "Not without you," she said, releasing the chair and nudging his head away from her breast. As he straightened, she turned and knelt in the chair, seizing the buckle of his belt and unfastening it. As she unzipped his trousers to free his erection, he unbuttoned and shrugged out of his shirt. His bare chest caught her attention and she ran her hands up his flat abdomen, feeling the dusting of dark hair under her palms. She surged up to lick one of his nipples. He wrapped his fingers around her shoulders to hold her there, his head falling back as he breathed out her name.

She slid one hand downward to encircle his cock while she lapped at his other nipple. He jerked in her hand. She cupped his balls and moved her mouth to the triangle at the base of his throat, exploring the hollow with her tongue. A tang of salt and a hint of lemon lingered on her taste buds. A vibration almost like a growl came from within him.

His grip on her shoulders tightened and he set her on her feet before he hooked his ankle around the chair leg and kicked it away. Crushing her against him, he locked his mouth against hers and drew her into an exploration that almost distracted her from the pressure of her breasts against his skin and his erection against her stomach. She felt him kneading her bottom through her jeans and she wanted to feel his fingers on her skin. Working her hands between them, she pushed away from him.

He eased his grip and lifted his head. "Too much?"

"Not enough," she said, working the button of her waistband loose.

His smile was sinful as he watched her unzip her jeans and shimmy out of them. She deliberately left her heels and lacy panties on. She grabbed the waistband of his underwear, shoving both them and his trousers downward. "Can't you take a hint?"

"I was mesmerized," he said, slipping off his loafers and stepping out of his clothes to stand spectacularly naked.

"Now *I'm* mesmerized," she said, watching the shadows play over the curves of muscle as the candles and fire flickered.

He reached out to hook his fingers into each side of her panties. "These are blocking my view," he said, slowly dragging them downward over her hips before letting them drop to the floor.

She fought the urge to cover herself as his gaze focused between her legs. He sank to his knees, curling his fingers into her buttocks to pull her toward him before he nudged her thighs apart and worked his tongue against her.

She grabbed his shoulders to balance herself on her high heels as a maelstrom of sensation spun through her. Before he could drive her to climax, she dug her nails into his shoulders and shook him. "I want you with me," she said when he dragged his mouth away from her.

He threw a glance around the room. "There's a couch in my office."

"There's a nice thick rug here," Hannah said, leaning on his shoulders as she lowered herself onto her knees in front of him.

"I wasn't expecting this," he said. "Not this fast." He wrapped his arms around her and drew her in for a kiss. She could taste herself on his lips.

"Please tell me you have a condom," she said.

His smile flashed in the candlelight as he snagged his trousers and rummaged in the pockets before holding up two foil packets.

"Thank goodness," she said, taking one envelope and ripping it open. She took her time rolling the condom onto him, enjoying the hoarseness of his breath as she stroked his erection.

"Let me be your bed," he said, tumbling them sideways before he rolled onto his back with her draped on top of him.

He flexed his fingers into her hips, urging her up and back. She put her forearms on his chest and pushed herself upward, feeling a strange sense of shyness about straddling him. Then he lifted her hips up to position her above his cock, its head just touching her.

"Are you ready?" he asked, his gaze burning into hers.

"Yes," she whispered.

He pulled her down and thrust upward at the same time, seating himself deeply inside her. The sense of being filled brought a momentary satisfaction before she tightened her inner muscles around him, giving herself a burst of pleasure and making Adam moan.

He allowed her a few seconds to adjust before he began to move, tilting his hips as he guided her up and down in a rhythm that wound the ball of sensation in her belly into a knot of pure want. She leaned forward to rest her hands on his shoulders, changing the angle of their joining so the friction grew stronger. The feel of his skin stretched over muscle under her palms, the huff of his warm breath against her neck, and the driving of his cock sent pleasure spinning through her. She came down hard and arched backward as an orgasm blossomed in the depths of her body and exploded outward like a supernova. She choked out his name as her muscles clenched and clenched again around him.

She felt him shift and thrust hard into her before he arched up under her, his shout of completion echoing off the glass and stone walls. She held herself still so she could feel him pumping inside her.

When they were spent, he cradled her on his chest, stroking one palm down her back. She lay sprawled on him, her legs splayed over his hips, all shyness burned away. What was left was a profound sense of satiation and bone-deep contentment.

"Is caviar an aphrodisiac?" she murmured against his throat.

"For you it is," he said, his voice laced with amusement. "I'll have to stock up."

"That could get expensive," she said, remembering the price on Ward's menu.

"Worth every penny." He gave her butt an affectionate caress. "Besides, it only required one bite to take effect, so my supply will last a long time."

She twined the fingers of one hand into the hair at the nape of his neck, exploring the thick, waving texture. His chest rose and fell underneath her, so the still-tight tips of her nipples tingled at the slight changes in pressure. It was a languid, undemanding pleasure, and she sighed at the deliciousness of it.

Then the doubts skittered in. She was playing Cinderella at the ball again, believing this brilliant, successful, gorgeous man wanted her above all other women. He was just grateful to her for helping him with his son. She must have shifted as she wrestled with her nasty little demons.

"What is it?" Adam asked.

"I've cooled off now that we've stopped exercising," she lied.

He eased her over onto the rug and surged to his feet in an eye-catching display of flexing muscles under bare skin. With a few quick motions, he shifted the food first to one side of the tablecloth, folded it, and shifted the food back to the bare table. Whipping the cream-colored brocade off the table, he spread it over her where she lay curled on the floor. He lay down beside her and slid under the tablecloth, pulling her back up against his front.

He wrapped his right arm around her waist, tucking his hand under her hip. The front of his thighs fit against the back of hers like a warm, living puzzle. His breathing feathered through her hair, and his left arm pillowed her neck.

As she drifted down into slumber, the images of the last few days floated randomly through her mind.

All desire to sleep fled as one scene rose with shocking vividness. Matt stood in Satchmo's stall, his hands thrust in his jeans pockets, his voice raw with pain, as he said, "He's trying to find someone from my mother's family to adopt me."

She couldn't put it off any longer. She needed to know the truth.

Chapter 17

*H*ANNAH WAS WIDE AWAKE NOW, AND SHE TRIED TO keep her voice casual. "Matt said the strangest thing to me last night."

"Strange how?" Adam's voice held the rumble of drowsiness.

"He told me you were looking for a family member to adopt him."

He didn't tighten his grip on her or flinch. He went completely still. Even his breath no longer ruffled her hair. "Where did he get that idea?" he asked after what seemed like a long silence.

"From you, he said." She waited for the categorical denial.

"I never told him that."

Not as categorical as she had hoped. "I was surprised because you were so upset about being refused a part in his life."

"I'm upset, but I have no right to feel that way." The arm he had flung around her waist tensed.

"Emotions have nothing to do with rights. But why would Matt think that?"

There was a moment's hesitation. "Matt's mother Maggie was repudiated by her parents when they found out she was pregnant and had no intention of marrying the father. So Matt never met any of the McNallys. I've located some of his relatives in Boston, a cousin and her husband. I'm going to fly up to meet them next week, as long as Satchmo remains stable."

"You told him that?"

"He must have overheard something."

Ward had used that same careful tone when he suspected a conversation wasn't going his way. Trying to pin him down had always resulted in a fight. She didn't know Adam well enough to push him. "If the McNallys shunned Matt's mother back then, why are they interested in him now?"

"They didn't know he existed until I contacted them." His voice was surer now. "They didn't even know Maggie had died."

A horrifying thought struck her. "What happened to Matt when his mother died? Was he all alone?"

"Fortunately, no. Maggie's neighbor babysat Matt when he was younger, so she took him in. Maggie understood how precarious it was being a single parent, so she made sure the neighbor knew to contact me if something happened to her." He had to stop to clear the gruffness from his voice. Clearly, he didn't like to think about what might have happened to Matt either. "They reached me within twenty-four hours."

"That's a relief. I'd hate to think of him . . ." She couldn't finish the sentence as the image of a grief-stricken Matt left without someone to comfort him clogged her throat with tears.

He pulled her closer to him. "I know. I went to pick him up that day." Huffing out a laugh without any humor, he said, "Although I think he would have preferred to stay with the neighbor."

"Maybe at that moment, but not in the long run." She ran her hand along his arm where it encircled her waist. "You feel it's important he know these cousins, so think how much more important it is to know his father."

That made him shift. "With some fathers, it's better not to know them."

"Why do you think you're not capable of being Matt's father? All I've seen from you is concern and caring and commitment."

His sigh blew strands of her hair across her face. "None of that changes what I am." He sat up, pulling her with him. Smoothing her hair back to expose her neck, he laid a trail of kisses down to her shoulder. "Let's finish the caviar."

The brush of his warm lips sent pure delight tingling through her. It was easier to let him change the subject than to keep beating against the implacably dark image he had of himself. Where she saw a man of profound kindness and extraordinary awareness, he saw an alcoholic who was unworthy of love. An ugly little gremlin of doubt crept into her mind. Could Adam's grim vision of himself lead him to give up his son in a misguided burst of altruism? His cautiously phrased answers to her question pointed in that direction.

Shoving the uncomfortable thoughts out of her mind, she tried to wrap herself in the circular tablecloth only to find it wouldn't stay tucked in. "May I borrow your shirt?" she asked.

His smile went sinful as he scooped the shirt off the chair. "If that's *all* you wear."

"Deal."

He held up the dark garment for her to slide her arms into while the tablecloth crumpled down around her ankles. The shirt's fine fabric whispered over her skin and she caught the scent of spice that she associated with him. The sleeves fell down to her fingertips, so she rolled them back.

Adam pulled on his trousers, leaving the belt unbuckled so they rode low on his hips. He seized the tablecloth and snapped it wide open, letting it drift to the carpet right by the hearth. "We'll picnic in front of the fire to keep you warm," he said, moving plates, glasses, and the champagne bottle to the cloth.

"I'll handle caviar transport," Hannah said, carefully balancing the dish on its tray as she walked to the fireplace.

Once the food had been shifted to the warmer location, Adam sat cross-legged and covered each diamond of toast with perfectly piled mounds of caviar and laid them on the serving tray. With his back to the fire, the tips of his hair and the arcs of his shoulders were outlined in gold, but his face was in shadow. Only his eyes caught a glint of the candle flames still burning around the table.

He looked like the kind of seducer the devil sent to persuade you to sell your soul. Hannah shook her head to rid herself of that unfair idea. Ward was the one who had sold his soul. Adam still battled to reclaim his.

She raised her champagne glass in a toast. "Here's to second chances."

"Amen," he said, touching her glass with his. Was she thinking about her problems in Chicago or his problems in Sanctuary? He needed third, fourth, and fifth chances.

Hannah stared into the fire, twisting the stem of her champagne glass between her fingers. The light shimmered along the flyaway strands of her flaxen hair and gilded her creamy skin. Giving her the black shirt had been a mistake. It covered too much of her beautiful body and looked like a dark shadow casting a pall over her glow. Or maybe that was cast by his half-truths.

He slid down onto his side and picked up a toast point, shoving it in his mouth and chewing without really tasting the precious caviar.

How had Matt found out about his quest for an adoptive family? Shame had driven Adam to keep it a secret from everyone except the private investigator. Matt must have discovered something about the Boston cousin and drawn his own conclusions.

A razor blade of guilt sliced through him as he thought of how his son must feel.

Adam had called Ellen O'Brien from the restaurant that afternoon. The image of Matt with his fingers buried in Trace's fur had forced his hand. Despite his resistance, Matt was growing attached to his new life. The pony. The dog. Hannah. Maybe even his father.

The razor blade expanded to a machete hacking at Adam's chest as he imagined sending his son away. It would be kinder to both of them to make the break quickly.

He must have uttered some sound because Hannah's gaze swung around to him. Her soft, warm eyes scanned his face, searching for whatever needed healing. "Are you all right?" she asked.

He could spill his guts about yearning to be Matt's father but knowing he was the worst possible candidate for the job. She might understand the terrible choice he was forced to make. Or she might gather up her clothes and stalk out of his life in disgust. "I was just thinking I don't like black on you."

She glanced down at his shirt. "But it's a classic."

"All right. I don't like clothes on you."

"Ditto on you." She smiled and picked up the last caviar-loaded toast point, holding it out to him. "Someone should eat this before we get distracted again."

As he reached out for it, she pulled her hand back. "Open your mouth," she said, using her other hand to flick the top button of her shirt out of its hole. She leaned toward him so the fabric gapped open to display the curves and shadows of her breasts.

He took the bite of toast and nearly swallowed it whole in his haste to yank the shirt up over her head.

"Hey, you're supposed to savor expensive food," she said, as he pushed her backwards to sprawl onto the carpet. "You told me that."

He knelt above her and skimmed his hands down over her breasts, along the indent of her waist, and around the out-swell of her hips before he buried his fingers in the liquid heat between her thighs, making her eyelids close and her pelvis arch up against his palm on a gasp.

"I'm going to savor something so much better than food."

Chapter 18

*T*HE SIGHT OF TIM ARBUCKLE'S ENORMOUS, GREEN SUV in the parking lot behind the veterinary clinic sent both relief and trepidation through Hannah as she pulled in first thing Monday morning. Handling the entire practice in his absence had been tougher than she expected, and she looked forward to discussing Satchmo's case with her more experienced boss.

However, she also needed to tell him about Mrs. Shanks. And possibly offer her resignation.

Her knuckles went white as she gripped the steering wheel.

The cell phone chimed with an arriving text message, and she scooped it up from the center console of her car, relaxing as she saw Adam's name. He'd declined to make a late-night visit yesterday because she had to work today. She swiped the text open.

I got another shipment of caviar this morning.

Heat spread through her body. She leaned her cheek against the cold glass of the car window, trying to cool the flush warming her face and her breasts.

All it took was one text message to make her want to roar up the mountain to Adam's house, ripping her clothes off as she went. The glimpses she'd had of Adam's demons should have sent her screaming in the opposite direction, but instead she let herself be drawn closer and closer to him.

Looking back down at the phone, she tapped her reply on the screen: *Chocolate works just as well and it's cheaper.*

She turned off the car and grabbed her bag, opening it to shove the keys and the phone in when the chime sounded again. She looked at the new message. *I'm famous for my chocolate cake with caviar ganache. Would you like to taste it tonight?*

"Oh, my goodness," she said, as yearning coiled in her belly. *Yes.*

She waited a couple of seconds for his response to arrive. *I'll be there at 10:00.*

The day stretched before her like an eternity.

❖

"Welcome back," Hannah said, sticking her head into Tim's office. "Did you have a great trip?"

Her boss sat at his desk, dressed in his customary work outfit of polo shirt and khakis, staring at the long list of emails on his computer screen. A slow smile spread across his face as he swiveled his chair around toward her. Hannah understood why Tim's wife, Claire, had fallen for that smile.

"Come on in and have a seat," he said. "The trip was great but it's good to be home. Looks like you've been busy here." He gestured toward the computer. "I feel guilty about leaving you with all this, but you did a fine job of handling it. Couldn't have done better myself."

The compliment warmed her as she dropped into the chair in front of his desk. "Thanks. It kept me out of trouble." She felt the glow fade as she took a breath. "There are two issues I want to discuss with you."

Tim leaned back in his chair, making it creak. He was a giant of a man who moved through the world with a deliberateness that concealed a laser-sharp mind. His solid presence was both comforting and slightly intimidating. "Sounds serious."

She led with the simpler of her two concerns.

"There's a pony named Satchmo at Healing Springs Stable who's been ailing since he arrived there. The test results were inconclusive, but I started treating him for EPM. Friday night he took a turn for the worse, and I nearly lost him." She flipped her ponytail back behind her shoulder. "I'd like you to take a look at him and see if you agree with my diagnosis."

Tim nodded. "I read through your notes and the test results in the database. Sounds like you got him through the crisis just fine, but I'll pay him a visit later today."

She twisted a button on her lab coat. "Satch is important to a kid who doesn't need any more death in his life right now."

"Which kid is that?"

"Adam Bosch's son."

"I didn't know Matt was a rider," Tim said.

"He's learning." She twirled the button in the other direction. "Have you heard Sharon Sydenstricker talk about whisper horses?"

Tim's smile was both luminous and private. "You could say that."

"You seem to know something about them," Hannah prodded.

He pushed a hank of auburn hair off his forehead. "Claire has a whisper horse named Willow."

"So you believe in Sharon's theory?"

His smile hovered. "Well, Willow was a member of our wedding party."

"This is a story I want to hear."

"Ask Claire about it. She's the true believer," Tim said. "Does Sharon think Satchmo is Matt's whisper horse?"

Hannah nodded. "Even more important, Matt thinks so. I guess you're aware of his history."

"The kid's had a rough time of it, and so has his father." Tim's expression turned serious. "We'll make sure the pony gets better."

She wanted to ask him to expand on his comment about Adam, but she couldn't come up with any work-related reason to do so. "Great," she said and fell silent.

"You wanted to discuss something else?" Tim prompted.

Hannah laced her fingers together in her lap. "I think I lost you a client last week."

"You know as well as I do that we can't save all our patients," he said.

"The patient didn't die. His owner refused to let me treat him because of what happened in Chicago. She took her cat to another vet."

"That's her prerogative, but she won't find a better vet than you."

"I appreciate the vote of confidence." She looked away as she fought to control her surging emotions. The array of diplomas hung on his wall caught her eye. His credentials were impeccable, while hers were sullied. "I don't want to damage your practice."

"I can afford to lose a client or two," he said with what appeared to be genuine unconcern.

"What if you lose more than that? Mrs. Shanks announced it to the entire waiting room. It's a small town. Word will spread." Hannah gave him a direct look. "I should resign."

Tim leaned forward, his big hands gripping the arms of his chair. He seemed to swell with the anger she could see in his eyes. "Bertha Shanks isn't worth wasting another thought on. You are an outstanding veterinarian who uses a brilliantly intuitive approach in treating your patients. Anyone who takes their business elsewhere is doing a disservice to their animal."

Hannah rocked back in her chair. "I . . . I'm glad you feel that way. Thank you, but—"

He held up his hand to stop her. "No resigning."

"All right." A wave of relief rolled through her. She didn't want to leave Sanctuary.

He lowered his hand. "It's for my own benefit. Claire is headed for Croatia in about six weeks, and I don't want to miss the trip. It would be tough to replace you on such short notice."

He gave her a wink, and she managed a weak smile. "It's good to know you're only thinking of your own self-interest." Her tone was dry.

He nodded and swiveled his chair back to the computer. "Let's see when we can work in a visit to Satchmo. Looks like we can sneak over at lunchtime if you don't mind eating in the truck."

"I'll get Estelle to order us a couple of sandwiches."

"Make it more than a couple for me," he said.

At four thirty, Hannah pulled into her driveway. As she gathered up her handbag and go-cup, she felt a sense of buoyancy. After Tim had examined Satchmo and listened to Sharon's comments, he had turned to Hannah and said, "That was a difficult diagnosis. Well done." But it was the look of genuine respect in his eyes that sent a thrill of pride through her.

She opened her car door and jumped out, saying, "Take that, Bertha Shanks!" before she slammed the door shut.

As she started across the winter-dull grass to reach her front door, she heard another car door open and close.

"Hannah!" a man's voice called.

It was a voice that didn't belong here. She whipped around in shock to see her ex-fiancé, resplendent in a navy blue suit and red power tie, strolling across the street from a shiny, black sedan. The sun turned his sandy hair into a gleaming halo, and for a terrible moment she felt her heart leap at the sight of him. She wanted to rip it out of her chest. "Ward? What are you doing here?"

Her lack of welcome didn't stop her ex.

"It's been a long time," Ward said, crossing the lawn and leaning forward as though to kiss her.

She took a step back, making him sway into empty air. "You should have let me know you were coming. I don't have much time."

Although she would have preferred not to have Ward in her house, she didn't want to make a scene outside. She stalked up the sidewalk, feeling his presence as he followed her. She dug her keys out of her bag and opened the front door. Instead of giving her dogs the sit-stay command, she let them jump all over her and Ward.

It depressed her to see how happily they greeted him, but she couldn't blame them. He'd wooed them with treats the same way he'd wooed her. Once he'd won them over, he'd reverted to an occasional pat on the head. Both she and the dogs had been grateful for getting even that. Satisfaction bloomed inside her when she noted dog hairs speckling his pristine suit.

"They sure know how to make you feel welcome," Ward said, trying to brush off some of the hair as the dogs' excitement subsided.

"If they thought you were threatening me, they'd sink their teeth into your leg."

"Man's best friend," he said, resorting to cliché as he always did when he got caught in an unpleasant corner. "Nice place," he said, making a show of casting an admiring gaze around her living room with its mishmash of furniture.

"It's a rental." Hannah tossed her bag and keys on the foyer table before turning to Ward with her arms crossed over her chest. "Why are you here?"

He held his hands out at his side and gave her a cajoling smile. "Don't I even rate a glass of water after traveling all the way from Chicago?"

That glinting smile with its false hint of self-deprecation had once charmed her right into his bed. "If I give you a glass of water, will you leave?"

That wiped the smile away. "We need to talk," he said, all the previous coaxing absent from his voice.

"Then talk."

"Let's sit down like civilized human beings."

"Is that how you see yourself? Because I disagree." When Ward had dumped her, she'd been too devastated to fight back. Now her stoked anger burst into a roaring bonfire, and it felt good to blast him with it.

He turned on his heel and stomped into the living room, yanking a dog blanket off an armchair and seating himself. Clearly, he wasn't leaving until he'd had his say, so she and the dogs followed him in. The dogs stayed by her side as though they had picked up on her antagonism toward her ex.

She dropped down onto the couch and crossed her arms again, her gaze on his face.

He hated silence. When they lived together, either the television or radio was always on and tuned to news. He claimed it was important for his job as Robert Sawyer's right-hand man.

Ward adjusted his cufflinks and crossed his legs. "What are you trying to prove, Hannah?"

Thrown off balance by the unexpected question, she had no cutting comeback. "What are you talking about?"

"My sources say someone is asking questions about the incident with Senator Sawyer's dog."

She thought of the letter she'd received and stuffed in the drawer. "Your sources are crazy. I've moved on."

"Somebody hasn't. Maybe your boss?" Ward made it a question and a challenge.

"Tim's been out of the country for two weeks. I don't think he was doing long distance espionage." Paul Taggart had brought up the possibility of clearing her name, but she'd turned him down and she couldn't picture him going forward without her permission.

Could it be Adam? He'd been furious after she had blurted out the reason for her distress over Mrs. Shanks' accusations. He might have decided to fix things for her because he felt an obligation to her for helping him with Matt and Satchmo.

"Who is it then?" Ward must have caught some hint of her thoughts in her expression.

"I have no idea. Your buddies are just paranoid."

"Look," he said, smoothing his trousers over his thighs, "I know I caused you pain, and I'm sorry. It hurt me as well when our relationship ended."

"Ended?" Furious disbelief crashed through her. "You make it sound like it just petered out. You dropped me like a hot potato as soon as Sophie's death got into the newspaper."

He winced. "It was just damage containment. I needed to separate your name from the senator's. My heart was breaking, though."

She tucked her hands under her thighs, so she didn't launch herself across the room and strangle him. "I hope you don't think I'm stupid enough to believe that."

"I'm hoping you'll remember the great times we had together, and call off whoever's stirring the pot in Chicago." More clichés, stacked on top of each other. He must be desperate.

"What exactly do your sources say is going on?" Maybe some details would give her a clue as to who was behind this, unless Ward's cronies were riled up over nothing.

His lips thinned. "I'm not at liberty to share that."

"Oh, for Pete's sake, can't you talk like a normal person instead of a walking sound bite? If you tell me more, maybe I can figure out who's involved."

"Someone's been exploring the possibility of filing a lawsuit for slander," he said, his voice tight with reluctance.

That sounded like a lawyer—which meant Paul—but she just wasn't seeing him as the force behind the pot-stirring. She shook her head.

"What is it? Do you have an idea?" Ward asked.

"I'm still baffled," she said with total honesty, as she leaned forward to pet Annabelle, who lay at her feet. She wanted Ward to leave, so she raised her gaze to his and put every ounce of sincerity she could into her voice. "I promise you I'm not involved in whatever is going on in Chicago. And I'm pretty sure no one can file any suits without my cooperation. Are you satisfied?"

"What if someone came to you and said they had enough evidence to file a suit? What would you do?"

She sat back. She'd made the decision to turn and run months ago. "Nothing. The damage has all been done, and I've come out the other side."

His gaze bored into her for a long moment before his face softened. "I wouldn't believe anyone else, but, well, I always said you were too good for me."

He was convincing, and she had to fight the compulsion to believe he meant it. She leapt to her feet. "On that note, why don't you head back to Chicago?"

"I was hoping to take you out to dinner," he said, rising more slowly.

"I have plans for the evening already. Besides, The Aerie is closed on Mondays."

"The Aerie? I was going to take you to the Laurels," he said, giving her a sharp look. "That's where I'm staying."

"Oh, I just assumed you'd want to go to the most expensive restaurant in the area." She was so wrapped up in Adam that she hadn't considered the possibility of any other restaurant.

Her slightly insulting explanation seemed to ring true with Ward because he dropped the subject. He crossed the space between them and reached for her hands. Short of whipping them behind her back, she couldn't avoid his touch. As his fingers folded around hers, she braced herself for a surge of physical memory. His grip was warm and firm, as befit a politician's, but it didn't send any sparks zinging through her. She let out her breath in a sigh of relief. She'd been blindsided by his arrival; now that her brain had caught up, she was free of him.

"I'd like to put the past behind us and become friends. You are a special person, and I want to keep you in my life." His pale-blue eyes held a fine sheen, as though he might be tearing up.

She remembered the horrible scene when he'd read the first media report, where they'd interviewed her about her decision to euthanize Sophie. He had hurled the newspaper across the room and rounded on her with a face contorted by fury. "How could you do this?" he'd shouted, the tendons in his neck standing out. "Don't you care about my career?"

She'd been afraid he was going to hit her and had put a couch between them. Instead, he'd taken her apart verbally and left the pieces strewn all over the floor before he ground them into the carpet with his heel.

The next day he'd sent her a giant bouquet of flowers, taken her out to dinner, and apologized. His regrets had been barbed, though, filled with subtle putdowns about how unskilled she was as a political fiancée. After that she'd felt as though she was walking on eggshells, watching every word she said in public.

Maybe he had done her a favor in breaking their engagement.

She tugged her hands out of his and shook her head. "We live in very different places."

His jaw tightened, but his voice remained persuasive. "May I call you every now and then?"

She couldn't imagine what they'd have to talk about. "I'd rather you didn't."

His nostrils flared and a flush climbed his neck. "If you won't be friends, then I'll have to consider you an enemy." He brought his face closer to hers. "And you don't want to be my enemy."

"Are you threatening me?" She couldn't believe it. Why was he worried about her, hiding down here in the mountains of West Virginia?

He took a step back, a nasty smile thinning his lips once again. "Of course not. I have no reason to, do I?"

His B-movie dialogue was as absurd as his idea that she was out to get him, and it sent a nervous laugh up her throat. She covered her mouth and turned it into a cough.

After watching her with narrowed eyes for several seconds, he asked, "Do you need a glass of water?"

She shook her head.

"Then I'll say good-bye," he said.

She took a deep breath and conjured up an image of Satchmo lying on the straw of his stall as he slipped toward the edge of death. That killed the last of her desire to giggle.

"Good-bye, Ward," she said. As a peace offering, she stood on her toes and kissed the air beside his cheek, catching a whiff of his cloying cologne.

He lifted a hand as though to stroke her hair and then dropped it. "I wish I could turn back the clock." He turned and walked to the door, hesitating a split second before he twisted the knob to open it. He paused there again.

Did he expect her to run after him and say she wanted to be friends after all?

Courtesy urged her to wish him a safe flight, a good sleep, something to bridge the charged silence. She pressed her lips together and waited until he stepped outside and closed the door. As soon as the latch clicked, she flew to the door and threw the deadbolt.

She hoped he heard it snick into place.

Chapter 19

EFTING THE LOADED COOLER, ADAM RANG Hannah's doorbell and waited, the frozen clouds of his breath glowing amber under the porch light. The temperature had taken a sudden plunge downward, and there was snow in the next few days' forecast. That always complicated the restaurant's food deliveries because everything came in fresh.

A spate of barking acknowledged his presence before he heard Hannah's voice issue a firm but unintelligible command. The dogs fell silent. He dropped his business worries and smiled at her relationship with her dogs. She loved them, but she'd taught them good manners. She'd make a great mother.

The thought killed his smile as it pulled him back to his dilemma with Matt, one he had yet to resolve. He wished he could discuss it with Hannah, but he didn't want her to know what a coward he was. He wasn't ready to have her turn away from him in disgust.

The door swung open to reveal her surrounded by furry creatures, her pale hair floating around her head like skeins of golden thread. There was welcome in her face, but a subtle unhappiness threw a shadow over it.

Her gaze settled on the cooler. "That's a lot of caviar."

"There are a few other ingredients." He stepped in the foyer and set the cooler down, so he could wrap his hands around her slim shoulders and watch her expression. "Is something wrong?"

She slipped her hands around his neck and stood on tiptoe to press a kiss on his lips. The pressure of her breasts on his chest and the brush of her thighs against his sent a bolt of heat straight to his cock. He tightened his hold on her as he deepened the kiss. She shuddered and melted into him, freeing him to send his hands roving down to the delicious curves of her bottom. When he flexed his fingers, she moaned.

Images of stripping off her jeans and panties and sinking himself inside her flashed through his mind, but he banished them as he eased his grip. He needed to chase the sadness from her eyes before he could make love to her without guilt.

Lifting his head, he shifted his grip to her hands. "Come sit with me," he said, turning her toward the sofa.

"What about dinner?" she said, glancing at the cooler, which was the object of her dogs' rapt attention.

Adam twined his fingers into hers. "I'd rather hear about what's got you upset."

"I'm not upset. Just . . . confused."

"Tell me." He guided her down onto the cushions, seating himself beside her.

"I had a visitor from Chicago today," she said, twisting her hands together in her lap.

"An unwelcome one?"

"Very."

He waited. He felt her suck in a breath and let it out.

"My ex-fiancé," she said. "Ward Miller. Have you heard of him?"

Her question sounded casual but he sensed a purpose in it, so he thought carefully. "Maybe. A rising politician?"

"That's the one." She lifted her eyes. "Do you know anything else about him?"

She seemed to think he should, but he shook his head. "I don't follow politics all that closely. It makes it easier to be cordial to my guests at the restaurant."

She gave him a slight smile but her gaze remained serious. "He says someone's raising questions about the incident that made me leave Chicago. And he's not happy about it."

"Was he involved?" This was news to Adam.

"He's Senator Sawyer's protégé and former campaign manager, so he's very involved."

The pieces fell together in his mind. He'd known there was more to her story than unfavorable press over euthanizing a sick, elderly dog. "Is that why you left?"

"He told me I wasn't cut out to be a politician's wife."

Anger flared as he considered how her ex-fiancé had deserted her when she most needed him. He unclenched a fist to brush a finger along her cheek. "I'd take that as a compliment."

"It knocked my world sideways."

He wrapped his arm around her and brought her against his side. "You've righted your world."

"Seeing him again gave it a whack, though. It's amazing how strong old feelings can be."

So she wanted to use him to wipe away those old feelings. He could live with that. "Do you regret what you did back then?"

She stiffened, as he had expected her to. "For Sophie? Not a bit. All I regret is that I didn't manage to persuade Mrs. Sawyer to put her to sleep before they left on vacation."

"Did you ask Ward for help contacting Sawyer? He must have had the senator's cell number."

A moment of silence. "No. We'd had a fight about the fact that Mrs. Sawyer wouldn't agree to euthanize Sophie. He said I wasn't considering the children's feelings. I asked him why they were more important than the dog's suffering. It was ugly."

He kissed the top of her head and held her, waiting for the rest of her guilt to spill out.

"I didn't want him to tell me I couldn't put Sophie to sleep until the Sawyers got back from vacation. So I didn't call him, although I knew he could contact the senator. I went through the regular channels," she said with a bitter edge to her voice. "Except Sawyer had blocked those."

His anger swelled again. He reined it in so as to not crush her with his grip. "Would Ward have given you Sawyer's cell phone number?"

"I've asked myself that a thousand times," she said. "I didn't give him the chance."

"Because you knew the answer," he said. "He would have told you not to bother the Sawyers, to keep Sophie alive."

"How can you be sure of that?"

"He let go of something far more important in his life in order to protect Sawyer. You."

She stirred and pushed away from him, rising to pace over to the dead fireplace. When she turned back to him, there were tear-streaks on her face, but she looked relieved. "I needed you to say it for me to believe it."

He wanted to pummel her ex with a stainless-steel ladle. No, with his bare fists. More satisfying that way. "He doesn't understand what you did for him. You knew you had to release Sophie from her suffering and you did it alone, for his sake."

"No one else understood that." She waved her hand in a gesture of apology. "I'm sorry. You always seem to get the worst of me."

"No, the best," he said. "The real honesty of you." It was his fault Ward had intruded on her in Sanctuary, and Adam decided he needed to own up. "I'm the one who should apologize."

"You?"

"I brought Ward down on you." He forced himself to continue. "After you told me the story of Sophie, I went to see Paul Taggart. I persuaded him to look into the situation with an eye to clearing your name."

She looked flabbergasted. "You went to Paul? But I already told him not to bother about it."

"I know. He put up a good fight, but—"

"But he wanted to do it as much as you did," Hannah said, shaking her head.

"It's none of our business, but we were both pissed off on your behalf."

She gave him a strange, unreadable look.

"Go ahead and tell me to butt out," he said.

"Would you?"

He nodded. "I've done enough damage."

"I'm not used to this," she said, her voice tight.

"To people sticking their noses in your business?"

"To people caring enough to take up the fight when I've given up." She came back to the sofa and sat down beside him, putting her hand on his where they were clenched together between his knees.

Her generosity astounded him. He'd be furious if someone had stirred up his past without his permission.

"I'm glad Ward came down here," she said. "It clarified something for me."

He turned his hands up to envelope her small one. "I'll tell Paul to call off the dogs."

"I'm not sure I want you to," she said, using her free hand to trace over his knuckles. "Two very smart men think I should clear my name." She looked up at him with a slight smile. "Maybe they're right. Maybe I owe it to Tim."

"Tim doesn't—"

She held up her hand to stop him. "Ward and the scandal over Sophie were so tangled up in my mind that I left Chicago not knowing which I was running from."

"Ward," he guessed.

"And now I've faced him." She wrapped her hand around his. "So let Paul work his magic."

The tension in her shoulders and her convulsive hold on his hands told him this wasn't an easy decision for her. "Don't do this for anyone but yourself."

She looked him in the eye. "That's exactly who I'm doing it for."

Chapter 20

 T ONE O'CLOCK THE NEXT DAY, HANNAH SAT IN HER car in front of Paul Taggart's white frame law office. He'd scheduled her in at lunchtime without any questions, telling her he'd order sandwiches for both of them.

She felt wrung out, both physically and emotionally, from the night before. After she'd spilled her guts about Ward, she and Adam had eaten his delicious inventions featuring caviar. Somehow he'd even made it work with a dark chocolate mousse, the salty taste of the fish eggs contrasting with the richness of the cacao.

Weight gain might have been a concern, except they'd made love twice after eating. She'd deliberately seduced Adam because she wanted to forget all about Ward and the ugliness he'd dragged into her house. Not that Adam was reluctant, but guilt still twined with the heat flickering through her at the memories.

Shaking off those thoughts, she stared down at the crumpled copy of Sophie's intake form, which she'd dug out of her junk drawer that morning. She placed it on her knee, trying to smooth the wrinkles out before she gave it to Paul. Fortunately, the slash through the line requesting an emergency contact number was still clearly legible, as was Robert Sawyer's signature. Folding the paper, she slipped it into her handbag before taking a deep breath and opening her car door.

She strode across the porch and through the front door, not allowing herself to hesitate and fall prey to second thoughts. An older woman with the thickest mascara she'd ever seen was seated at a heavy, oak desk, keyboarding at superhuman speed. Without slowing, she smiled at Hannah. "Dr. Linden? Mr. Taggart's expecting you. Go right on in." She tilted her hairspray-lacquered head in the direction of an open door beyond her desk.

Hannah said thanks and walked through the doorway, finding Paul at his desk with a telephone headset hooked over his ear. He flashed a smile at her, held his index finger up in a request to give him a minute, and waved her toward a green, leather sofa. On the coffee table in front of it were platters of quartered sandwiches, pickles, Cole slaw, sweet potato fries, and bottled water. She shrugged out of her jacket and draped it over the sofa's arm.

Paul finished his call and crossed to where she sat. "My apologies, but I made the mistake of taking that call from Bill Lassiter. He could talk the ear off an elephant." He folded himself into an armchair before passing her an empty plate.

As she served herself, he sat back. "Adam told me your ex-fiancé paid you a visit yesterday. I guess I wasn't as subtle in my inquiries as I thought. Adam and I both regret any distress it caused you. Say the word and I'll stop all further investigation." His tone was remorseful.

"No." Hannah put her plate down with a clatter and dug into her handbag. "I want you to keep going." She pulled out the form and handed it to Paul, who had straightened up in surprise. Evidently Adam hadn't mentioned her change of heart. "This should help."

He unfolded the paper and scanned down it, his lips stretching into a feral smile. When he looked up, she got a glimpse of what he must be like in the courtroom. "Gotcha, Senator Sawyer," he said.

"Three of the vet techs are prepared to testify about Sophie's condition on my behalf," Hannah said, "but I'd prefer not to involve them. It might affect their jobs."

"This won't ever get to court," Paul said, his pale-gray eyes lit with satisfaction. "Sawyer won't let it. We just have to decide what you want from him."

"What do you mean?"

"A public apology in the media. Compensation for the economic damage to your career." He held up the paper. "This and a little back-door pressure will get you both of those."

"I wouldn't touch a penny of his money," Hannah said. "I just want my name cleared in a way that will silence Mrs. Shanks and her sort."

"How much crow do you want Sawyer to eat?"

Hannah remembered the suffering that Sawyer's selfishness had put Sophie through and was tempted to make him grovel for that cruelty. Then she had a better idea. "As long as the blot is removed from my work record, he can blame it on one of his aides or absentmindedness or whatever he wants to do to save face. However, he must make a large donation to the local animal welfare society. I'll get their contact information for you. He can even spin it as a gesture he's making of his own free will in Sophie's memory."

"I like it," Paul said. "You demonstrate your power by letting him present it his way, knowing all the while you can reveal the raw truth whenever you choose."

"I'm not sure how you're going to do all this without legal action," Hannah said.

"Trust me, the senator will accept your terms without a word of protest." Paul snagged a sandwich from the platter. "He wouldn't have sent Ward down here if he wasn't already worried."

She raised her bottle of water in a mock toast. "To Sophie's memorial fund."

Chapter 21

ELLING THE CABBIE HE'D PAY HIM TO WAIT, ADAM jogged up the cement steps to the front door of a modest frame house in a suburb of Boston. The yard was small, the grass a frost-killed brown, but the short, concrete sidewalk was bordered with winter cabbages. While the house was a simple square box with little charm, its green paint peeling in a few places, the front door was a cheerful, glossy rust color, and the brass of the Irish-harp-shaped knocker gleamed.

He hesitated on the porch, remembering Matt's tense, unhappy face as he said good-bye to him this morning. No matter how much he hated seeing his son looking miserable, he couldn't lie to him outright, so he'd offered no words of reassurance. Just a quick hug that had been shrugged off with an edge of resentment.

He'd spent the two flights it had taken to travel here from Sanctuary reading the newly expanded file on the O'Briens, trying to find the flaw that would make them unsuitable to adopt Matt. He'd asked Gaspari to dig deep. There were a few parking tickets, one minor automobile accident, and one contempt of court citation for failing to show up for jury duty twenty years ago. No serious medical conditions came to light, nor did there appear to be any issues with alcohol, drugs, or gambling.

Instead he read of Ellen's job recruiting and coordinating tutors for at-risk children, and Pat's years of service as a librarian.

Hoping to discover a bitter marriage or a filthy house, Adam gave the bottom of his leather jacket a downward tug and rang the doorbell.

The yapping of a small dog came from inside. "Oh hell, they even like animals."

He heard a woman's voice admonishing the dog to hush. The door opened. "Mr. Bosch?" the red-haired woman asked with a tentative smile.

He made himself smile back as he held out his hand. "Mrs. O'Brien, please call me Adam."

Her face relaxed into genuine welcome and she took his hand between hers. "And I'm Ellen."

A man joined her. "Adam, good to meet you. I'm Pat," he said, giving Adam a firm handshake. "Come in."

A muffled yip sounded from behind a closed door. Pat said, "That's Hattie. We don't want her begging while we eat."

Adam nodded as he followed them through the small hallway into a living room filled with dark, polished wood furniture and china knickknacks. Faux Tiffany lamps cast a pale glow in the dimness of the winter afternoon. The scent of hot tea and fresh baking wafted to his nostrils.

On the oval coffee table sat a tray laden with a delicate china tea service and a plate of scones with clotted cream and jam. The gourmand in him appreciated the classicism of the offering, while a more basic reaction to the aroma set his mouth watering. He'd eaten nothing but a bag of pretzels on the journey.

Ellen waved him to the couch while she sat on one overstuffed armchair and her husband took the other one. "We like to have a real Irish tea," she said, picking up the pot and pouring the steaming liquid into a cup. "I know you're a grand chef and all, so I hope you won't mind my scones. Pat swears they're the best in Boston." She cast her husband a laughing, sidelong glance that made her blue eyes gleam, and Adam felt the first twist of pain. No ugly nagging here.

"I'd never turn down a homemade scone," Adam said, taking one from the plate proffered by Pat.

"I'm thinking you know how to eat it properly too," Pat said, putting one on his wife's plate before taking his own.

As Adam slathered cream and jam on his scone and made small talk, he examined the O'Briens. She was dressed in gray, wool slacks and a cream sweater that seemed a little bulky on her slight frame. Her red hair was twisted in a knot on top of her head, reminding him of Maggie when she was waitressing.

Pat's wiry body was clothed in green trousers and a pressed, plaid flannel shirt. His sandy hair was shot through with silver, but his face was barely lined and sported a sprinkling of freckles across his nose and cheeks. Pale, amber-colored eyes were a surprise with such Irish coloring.

Engrossed in his observations, Adam bit into the scone without thinking. The burst of flavor brought him up short, and he closed his eyes to concentrate on the perfect combination of sweet, sour, and yeast, as well as the exquisite blending of textures.

"You did it again, love," Pat said. "You got him with your scones."

Adam opened his eyes. "I'm putting these on my menu. How many can you bake every day?"

"Oh, about five dozen," Ellen said with a wink. "Pat takes them to the firehouse where his brother works."

They had a fireman in the family. It just kept getting worse.

"I'll buy them all and arrange for a courier to pick them up." Adam was only half-joking. He took another bite and nodded.

The scones were brilliant, perfect for a late fall luncheon. He hated that she could bake so beautifully.

He hated even more the way the couple teased each other and took turns refilling teacups and plates like a practiced team. And although they were ten years older than he was, they looked healthy and active—perfectly capable of dealing with a teenager.

As soon as she was satisfied everyone was well fed, Ellen fixed her blue eyes on Adam. "You've come a long way, and we're very eager to hear more about our young cousin. Do you have a photo by any chance?"

Adam reached into the carry-on bag he'd brought with him and pulled out a manila envelope containing copies of Maggie's photos of her son, as well as Matt's current school portrait. "These are for you to keep," he said, handing it to Ellen.

Her fingers shook slightly as she fumbled with the flap, opening it to spill the pictures onto the coffee table so Pat could see them at the same time. "Oh my goodness, he's so handsome," she said as the portrait slid out on top. She glanced up at Adam. "He looks just like you."

A jolt of pleasure tinged with anguish made him wince.

"I'm sorry, was that the wrong thing to say?" she asked, distressed. "I meant it as a compliment."

"No, of course you did. Thank you." Adam turned her attention back to the photo. "He has Maggie's eyes."

"And a bit of her smile," Pat said.

"I don't understand it. Why did she not tell the family about Matt?" Ellen asked after they'd gone through all the images once and begun again.

Adam laced his fingers together and frowned down at them, choosing his words carefully. "When she told her parents about her pregnancy, she didn't get the support she expected." He met Ellen's gaze. "I think she was protecting Matt."

"Those old so-and sos!" Ellen exclaimed. "I'd like to give them a piece of my mind."

"She didn't tell me about it either," Adam said.

"But why—?" Ellen began.

"It's not our business, love," Pat said. "We should be thanking Adam for letting us know Matt exists."

"It's not something I hide," Adam said. "I'm a recovering alcoholic, but when Maggie knew me, I was on a downhill slide. I don't blame her."

Pat nodded. "You seem like a responsible sort. I wondered why you hadn't married her."

"When can we meet Matt?" Ellen asked, unconsciously stroking the portrait with one finger. "That is, if we've passed muster."

They'd passed muster and then some. It wrenched his gut but Adam smiled. "I was hoping you might come down to Sanctuary for Thanksgiving or the day after, if it wouldn't upset your plans too much. I know it's only two weeks away, but it would be nice for Matt to have real family to celebrate with."

Ellen and Pat looked at each other before turning back to Adam. "Will you allow me in your kitchen to make my special sweet potatoes for Thanksgiving Day?" she asked.

"You'll want to add them to the menu too," Pat said. He reached out and took his wife's hand. "Ellen doesn't have any family left here in the States, so she's adopted mine and that's where we usually have our holiday, but it will mean the world to both of us to get to know Matt."

"We married late and weren't able to have children of our own," Ellen said. "So, well, I hope we'll see him often."

Adam wanted to curse William Gaspari for finding this couple. Instead, he insisted that he be allowed to pay for their plane tickets and that they treat his house as their own.

As he stood on the front steps saying good-bye, Ellen reached out to touch his arm. "Thank you for giving Maggie's family another chance. We would have helped her if we'd known. Please believe that."

He looked at these two people with nothing but concern and gratitude written on their faces, standing with their arms twined around each other's waists, and believed it wholeheartedly.

His stomach clenched into a knot.

Chapter 22

HANNAH SLID OPEN THE BACK PATIO DOOR TO LET the dogs out for their post-supper outing. Floyd bolted out the door, Ginger trotted onto the patio, and Isabelle strolled at a stately pace. As she watched them patrol the yard, she continued her internal lecture about getting too involved with the Bosches. She'd been going in the same circles ever since she got home from the stable, where she'd run into Matt.

The poor kid had looked so forlorn when he told her his father was in Boston looking for his relatives. She wanted to tell him not to worry, but her conscience wouldn't let her. Adam's answers to her questions on the topic had not reassured her.

She had to stop kidding herself that her relationship with Matt's father was purely physical, even if the lovemaking was intense. Which meant she needed to take a long, hard look at the man she was falling for.

There was the charming, sensual lover who fed her caviar and made her feel beautiful when he touched her.

There was the brave but damaged soul who successfully fought his addiction to alcoholism and helped others fight theirs.

There was the brilliantly creative chef and the shrewd, workaholic restaurateur who built The Aerie into a world-class destination for those who cared about fine dining.

There was the father who thought he didn't deserve his son.

Did she want to fall in love with a man as complicated as that?

"Can I stop myself?" she muttered.

The dogs finished their circuits, walking through the open door just as the phone rang. The caller ID announced Adam's name, and Hannah felt her heartbeat pick up speed. "I just answered my own question." Forcing herself to walk slowly to the phone by the couch, she picked it up.

"Hannah, am I interrupting dinner? I can call back later." He sounded tired and keyed-up at the same time. Shockingly, her body responded to the deep timbre of his voice spiraling into her ear. Awareness feathered over her skin and pooled between her thighs.

"Nope, the dogs have eaten." Sinking onto the couch beside Floyd, she stroked his wiry fur. "Are you still in Boston?"

"Yes. How did you know I went today? It was a last-minute trip."

"I saw Matt at the stable."

"Is Satchmo all right?" His worry came through clearly, and whatever resolve she was trying to build against him was undermined.

"He's doing great. As Matt proudly pointed out, he's eating everything in sight, just like a regular pony."

"That's a relief!"

Ginger nosed under her elbow, demanding her attention, so she shifted to pet her. "Did you meet Matt's cousins?" She held her breath, not sure how he would respond to her prying.

"Yes." His voice was tight with tension. "My worst nightmares came true."

"Oh no!" Her heart sank for Matt's sake. "What's wrong with them?"

"They're kind, intelligent people who love each other and desperately want to meet Matt. They live in a modest but comfortable house and have a small, spoiled dog. Ellen's an incredible baker. I want to put her scones on The Aerie's menu. To add the crowning blow, Pat's brother is a fireman."

He wasn't making sense. "So where do your worst nightmares come in?"

She heard him blow out a long breath before he said in a voice so low and strained she could barely hear it, "I have no good reason to stand in the way of them adopting Matt."

He'd admitted it. She was less shocked than sad. When he hadn't categorically denied Matt's accusation, some part of her had known the truth. Adam didn't trust himself with his son.

She sat bolt upright, startling the dogs so much they jumped off the couch. "Did you ask them if they wanted to adopt him?"

"Not yet. Matt needs to meet them," he said.

She sagged back at the reprieve. He hadn't done anything rash. She still had time to attempt to change his mind. Adam and Matt needed each other.

"But they made it clear they want to be a part of his life. They weren't able to have children of their own," he continued. "I've invited them to come for Thanksgiving, and they rearranged all their plans to be there." He paused and his voice took on a note of entreaty. "I hope you'll join us. Your presence would mean a lot. Matt thinks you hung the moon."

A tangle of emotions spun in her chest. Gratification that he wanted her to be present for such an important event in his and Matt's lives. Jangling apprehension at the implication that her opinion could influence his decision. A brief flare of self-preservation saying she shouldn't be drawn further into Adam and Matt's orbit because she couldn't handle being rejected again.

"You already have plans," he said. "I understand."

Tim and Claire had insisted she come to Thanksgiving at their home, but she knew if she explained why she needed to back out, both of them would understand. The question was, should she give into the frighteningly intense yearning to be part of the critical meeting between Matt and his family members? If she had been worried about the depth of her involvement before, how much more deeply would she be ensnared after this?

"I, uh . . ." She recalled the anguish of Adam's statement that he had no reason to keep the O'Briens from adopting Matt. "I'll be there."

"Thank you." His gratitude was palpable. "I'm closing The Aerie for the day. I felt Matt should have a real family holiday, even if it was only going to be the two of us."

And he'd included her. Her heart was beating too fast again. She took the plunge. "You wouldn't really send him to live with strangers, would you?"

His inhale whistled harshly in her ear. "*I* was a stranger until four months ago."

"You're his father. He loves you."

"He does not love me." His voice was low. "And that's why I need to make this decision now. Before he loves anyone in Sanctuary."

She groped for something to say.

"You're thinking I'm a terrible person," he said, "and I won't disagree with you, but I'm doing this for Matt's sake."

She heard the raw pain in his voice. "Why do you insist you're not fit to be Matt's father?"

"You know my problem." There was impatience in his tone.

"Yes, and you've got it under control. You even help other people with their problem."

His laugh was brittle. "It's never under control. Remember the night we met at Moonshine? You left a half-full glass of wine on the table, and it took every ounce of my willpower to carry it to the bar and pour it down the drain."

"But you did it."

"What if I hadn't?" he asked. "What if I drank that glass, and the next one? What if Matt walked in and gave me attitude and I backhanded him across the face because I was too drunk to restrain my anger?"

Horror gripped her at the idea. "I don't believe you would ever do that," she whispered.

"It runs in the family."

"Alcoholism?"

"Violence," he said, his voice dropping. "My father . . ." He stopped.

"Hit you?" Her throat went tight and she had to swallow hard.

"Me. My mother." He sounded exhausted. "Only when he was drunk."

"You're not your father." She was sure of that. Adam would never hit a child or a woman.

"Oh, but I am," he said, his voice taking on a mean edge. "I started drinking at the same age. He told me so. I got a woman pregnant, just like he did. Only he married my mother and made her life hell. At least I didn't have the opportunity to do that to Maggie."

"Have you ever been violent when you were drunk?"

"Yes."

Shock rocked her back against the cushions. "When? In what situation?"

"It doesn't matter," he said. She heard the anger drain out of him.

"Yes, it does. Was it a bar fight? That doesn't count."

"It was in the kitchen. I punched another sous-chef."

"Why?"

"He was bothering a waitress."

"You were defending her."

"I could have just told him to lay off," he said. "He would have. Instead I smashed his nose."

"How long ago was that?"

"Right around the time I got Maggie pregnant." Bitterness laced his words. "You're not going to turn me into a white knight, no matter how hard you try."

"I'm trying to make you realize what you already are: a great father to a boy who needs you."

"Aside from my personal issues, there are professional ones," he said, all emotion banished. "My busiest hours begin exactly when Matt comes home from school. I work virtually every night." A pause. "Chefs have one of the highest divorce rates of any profession."

"You can work all those things out."

"You're a creature of light, Hannah. You can't understand."

"I'm trying." She could feel him shutting down the discussion.

"Don't. I don't want my shadows falling on you." His tone softened. "I wanted to hear your voice, but I should go now."

After they said good-bye she realized it wasn't his shadow that had fallen on her. It was his spell.

Adam dropped his cell phone on the hotel bed, where it sank into the puffy tan comforter. He huffed out a breath and paced over to the window. Twitching aside the sheer curtain, he looked out at the lights of Boston, trying to forget the conversation he'd just had with Hannah.

When he'd dialed her number, he'd intended to talk about anything other than the dilemma staring him in the face. But when she'd asked about Matt's cousins, the urge to spill his guts had overwhelmed his good sense. It had been a relief to admit to someone how he really felt about the visit with the O'Briens.

If he'd stopped there, it wouldn't have been a problem. But he'd told her about his father, about the violence in his own makeup. Her refusal to believe it had been a balm to his scarred soul, but he couldn't allow himself to enjoy it. The idea would worm its way into her mind, and she would begin to wonder.

He pivoted and went to the minibar for a bottle of water. Unlocking the door, his gaze fell on the array of miniature liquor bottles gleaming in the interior light. Craving climbed up his throat, making his mouth feel as parched as burnt toast. He grabbed a bottle of water and slammed the door shut, twisting the key hard in the lock before yanking it out. He practically ripped the cap off the water before tipping it up and gulping down huge swallows.

Finishing, he swiped his sleeve across his mouth and chin and hurled the plastic container into the trashcan across the room.

Matt. He had to call Matt. His son knew something was up when Adam had announced he was leaving for Boston. It was time to tell the boy about his relatives.

He scooped up his phone and hit the speed dial for his house, knowing the housekeeper would answer if his son didn't.

The phone rang three times before someone picked up. "Hey." It was Matt, his tone neither hostile nor welcoming.

"Hey," Adam said in return. "How's it going at home?"

"Fine."

"I hear Satchmo's doing great." He wanted to take it back as soon as he said it, because it would indicate that he'd talked to Hannah before he'd called Matt.

Matt didn't appear to connect the dots, and his voice took on a note of eagerness. "Yeah, Doctor Linden couldn't find any serious symptoms and he's eating grass now. I think he's going to be okay."

"That's good news." Adam turned toward the window again. "Matt, I met one of your cousins today, a really nice woman named Ellen O'Brien. She was a McNally before she married her husband Pat."

Matt was silent.

Adam kept going. "They're a little older than I am, and they live outside Boston. Ellen works for an organization that helps at-risk children. She bakes a mean scone too. Pat's a librarian."

Still no comment.

Adam looked down at the geometric pattern in the carpeting. "I thought you'd like to have more family than just me," he said in a low voice. He didn't add that he never wanted his son be left completely alone with a stranger again.

"Mom said they were all in Ireland."

Adam had forgotten that wrinkle in the story. "Your mom may not have known about Ellen because her married name was different. They're your second cousins, once-removed, so not really close family."

"How did *you* find them?"

What was the right answer to that question? "A lot of research," he hedged.

"How long have you known about them?"

"A week or so. I wanted to meet them before I told you."

"In case they weren't interested." The rawness in his son's tone clawed at Adam's throat.

"No, I wanted to make sure they would be a positive presence in your life," he said. "There are some relatives who can be worse than no relatives."

Silence stretched through the phone connection. "I invited them to come down for Thanksgiving," Adam said. "They really want to meet you."

He held his breath.

"I thought it was just going to be you and me," Matt said, his voice so low Adam had to strain to hear it.

The implication of the words sank in slowly. Had Matt *wanted* it to be just the two of them? Something warm and feathered fluttered in Adam's chest. Before he could think about the complexities of the arrangements he'd have to make for The Aerie, he said, "How about you and I do something alone together over the Thanksgiving weekend after the O'Briens leave? Maybe go away somewhere."

"Maybe." Adam could practically hear the shrug in his son's voice. But Matt hadn't said no.

He wondered how many strings he'd have to pull to swim with the dolphins in Disney World on a holiday weekend. Or maybe that was a bad idea, because it would remind Matt of his mother. He squeezed the bridge of his nose between his thumb and forefinger, trying to figure out what was right and what was wrong. "I'll see you after school tomorrow, so we can talk about it then. I just wanted you to know there are McNallys who care about you."

He heard what might have been a strangled sob. "Yeah. Great," Matt said.

"Good night, Matt." He hesitated before deciding to go for broke. "I love you."

"Yeah. Bye . . ."

Disappointment drained the life from Adam. He sagged down onto the foot of the bed.

Then Matt spoke one more word that set the wings of hope pumping again. ". . . Dad."

Chapter 23

ANNAH MOVED THROUGH HER MORNING appointments with half her mind on her patients and the other half on her conversation with Adam. He felt ashamed of defending the waitress, while she found it admirable. What disturbed her was his confession that his father had hit both Adam and his mother. She kept picturing Adam, looking just like Matt, cowering away from the hulking man who was supposed to protect his son and instead had his arm drawn back to strike him. A shudder ran through her as she practically felt the blow land. How could Adam believe he would ever do something like that?

Just as Hannah slipped into her office to wolf down the sandwich Estelle had ordered for her, Tim showed up in the doorway, his hands shoved in his lab coat pockets. "Paul Taggart called while you were in with Brillo. He wants you stop by on your way home this afternoon if you're free. He said any time after four was fine."

She tried to read Tim's expression to see if the news was good or bad, but his placid countenance gave nothing away. He noticed her scrutiny. "He didn't tell me anything. Lawyer-client confidentiality."

"Right. I wasn't sure if lawyers stuck to those rules in Sanctuary." She glanced at her computer screen. "My last appointment should be over about 4:30. Do I need to call and tell him?"

"Nope. Just show up on his doorstep." Tim's expression turned serious. "I don't know what you and Paul are working on, but I can take a guess. Whatever happens, you know I back you one hundred percent."

Hannah looked at her giant of an employer and felt a glow of comfort. Tim could carry any burden on those massive shoulders, and his unflappable personality would be an anchor in a storm. "Thanks, boss. It's good to have you on my side."

He nodded and stepped out of the room. She'd just unwrapped her sandwich when she heard Adam's voice in the hallway. Its rich timbre danced along her skin like the brush of his fingertips. All he said was, "I know where her office is," and her breathing sped up. She stood up to take a firm grip on the back of her desk chair, trying to get an equally firm grip on her response.

"Hannah!" He wore his black leather jacket over black jeans and an open-necked black shirt. His presence was magnetic.

He stopped halfway to her desk, clearly trying to gauge her reaction. She couldn't bear his hesitation. Releasing her chair, she circled the desk and walked into his arms, feeling his exhalation of relief whiffle through her hair.

"I wasn't sure you'd want to see me after what I told you," he murmured before he lowered his head for a kiss.

She wound her arms around his neck and dove into the sensation of his lips on hers, trying to pour both regret and comfort into her touch. "What you told me just made me want to see you more," she said when they both came up for air.

His mouth twisted and she saw his mood go somber. For a moment he seemed about to say something, but then he shook his head and brushed his fingers down her cheek. "How much time do you have for lunch?"

"An hour. I was going to check on Satchmo."

He framed her face with his hands and tilted it up. "Come to my house instead. I'll cook for you. And maybe do a few other things."

Her already sparking nerve endings nearly combusted at the sexy growl of his last few words. "How can I turn that down?"

She grabbed her barn jacket from the coat rack. Before she could swing it over her back, he took it and held it as she slid her arms into the sleeves. When he lifted her hair to gently tug it out from under the collar, she closed her eyes to appreciate his touch against the sensitive nape of her neck.

Out in the parking lot, his Maserati stood gleaming in the thin November sunlight.

Hannah frantically brushed pet hair off her khakis as Adam swung open the door of the beautiful car. She slipped into the rich, leather seat with a twinge of guilt. "I feel underdressed."

Leaning in, he said, "Just the opposite. You have on far too many clothes."

She couldn't resist tugging one of the thick strands of his hair. "Patience."

His eyes lit with desire. "Not my long suit when it comes to you."

She ran her fingertips over the polished wood on the dashboard, trying to quell the anticipation humming through her body. It clouded her brain when she had things that needed to be discussed. For now, though, she was going to put those aside. Maybe it was just an excuse for her to make love with him, but she felt that intimacy was the key to knocking down the walls around his heart. The closer she could get to him, the better chance she had of changing his mind about himself.

As they pulled out of the lot, Hannah said, "Tim says Paul wants to see me. Do you know what's going on?"

Adam shook his head. "I felt I'd done enough damage, so I bowed out."

"Damage?" She was incredulous. "You're the one who made me understand the past affects the whole fabric of our lives. If a thread gets twisted, it fouls up all the threads that are woven in after it." She looked sideways to study the angles of his profile.

"Sometimes I get lucky," he said.

"No, you draw on your own experiences to help other people understand theirs. It's a brave and generous thing to do."

"I'm just around when people are ready to face their own demons."

She pressed her lips together in frustration. Then the truth about her feelings seeped into her brain. She'd found the strength to put Ward behind her because of this man. Whatever lingering emotional echoes there had been from her broken engagement had been silenced by her relationship with Adam.

She sucked in a sudden breath as the revelation blossomed. It wasn't just sex, and it wasn't some transference of her affection for Matt. It was love, pure and simple. She'd gone and fallen in love with this complex, damaged man.

Staring through the windshield without seeing the scenery, she tried to reconcile the way her heart both swelled and quailed at the knowledge. It was glorious to be in love with Adam, but it was like standing on the edge of a shadowy gorge with a bungee cord wrapped around her ankle. If she jumped it would be a hell of a ride, but she didn't know if she would hit the bottom before the bungee cord snapped her back up.

"You've gotten quiet," Adam said.

She pulled herself away from the lip of the abyss she was staring into. "Sorry. Just wondering what Paul might have to tell me."

"Knowing Paul it will be good news," Adam said. "He's exceptional at his job and he's very well-connected." He threw her a reassuring glance. "He'll get your reputation polished until it sparkles again."

She didn't want to think about the past anymore, not with the discovery she'd just made about her present . . . and the decisions she needed to make about her future. "So what are you serving for lunch?"

"It depends on how long I have to cook it," he said, taking one hand off the steering wheel to stroke along the inside of her thigh.

She choked on a moan as his fingers slid higher up the seam of her trousers, getting closer to the place she wanted him to touch. Then he withdrew, grabbing the steering wheel to negotiate a sharp bend in the road.

"How about something from the microwave?" she said, squirming against the seat in frustration.

"Not even if hell freezes over," he said, with a look of horror. "But I can throw together a meal in five minutes flat, if necessary."

By the time he swept up the driveway to his front door, she thought she would spontaneously combust.

He came around to open her door, offering his hand to help her out of the low-slung sports car. As soon as she was upright, he pinned her against the Maserati, kissing her while he let his hands roam up and down her body, insinuating them under her jacket and then her silk tee-shirt with an almost desperate determination. His fingers were slightly chilled, contrasting deliciously with her heated skin. Being sandwiched between the cold, rigid metal and his warm, lean body forced the breath from her lungs, but she felt no need for oxygen.

"I thought about you all the way back from Boston," he murmured.

She tried to slip her hands between them to start unbuttoning his shirt, but he pulled away. "Too cold out here," he muttered, twining his arm around her waist and pulling her toward the house, half-carrying her to keep up with his long, impatient strides.

He unlocked the door and swept her through. Hannah stopped short. Trace sat in front of them, his triangular ears ramrod straight, his tail sweeping back and forth across the floor. He quivered with the intensity of his desire to launch himself at them in greeting but he kept his butt down on the ground.

Adam gave the dog a quick pat on the head. "Trace, go to—" he began.

"Just a minute," Hannah said, unable to resist the eager dog. She knelt down to massage Trace's ruff while he licked her face. She threw a teasing look up at Adam. "Trace has more self-control than you do."

"Is that so?" Adam's tone dropped into silky dangerousness. "Let's see how good your self-control is."

He reached down and took her hand, drawing her to her feet as he commanded Trace to go to his bed. The dog padded slowly across the living room with a pitiful backward look.

Adam threaded his fingers into her hair and pulled her head back so he could drag his lips down her throat to the V of her neckline, where he flicked his tongue into the hollow of her cleavage. He ran his other hand up under the hem of her shirt and found her already taut nipple, thumbing it through the flimsy lace of her bra.

"Ahhh, yes, there," she said, letting her head fall backward into his hand and forgetting all about Trace.

He moved his mouth back up the side of her neck to nip at her earlobe, making her squeak at the jolt it sent zipping through the center of her body. He found the front fastener of her bra and flipped it open. Her breast spilled into his waiting palm, the contact of delicate nipple with calloused male skin exquisitely erotic.

He massaged her in gentle but insistent circles. She arched into him, straddling one of his thighs and gasping as the friction intensified the building tension created by his touch.

He blew out a breath against her ear, making her shiver. "Patience," he repeated back to her.

"Hmm." She pulled his shirt out of his waistband and walked her fingers up the six-pack of his abdomen to flatten her hands beside his nipples, letting her thumbs brush across the small but hardening peaks. He shuddered under her touch and she smirked.

Lifting his head, he caught her expression. "So you think two can play the same game?" he said, his eyes gleaming with banked arousal.

"I figure there will be no losers, no matter who wins." She brought her thigh up to rub against the erection straining at his jeans.

"Maybe we need to set a forfeit for the loser," he said. She could tell he was fighting back a groan.

"Like what?" She ran her hands around to his back and thrust them down under his jeans and briefs to palm his buttocks.

He moaned before lowering his head to tongue her nipple. An arrow of heat and desire shot straight from her breast to the coiled yearning between her legs. "Adam!" She dug her fingers into the muscles of his behind.

He straightened. "A massage."

"What?" Her brain wouldn't process the word.

He ran the edge of his teeth up along her jawline, stopping beside her ear. "The winner gives the loser a massage," he murmured.

"Deal," she said, picturing the length of his nude body on the black satin sheets she'd imagined on his bed, while she kneaded the lines and curves of muscle under his golden skin. "Wait, shouldn't the *loser* give the *winner* a massage?"

He pressed his thigh between her legs, making her hips pulse involuntarily. "How about if we make it winner's choice?" His lowered voice was like liquid sex pouring in her ear. "Because I want to put my hands on every inch of your body."

"Oh," she breathed, feeling the tension in her core wind tighter. Now her imagination was painting the scene where she was lying on the bed, bared to *his* eyes and *his* touch. "I'm not finding much incentive to win."

"Bragging rights," he said, bending down and slinging her over his shoulder.

"Hey!" She sputtered as she found her face mashed against the leather covering his back.

He carried her to a sectional couch that stretched in front of a huge window giving onto a spectacular mountain view. Lowering her to a sitting position on the couch, he knelt at her feet, his fingers busy with the button on her waistband. "We'll both have a view to enjoy," he said with a wicked smile as he tugged her zipper downward and coaxed her trousers and undies down over her hips to her ankles, where he stripped them free.

The nubby texture of the couch cushions against her bare skin made her doubly aware of her nakedness. He locked his gaze with hers as he ran his hands along the tops of her thighs to her knees, grasping them and gently pressing them apart. "Prepare to lose," he said and lowered his head.

She admitted defeat as his mouth sent wave after wave of pleasure coursing through her until she disintegrated into a screaming orgasm. When he had confirmed her unconditional surrender, he laid her down on the couch and sent her spiraling into another climax when he found his own release deep inside her.

They lay tangled with each other, still panting, as they came down from the detonation between them.

She felt a tremor of nerves at the intensity of what he made her feel and how easily he annihilated any instinct for self-preservation she might muster. Here she was sprawled half-naked on a couch in broad daylight in front of a plate glass window with no curtain, entwined with a man still wearing all of his clothes, including his leather jacket. She'd let him spread her open to his eyes and his mouth without even a blush.

Even worse, she loved him.

Chapter 24

ADAM LET HIS GAZE GLIDE DOWN HANNAH'S BARE curves, savoring the way her fair skin contrasted with his black jacket and jeans. If they hadn't both just come in a near-nuclear blast, he'd be letting more than his eyes roam over her body. Now he held her against his chest and stroked her corn-silk hair.

"Mmm," she murmured against his leather jacket as she gave a little shiver.

"Cold?" he asked, looking around for something to throw over her.

She nestled closer and wrapped her fist around his lapel. "Nope, just aftershocks."

He closed his eyes and concentrated on the feel of her against him. He wanted to etch her on his memory because he knew this couldn't last. He could make her happy in bed and in the kitchen, but that was all he had to offer.

Something twisted painfully in his chest, making him grimace. Yes, he'd fallen in love with her, but that changed nothing. She deserved a whole man who could love her without fear, not the scarred and damaged creature he was.

He dragged his mind away from the torment of feelings he couldn't speak out loud and stroked lower, tracing along the slope of her waist to the swell of her bottom. When he pressed his fingertips lightly into the softness of her flesh, she shuddered again.

"More aftershocks?" he asked against the top of her head as he inhaled her fragrance, adding to his sensory stores.

"They might be before-shocks if you keep that up," she said, making his cock harden again.

Then her stomach growled, and guilt smacked him. She needed to eat before she went back to work. "Time for lunch," he said, shifting her gently off him and rolling her toward the back of the couch. Swinging his legs over so he could sit up, he stopped to enjoy the sight of her stretching, from her up-flung hands to her pointed toes, before she levered herself up on her elbow, her flaxen hair drifting over her bare breasts. The smile she gave him was pure feminine satisfaction.

"Let's eat fast so we have time for dessert," she said.

He laughed and bent to gather up the clothes he'd so ruthlessly stripped off her, handing them to her before he brushed his lips along her shoulder. "The door over by the stairs is the powder room. Meet me in the kitchen through there." He pointed toward the opening to the dining room.

She reached up and traced her finger along his jaw as a shadow crossed her face. It reminded him of when she'd gone quiet during the car ride up. He wasn't going to ask her what she was thinking. Right now he didn't want to know.

Hannah walked into the kitchen and stopped dead, not because of the impressive, professional-level appliances, nor the enormous, stainless-steel island overhung by a rack holding myriad pots and pans, nor the vividly hued winter garden beyond the glass wall.

It was the sight of Adam standing in front of the massive range, the black of his clothing outlining his tall, sinewy body against the gleaming silver, as he lifted a spoon to his lips and tasted the dish he was cooking with such utter concentration he didn't even realize she was there. The air around him vibrated with his passion as he scanned a grouping of small, glass bowls beside the stovetop, each filled with a different colored ingredient. His hand moved so fast and with such certainty it almost blurred as he selected what he wanted and stirred it in.

She understood as she never had before that he was an artist. The Aerie wasn't a business for him; it was the embodiment of his creative genius.

He stirred the pot again, sending the aroma drifting past her nostrils. One inhalation and her eyes drifted shut on a groan of appreciation.

A satisfied chuckle made her force her eyelids open.

"Smells good?" Adam asked, plucking a plate down from a cabinet and filling it with the contents of the various pots and pans around him.

"That would be an understatement," Hannah said, starting toward him.

He waved her toward a sleek, mahogany table set by the glass wall that looked onto the garden. "Sit. I'll bring it over."

She slid into a leather-and-chrome chair, finding its stark shape surprisingly comfortable. The table was already set with clean-lined flatware and forest-green glasses set on brown leather placemats. She filled both glasses with ice water from the matching pitcher as Adam came across the room with plates balanced up both arms.

"I had to be quick, so it's just homemade fettuccine with crimini, oyster, and shiitake mushrooms grown locally," he said, setting the dishes in front of her. "And some fresh greens for salad."

"*Just* homemade fettuccine," she said, plunging her fork into the pasta and bringing it to her mouth. The flavors burst on her tongue and sent pleasure signals beaming to her brain. "Oh, yes!"

"If you say it's better than sex, I'm not cooking for you again," he said.

"How did you guess?"

His smile turned hot. "The way you said 'oh, yes'. Very similar to your tone on the couch earlier."

"So you'd rather be loved for your body than your cooking?" she asked, teasing.

The smile faded as he turned his gaze to the garden. "If I had to choose."

She'd struck some nerve she didn't even know existed. "Well, it's a good thing I don't have to choose," she said, trying to retrieve the lighter mood, "because I love you for both."

Poor choice of words. She winced, hoping he wouldn't notice the "love" part of her comment.

He turned back to her. "I can handle your most basic needs at least." His tone was humorous, but his eyes were opaque.

"This pasta is not basic in any way." She allowed herself a few more delicious bites before she brought up the subject hanging over them. "So tell me more about the O'Briens."

He twirled some fettuccine onto his fork. "They're perfect." His voice was flat. "My private investigator can't find a thing wrong with them."

"And you've told him to try as hard as he can."

He nodded and put the pasta in his mouth, chewing without any noticeable pleasure.

Hannah put down her fork. "You don't have to keep looking for flaws in the O'Briens."

He lifted his eyebrows in a silent question as he took another bite.

She leaned forward. "You don't need an excuse to keep Matt. You're his father."

His fork clattered onto his plate. "I've been his father for all of four months."

"You'll be his father for the rest of his life."

"We went through this last night," he said, making a short, sharp gesture. "How can I be his father when I work seven days a week, twelve hours a day? And those hours are exactly the ones when he's home and needs a parent. How can I be a father when I don't even know if I should take him to Disney World to swim with the dolphins, or if that would break his heart because his mother wasn't there with him?" He flung out his hand again. "How?"

"Every parent has to figure those things out. Sometimes they get the answers wrong at first, but it doesn't matter because you love Matt. That's all he's going to care about."

Adam stood up, making the chair scrape backward with a squeal of metal on tile. "One thing I learned young is that love is not enough. Children need to be protected as much as loved."

"You've already protected Matt by making sure the O'Briens would be welcoming to him."

"I can protect him from outside things," Adam said. "I can't protect him from myself."

"Are you still worried about punching the sous-chef?" she asked. "Because that was a long time ago and you were a different person."

"No, I'm the same person." He leaned forward across the table. "Last night I opened the minibar in my hotel room and saw all those tiny bottles of oblivion beckoning to me. The only way I kept myself from drinking them all was to call Matt. It's a battle I fight every day." He banged his fist on the table, making the dishes jump. "Every. Single. Day."

He lowered his head so she could no longer see his face. His despair seemed to weigh down even the air between them.

"And every day you don't give into that urge," she said. "You do the right thing every single day."

He shook his head without looking at her.

"Matt would help you, just like he did last night," she said. "Maybe that's what you're missing: a reason not to dive into the bottle."

That got his attention, and she almost wished it hadn't. The look he gave her was scorching in its fury. "You think running a multimillion-dollar business isn't a good enough reason to stay sober?"

"You tell me. Is it?" She had the napkin in her lap rolled into a ball and was crushing it in her hands.

He avoided her question. "I'm not going to use Matt as some sort of life preserver."

She wanted to reach out to him, to soothe him the way she would an abused, frightened animal who won't allow anyone to come near. Except Adam was afraid of himself and the damage he might do to someone he loved.

"What about me? Will you let me stay around?" she asked, knowing the answer meant more than she wanted it to.

His head snapped back, almost as though she'd struck him. "What do you mean?"

Not good. "Well, it seems as though we're going down the road to a relationship," she said. "I'm wondering about where it will take us."

He closed his eyes, the tendons in his neck standing out with tension.

"I don't expect a declaration of undying love," she back-pedaled, "but if there's no hope for the future, I'd like to be prepared."

After a long silence, his stance went from strained to relaxed and he opened his eyes. "It's a legitimate question," he said, his voice level and rational. "I should have told you right from the start that former alcoholics are a bad bet for long-term relationships. I already mentioned the track record for chefs when it comes to divorce."

"If I believed in nothing but statistics, I wouldn't bother treating many of my patients. But I've seen how the love between a human and an animal can heal them both. Look at how strongly you feel about Trace." She stood up and gestured toward the dog, where he lay with his gaze firmly on his master.

Adam's expression softened as he glanced toward the dog, but his voice was bleak. "Trace has been seriously injured twice while he's been with me."

"No one can keep another being safe all the time. Life is risk. Your love helped him heal both times." Frustration made her voice rise, so she lowered it. "You're pretty arrogant if you think you can't be healed by love as well."

"Arrogant? Of course, I am. I'm a chef." He shook his head, a humorless half-smile curling his lips. "No, in this case, I'm realistic." He took a step back from the table.

She wanted to leap across the barrier between them, grab fistfuls of his shirt, and shake some sense into him. Instead she hurled her napkin on top of her unfinished plate. "Why did you start something you had no intention of finishing?"

The made him flinch and look away. "I didn't intend to start it." He swung his gaze back to her with that same half-smile. "You're a beautiful woman who bathes everyone you know in warmth and light. I'm a selfish man and I couldn't resist you."

She felt the anguish of loss hollow out her chest. "Don't try."

He took another step away from her. "If we keep going, I won't have the strength to stop it."

"Stopping doesn't take strength. Letting yourself love someone does." She grabbed the back of her chair. "I'm willing to risk being hurt to prove you have that strength."

He dragged both his hands through his hair. "If I hurt you, I couldn't live with myself."

Anger burned through her, and she shoved herself away from the chair. "Maybe you should stop avoiding trouble and face up to it instead. You pushed me to do that."

She started to walk out of the kitchen when she remembered he had driven her to his house. Keeping her back to him, she thrust her hand out to the side, palm up. "Give me the keys. I'll drive myself back to work. You can pick up your car there later."

"It's not an easy car to drive. Let me—"

"No!" She couldn't bear the thought of being shut in the enclosed space of the Maserati with him for the long drive down the mountain. "Don't worry. I'll go slowly and carefully. I won't wreck it."

"Hannah, I don't care about the car. You're upset. I don't want you to get hurt driving it."

"I know how to drive a stick shift. The keys," she said, shoving her hand out further.

She heard his footsteps on the tile floor and a jingling sound before the cold weight of keys dropped into her hand. She made a fist over the metal, letting the sharp edges dig into her skin to counterbalance the stabbing ache in her chest. "I'm an adult, so I'll get over you. But Matt won't. He will always feel rejected by his father, no matter how hard you try to pretend he'll be happy with some other family." Taking a breath, she turned to meet Adam's eyes. "I hope you find the courage to love Matt. For his sake."

He went completely still, his face as hard as though it was carved from the local limestone.

"Why do you think I'm an alcoholic?" His breathing was audible. "It's because I don't have the courage to face each day without blurring the edges. I'm a coward, Hannah."

She wanted to scream that she hadn't meant it that way, but he was already walking past her to the front door, his shoulders held stiffly.

She followed him in silence, wishing she could yank back all the words that had spilled out of her mouth in the last few minutes. Wishing they could go back to being tangled together on the couch, their bodies attuned to each other in a way their emotions were not. How had she created such a catastrophe?

She swallowed hard. She was trying to save him from making a decision that would haunt him for the rest of his life.

If Adam gave his son away, he would never heal from the wound.

Adam walked back into the house after watching the taillights of his car disappear around the bend of his driveway. Trace sat waiting for him, his tail sweeping across the stone floor.

Anguish swamped Adam, and he moaned through gritted teeth. Trace shoved his head under Adam's hand, whining.

A bigger wave, this one laced with regret and guilt, crashed over him. He dropped to his knees to bury his face in Trace's thick ruff. His fingers burrowed into the dog's warm, comforting fur. The sound that wrenched itself from within his chest made Trace whimper and lick Adam's ear.

Adam stayed there, holding onto Trace, using the dog's living, breathing presence to brace himself against the longing for a drink that was building inside him, making him nearly dizzy with the desire for the oblivion alcohol could bring. The chilly, stone floor made his knees ache as he waged a silent battle deep within himself.

Finally, he let out a nearly inhuman groan and released the dog. Grabbing a set of keys from the hook by the door, he slammed out the front door and strode down the shaded path to the rear entrance of The Aerie. Letting himself in, he nodded to a couple of staff members as he made his way to a utilitarian staircase leading down into the bowels of the mountain.

He stopped in front of a heavy oak door and tried to fit a shiny silver key into the high-security lock. His hand was shaking so hard it took him two tries to insert it in the keyhole.

He stood with his other hand flat against the wood for a long moment before he turned the key and stepped inside the dimly lit room lined with bottles, the glass gleaming beneath a thin film of dust.

In the center was a rectangular table surrounded by eight chairs upholstered in cognac-colored leather held in place by brass nail heads. It was overhung with a rack containing crystal wineglasses of all shapes and sizes. This was where The Aerie held professional-level wine and Scotch tastings a few times a year.

Adam slid a large wineglass from the rack and set it in front of the chair at the head of the table. Then he prowled through the racks until he found a Pétrus, one of the rarest and most expensive bottles in The Aerie's elite wine cellar.

"Even though it doesn't matter a damn as long as there's alcohol in it," he muttered, dusting the bottle off with a linen napkin.

He retrieved a simple waiter's corkscrew from the rack and removed the cork with a flex of his wrist. The wine deserved to be decanted and allowed to breathe, but he didn't have time for that. The craving swelled inside him, and with an unsteady hand, he poured the rich, red liquid into the glass, spilling a few drops in his haste.

He sat down in the chair and curled his fingers around the stem of the glass, staring into the luminous depths of the wine. Lifting it, he swirled it under his nose, closing his eyes as the exquisite scent filled his nostrils and fed his yearning.

A nagging voice in the recesses of his brain made him set the glass down again as he wrestled with the knowledge that he was about to wipe out nine years of hard-won discipline and agonizing self-denial.

But then Hannah's voice whispered through his mind, speaking the truth he hated most about himself. *He'd spent his life running away.*

He brought the glass to his lips and tilted the bottom high, letting the elixir of forgetfulness flood his mouth.

❖

Adam sat on the stone terrace of his house, staring out over the graying mountains as the late afternoon light faded around him. The chill sank through the thin wool of his trousers and suit jacket, but he couldn't unclench his grip on the arms of the chair, even though the hard edges dug into his tendons. He needed an anchor to hold himself together after his trip to the cellar.

One of the French doors swung open, and he turned his head slowly to see Matt saunter toward him, dressed in jeans and a forest-green, hooded sweatshirt, with Trace at his heels. "Hey," his son said. "Mrs. Duckworth said you had something for me."

"I'm sorry I didn't pick you up. How's Satchmo?" Adam asked.

Matt's blue eyes blazed with happiness in the dusk. "He's doing good. Ms. Sydenstricker let me take him out on the lead line on a trail by myself. She said the change of scenery would do him good, and she trusted me to keep him from taking off at a gallop." Matt gave a lopsided smile. "That was her little joke since Satch still isn't Mr. Energetic these days. But he liked it. I think he was walking faster at the end of the walk than at the beginning."

Adam watched the expressions play across his son's face, trying to memorize each one. "Sounds like he's on the road to recovery."

"Yeah," Matt said, plopping down in the chair next to his father's while Trace lay down between them. "Dr. Tim came out to check on him and said Dr. Linden did an amazing job."

"Dr. Linden didn't come?" Adam felt the pinch of regret. She probably didn't want to risk encountering him at the stable.

"Nah, she had some meeting or something."

He remembered now. Paul Taggart had news for her. He hoped it was good. "She'll be back tomorrow, I'm sure." He tightened his grip on the wooden arms as it occurred to him that she probably wouldn't be coming to Thanksgiving. He'd driven away his one ally in introducing Matt to his relatives. "The O'Briens are looking forward to meeting you. They're arriving Wednesday afternoon before Thanksgiving and staying until Friday morning."

"Yeah," Matt said, slumping down into the chair and staring out over the mountains.

"They're excited to have discovered a new cousin." Adam let go of the chair arm to reach into his breast pocket. Pulling out the photo Ellen had given him, he stretched his arm toward Matt. "They thought you might like to see what they look like."

The boy looked at the proffered photograph as though it might bite him. Finally, he took it and dropped it in his lap without even glancing at it. "What are we doing after they leave?"

Adam wrapped his fingers around the hard wood again. "I don't know." He decided to take the plunge. "How would you feel about Disney World?"

"Disney World? Seriously?" Matt had pivoted in his chair and was gaping at his father.

"I can't tell if that's a yes or a no."

"Yes!" Matt said, in the teenage tone that indicated his father was in idiot. "That would be so cool."

"That's what we're doing." He'd deal with the dolphin question later. He'd barely made it through the Disney issue, and he was going to have to pull a lot of strings just to get a room at this time of year.

"Cool," Matt said again. "Thanks, Dad."

His son's last word sent a spear of pain slicing through him.

"Are you okay?" Matt asked. "You look kind of weird."

"Just tired from all the flights." Adam levered himself out of the chair. "I have to go to work." Trace stood up before Adam signaled him to stay.

"Right." Matt's voice was flat. He yanked his hood up over his head and slouched down in the chair.

Adam walked to the door Matt had left ajar. Looking down at his hand on the doorknob, in a voice hoarse with emotion, he said, "I love you, Matt." Then he strode through the door and pulled it shut behind him.

Chapter 25

$\mathcal{G}$ UILT JABBED AT HANNAH WHEN SHE CAUGHT SIGHT OF Adam's Maserati standing alone in the nearly empty parking lot. Heading to her own car she hesitated, wondering if she should retrieve his keys from Estelle's desk in case he wanted the car after the animal hospital closed.

"Get a grip," she muttered to herself, yanking open the door of her Subaru. "He's got to have a spare for that fancy car."

And he wouldn't want to see her anyway. She'd sleepwalked through her afternoon appointments with half her mind on her patients and the other half on whether she should apologize to Adam for the awful things she'd said. She'd tortured herself by remembering all he'd overcome to get where he was, admitting to herself that she didn't know whether Matt would be better off with his father or with the seemingly perfect O'Briens, no matter what her instincts told her.

She forced herself to drive to Paul Taggart's office, although the last thing she wanted to do right now was dredge up the horrors of her past in Chicago.

The windows of the law office glowed gold and welcoming in the late afternoon dusk. Paul's secretary waved her through to his office with a smile and a flash of enormous rings on every finger.

Paul stood up behind his desk, coming around to give her a peck on the cheek. "Hello, doc. Something to drink?"

She swallowed and noticed her throat was tight. "Water would be great," she croaked.

He opened the refrigerator and brought two bottles over to the couch. "Good news," he said, unscrewing the cap and handing her the water. "Sawyer has agreed to admit he was misinformed, and blamed you and your veterinary practice wrongly. He's also going to make a handsome donation to the local animal shelter in Sophie's memory. You just have to decide how you want him to get the word out to the media. He's willing to do whatever you want on that front."

Hannah waited for the flare of jubilation but her despair over Adam muffled every other emotion. She tried to sound enthusiastic. "You got Robert Sawyer to let me decide how he should apologize? You're a miracle worker."

"No, I just have leverage." His excitement faded slightly as his gaze met hers. "Are you worried about the media? Because we can keep it low-key if you prefer."

She made a face. "I'd prefer to have no media at all, but that wouldn't accomplish what I want."

"Which is?"

"To make sure everyone in Sanctuary knows Tim didn't hire some sleazy veterinarian to take care of their animals. And to clear my partners in Chicago of any lingering stain on their reputation."

"Tim isn't worried about that, and your former partners threw you to the wolves," Paul said. "So you don't really need to deal with the press, if it makes you uncomfortable."

She thought of Adam's constant battle with his past. He couldn't come to terms with it, so it was warping everything he did. She took another sip of water and shook her head. "I tried to run away from the situation the first time. Now I need to meet it head-on. Otherwise it's going to follow me around for the rest of my life."

"You're sure?"

She squared her shoulders. "Invite every reporter in the city of Chicago."

Hannah woke up early the next morning, feeling as though a heavy blanket of misery lay on top of her. Trying to escape the memory of yesterday's disaster, she rolled over and squeezed her eyes shut. That's when she realized she didn't just feel horrible on the inside; her body ached all over. Laying the back of her hand against her forehead, she moaned as she felt the heat against her skin.

"It's probably psychosomatic," she muttered, wriggling out from under Floyd and Ginger to pad into the bathroom for a thermometer and aspirin. She swallowed two pills before shoving the electronic thermometer in her mouth until it beeped. "Oh, crap! A hundred and two degrees."

Great. Now she could spend all day in bed alone, obsessing over the terrible things she'd said to Adam and worrying about the upcoming press conference in Chicago.

She grabbed her favorite fuzzy purple robe and shuffled into the kitchen to make a cup of tea. Maybe she'd feel well enough after ingesting a hot, caffeinated beverage that she could drag herself into the office for distraction's sake.

It didn't work. Two cups of tea later she had to admit that even feeding the dogs was so exhausting she needed to lie down again.

She called Tim, who threatened to send a doctor over. "Geez, do they really still make house calls around here?" she asked.

"I make house calls, so the human docs can do the same," Tim said with a certain ambiguity.

"You mean you'd call in a favor to get someone to come here," she said. "Thanks, but it's just a flu, I'm sure. If I need stronger medicine, I'll get you to bring me some Oroquin-10, seeing as it worked for Satchmo."

Her employer chuckled. "I'll call and check in on you at lunchtime, unless you'd rather not be bothered."

"No, that would be nice," she said, tears welling up at the concern in his voice. She always got weepy when she was sick. "But don't worry about me. I have lots of furry company."

"They're good for moral support, but they can't bring you ginger ale or chicken noodle soup," he said. "Don't think about coming back to work until you're one hundred percent."

She didn't tell him that she'd be back as soon as she hit even fifty percent.

Her next call was to cancel her dog walker. She didn't want to deal with any humans when she was feeling lousy. The dogs would be content with going out in the yard.

Heading for the couch, she lay down and drifted into a feverish dreamland that mixed together Adam, Ward, Matt, Satchmo, and a chorus of barking dogs. The barking finally became so insistent it jerked her awake to hear the doorbell ringing.

Glancing at her watch, she discovered she'd been asleep for three hours. The doorbell rang again. She rolled off the couch and trundled to the door as she shushed the dogs. Peering through the frosted glass pane beside it, she saw the blurry form of Sonya, the vet tech she'd foisted Matt on that fateful Saturday morning.

Hannah retied the belt on her robe and cracked open the door.

Sonya held out a canvas tote bag with "Sanctuary Animal Hospital" printed on it. "I come bearing chicken soup from Clingman's Market," she said. "Dr. Tim sent me. He said it's more effective than Oroquin-10."

Hannah managed a weak smile as she took the tote and held the door wider. "Sounds great. You're welcome to come in, if you're not afraid of my germs."

"Just for a minute to check on you," Sonya said, stepping inside and unzipping her parka. "What's your temp?"

"I just woke up, so I don't know."

Sonya's gaze went past Hannah to the three dogs, who sat looking longingly at her. "Hey, guys! C'mon and get some lovin'." She knelt in front of them and began a petting-fest.

"They're your slaves for life now," Hannah said, leading the way into the kitchen where she stowed the chicken soup in the refrigerator.

"You're supposed to eat that," Sonya pointed out.

Hannah grimaced. "I'm not really hungry."

"You're forcing fluids, though, right?"

"Well, I was sleeping until you rang the bell," Hannah said.

Sonya chuckled and went to the refrigerator. After surveying the meager contents, she pulled out a bottle of fruit juice and poured Hannah a tall glass. "Drink it, and then I'll leave you alone. After we take your temperature."

"Are you qualified to treat humans?" Hannah asked, feeling grumpy, although she picked up the glass and took a sip.

"Two years of med school," Sonya said. "I dropped out when I got pregnant with Danny."

"Oh." Hannah had no idea about Sonya's history. "In that case . . ." She took another sip.

The vet tech perched on a stool, her hands thrust into her jacket pockets. "The truth is I found out I'm good with animals, so I like what I'm doing. Maybe when Danny gets older, I'll go to veterinary school."

"I'll write you a glowing letter of recommendation," Hannah said.

"Thanks, doc. Now where's your thermometer?"

"In the bathroom. I'll get it." She didn't want Sonya to see her messy bedroom, so she shuffled there and back, sitting down and putting the thermometer in her mouth.

When it beeped, Sonya took it and checked the reading, her eyebrows rising. "One hundred two point five. Doc, you're pretty sick."

"I always run a high fever with the flu. It's no big deal. Really," Hannah added as she saw the skepticism on Sonya's face. "I'll take another dose of aspirin in an hour and it'll go right down."

"I don't know. Maybe you need someone who can write you a prescription for human meds." The vet tech looked worried.

"A day of bed-rest and I'll be fine."

Sonya grinned. "I get the message. I'm going." She jumped off the stool and headed for the front door, stopping to say good-bye to her new canine friends. As she walked out, she said, "Make sure you eat that chicken soup or Dr. Tim will have my head."

"Promise." Hannah closed the door and slumped against it. Her knees felt like they were made of rubber and even her hair seemed to pulse with achiness. "Ugh. Back to bed," she said, pushing herself upright and stumbling to her bedroom. She remembered to put the aspirin on her bedside table before she collapsed.

Her dreams grew darker. Satchmo lay motionless on the straw as Matt crouched over him and sobbed, while Hannah tried to do a spinal tap on the dying pony. The stall door flew open with a bang and Adam reeled in, clutching a bottle of whisky. He staggered and thudded against the wooden wall. The sound of barking dogs started up again, and she snapped into consciousness.

Her clock showed an hour had passed, so she fumbled open the aspirin and swallowed three. The banging from her dream moved to the real world and she realized someone was knocking on her front door again.

Groaning, she flipped back the covers and swung her feet to the ground. "Don't they know a sick person needs rest?" she grumbled as she trundled to the door. She didn't recognize the woman standing outside.

"Just what I need . . . a total stranger." She yanked open the door. "Hello?"

The stranger was about her age, dressed in a belted, black wool coat and high-heeled, black pumps, her blonde-streaked brown hair twisted into a neat bun. A wheeled cooler sat at her elegantly shod feet. She made Hannah feel like a walking mess.

"I'm Lucy Porterfield, a hostess at The Aerie, and I'm real sorry to bother you," her lovely visitor said, "but Mr. Bosch heard you were feeling poorly and wanted you to have this." She gestured to the cooler with a smile.

"Mr. Bosch?" Hannah closed her eyes briefly as a confusion of emotions roiled in her chest. Maybe Adam didn't hate her too much.

"I don't want you to have to pull this heavy thing, so if it's okay I'll just wheel it in and put everything away for you." Lucy reached down and flipped up a handle. She waited with an expectant look as Hannah tried to absorb the implications of Adam's offering.

"Sure. Fine. Thanks." Hannah thrust the door back so Lucy could tug her burden inside. "Let me guess. There's chicken soup in there."

"Three kinds," Lucy said, following Hannah into the kitchen after she said hello to the canine greeting committee. "And lots of other goodies."

"How did Mr. Bosch find out I'm sick?"

"Oh lord, everyone finds out everything here in Sanctuary," Lucy said. She flipped up the top of the cooler and began stowing containers in the refrigerator. "To tell the truth, I volunteered to come. Mr. Bosch was as cranky as a black bear who can't get the lid off a garbage can."

That startled a snort of laughter out of Hannah as she pictured Adam wrestling with a galvanized-metal can.

"My granny always told me laughter's the best medicine," Lucy said. She brushed her hands together in a gesture of accomplishment. "There. It's all put away. Everything's labeled with contents and warming directions."

"Is Mr. Bosch often cranky?" Hannah asked.

"Hardly ever." Lucy tilted her head as though considering. "He looked kind of tired when I first came in, but it wasn't until he burst out of his office, saying he needed to make chicken soup, that he seemed kind of upset." She looked at Hannah. "I guess he's worried about you."

Hannah sank onto a stool. Had he forgiven her? "Is there any caviar in there?"

Lucy frowned at the array of nonperishables on the counter. "Caviar? I don't think so. Mr. Bosch probably thought a sick person wouldn't like the strong taste of it. But if you want, I'll ask him for some."

"No, no, *please* don't do that," Hannah said, waving her hands frantically as though to erase her words. "I was joking." She didn't know what possessed her to ask that. Except that it might have meant Adam wanted to see her again.

Lucy picked up the handle of the cooler. "I'm sorry I woke you, but I wasn't going back to face Mr. Bosch without delivering the food." Her heels clicked on the tile floor of the foyer as she rolled the cooler to the door and waved. "Hope you feel better real soon!"

Hannah followed her to bolt the door before padding back into the kitchen. Pulling open the refrigerator door, she randomly chose one of the pale-green containers marked with the soaring-eagle logo of The Aerie. Handwritten on the top was "Curried Chicken Soup. Heat in a saucepan to desired temperature." She didn't know if it was Adam's writing or not, but it was bold and finished with a flourish. She picked up another container. "Hearty Chicken Soup." Same cooking directions. Finally, there was "Chicken, Brie, and Artichoke Soup."

Lucy said Adam had made it for her. She had a vision of him standing in front of the stove, his hands hovering over the ingredients, choosing the ones he thought she'd like the best. She closed the refrigerator door. "Time to go back to bed before you get any more pathetic."

When the barking dogs jerked her awake for the third time, she discovered her fever had broken, leaving her pajamas and the sheets soaked in sweat. "Ugh," she said, climbing out of bed and flipping the covers back to air out.

The doorbell was ringing, but she couldn't greet a visitor in her soggy pj's so she quickly changed into new ones and grabbed her robe. Shuffling to the door as she finger-combed her damp hair, she squinted through the glass to see the vivid, red mane of Paul's wife, Julia. The artist carried a glass vase of tall, yellow flowers in one hand and had a picnic basket hooked over her other arm.

By now Hannah had resigned herself to the fact that people took care of each other in a small town whether you wanted them to or not. Maybe she'd call the dog walker back, as her sleep kept getting interrupted anyway.

Hannah tightened the belt on her robe and cracked open the door, hoping Julia would hand her the flowers and basket and leave.

"Oh, dear, you look terrible," Julia said, her gaze sympathetic. Then she looked horrified. "I mean, you look like you *feel* terrible."

"It's okay. I'm sure both are true," Hannah said. Julia's faux pas had dissolved her annoyance, so she opened the door wide.

"I won't stay long, but Claire was worried when she found out you were sick. She got tied up at the gallery, so she sent me with her food." Julia stepped inside and set the vase down on the hall table. "I added the Dancing Lady orchids because I think beauty helps heal just as much as chicken soup does."

Hannah looked at the blaze of yellow flowers lighting up her little foyer. "You might be on to something there."

"Oh, hello," Julia said, surveying the three dogs who had joined Hannah. "You've got nurses, I see."

"Anabelle, Floyd, and Ginger," Hannah said, liking Julia's guileless presence more and more. "Come on in."

Julia gave each dog a greeting pat and bustled into the kitchen. Setting the basket on the counter, she proceeded to unload an array of containers. "Chicken noodle soup and homemade pumpkin pie ice cream from Tammy's Place. Nice combination, right? I'd dig in there myself. A selection of herbal teas from the Bean and Biscuit. This one is supposed to reduce fevers, so you might try it first." Julia lifted the box and sniffed at it, wrinkling her nose. "Although it smells nasty." She went back to her catalogue. "Organic ginger ale and homemade cheese bread from Bellefleur. Hot chocolate from Jezebel's. Crackers and cheese from Moonshine. And meat loaf from the Library Cafe. That's for when you're feeling better, so I'll put it in the freezer."

Hannah slid onto a stool to watch in fascination as Julia arranged the offerings in a beautiful display on her battered countertop. When the other woman was done, she looked at Hannah. "I have orders to make sure you eat some of the chicken noodle soup before I leave."

"You and everyone else in Sanctuary," Hannah said.

"I'm not your first visitor?"

"Not even close."

"Small towns," Julia said with a sympathetic grimace.

"I don't want to infect you, but would you join me in a bowl?" Hannah said. Now that her fever was down, she found she'd like to have some company. "I'll stay on this side of the counter and you can sit over there."

Julia's face lit up. "I never get sick, so I'd love to. Tammy makes the best soup, and I have my eye on the pumpkin pie ice cream too." She stowed the ice cream and meat loaf in the freezer before opening the fridge to stash the cheese. She turned to look at Hannah, her eyes wide. "You got food from The Aerie? Maybe we should have that."

"No, let's eat Tammy's soup while it's hot." Hannah didn't want to eat the soup Adam had made for her in front of Julia. *Stupid.*

Julia nodded and followed Hannah's directions about where to find dishes and silverware. It was pleasant to have a steaming bowl of soup, a piece of cheese bread, and a frosty glass of ginger ale appear in front of her without any effort on her part.

"I'm glad you let me stay," Julia said, dragging a stool around to the opposite side of the counter. She took a spoonful of soup and swallowed. "So, tell me about you and Adam Bosch."

Hannah choked on a noodle. "What do you mean?" she croaked.

"Well, The Aerie doesn't do take-out except for special people. Tim gets it because he patched up Adam's dog after a bear attack. So you must have some strong connection."

"Um, Adam's son likes me. I take care of his whisper pony."

"If I weren't madly in love with Paul, I'd be madly in love with the dark and mysterious Adam. He's gorgeous and he can cook. And he clearly has secrets that need prying out of him."

"Not so easy to do," Hannah said, without thinking, as she took another bite of soup.

"So you've tried?"

Hannah cursed her loose tongue. Something about Julia's clear green eyes and lopsided red bun disarmed Hannah. She had no close friend to discuss her troubles with here in Sanctuary.

Hannah knew the germs were undermining her willpower, but tears streaked down her cheeks before she could hide them.

"Oh, Hannah, I'm sorry!" Julia reached across and squeezed her hand. "I've never learned to behave in polite company."

"No, that's not it," Hannah, said shaking her head as she pulled a crumpled tissue out of her bathrobe pocket. "I need to talk to someone about Adam."

"I'm listening." Julia put down her spoon and sat forward to plant her elbows on the countertop and rest her chin on her laced fingers.

More tears burned in Hannah's eyes. "I, well, I said some awful things to Adam yesterday. And I don't know whether I should try to apologize or whether I should leave him alone since I'm pretty sure he never wants to see me again."

"And that upsets you because?"

"Because I'm an idiot." Because she was in love with him. Hannah picked up her napkin and tore it in half before she tore each half into quarters.

Julia sat back on her stool. "Tell me what you said to him."

"I called him a coward because he's found a nice couple up in Massachusetts who are Matt's second cousins or something like that. He thinks he's not good enough to be Matt's father, so he wants the O'Briens to adopt Matt. He went up to Boston yesterday to meet them." Hannah ripped the napkin into ever smaller pieces. "He admitted he was hoping there would be something wrong with them, but he says they're perfect."

"Oh, lord, this is terrible," Julia said, her face tight with concern. "Is it because of his alcoholism?"

"Mostly," Hannah said, "but it's also his job. He admitted he uses the business to distract himself from his craving for liquor. And The Aerie is the one achievement in his life he takes pride in."

"I hear a teenager can be a pretty big distraction."

"That's what I tried to tell him." Hannah rolled the napkin shreds up into a ball. "Matt doesn't help. He's so afraid of being hurt again that he puts up this barrier between himself and Adam. Only Satchmo has been able to build a bridge between them."

"Thank goodness for whisper horses!" Julia said. "If it hadn't been for Darkside, I'd be single and miserable back in North Carolina, painting greeting-card landscapes."

"You really believe in this whisper horse idea?"

Julia nodded. "As a vet, you see the bonds between humans and their animals all the time. Why is it hard to believe a horse can share your troubles with you? They're strong and have broad backs for carrying heavy burdens."

"Sharon thinks there's one special horse for each person."

"That's just her way of saying you find the right horse when you need one." Julia smiled. "Although I'd been painting pictures of Darkside before I ever saw him in person."

Just when Hannah thought the explanation began to make some sense, Julia had injected that suspect note of mysticism again. "It's Adam who needs the whisper horse right now," Hannah said. "Matt can whisper in Satchmo's ear all he wants, but it's not changing his father's mind."

"Satchmo might need some human assistance," Julia said, picking up her spoon again. "Now tell me about the O'Briens."

"They're coming for Thanksgiving."

Julia sat bolt upright. "You have to go too."

"But—," the flu was fogging Hannah's brain, "—I'm going to Claire and Tim's."

"I'll explain why you can't. They'll understand."

"What makes you think Adam would want me there?" Hannah pulled apart the cheese bread and arranged the pieces on the bread plate. "I accused him of cowardice."

"That was just to get his attention. He must realize that now."

"It's more complicated." Hannah took a deep breath, making herself cough. "We sort of broke up too."

Surprise transformed into sympathy in the artist's gaze. "I thought there might be a little more to the story." Julia reached across the counter to touch the back of Hannah's hand. "You care about the father as much as the son, don't you?"

Hannah swallowed hard and nodded.

"Did you break up because you told him off, or was there some other reason?"

"Both." Hannah clenched her fist around the balled-up napkin. "The way he feels about Matt spilled over into the way he feels about me."

"If he's not worthy to be Matt's father, he's not worthy to be your lover?"

A wave of exhaustion rolled over Hannah, and she slumped on her stool. "That's what he believes."

"Men are so stupid and stubborn!" Julia slapped her palm on the counter, making Hannah jump. The artist leaned across the Formica. "You have no choice. You're Adam and Matt's last hope."

After Julia left, Hannah slid into a heavy, dreamless sleep. At 5:30 the dogs made their needs known, so Hannah forced herself out of bed to feed them.

Her fever had risen again but only to 100 degrees. Thrusting her feet into a pair of slippers and pulling a ski jacket out of her closet, she trailed out the sliding back door and plunked down in a lawn chair to watch the dogs cast around the yard in the near dark. It felt good to pull in a lungful of sharp, clean air, even if the chill scraped at her throat.

Besides, it warmed her to think of all the chicken soup in the refrigerator. In Chicago she would have fended for herself; Ward wasn't the sort to play nursemaid to a sick fiancée. Here half the town worried about her.

Including Adam. A shiver pulled her out of her reverie and she stood up, calling the dogs to come in.

It was time to taste his soup. She dumped half the container marked "Hearty" into the saucepan, recalling his disdain for the microwave, which would have worked just as well for this task. Plunging her spoon into the pot, she took a sip and moaned at the deliciousness of the subtly herbed broth, the tender chunks of white meat, and the slightly sweet peas and carrots.

"Do I love him more for his cooking or his lovemaking?" she asked the dogs who watched avidly in the hope she'd drop some of the wonderfully scented food. You couldn't separate the two aspects of him; they sprang from the same streak of innate sensuality.

As she swallowed spoonfuls of the warm, soothing soup, it rinsed away some of the ugliness of the scene between them. Maybe she *could* face him at Thanksgiving . . . if the invitation was still open.

After scraping her spoon on the bottom of the pot, she deposited it in the sink, too weak even to rinse it for the dishwasher. With the dogs' escort, she wandered into her office, a converted second bedroom that held an Ikea desk and chair she'd bought in Chicago, as well as a wall of overflowing bookshelves. She flicked on the computer screen and scrolled through her emails to see if any required answering.

Paul Taggart's name caught her eye and she opened the message from him.

Dear Hannah,

I'm sorry to hear you're feeling under the weather and hope you are on the mend soon. Julia says you are well supplied with chicken soup, Sanctuary's favorite cure-all for what ails you. If you need anything else, let us know. We're here to help.

The arrangements for the press conference are going forward. We have agreed on next Thursday afternoon as an appropriate time. I requested it before I knew of your illness, so I hope you will be recovered by then. Anything later will get lost in the Thanksgiving/Christmas holiday rush, and I want Sawyer's apology to be heard by as many as possible.

I've already booked round-trip tickets to Chicago for both of us (see attachment), since our airport doesn't run to many flights. If you prefer to travel at another time, don't hesitate to say so.

"He's coming with me!" Hannah marveled at the support her new allies in Sanctuary gave her.

We will continue to work with Sawyer's staff to develop the format and final location of the conference, pending your agreement. You may play as large or as small a role as you choose.

In order not to disturb you, I decided to email rather than call, but feel free to give me a ring if you have any questions.

Best regards,
Paul

Hannah sat back in her chair. The high-and-mighty Senator Robert Sawyer was going to eat crow in front of the local press. The thought brought a rush of satisfaction and a flutter of nerves. She didn't want to face the reporters with their cameras and their microphones again.

She thought of Adam and his openness about his struggle with alcoholism. If he could tell the world about his disease, she could put on a game face for one afternoon to remove the blot on her record. It affected more than just her own life; Tim and her former partners benefited as well.

Hannah leaned forward to type a reply, outlining what she wanted to have done at the press conference. She sat back, amazed at her sudden burst of daring.

Sawyer wasn't going to like it one little bit.

Chapter 26

"THANKS FOR GETTING ME OUT OF SCHOOL," MATT said, slinging his backpack into the Maserati without a snarky comment about the car.

"You and Dr. Linden are friends, so you should see her vindication," Adam said, steering the car out of the school parking lot and onto the road toward the Sanctuary Veterinary Hospital.

Matt threw him a look. "Meaning everyone says she didn't do anything wrong?"

Adam looked back at him. "You'll need that word for your SATs."

The boy snorted and slouched in his seat. "It's cool that Dr. Tim sent the cameraman to Chicago so we can all watch."

"He wants everyone in Sanctuary to know Dr. Linden made the right decision."

Without telling Hannah, Tim had arranged for a two-man crew from the local-access television channel to be present at the press conference in Chicago. He'd invited Hannah's friends and several influential town residents to the animal hospital to see it live.

"Do you believe she made the right decision?" Matt asked.

Adam's grip on the steering wheel became punishing as his feelings for Hannah writhed through him, dragging him back down into the wine cellar of The Aerie. He felt like one of the restaurant's fine, crystal wineglasses—brittle enough to shatter at any second.

When he'd heard Hannah was ill, his first impulse was to rush to her house. However, the memory of their last encounter smacked him back to his senses. So he resorted to his standard response to every problem: he cooked. In this case, every kind of chicken soup he could think of, sending it all to Hannah with the hope she'd understand his unspoken apology and wishes for her speedy recovery.

He'd been relieved to hear she was well enough to go back to work on Tuesday, but he couldn't face her. He thanked his lucky stars that Satchmo continued to improve, so he didn't have to risk a meeting at the stable. In fact, if it hadn't been for Matt, he would have avoided seeing Hannah even on television.

"Dad?"

What had Matt asked him? About Hannah's decision. "I would never question anything she did for an animal's well-being. Look at how she saved Satchmo."

"Yeah, she's awesome."

When they pulled into the last empty space in the parking lot at the veterinary office, Adam turned to Matt. "Want to give me a hand with the coolers in the trunk?"

"Sure. I bet they'll be happy to see us bringing in some of your food." His son clambered out of the car as Adam sat stunned. He had braced himself for the usual accusation of trying to bribe people with his cooking. Shaking his head, he followed his son more slowly.

Matt's prediction proved correct. The chorus of greeting was enthusiastic. Tim had set up a big-screen television in the waiting room with chairs arranged in rows facing it. Estelle cleared her desk to create an impromptu buffet table and helped Adam lay out the mid-morning snacks he'd brought. Soon the staff was scarfing down mini-quiches made with bacon, Gruyere, and zucchini, freshly baked sweet rolls, and croissants filled with ground lamb and mushrooms.

"Oh my gosh, this pastry melts in your mouth before you can even chew it," Sonya sighed as she bit into an orange-cinnamon swirl. Adam felt a twinge of bittersweet amusement when he saw Matt hovering near the beautiful vet tech. He envied the boy his uncomplicated crush.

"You could have made them a little bigger," Tim grumbled, his big hand dwarfing the bite-sized quiche he'd picked up.

"I'm used to feeding normal-sized people, not human mountains," Adam said, surprised by the friendly ribbing.

"We grow 'em big here in Sanctuary," one of the town councilors said. He added another croissant to the pile on his plate before he took it to his chair in the front row.

Tim's wife, Claire, appeared beside Adam. "Thank you for providing the refreshments," she said in a low voice as she watched the mayor and two more officials load up their plates. "Good food always puts politicians in a receptive mood."

"I considered bringing hot buttered rum," Adam said, "but Tim said he wanted his staff sober enough to work the rest of the day."

"We wouldn't want them sleeping it off on the examining tables." She gestured with her plate. "Those two women coming back for seconds are reporters. One's from the *Sanctuary Sentinel* and the other's from the *Tri-County Crier,* so we'll get some regional coverage."

"Tim orchestrated this brilliantly."

"If you hadn't persuaded Paul to start his inquiries, this wouldn't be happening."

Adam shook his head. "It wasn't any of my business, but I hated to see Hannah's reputation being smeared."

"It's always the business of good friends to help each other," Claire said, giving him her serene smile.

Tim's voice broke through the hum of conversation. "It's nearly eleven, so find yourself a place to sit, and I'll turn up the sound on the television." He picked up the remote control and increased the volume, so a televised debate over the best diet for dairy goats became audible.

The crowd moved to their seats. Adam watched Matt settle beside Sonya and crane his neck around until he met his father's gaze. The boy jerked his head toward the empty seat beside him, his wordless invitation making Adam feel as though he'd won the lottery.

Sonya leaned forward as Adam sat down. "Mr. Bosch, you are a wizard with food," she said. "Now I want to eat at The Aerie in the worst way."

"Come anytime," he said. "I'll put your name on the special guest list, and they'll always find you a table."

"Thanks, but it's beyond my budget."

"You'd be my guest. No charge."

She shook her head. "I couldn't do that, but it's nice of you to offer."

Adam frowned. He'd been living in isolation on his mountaintop, absorbed in turning The Aerie into a success. He'd made a point to hire locally, but he hadn't thought about the fact that many people who lived in Sanctuary couldn't afford the prices at the famous restaurant just outside their town. Maybe he could offer local residents a discount or a series of "Sanctuary Nights" where he invited them for a private party.

He was still thinking about how best to organize an event when Matt sat up straight beside him and said, "It's starting."

Adam braced himself.

Hannah stood in the cramped foyer of the animal shelter, making polite conversation with the shelter's director, a stocky, young, blond man named Nick Wodarski. Paul had positioned himself by the glass front door, his gaze on the street. "Showtime," he announced, smoothing his hand down his necktie. Hannah turned in time to see two shiny green sedans sweep up in front of the shelter's cracked cement steps.

The first car's four doors all swung open simultaneously, disgorging three men and one woman dressed in dark overcoats and business suits. One man went to the trunk and pulled out a large, cardboard sign, which Hannah guessed was the symbolic check Robert Sawyer would be handing to the shelter's director to open the Sophie Memorial Fund.

The second car's doors remained closed until a news van pulled up, its roof bristling with antennae. Then the senator's driver emerged and walked around to hold the door for Sawyer. Hannah hissed in a breath as she recognized the man who exited from the side of the car opposite Sawyer.

Ward. She was surprised he'd want to be involved on the wrong side of a public apology.

"You okay?" Paul asked.

She nodded as she smoothed her damp palms down her belted, gray coat. "Just had a momentary flashback." She decided Paul should be clued in about the unexpected guest. "That's my ex-fiancé in the blue shirt and yellow tie. Ward Miller."

The lawyer frowned. "I can ask him to leave."

"No, I'm glad he's here. He was part of the problem." She wanted Ward to watch her take back her life.

At the sight of Sawyer, a gaggle of reporters appeared out of the cars parked along the rundown street, converging on the senator. He stopped to talk with them, smiling and at ease. As she watched the reporters laugh at something he said, Hannah felt a surge of distaste for the coziness of the relationship between the press and the popular politician.

Sawyer made his way up the steps and waited as one of his aides opened the door for him. Evidently it was beneath his station to touch a door handle. Tall, with iron-gray hair, a long, patrician face, and a dazzling smile that she suspected required regular trips to the dentist, he strode in as though he owned the world.

"Senator Sawyer," Paul said, stepping forward. "I'm Paul Taggart, and this is my client, Dr. Linden."

The senator's smile never wavered as he held out his hand to Hannah. "Dr. Linden, I'm glad we're getting this misunderstanding straightened out to everyone's satisfaction." He turned to shake Paul's hand. "I hear great things about your Pro Bono Project, Mr. Taggart."

Hannah nudged Nick forward. "Senator, this is Nick Wodarski, the director of the All Paws Onboard Shelter. He does fantastic work for animals in this area of the city."

"Mr. Wodarski, I'm glad to support your impressive organization," the senator said, clasping Nick's hand.

"Thank you, sir," Nick mumbled before he flashed a look at Hannah. "And thank you, Dr. Linden, for connecting us with Senator Sawyer."

Maybe Nick wasn't as shy and retiring as she'd thought.

One of the senator's staff members came through the door. "We're all set up outside, senator."

A thrill of nerves thrummed through Hannah. She pulled her belt a notch tighter as she squared her shoulders. Now she just had to make sure she didn't trip over anything in the high-heeled pumps she'd worn in order to project an air of professionalism.

"Excellent!" Sawyer said. He turned to Hannah. "I have what I believe you'll find a pleasant surprise."

His words nearly undermined her tenuous poise. There weren't supposed to be any surprises; Paul and the senator's staff had worked out the ten minutes of scripted action to the last comma and period. She glanced at the lawyer beside her.

"Senator, what—?" Paul began, but Sawyer was already out the door. "We'll just have to go with it," Paul muttered, pushing open the door. As Hannah passed him, he gave her a reassuring smile and a quick squeeze on her shoulder.

A portable podium and microphone had been set up at the top of the steps. Senator Sawyer stood behind the podium, bantering with the reporters who'd taken up stations at the foot of the stairs. She was surprised to see not one but two video crews. They'd expected only the local television station.

Hannah walked over to Sawyer's left while Paul directed Nick to the senator's right. She gritted her teeth when she noticed Ward stationed just behind the senator, holding the giant cardboard check.

Everyone's head turned when a door banged open on the side of the shelter building and a procession of people wearing yellow T-shirts printed with "We ♥ Dr. Linden" marched out and arrayed themselves behind the press.

Hannah had the satisfaction of seeing a flicker of dismay cross Sawyer's face as the sea of yellow overflowed the sidewalk onto the street, and the video cameras turned to pan over the crowd. She glanced at Nick and caught the broad smile on his face as he nodded to the group.

Sawyer recovered quickly, taking a pair of glasses from his breast pocket before bracing his hands on the podium and surveying the scene below him with a friendly air. "Good morning!"

His audience responded with a hearty "good morning" in return.

"I'm here to put the record straight about a very special dog and a very special veterinarian," Sawyer said. "Sophie, our golden retriever, was part of our family for eleven years when she developed cancer. At first, Dr. Linden—" he nodded toward Hannah with a grave smile "—was able to use her considerable skills to keep Sophie comfortable and functioning as part of our family. Unfortunately, we had a vacation scheduled just as Sophie's condition began to deteriorate. We chose to leave Sophie in Dr. Linden's more than capable hands while we were away, with full confidence that she would make all the right decisions about our beloved dog's health."

He swept the crowd with his gaze.

"While Dr. Linden made heroic efforts to control Sophie's pain, the cancer in our sweet dog's body continued to grow. At last, our poor golden was in too much agony to prolong her life any further, and Dr. Linden made the absolutely correct judgment call. Our Sophie had to be put to sleep."

Sawyer pulled a handkerchief out of his pocket, removed his glasses, and swiped the cloth over his eyes. Hannah wanted to snort in disbelief at the play-acting, but controlled herself as she noted the glowing, red lights signaling that the cameras were recording.

The senator replaced the handkerchief and glasses. "Unfortunately, due to an oversight on my part, I neglected to leave my cell phone number at the veterinary office in the event Dr. Linden needed to reach us, and this is where the misunderstanding occurred. She explored every possible avenue available to her to track us down, calling both my office and my home number to beg someone to contact us."

He paused to make a wry face. "I am lucky to have very loyal staff members. They felt my family needed the vacation and did not wish to disturb us with such sad news, so they refused to allow Dr. Linden access to us." He drew himself up to his full height, his voice increasing in volume and resonance. "I take full responsibility for this breakdown in communication. I should have given Dr. Linden my cell number or left instructions with my staff to put her through to me. My lapse created much trauma for my family and for the doctor."

His tone shifted from solemn to regretful. "My children were understandably upset to discover their wonderful Sophie had died in their absence. I'm afraid I overreacted to their distress without knowing all the facts."

Hannah tensed. Her moment was coming soon.

"To atone for my error, I would like to state unequivocally that Dr. Hannah Linden of the Roscoe Veterinary Hospital acted appropriately at every stage of the situation. I deeply regret any past statements I have made to the contrary." Hannah had to give him credit: Sawyer's voice boomed as he spoke the words of apology. "To prove my sincerity, I am making this donation to the All Paws Onboard Animal Shelter to create the Sophie Memorial Fund in Dr. Linden's honor."

That was the cue for Hannah and Nick to step forward. Ward handed Sawyer the check, and the senator handed it to Nick as they shook hands and cameras clicked. Nick spoke a few words of thanks before holding the check above his head as the T-shirted spectators cheered. When Hannah caught sight of the amount she blinked: it was twice what the senator had agreed to.

Hannah was about to step up to the vacated podium when Sawyer took the microphone again. "Because Dr. Linden has made a believer out of me, I will be introducing a stringent animal rights bill in the Senate. My staff members have copies of the proposed legislation for any who would like to read it."

So that was his surprise. He'd found a way to turn the apology into a political opportunity, appealing to the animal activists in his constituency. It might be pure calculation on his part, but she hoped some good would come of it.

Sawyer backed away with a graceful gesture indicating she should take the podium. Taking a deep breath, she walked up and bent the flexible mic down to her level. "Thank you, Senator Sawyer." She sent a cool smile in his direction before she turned back to the assembly in front of her. "It takes a big man to let the world know he's made a mistake, and I appreciate the senator's willingness to do so."

She waved to the building behind her. "This shelter does remarkable work for the animals in this community and beyond, and Senator Sawyer's generous donation will support many worthwhile programs." She took a page from his book and paused to let the yellow shirts applaud. "His sponsorship of such necessary animal rights legislation is a wonderful bonus. I am thrilled to have made a convert to the cause of those creatures who so enrich our lives yet cannot speak or fight for themselves." More applause. She decided to express her gratitude to those who truly deserved it. "Many thanks to Nick Wodarski for doing such a great job in organizing this event, and to all of you who came out to show how important our animal friends are."

As choreographed, she turned and held out her hand to Senator Sawyer, something Paul said she had to do for the press, even though it made her skin crawl. The senator took it in both of his and spoke in voice too low for the microphone to pick up, "I hope this is behind us now." He gave her a warm and entirely false smile.

She smiled back just as insincerely as she nodded. "I look forward to reading the bill you're sponsoring."

A gleam of grudging admiration shone in his eyes. "You're a tough young woman, and you've got yourself a good lawyer."

"The best," she said, withdrawing her hand from his grasp and walking back to her spot in the background.

Two of Sawyer's aides stepped forward to distribute copies of the proposed animal rights bill while a couple of reporters tossed a few questions at the senator about its content. He answered them without hesitation before making his way to his car. The press dispersed almost immediately, and with a sigh of relief Hannah turned to head back into the shelter.

She halted as Ward blocked her way. "Hannah," he said. "The animal rights bill was my idea," he said.

"Great," she said, starting to walk around him.

He grabbed her wrist, his voice pleading. "I thought you'd like that."

She shook loose from his grip and let her gaze drift over his pale-blue eyes and sandy hair, his navy blue suit. A vision of Adam rose up in her mind, his dark complexity making Ward look like a cardboard cutout. "Should you keep the senator waiting?"

"He knows I need to talk to you." Ward started to reach for her again, but she skewered him with a look. He dropped his hand. "I'm sorry about what happened. I overreacted."

"You and Sawyer both, except he wasn't living with me," Hannah said. Ward had the grace to flinch. She thought of her conversation with Adam. "If I'd asked you for Sawyer's private cell phone number, would you have given it to me?"

Her ex-fiancé looked down at his polished wingtips. "I realize now you were protecting me by not asking." He raised his gaze to meet hers. "I'd like to think I would have given it to you."

At least he was honest enough not to pretend outrage about her doubts. "I'd like to think so too. Good-bye, Ward." She stepped sideways and continued to the doorway where Paul stood waiting for her. He swung open the door and she walked into the shelter.

A splash of yellow T-shirts greeted her, and a cheer went up. "Han-nah! Han-nah!" She smiled and waved before she threw a beseeching look at Paul. He took her elbow and led her through the chanting crowd to Nick's office, closing the door behind them. Hannah sagged into a plastic chair, the adrenalin draining from her body and leaving exhaustion behind.

"You were great," Paul said, leaning his hip against a desk. "Does it feel good to know your reputation has been restored?"

Hannah had been so focused on surviving the press conference she hadn't yet absorbed the end result. "It feels like a black cloud just cleared away between me and the sun." She hadn't realized how much it had bothered her until the shadow was gone.

"That was a nice ad lib of yours about the animal rights bill," Paul said.

Hannah allowed herself a short bask of pride at holding her own against the well-practiced Senator Sawyer. "Ward claimed it was his idea. I can't decide if he considered it a sop to his conscience or a political opportunity."

"Hey, cynicism is *my* territory. You're the kind, warm-hearted healer," Paul said.

"Only when it comes to animals," Hannah said, leaning her head back against the wall behind her and closing her eyes.

Adam peered past the local reporter on the television screen, his gaze riveted on Hannah as she stopped to speak with one of the senator's entourage before she disappeared into the shelter.

His attention shifted back to the white-haired woman with the microphone as she said, "Dr. Hannah Linden of the Sanctuary Veterinary Hospital should feel real good about today. She's been cleared of any wrong-doing *and* she's turned a powerful U.S. senator into an animal-rights supporter. I'd say we're mighty lucky she moved down to our neck of the woods. This is Gladys Weikle, signing off for Channel 44."

As the screen switched to a scroll of upcoming events accompanied by country music, applause rippled through the spectators.

Tim stood to turn off the television. "Our Dr. Linden is one impressive lady."

"She looked as cool as a cucumber," Estelle said. "That highfalutin' senator didn't bother her at all."

"What'd you think, Dad?" Matt asked quietly as other voices chimed in with praise of Hannah's performance.

"I thought she was magnificent," Adam said, working hard to keep his voice even. And heart-shreddingly beautiful. Her poise in the face of the powerful politician, her warmth toward the crowd, and her all-too-well-remembered body, clothed in a tailored coat, had sucked the air out of his lungs.

"That guy was a real jerk for thinking his vacation was more important than his sick dog," Matt said. "He was lucky Dr. Linden had the guts to do the right thing without his permission."

"You're a smart guy. A lot smarter than Senator Sawyer."

Matt's face glowed. "Maybe I just know Dr. Linden better."

"There's some of Adam's good food left," Tim announced, "so let's finish it up before we get back to work."

"It's time for you to get back to school," Adam said, even though he wanted this moment of unexpected bonding to go on forever.

"Don't you want to wait until you can take all the empty platters?" Matt asked.

"Nice try," Adam said, one corner of his mouth twitching upward in amusement. "I'll get them on my way home."

Matt shrugged as he picked up his jacket. "It was worth a shot."

Adam's heart twisted at the exchange. It was nothing, just a typical wrangle between a parent and a child about going to school. Which made it enormous.

Hannah's words echoed through his mind: "You don't need an excuse to keep Matt. You're his father." At times like this, he could almost convince himself she was right.

Then he remembered where he had gone after Hannah left him that day. Straight to the wine cellar.

As Paul stopped his Corvette in front of her house, Hannah gave him a rueful smile. "I apologize for sleeping almost the entire trip."

Paul waved a hand in dismissal. "You've had a tough week, and I got a lot of paperwork done, so no apology is necessary."

"I can't thank you enough for getting my name cleared and for—" she began.

"You've thanked me more than enough."

"Well, if you ever get a pet, all veterinary care is free," she said.

"I've always wanted a boa constrictor. I just haven't been able to talk Julia into it," Paul said with a wink.

"She seems more like the tiger cub sort."

"Don't put that idea into her head," Paul said, unbuckling his seat belt. "It's hard enough to have a bad-tempered stallion as her whisper horse."

"Darkside? He's just high-spirited." Hannah reached for the door handle.

"You're as crazy as my wife," he said in a tone of affectionate exasperation. Hoisting himself out of the car, he headed for the trunk to grab her overnight bag.

He insisted on carrying the bag to her door, where once again she tried to express her gratitude.

"You should thank Adam," Paul said. "He's the one who started the ball rolling."

Adam's name sent a shock of sorrow through her, and she looked away. "I'll make sure to do that."

As Paul strode back down the sidewalk, Hannah unlocked her front door and was treated to a warm welcome from her three dogs. The cats even strolled out to claim their share of her attention as soon as the flurry of barking and licking had calmed down.

"You guys were always on Sophie's side, weren't you?" she said, rubbing and scratching and smoothing all the different textures of fur. She blew out a sigh. "It feels good to be free of all that." She looked down at the expectant faces and said, "Want to go out?"

Three dogs streaked to the back slider, where they stopped to look over their shoulders as Hannah followed more slowly. Gliding the door open, she let the dogs bolt through before she stepped outside onto the cement patio.

Shoving her hands into her coat pockets, she drew in a lungful of the sharp-edged mountain air and let her gaze drift over the gray-blue ridges rising in the distance. The kaleidoscope of the last couple of days stopped whirling, and the pieces settled into a pattern of welcome familiarity. This was home in a way Chicago hadn't been. Maybe it was because she no longer had a need to defend herself and her actions, but she felt a soft wash of peacefulness flow through her as she inhaled another clean, chilly breath.

If only she didn't ache with a constant undercurrent of misery about Adam and Matt. Was she still invited to their Thanksgiving celebration? She wanted to meet the O'Briens, but she hated the thought of watching Adam suffer as he pushed his son toward these strangers. He probably wouldn't want her there to witness it either.

But he'd sent her chicken soup every day she'd been sick. Coconut curry chicken soup. Chicken and sweet corn soup. Chicken soup with polenta herb dumplings. Creamy potato leek and chicken soup. She and Lucy Porterfield had forged a budding friendship during the daily deliveries.

Didn't that mean he wanted her to come for Thanksgiving?

A chill shuddered through her as the cold penetrated the dressy winter coat she'd worn for its style, not its warmth. She pivoted on the heel of her pumps and went back into the heated interior of her rental house. She looked around at the mishmash of furniture she'd shoved into place. The house itself had no charm; she'd chosen it for the size and security of its fenced yard.

"I need to buy a house. A home."

The depth of her longing rattled her. She'd rented in Chicago and been happy with the arrangement. Now she wanted to put down roots in a town she'd once viewed as nothing more than a hiding place.

Chapter 27

*S*ATCHMO LOOKS AMAZING," HANNAH SAID TO MATT, as she gave the pony a gentle pat on the rump. Tim had forbidden her to come into the office until Monday, saying she needed extra time to recover from her trip and her flu, but she couldn't wait that long to check on Satchmo. However, she'd been cowardly enough to delay her visit until noon because she knew Adam would be so busy at The Aerie at lunchtime on a Saturday there would be no chance of running into him.

As it turned out, she had to track down Matt and Satchmo on one of the trails radiating out from Sharon's farm. The boy had gotten Sharon's permission to lead his convalescing whisper pony on leisurely walks, as long as he told her which trail he was taking and stuck to it. This path wound around the foot of a mountain and was edged by bare-limbed trees and rhododendron bushes with deep green, cold-curled leaves.

Matt ruffled Satchmo's pale bush of mane. "His coat is even starting to shine, sort of like a penny. I brush him every day."

Hannah ran her hand down the pony's shoulder. Matt was right about the burgeoning gloss of his coat. "I consulted with Sharon, and we agreed you should be able to start riding Satch in a few days. Slowly, of course, until he gets his strength back."

Her heart squeezed as Matt gave her a delighted grin. He looked so much like a younger, carefree version of his father. "You hear that, Satch. You get to start teaching me to ride again," he said into the pony's ear before turning back to Hannah. "Hey, you were really good on television. I think that senator is a major jerk, even if he's being all about animal-rights now. I'm glad you made him apologize where everyone could see it."

"Sometimes it's necessary to stand up for yourself," Hannah said, thinking it was a lesson Matt might need in the future. "The senator was hurting more people than just me. It was damaging Dr. Arbuckle's practice, and my former partners. That's why I decided to make it public."

"It got me out of school for the morning, so I was okay with it," Matt said.

Hannah resisted the urge to rumple his hair the way he'd done Satch's. She didn't think a thirteen-year-old would appreciate the gesture. "You go ahead and get Satchmo back in shape," she said, stepping off the trail so Matt could lead the pony past her.

She stood and watched the boy and pony amble up the slight slope of the wooded trail, Satchmo's tail gently swishing behind him. The bond between them was evident in the way Matt kept his free hand resting on Satchmo's neck, and the pony occasionally bumped his shoulder against the boy's side.

"It makes you believe in whisper horses."

Hannah jumped and spun around to find Adam standing in the middle of the path, his hands shoved into the pockets of a long, black coat hanging open over his working uniform of black suit, shirt, and tie. The late-autumn breeze ruffled his dark hair and sent the coat flapping around his long legs.

Her body seemed to catch fire, the heat licking along her skin. She yanked the zipper of her barn jacket down and let it blow open. "Why aren't you at The Aerie? It's lunchtime."

"I bribed one of the stable hands to call me if you showed up here," he said.

For a moment hope blossomed, but it withered again as she studied his unyielding stance. He didn't look like a man who'd come to admit he'd made a mistake. She copied his rigid pose by shoving her hands into her jacket pockets. "I see."

"Congratulations on getting the long-overdue apology from Sawyer," he said. "We watched it in the waiting room of the animal hospital. You managed it like a pro."

Hannah had heard about Tim's arrangements on her behalf, including Adam's donation of food. She remembered another reason she owed him gratitude. "Thanks for all the soup. It was delicious."

He nodded. They stood looking at each other for a long moment, the air between them crackling with tension. As she scanned his face, her heart twisted. There were shadows under his eyes, as though he hadn't slept well for some time, and the angles of his jaw looked sharp and tense.

He shifted slightly. "I hope you'll still come to Thanksgiving dinner. For Matt's sake."

She had to make her decision. The image of Matt's happy grin flashed through her mind. "I'll be there," she said. "For Matt's sake."

He flinched at her last words. "I'm sorry." His voice was so low she barely heard him.

"For what?"

"That you're not coming for my sake."

A flash of anger tempered her spine into steel. "You made that choice."

He dropped his gaze. "It was the right one."

Overwhelming sadness undercut the flare of anger. Pulling one hand out of her pocket, she waved it in a gesture of frustration. "But you still have the chance to make a different choice for Matt."

He shook his head. "We're going to Disney World the day after Thanksgiving."

She felt a flutter of hope, for Matt this time. Then she understood. This was Adam's farewell gift to his son. One long weekend of togetherness before he sent him away to the O'Briens. "I'm sorry for both of you," she said, grief slicing through her. "And what about Satchmo?"

"I'm still trying to work that out."

She tried one more time. "You're a better man than this."

A spasm of pain contorted his features for a moment. He took one hand out of his pocket and shoved it through his hair before he met her gaze straight on. "I came to say thank you. For saving Matt's whisper pony. For giving me a relationship with my son. For—," he took in a deep, shuddering breath. "For the time we had together."

She'd been wrong about the daily soup, and the food for Tim's party, and the invitation to Thanksgiving. They weren't an apology; they were a good-bye.

The wind pierced the cotton fabric of her polo shirt, making her shiver. With slow, deliberate motions she slotted the zipper back into its tab and pulled it upward until her jacket was closed all the way up to her chin.

He half-turned as though to go, and her body started to tremble with the churn of emotions. "I don't want to leave you here alone," he said.

"You've already done that." She curled her hands into fists in her pockets, digging the nails into her palms, willing him to go before she fell apart.

"Hannah, I . . ." He stopped with a huff of frustration before he pivoted and strode away, his coat billowing behind him.

Hannah held herself still until his silhouette vanished around a bend in the trail. Then she dropped to her knees on the frozen earth.

Chapter 28

I APPRECIATE YOU COMING TO MY HOME, DR. LINDEN," Louise Crickenberger said, as she opened her front door. "You've done so much for Ferdie, but now I think it's time to let him go." The elderly woman's voice cracked on the last words.

Hannah's grip tightened on the handles of her medical bag. She'd thought her Monday couldn't get any more miserable until Estelle caught her on her way out the office door at the end of the day, saying there was an urgent phone call.

"He could barely get up to do his business this morning." The elderly lady blotted her red-rimmed eyes with the tissue she was carrying. "Now his breathing sounds like it's hurting him something terrible."

"Let's make sure there's nothing we can do for him before we make the final decision," Hannah said, following her down the hall toward the back of the house.

By unspoken agreement, Tim had handled all euthanizing since Hannah came to Sanctuary, but this afternoon he was out delivering twin foals. Sawyer's ghost might have been banished, but Sophie's still haunted her.

Mrs. Crickenberger led her into a small den and gestured toward an upholstered chair. Ferdie lay stretched out on top of a tattered and stained yellow blanket, his eyes closed, his side rising and falling while his breath rattled in his throat. The small, brindled dog, with his floppy ears and long body, was a mix of so many breeds Hannah couldn't even guess at the dominant one.

She knelt beside the chair and pulled out her stethoscope, already knowing what she was going to hear. After listening to Ferdie's lungs and his heart, she took the earpieces out of her ears and turned to the older woman. "I'm very sorry, but his lungs are full of fluid and his heart is laboring. The best thing is to help him go without any further struggle."

Mrs. Crickenberger gave a sob as the tears streamed down her face, but she nodded. "I knew it was his time."

Hannah stood and put her arm around the woman. "Would you rather not be in the room when he goes? It will be very quick, and I'll hold him myself, I promise."

"No, I'll stay. I held my Tommy when he passed, so I'll be here for Ferdie too."

"You're very brave," Hannah said, meaning it. She moved her bag out of Mrs. Crickenberger's sight as she pulled out the syringe and calculated the proper dosage for Ferdie's body weight. Her hands shook slightly as she drew the liquid into the glass cylinder. She took a breath and counted to ten before letting it out. When she turned back to the woman, she held the syringe behind her back, both out of consideration for Mrs. Crickenberger and to conceal any nervous tremors.

The woman had gathered Ferdie up from the chair and sat down with the dog and his blanket on her lap. She stroked him and told him what a beautiful dog he was and what a wonderful companion he'd been to her, especially after her Tommy died. The dog's tail moved a fraction of an inch in an attempt to wag.

The knot of anxiety in Hannah's chest unraveled. This was what she had wished for Sophie's last days: being in her own home with someone she loved. Peace flowed through Hannah at the knowledge she was giving Ferdie this gift.

"If you want more time with him, I can wait in the other room," Hannah said. "There's no rush."

Mrs. Crickenberger looked up as two tears trickled down her cheeks. "That's kind of you, dear, but it won't change what needs to be done. You go ahead."

Hannah knelt again and gave the dog the injection as unobtrusively as she could. She rested her hand on his side, and it didn't take long before she felt his body go slack. Mrs. Crickenberger felt it too. She bent over her longtime companion and wept quietly.

Hannah slipped her stethoscope into her ears again and checked for a heartbeat. There was none.

She gave the little creature's fur one last stroke before she laid her hand on the woman's forearm. "I'm going to leave you with Ferdie for a little while. Then I'll take his body to the hospital."

Hannah retreated into a kitchen that hadn't been redone since the fifties, where she allowed herself to slump against the orange Formica countertop. Putting a dog to sleep always drained her emotionally, but she was relieved she'd finally gotten past the ghost of Sophie.

To distract herself, she drew her phone out of the medical bag to check for messages. She'd silenced it when she'd pulled up in front of Mrs. Crickenberger's house.

Five missed calls showed in the notifications bar, but no one had left a voicemail. When she swiped it down to look at the details, Adam's phone number came up for all of them.

"Why would he call me so many—?" A thought struck her. "Oh no, something's happened to Satchmo!"

She froze for a moment, torn between her sympathy for Mrs. Crickenberger's grief and her anxiety over Adam's repeated calls. Shoving the phone in her back pocket and slinging her medical kit over her shoulder, she tiptoed down the hall and peeked into the den. The elderly woman still sat in the chair, but she was carefully wrapping Ferdie's body in the blanket. She finished and looked up as Hannah stepped through the doorway. "I've said my good-byes. He's gone to heaven now, and it's time to let his body go back to the earth."

Hannah crossed the room to lift the little bundle from Mrs. Crickenberger's lap, cradling it against her chest. "I'll bring his ashes back to you tomorrow."

The woman gripped the arms of the chair and slowly pushed herself to her feet. She looked around the room as though she didn't recognize it before turning back to Hannah. "I hope it doesn't sound cold-hearted to you, but if you hear of another small dog who needs a good home, let me know."

"It's the opposite of cold-hearted," Hannah said. "It's warm and generous and perfect." She didn't want to rush her farewell, but the phone seemed heavy in her pocket. She started for the door. "I'll stop by tomorrow to see how you're doing."

"That'll give me a good reason to bake up a batch of snickerdoodles."

"Please don't go to any trouble for me." Hannah contained her impatience as she matched her steps to the slower pace of the elderly woman.

"No trouble at all. Baking will take my mind off Ferdie."

Hannah finally got out the front door with her burden and practically jogged to her Subaru. She placed Ferdie tenderly in the container she'd brought along, the blanket flecked with melting snowflakes. Then she leapt into the driver's seat and drove around the corner to park, so her car was out of Mrs. Crickenberger's sight.

It took her two tries and several swear words before she got the call to go through on the weak cell signal.

"Hannah!" Adam's voice sounded far away but his agitation came through the receiver clearly.

"Is it Satchmo?" Hannah braced herself.

"It's Matt. And Satchmo. They're gone."

"Gone! What do you mean 'gone'?"

There was a moment of silence before he spoke more calmly. "Matt took Satchmo out for a walk on the trail. He was supposed to be back half an hour ago. He's not answering his cell phone, and it's getting dark." Another silence before Adam spoke again. "I'm afraid he's run away."

Hannah stared through the windshield into the gathering gloom of the late-November afternoon. It had been spitting snow on and off all day, although none had accumulated on the ground yet. She didn't want to think about the boy and the pony wandering lost in the frigid darkness. "Sharon must know which trail he was taking. He always tells her."

"She's sent riders out on all the trails. No one's found them yet." She heard him draw in a ragged breath. "Please come."

"I'm already in my car. I'm going to put you on speaker." She hit the wireless connection and slotted the phone into its dashboard holder before putting the car in gear. "Have you called the police?"

"Not yet. I don't know if I should."

It spoke volumes about his state of mind that he couldn't decide. She hesitated for a moment as she turned onto the highway. "It wouldn't hurt. They could start looking on the roads."

"I don't want to scare him into hiding." Adam's voice was laced with anguish.

"Ask them to be subtle about it. No sirens. Talk to Robbie McGraw. He'll handle it the way you want."

"I'll call you back."

Hannah disconnected and hit the accelerator. She concentrated on steering her car through the sharp mountain curves so her mind wouldn't keep conjuring up images of Satchmo suffering the agony of a broken leg or Matt lying still at the bottom of a ravine. Or both.

One of Adam's comments nagged at her. Why would he think Matt had run away? They were going to Disney World. Surely the boy was looking forward to that.

Then she remembered. Today was the Monday before Thanksgiving, and Matt's newly discovered relatives would be arriving in two days. Had Adam said something to his son about going to live with them?

The car skidded on a turn, and she eased her pressure on the accelerator. Her headlights lit the thickening snowfall, and she swore at the weather as anxiety began to tighten her throat.

At last she turned through the brick gateposts marking Healing Springs Stables. The barns were ablaze with lights when she parked in the lot. She was relieved to see a police car pulled up in front of the big stable door. Robbie must have been close by when Adam called.

Grabbing her medical bag and dashing across the whitening gravel, she collided with Sharon as she ran through the barn door. "Whoa there, doc," the other woman said, grabbing Hannah's arm to steady her. "We don't need *you* gettin' hurt."

Hannah froze. "Did you find them? Is someone hurt?"

"No, no sign of them yet," Sharon said with a shake of her head.

Her spike of fear eased. "Where's Adam?"

Sharon nodded toward the barn's central corridor. Hannah pivoted and saw Adam talking to a police officer whose back was to her. "What's happening now?" she asked Sharon.

The woman's face went grim. "I just called in all my riders. It's too dark to risk the horses out there any longer. If they haven't found them by now, they're not on any of the trails."

Hannah fought back her panic as she walked toward Adam, who was too engrossed in his conversation to notice her. He wore his standard casual attire of black jeans and a black leather jacket.

How could she still feel that gut-deep thrill at the sight of him when he'd been so brutal about ending things between them?

Then she saw his face, and compassion swamped every other emotion. His eyes were haunted, and the lines around his mouth were so sharp they appeared to be carved into his skin. He looked like a man who'd lost everything.

His gaze shifted from the policeman to her, and for a moment his eyes lit with relief and welcome. "Hannah!" He said something to the officer and strode forward to meet her, his hands outstretched with the palms up. She saw the exact moment when he realized he no longer could expect her to greet him with the same warmth.

But this was not the time to deny him whatever comfort she could give. She took his hands in hers, feeling the heat and strength of his touch. "I—" he began before shaking his head, the momentary light extinguished from his gaze.

"I have an idea," she said, leaping past the awkwardness. "You said Trace was trained as a police dog. I think you should bring him here, along with a piece of Matt's clothing. Maybe he can help us find Matt and Satch."

"Why didn't I think of that?" His grip tightened on her hands as hope flickered across his face. "I'll call my housekeeper, Sarah. Trace will get in the car with her, I'm sure." He released one of her hands to brush his fingertips down her cheek. "I knew you would help." He let go of her other hand and pulled out his cell phone, walking away to make the call.

Hannah shivered as his touch seemed to ricochet through her. Scrubbing at her cheek to erase the sensation, she hurried to join Sharon and Robbie McGraw, the police officer. They were discussing where the trails intersected the local roads and highways while the policeman took notes.

"We'll use unmarked cars," Robbie said, "so we don't spook them. I'll get on the radio in my cruiser and direct the search."

He flipped his notebook closed and blew out a breath. "In this weather, we need to find them sooner rather than later."

As the officer walked away, Sharon turned to Hannah, worry disrupting her normally unflappable calm. "I just don't see Matt doing something as irresponsible as running away with Satchmo. He loves that pony and he wouldn't risk having him come to harm."

"Adam's arranging to get his dog Trace here. I think we should take the dog out on the trail Matt said he was taking. If anyone can find a boy and a pony, it's a police-trained German Shepherd."

"That's using your noggin," Sharon said. "Let's get a search party equipped."

"I think we should keep it to Adam and me," Hannah said. "If Matt is hiding for some reason, he might not want to show himself to a large group. He trusts me, so I'm hoping he'll respond if he sees or hears me."

Adam walked up to them in time to hear her last comment. A shadow crossed his face, but he nodded in agreement. "Sarah's bringing Trace as fast as she can."

Sharon pulled a paper from her jacket pocket and unfolded it. "Here's the same trail map I gave Matt. He told me he was taking the Rhododendron Trail." She traced a green line that wound along the foot of the mountain in a misshapen loop, twice crossing a blue line marked "Second Creek."

"How deep's the creek?" Hannah asked.

"Depends," Sharon said. "But this time of year it wouldn't be above Matt's waist, even at the deepest point. And those bridges are solid. We inspect them every six months."

A fleeting look of relief crossed Adam's face as he tucked the map into the pocket of his jeans.

Sharon eyed his fashionable jacket and smooth-soled leather boots. "While we're waiting for Trace, let's get you two some warm clothes and a thermos of hot chocolate for when you find Matt. Neither one of you is dressed for hiking through the woods in the snow."

She led the way to the tack room, where she pulled open a door to reveal a walk-in closet housing a kaleidoscopic array of boots, jackets, gloves, and hats. "People leave stuff here all the time and never claim it. If you can't find anything that fits, let me know, and I'll borrow something from one of the stable hands." She left them alone in the small space, saying she would be back with the thermos. "And I'll load your medical supplies into the backpack as well."

Feeling Adam's presence acutely, Hannah pulled a puffy, quilted jacket in bright turquoise off a hook. "Too small." She hung it back up and randomly yanked down a black fleece.

"I had no right to call you." His voice vibrated down her spine.

She turned to face him, hugging the fleece to her chest. "What happened between us doesn't change my feelings for Matt . . . or Satchmo."

His posture sagged but his gaze never left her face. "Your feelings for me have changed, though."

It was almost a question, but Hannah wasn't going to answer it. Her feelings for him had *not* changed. That was the problem. She turned and blindly snatched another coat, fumbling at the collar for the tag.

She sensed him behind her before he took her shoulders in a gentle grip. "Thank you for being here." His breath moved through her hair, so she knew his lips were very close.

"We'll find them," she said, fighting the urge to lean back against him.

As she'd half-hoped, the reminder of their purpose made him release her. She heard fabric rustle against fabric. When she glanced over her shoulder, he'd shed his jacket to reveal a black silk T-shirt.

Wrenching her gaze away from the column of his throat, she focused her attention on locating the right clothes. It took only a few minutes, despite the distraction of Adam shrugging into a maroon ski jacket mere inches from her.

"You couldn't find a black one?" she asked without thinking, as she wound an orange-and-blue wool scarf around her neck.

The ghost of a smile touched his lips. "I'm branching out." He thrust his hands into the jacket's pockets and pulled out a black ski glove from each one. "Not far, though."

She looked down at his boots. "You're not going to get far in the snow in those." Luckily, she was wearing the Timberland boots Matt had teased her about, now scuffed to fashion perfection. The memory of that first tentative connection over his red high-tops brought her fear back to the forefront. "It'll be quicker if we both look through these. What size do you wear?"

"Ten and a half," he said, removing his unsuitable shoes. As he padded over to the footwear shelf in his stocking feet, a pang of memory hit her. She remembered him stretched out in front of the fire, wearing his trousers with his long, narrow feet bare. She shoved the image away and grabbed the first boot on the shelf.

"Not my style," he said, as she looked down to see pink and purple kitties prancing across the child-sized rubber footgear.

"I was moving it," she said, setting it on the floor and choosing a giant L. L. Bean boot. It was a size 13.

"Got them," he said, dropping a black, furry mukluk on the floor beside his feet.

"Still with the black." It felt comfortable and somehow right to be teasing him about his clothing choices to distract him from the frightening situation. Yet he wanted to cut her off from that kind of intimacy.

She tugged a balaclava over her head, tucking the mouth covering down under her chin before she shoved her hands into a pair of insulated purple mittens. "I'll see you outside," she said, barging out the door.

She found a hay bale to sit on in the barn's corridor. The riders had returned and were swinging saddles off the backs of steaming horses before rubbing them down and leading them back to their stalls. The usual barrage of humorous insults was absent; the riders took care of their mounts with swift efficiency before congregating near the tack room door.

Adam emerged, the borrowed clothes looking as though they'd been styled just for him. One of the stable hands stopped him. "We want to go out on foot to keep looking."

He surprised her by saying, "I'll take all the help I can get. I'm bringing in a tracking dog, so let's talk to your boss about how to coordinate our efforts."

Sharon emerged from a nearby door, and the group converged on her, making their offer again. She glanced at Adam with a question in her eyes. He nodded his permission. Within minutes she had parceled out assignments and sent off several grooms to locate more flashlights. "But nobody moves until we give the dog a chance to work," she reminded them.

A murmur of assent went up from the group as they settled around the corridor in small clumps, speaking quietly among themselves out of respect for a father's worry.

Hannah sat on the hay bale, listening to the soothing sounds of the horses munching on hay, rattling water buckets, and rustling around in their bedding. She wanted to close her eyes and let the scent of the big, warm bodies calm her, but she couldn't tear her gaze away from the figure pacing back and forth in front of the half-open barn door, his gaze swinging out to search the thickening snowfall every few seconds.

Finally he was rewarded with the flash of headlights and the sound of car tires crunching over the gravel. Hannah shoved to her feet as the engine went quiet, and a dark shape streaked in through the door. Adam knelt to press his face against Trace's thick fur for a brief moment, and she knew he was drawing comfort from the dog's presence. Then he rose to take a folded bundle of fabric from the woman who hurried through the doorway.

Hannah walked up to the two of them, greeting the housekeeper before she turned to Adam. "Sharon's bringing something of Satchmo's too. Can he handle two scents at once?"

Adam frowned. "I'm not sure. Maybe I could hold them together and give him the command."

Sharon jogged up the corridor, carrying a flashlight, a lantern, a backpack, and a saddle pad. Adam grabbed the backpack and shrugged it on before Hannah could object, so she took the lantern and flashlight. Adam bunched Matt's shirt and Satchmo's saddle pad together in one hand and reached for the flashlight.

"One last thing," Sharon said, pulling a long-distance walkie-talkie out of her back pocket. "This is better than a cell phone up here in the mountains. Give me a beep with this every fifteen minutes, so I know you're still searching. And holler if you need any help."

Sharon's brief instructions left unsaid all the possible scenarios of disaster that none of them wanted to contemplate. "I'll take that," Hannah said, holding out her hand for the walkie-talkie and looking at Adam. "You'll need to keep an eye on Trace."

He nodded, his mouth a grim, straight line.

Hannah switched on the lantern. "Let's go."

Chapter 29

Yanking up her balaclava, Hannah stepped out into the swirling snow. The weather was going to make Trace's job more difficult. She prayed Matt and Satchmo were together so the boy could use the pony's body heat to stave off the cold.

"Damn it," Adam muttered beside her, obviously plagued by thoughts similar to hers. He set off at a fast walk, with Trace's dark shape gliding along beside him. Hannah had to jog to keep up, but she didn't complain.

They wound past the barns and paddocks, arriving at the beginning of the trail Sharon had pointed out on the map. Adam knelt beside Trace and let the dog snuffle at the bundle of fabrics in his hand. He stroked the dog's sleek head once before saying in a voice almost harsh with command, "Go find!"

Trace's big, triangular ears flicked straight up as he took one last look at his master before lifting his nose into the snowy air and sniffing.

Hannah watched in fascination as Trace cast back and forth across the trail, first with nose up and then with nose to the ground. Adam had the flashlight turned on but aimed away from the dog so as not to distract him. She held her breath, waiting for some sign the dog had picked up a scent.

Trace stopped and looked down the trail with a whine.

"Go find!" Adam repeated. Once again, the dog looked at him before he set off at a trot, his nose lifted.

"I think he's got something, but it must be faint," he said, turning the flashlight on the trail just in front of them. "Otherwise he'd be more excited."

Disappointment nagged at her as they started after Trace. "You don't think he's confused by having two scents to follow, do you?"

"I wish I knew." Adam was silent for several strides. "Trace has bonded with Matt, so I'm sure he recognizes that scent. And the pony is so much bigger his trail should be easy to follow."

Hannah pinged Sharon on the walkie-talkie and jogged a couple of steps to match Adam's long stride. The trail was well manicured; no roots or rocks offered hazards to stumble over. Which meant Matt and Satchmo must have wandered off it. Or had deliberately left it. "Why did you say Matt might have run away?"

The silence lasted so long she thought he wouldn't answer. "He doesn't want the O'Briens to come for Thanksgiving."

"He knows your plans?"

"*I* don't know my plans." His tone was abrupt.

Surprise made Hannah stumble slightly, and his grip closed like a vise on her elbow as he steadied and released her. The pressure of his hand lingered. Was he having second thoughts about the adoption? Hope bloomed inside her.

"Did I hurt you?" he asked.

She realized she was rubbing her elbow where he'd grabbed her. She dropped her hand. "No, I'm fine."

He pointed the beam of the flashlight into the flake-filled darkness in front of them, just catching the gleam of Trace's coat as the German Shepherd zigzagged across the path. The dog continued to move forward, which encouraged Hannah.

The trail left the cleared land of Sharon's farm and plunged into the woods, the heavy rhododendron thickets on either side of it creating a narrow tunnel. The snowfall became lighter as some of the flakes were caught on overarching branches.

"After you left on Tuesday, I—" He sounded as though the words were forcing themselves out of his throat. "I went to The Aerie. To the wine cellar."

A terrible pressure squeezed Hannah's chest. She'd driven him back to his addiction. "I'm so sorry."

"That's not why I'm telling you. I picked out the best bottle of wine down there, opened it, and filled a glass to the brim. I took a mouthful of it, a spectacular 1989 Pétrus."

Her free hand clenched into a fist as regret tore through her.

"And then I spit it out." He made a jagged sound that was meant to be a laugh. "I poured an entire six-thousand-dollar bottle of Pétrus down the sink."

"That's—that's wonderful!" She fought down the urge to throw her arms around him.

"Your face stopped me."

"My face?"

"It was there in front of me, and I couldn't disappoint you again."

She forced herself to keep walking beside him, even though she wanted to step in front of him to see his expression. "I–I'm glad you found the strength to fight it."

"I came far too close," he said. "Closer than I've come in years."

"You stopped!" She nearly shrieked at him. Why couldn't he see it as an act of strength instead of weakness?

"I shouldn't have started." He shone the flashlight ahead again. Trace had his nose to the ground twenty feet in front of them. The dog whined as the beam fell on him. Adam brought the circle of light in closer to them. "What happens the next time Matt pulls something like this? What keeps me from the Pétrus then?"

"I'll give you a photograph of myself you can pin up in the wine cellar," Hannah said, frustration driving her to sarcasm.

The sound of rushing water sounded in the tense stillness between them. She hadn't heard it before because she'd been so engrossed in her conversation with Adam. They must be approaching the first bridge over Second Creek. Not sure how much time had passed, Hannah hit the beeper on the walkie-talkie again. Adam pointed his light farther forward, picking up the metal railings of the short span.

Trace was nowhere in sight.

As one, they broke into a run, pounding up onto the wooden planks of the bridge.

"Trace!" Adam called, the surface of the stream glittering as he skimmed the flashlight's beam along the banks. "Come, boy!"

A short bark sounded from somewhere ahead and to their right. Adam sprinted up the trail, while Hannah ran behind. She could see the dog's footprints mingled with Adam's in the light dusting of snow.

"He's gone off the trail here," Adam called to her, stopping on the edge of the path and shining his light into the dense woods. "It's going to be tough to follow him through the rhodie thicket."

"He didn't come back when you called," Hannah said as she came up beside him. "That must mean he's caught a strong scent."

"I hope you're right." He pushed into the woods a few feet. "I'd tell you to wait here, but you've got the medical skills, so I have to ask you to come with me. Stay close behind me so you don't get slapped by the branches."

She didn't bother to tell him he couldn't have stopped her from following him.

They moved slowly through the trees, the sound of water growing louder. Now that they were off the trail, Hannah kept her gaze down to watch for stones, roots, and uneven ground. A dark patch she thought was a shadow turned out to be a rock. She stepped on it and twisted her ankle, clutching the back of Adam's quilted ski jacket to stop herself from falling.

He turned and caught her by the elbows. "Are you all right?"

"Thanks to Timberland I am," she said, testing her weight on the turned ankle. It was painful but it held her up.

"I'll go more slowly."

"Not on my account." She gave him a little push. "Move!"

She wasn't sure if he slowed down deliberately or because the trees grew so thick that it was hard to walk.

"Oof!" Adam had come to an abrupt halt, and she ran right into his back.

"Sorry," he said, his attention elsewhere. "There isn't enough snow on the ground to follow Trace's tracks here." The beam of light probed all around them.

The stream's rush had increased to a dull roar, blocking out any softer sounds. The thick, leathery leaves of rhododendrons and the intertwining tree branches formed a dense wall, so even Adam's powerful beam could only scour the ground in the small spaces between them.

Tears of frustration pricked at the back of Hannah's eyes. All they could do was stand there and hope Trace barked again or came back to them.

Adam must have sensed her distress because his arm came around her. "He'll let us know when he finds them," he said.

She couldn't help it. She leaned against him, letting her head drop against his shoulder. Her ankle throbbed, and cold was seeping through her jeans, but the strength of his arm and the solidity of his chest made her discomfort fade away. They stood in the near-embrace as he continued to probe the woods with the flashlight, illuminating nothing but ranks of bare, gray tree trunks and hulking clumps of bushes.

A volley of distant barks made them jump and shift away from each other. Adam aimed his flashlight in the direction of Trace's voice.

"Those are happy barks," Hannah said, cocking her head to listen. "He's found someone he's glad to see."

"Trace! Show me!" Adam shouted. She could see him practically vibrating with the need to move, but he was controlling himself until he knew where to go.

More barks, this time closer.

Adam started toward the sound, calling Trace and pushing branches out of his way as he went. Hannah followed at a safe distance so she didn't get smacked in the face by the spring-back. Either the dog was moving closer or they were going the right way because it was becoming easier to pinpoint Trace's location.

Suddenly a black shape streaked into Adam's flashlight beam. "Good boy!" Adam said, letting the excited dog jump on him as he praised and stroked him. "You're the best boy. Now, show me!"

Trace dashed off into the woods about fifteen feet before stopping to look over his shoulder at them.

"You go ahead," Hannah said, knowing Adam's long legs could carry him to Matt and Satchmo faster without her. "I can follow your light."

"Thank you," he said. He shocked her by pulling her against him for a brief, hard embrace. Then he was gone, his silhouette almost as dark as Trace's as the two of them wove through the trees.

Adam cursed as he tripped over a protruding root, but he didn't lessen his steady tracking of the dog. Thank God he'd found the strength to face his demons without alcohol. It was hard enough to navigate the dense woods stone-cold sober.

"Dad! Trace! Are you there?" The distant sound of Matt's voice flooded him with a relief that nearly made his knees buckle. At the same time, he felt an overwhelming urge to run, as though some sort of rope stretched between him and his son, and Matt's voice had pulled it taut.

"Matt! I'm coming!" he shouted, charging on, ignoring the branches that slashed across his face and thighs. The water's sound grew as he moved forward.

"Dad! We're over here!" The combination of joy and pleading in Matt's voice galvanized Adam into greater speed. Trace sensed his master's urgency and broke into a lope as Adam crashed along behind him.

The dog disappeared from view, and Adam pulled up just in time to avoid plunging down a sharply sloped embankment. His wavering flashlight caught the reflective glow of Trace's eyes as the dog looked up at his master from ten feet below and barked.

"Dad! Careful, it's steep!" Matt's voice came from below and to the left. "Satchmo and I fell down it."

Adam swung the beam toward the sound, spotlighting the boy standing, his hand shading his eyes, and the pony lying down with his legs tucked under him. Skidding down the muddy slope, Adam reached his son in three strides, sweeping the boy into his arms and holding him hard against him. "Matt! Thank God, you're all right."

"Dad, I'm sorry," Matt sobbed, his grip on his father as convulsive as Adam's. "I couldn't leave Satchmo."

"I know," Adam said, holding him and stroking Matt's snow-dampened hair as the boy shuddered against him.

He also knew that he was never going to let go of Matt again. No matter what it took, he was keeping his son. As the certainty swept through him, a sense of peace followed it, spreading a warm light that chased away the shadows shrouding his soul.

Hannah! Without releasing his son, he turned in the direction he'd come from and shouted, "Hannah! Wait! There's a dangerous drop-off. I'll come get you!" Squinting upward through the falling snow, he thought he saw the glow of her lantern.

"Okay," he heard her call back. "Did you find them?"

"Yes," he yelled. He took Matt by the shoulders and looked into his son's face. "I have to get Dr. Linden. I'll be right back."

Matt nodded as a shiver rattled his teeth. Adam remembered the thermos and shrugged out of the backpack's straps, handing it to Matt. "There's hot chocolate in here. It'll warm you up."

Adam shoved the flashlight into his pocket and scrambled up the embankment, using branches and rocks as hand and footholds. At the top he cupped his hands around his mouth. "Hannah?"

"Here!" A glow swayed to his left. She must be swinging her lantern to make it easier for him to see her.

"Got it. I'm on my way."

He dodged through the underbrush and found her leaning against a tree trunk, rocking her lantern in front of her. He wanted to enfold her in his arms and tell her of his decision, but he needed to make some amends first.

"How are they?" she asked, pushing off the tree and starting toward him.

"Matt is cold but seems fine. Satchmo is lying down. Matt says the pony fell down the hill."

"I hope nothing's broken."

"Are you limping?" he asked, noticing a stutter in her gait as they hit a relatively clear stretch.

"It's just a little sore from when I twisted it." She waved his concern away.

The least he could do was carry her to the top of the slope. He stopped and turned his back to her, saying over his shoulder. "Put your arms around my neck and jump up."

"What? No, I can walk." She gimped past him.

"Hannah, please. We need you in good shape." It also would allow him to touch her before the amends.

"Oh, fine." Her tone was grudging, but she wound her arms around his neck and gave a hop so he could catch her behind the knees and lift her upward.

Her warm breath tickled his ear. Having her thighs wrapped around his waist brought back vivid and erotic memories. He hoped like hell his amends would be good enough.

As she slid down from Adam's back at the top of the embankment, Hannah squeezed her eyes closed to imprint this last touch of his body against hers. It eased the pain of her twisted ankle. He went partway down the steep slope and braced himself before reaching up to her and saying, "Take my hands and lean on me. I've got a good foothold here."

She put her hands in both of his, trusting the power and steadiness of his grip. When her wonky foot slithered out from under her, he brought her against him for balance, their bodies synchronized in a way that echoed more intimate times.

At the bottom of the drop, he released her hands but wrapped one arm around her waist to take the weight off her ankle as he guided her to Matt and Satchmo. The boy stood beside the pony in a slight hollow filled with fallen leaves while Trace paced around them. A big rhododendron loomed above, providing some shelter from the snow and wind.

"Dr. Linden, I'm really sorry," Matt said. "I should never have taken Satchmo off the path, but he kept turning toward the sound of the water, like he was thirsty."

"It's okay, Matt. You didn't know he'd fall down the embankment." Matt looked so upset that Hannah gave his shoulder a quick squeeze. "Now tell me what happened."

Matt thrust his hand through his tousled hair in a gesture so like Adam's it made Hannah wince. She turned toward the pony, holding up the lantern. Satchmo blinked placidly in the electric light. He didn't appear to be in any immediate distress.

"I thought the water was close because it sounded so loud," Matt said, "so I just turned off the path and went toward it. It was still light enough to see, but I didn't expect that cliff to be there. Satch and I both kind of stumbled and skidded down it." Matt rubbed the back of his neck. "It was weird because I didn't see Satch hit any rocks or branches or anything but when we got to the bottom, he started limping real bad. I was afraid he might have broken something, so I led him over here and got him to lie down."

Matt bent down to stroke the pony's neck. "Then I tried to call the stable, but my cell phone's battery had died because it kept trying to find a signal and there wasn't one." His voice took on a burden of guilt. "I usually turn it off when I walk up here, but I forgot."

"You wouldn't have gotten a signal anyway," Adam said, putting his hand on Matt's shoulder. "Sharon sent us out with a walkie-talkie."

"Oh my goodness, I forget to tell Sharon we found them!" Hannah yanked the walkie-talkie out of her pocket.

"I'll do it," Adam said, taking the device from her. "You take care of Satchmo." He walked a few feet away, and Hannah heard a crackle of static and then Sharon's voice.

"Everyone from the stable went out searching for you," Hannah said, thinking it would make Matt feel better. "I guess you couldn't hear them because of the water, but they would have found you eventually."

Instead the boy gave her a look of dismay. "I didn't hear anyone."

Hannah knelt to run her hands over the pony's folded legs. "Which leg was he favoring?"

"I think it was the right front one." Matt squatted beside her, his brow furrowed. "It was kind of hard to tell because I didn't want to make him walk too far."

"There are no significant wounds, and I don't feel any noticeable breaks." She breathed out a sigh of relief. "Let's see if we can get him on his feet."

Matt went to Satchmo's head and wrapped his fingers around the cheek strap of the halter. Hannah forced herself not to limp as she went around to the other side of the pony. She didn't want Matt worrying about her too. Butting her shoulder against Satchmo's, she nodded to Matt.

"C'mon, Satch. Let's get up." Matt tugged and Hannah pushed.

Anticipating serious resistance, she nearly fell over when Satch surged obediently to his feet. "Well, that was easier than I expected." She pointed to a more open space. "Can you take him over there?"

Matt led the pony forward. Satchmo stumbled as he put weight on his right front hoof, and Matt stopped.

Hannah bent to probe down the leg with her fingers. "If there's a fracture, I can't find it. Could be hairline, so we'll need an X-ray. There's a little swelling around the knee, but nothing serious. The cold ground may have acted like a natural ice pack. Walk him a little farther."

Adam came up beside her, watching the pony as well. "Sharon's on her way with help." Satchmo took several more steps. "He doesn't seem that bad, does he?"

Matt wore a look of puzzlement. "He was limping a lot worse before. You know, with his head bobbing up and down every time he took a step."

Hannah checked his other three legs thoroughly. She didn't want to miss something. Stepping back, she let her hand rest on Satchmo's back as she frowned down at him. "I think he can walk back to the stable, as long as we can avoid that embankment."

"I'll find a way." Adam swung his flashlight up and strode along the foot of the slope, fading into the snow and darkness with Trace trailing along behind him.

Hannah knelt by Satchmo's right front leg, picking it up and bending it back and forth, watching for a reaction. All Satchmo did was turn his head to look at her and blow out a loud breath.

"Do you think Dad's mad at me?" Matt asked in a low voice.

Startled, Hannah glanced up to find the boy staring down at her. "Gosh, no! He's hugely relieved that you're okay."

Matt looked away. "I made a lot of trouble today. I mean, the stable hands looking for me and you hiking all the way out here in the dark and the snow. "

Her heart twisted as she realized he was afraid he'd given his father another reason to send him away. She shoved herself out of her squat. "I promise you he's not mad. He loves you, which means he was terrified something bad had happened to you. But now that we've found you and Satch, everything is fine."

Matt seemed unconvinced, but their conversation was ended by Adam's appearance out of the gloom. "The land flattens out that way," he said, pointing behind him. "Satch won't have any trouble negotiating it."

A heartbreaking mix of relief and uncertainty flitted across Matt's face when his father put his arm around the boy's shoulders and smiled down at him. "Did the chocolate warm you up?"

"It was so hot I burned my tongue."

"Good." Adam lifted his gaze to Hannah. "How're you doing?"

"What's wrong with Dr. Linden?" Matt swung around toward her.

"Nothing. I just stepped on a rock wrong."

"If Satchmo wasn't lame, I'd put the doc on his back," Adam said. "But it looks like she's getting another piggyback ride." He let go of Matt and turned his back to her. "Up you go."

Hannah stared at the expanse of ski jacket. Adam sounded almost playful. It must be that the release of tension after finding Matt was making him giddy.

"Thanks, but I can walk." She wasn't going to subject herself to the delicious torment of being draped over his back again.

"Too undignified for you?" She thought she saw his teeth flash in a smile. "Then lean on me." He pivoted to snake his arm around her waist, the firmness of his grip telling her she wasn't going to win this argument. "Matt, you take the lantern and follow right behind us."

As they set off, Adam drew her close against him so their hips jostled against each other as they walked. He let her set the pace, shortening his stride to a mere saunter as he threw frequent glances over his shoulder to check on Matt. Trace ranged back and forth beside them, his eyes occasionally blazing in the flashlight's beam.

What a strange little procession they made, yet contentment warmed Hannah. Despite her aching ankle and the sting of spitting snow, she relished the movement of Adam's body against hers, the arrhythmic thud of Satchmo's hooves as he limped along, Matt's murmured encouragement to the pony, and the jingle of Trace's dog tags.

Cocooned in the dark embrace of the woods, they could almost be a family.

"Hey, anyone out there?" Sharon's voice echoed through the woods, tearing the fabric of Hannah's illusion to shreds.

Soon the rescue party located them. A bevy of helpful stable hands attended to Satchmo, while Sharon handed Hannah a pair of crutches, removing her need to lean on Adam. When the cavalcade arrived back at the stable, Sharon insisted on icing and bandaging Hannah's ankle. Adam had come into the tack room to thank her before he took Matt home to a warm bed, but all the activity swirling around her had kept his acknowledgement formal and brief. He hadn't even given her a peck on the cheek.

Hannah couldn't decide if she felt cheated or relieved.

Chapter 30

THE NEXT AFTERNOON, HANNAH AND SHARON STOOD in the middle of the indoor riding ring, scrutinizing Satchmo as Lynnie led the pony back and forth in front of them. The snow had piled up during the night, so half a dozen other horses and riders circled around the outer path, the jingle and creak of their tack composing a soft music.

Other than a slightly swollen knee, Satchmo showed no ill effects from his previous day's misadventure.

"If that pony were a human, I'd say he faked the whole thing," Sharon said, crossing her arms.

"You don't think Matt got scared by the fall and overreacted?" Hannah changed positions to examine Satchmo from a different angle.

"Didn't he tell you Satch's head was bobbing up and down as he limped? No way Matt made that up."

"Maybe lying down on the cold ground for a couple of hours reduced the swelling and numbed the pain. I'll give you some more bute, in case he stiffens up, but otherwise I'd just continue to ice the knee," Hannah said, rummaging around in her medical duffel for the medication.

Her stomach growled, reminding her she'd skipped lunch to check on the pony. She hadn't waited until after work because she couldn't bear to run into Adam. Or Matt. She was afraid the boy would ask her more questions about his father, and she didn't have the energy to dance around the answers.

The throb of her twisted ankle and the tangle of emotions had kept her tossing and turning all night. She was exhausted physically and mentally. And she still had to face returning Ferdie's ashes to Mrs. Crickenberger. At least Satchmo was miraculously unscathed.

As she pulled the bottle of phenylbutazone tablets from her bag, she caught sight of a man's legs visible under Satchmo's belly. Clad in black trousers with a knife-sharp crease in the front and shod in elegant, black loafers marred by clots of damp sawdust, they could only belong to one person. She briefly closed her eyes to brace herself before she straightened to face Adam on the other side of the pony, his hands thrust into the pockets of his long, black overcoat.

"I never got the chance to thank you properly for all you did last night," he said.

She frowned. Something about him nagged at her, although at least the sharp lines around his mouth had eased. "There's no need. Everyone pitched in to look for Matt and Satchmo." She did a quick visual scan, drawing on her medical training in observing patients. "You're wearing a red scarf! And a red shirt!"

He freed a hand from his pocket to pick up the corner of the burgundy wool scarf, gazing down at it with a half-smile. "Matt loaned it to me. The shirt is from Walmart. I didn't have time to shop elsewhere."

"Oh." Thrown off balance, she turned to hand the bute to Sharon.

"How's Satch this morning?" Adam asked, running his palm along the pony's spine.

"He's made a remarkable recovery. There's a slight swelling in his knee," Hannah pointed, "but he barely limps now."

Adam's gaze went to Sharon. "I wonder if a whisper pony knows when he needs to exaggerate an injury."

"Since ponies are even smarter than horses, it wouldn't surprise me at all," the horsewoman said.

Lynnie snorted and shook her head.

Hannah grabbed the handles of her medical kit. "I have another appointment, so I have to head out."

"I brought you a gift," Adam said, reaching into his pocket and pulling out a small glass jar. He held it out over the pony's back, the scars on his fingers showing clearly in the sun.

Hannah sucked in a breath. She could see tiny round fish eggs pressed against the jar's side. Her eyes flew to his face as she took his expensive offering and cradled its cold, smooth weight in her palm. "Thank you."

Was he giving her this as an expensive thank you gift? Or was he sending her a more intimate message? She tucked it into her jacket pocket.

"May I speak with you a moment?" Adam asked, his gaze intent on her face.

She kept a firm hold on the duffel and didn't move. "Sure." Sharon started to signal Lynnie to lead Satchmo away, but Hannah sent her a pleading look. She wanted the pony between her and Adam.

He looked discomfited for a moment before the half-smile kicked up again. "I guess public amends are required." He took a step closer, so only the width of Satchmo's back was between them. "I'm adopting Matt. Paul Taggart started the process this morning. And Matt and I are going to swim with the dolphins in Disney World."

Joy for both Matt and his father surged through her. No wonder the strain in Adam's face had smoothed away. He'd wrestled his demons to the ground at last. "I'm so happy for you and

Matt." It was inadequate, but she couldn't throw her arms around him and kiss him. Hopefully, her wide smile told him enough.

She remembered Sharon and Lynnie could hear and wondered why they didn't jump in with congratulations. When she glanced in their direction, she caught expressions of rapt attention on their faces. Evidently, they didn't want to interrupt the conversation.

Adam laid both hands flat on Satch's back, leaning inward. "You were right. I can work out the details as long as Matt and I are together. It took a whisper pony and a woman brave enough to be brutally honest to convince me of it."

Hannah felt a flush heat her face.

"There's more you were right about." He breathed in. "The Aerie isn't enough. I tried to make it be, but what's that old saying? No one ever dies wishing they'd spent more time at work." He looked down at his fingers spread on the pony's reddish coat. "The emptiness I have inside me can't be filled by more hours at the restaurant or even by six-thousand-dollar bottles of Pétrus, although I certainly tried. It needs people to fill it. People I love."

His hands curled into fists. "Stupidly, I've pushed away those people. I thought I was being noble and unselfish, but you were right about what I really was." He looked straight into her eyes. "A coward."

Hannah heard a gasp from one of the women standing stock still at Satchmo's head, but she couldn't look away from the bleak honesty in Adam's gaze. She made a gesture toward the entrance to the riding ring. "Please, we can go—"

He shook his head. "I owe you this." Opening his hands, he held them out across Satchmo's back, palms up in invitation.

She dropped the duffel with a thud and put her hands in his, loving the heat and texture of his skin.

His voice dropped low. "I have no right to ask you this, but will you forgive me and try again?"

She wanted to leap across Satchmo and wrap her arms around Adam's neck. Instead she tightened her grip on his hands and said, "Yes! Absolutely, yes!"

"Oh, for heaven's sake, Lynnie, move the pony so she can kiss him," Sharon ordered, laughter in her voice.

Satchmo disappeared from between them, but Adam didn't instantly pull her into his arms. He closed his eyes a moment as though to absorb her response. When he opened them, she saw hope there. Still he didn't move. "I will always be an alcoholic, Hannah. It's a disease. But I swear to you I will fight it with every molecule of my being. And I will win."

She stopped waiting for him. Pulling her hands from his, she threw herself against him, seizing his lapels to bring herself closer. "Matt and I will be right beside you. *We* will win."

His arms came around her, and he bent his head to brush her lips with his. "Thank you," he breathed against her cheek.

She let go of his coat and threaded her fingers through his glorious, waving hair, smiling into his eyes. "Thank Satchmo, not me." She had no chance to say anything more because he swooped down on her mouth, no longer gentle with gratitude. His hands flattened on her back and her waist, pressing her against him as though he were trying to merge their bodies together. She moved her grip to his shoulders, digging her fingers into the fine wool.

His touch sent delicious zings of electric sensation fizzing through her body, and she hummed with anticipation at the thought of where he would kiss her later when they were alone.

"You two are makin' my heart go pitter-patter, but I got kids in here." Sharon's voice made Hannah try to pull away from Adam, but his grip on her was too tight. All she could do was turn her head to see the horsewoman grinning at them, Satchmo by her side. Sharon held out her hand. "Here's the key to the tack room. I'm not the only one who has a key, so make sure you throw the bolt after you go in."

Adam laughed. "As tempting as that is, I think we can find a more comfortable place to continue."

"Hey, you haven't lived until you've done it in a tack room," Sharon said, putting the key back in her pocket. She gave Satchmo's lead line a tug. "Your work here is done, whisper pony."

Hannah wriggled free of Adam's embrace and walked over to plant a kiss on the pony's velvety nose. "You've made a believer out of me, Satch."

Epilogue

Six Months Later

*H*ANNAH SIPPED HER CHAMPAGNE AND WATCHED Adam prowl down the length of the buffet table, his pale-gray suit throwing his dark hair and eyes into compelling contrast. He was in his element as the charming, attentive host, smiling and chatting with their guests. However, she knew he was also checking on every serving bowl and platter to make sure it met his exacting standards. He wanted this day to be perfect for Matt.

She stood under a huge green-and-white striped tent set up in Sharon's north paddock, the grass carefully groomed to remove all vestiges of horse manure. Satchmo had brought them all together, so Matt's whisper pony had to be able to attend the party.

Luckily, the weather had cooperated, giving them a day that was unusually warm for May in the mountains. The slight breeze carried the delicious and varied aromas of the dishes Adam and his staff had slaved over, wafting them to her appreciative nostrils.

"That confounded pony is at it again." Sharon shoved Satchmo away from end of the buffet table, a lettuce leaf dangling from the pony's mouth. "Lynnie! You have to keep a closer eye on this troublemaker."

Lynnie stood up from one of the nearby tables. "You know what an escape artist he is. I had tied him up tight so I could take five minutes to eat."

Hannah laughed and walked over to grab the short lead line hanging from the pony's halter. "I'll supervise him. You finish your lunch, Lynnie."

"Did you hear Satch's latest?" Sharon asked, retrieving her plate from the buffet table. "He decided he liked the hay in Willow's net better than his, so he unlatched his stall door, turned over a water bucket, pushed it over to Willow's stall, and used it as a stool for his front feet so he could reach the hay."

Hannah pulled the pony's chin up to look into his big, dark eyes. "Satchmo, you're going to get yourself exiled from Healing Springs Stables and then where will you live?"

"Don't worry about that," Sharon said. "Everyone at the barn loves him. He keeps us laughing."

Hannah smoothed the pony's thick, cream-colored mane, which someone had decorated with daisies for the occasion. "Thank goodness he recovered fully from the EPM. I was afraid there might be permanent aftereffects."

"Satch knew Matt needed him strong and healthy. Whisper ponies are smart that way," Sharon said, as she went off toward the table where Lynnie sat.

Tim Arbuckle strolled up hand-in-hand with his wife Claire. "Hello, partner." He stooped to give Hannah a kiss on the cheek.

She'd bought into the Sanctuary Veterinary Hospital's practice, signing the final papers a month ago. She was putting down roots in Sanctuary.

Claire released her husband's hand to give Hannah a hug. "I hear Bertha Shanks allowed you to treat Willie's hairballs, so you've been given the ultimate seal of approval."

"I was hoping she'd insist on Tim, but no such luck," Hannah said with a comic grimace.

"She decided that if a U.S. senator owed Hannah an apology, then maybe she did too," Tim said. "Now I'm headed for the buffet."

"For the second time," Claire said over her shoulder.

Hannah chuckled and led Satchmo over to a grassy patch so he could graze.

"Now that's a pretty picture!" Ellen O'Brien, Matt's cousin from Boston, sauntered up with her husband Pat. "You in your floating blue chiffon dress and the pony with flowers in his hair." Satchmo lifted his head to sniff at her pockets, and she tickled the pony's velvet nose. "Who prettied up your hair, Satch, my boy-o?"

"I suspect it was Julia Castillo, the red-haired artist who wanted to sketch you at Thanksgiving," Hannah said. "She was picking daisies right before this party started."

"That Thanksgiving seems like it was both long ago and just yesterday," Pat said, his silver-sandy hair gleaming above his green sweater vest. "We flew down here thankful that we'd get to see our young cousin and got the meal of a lifetime."

"It was quite a feast," Hannah agreed.

It had been quite a crowd too. Adam was so overflowing with gratitude and happiness after the drama with Matt and Satchmo that he'd wanted to share his good fortune. So he had issued last-minute invitations to the Arbuckles, Julia and Paul, and Sharon. And he'd left his staff to run The Aerie while he cooked nonstop for two days.

Ellen laid a hand on Hannah's arm. "You've been a wonderful catalyst for Adam and Matt. I can see the difference in both of them just since that Thanksgiving Day. They're so much more at ease with themselves and each other."

"Thank you. I think we've all come a long way," Hannah said.

"Okay, I'll take the little rascal now," Lynnie said, taking the lead line from Hannah.

The O'Briens left to sample the buffet. Hannah spotted Matt talking with Julia and Paul and ambled over to join them. Trace sat beside Matt with the boy's hand resting on his head. The German Shepherd had become a two-man dog since the night he'd tracked Matt through the woods.

"I was just admiring the colors of Matt's boutonniere," Julia said. "He tells me it's also full of symbolism."

Hannah had wanted to give her two men something meaningful for today, so she'd consulted with Lucy Porterfield, The Aerie's hostess and floral arranger, about choosing the flowers. As she'd pinned them on their lapels this morning, she'd explained what each blossom meant.

Matt tucked his chin in to look down at the petals glowing against his navy suit. "I know this blue one is rosemary for remembering my mom." A shadow of sorrow crossed his face, and Hannah's heart twisted a little before he broke into a grin. "And the yellow one is to remind me that no matter how obnoxious I am, you'll still put up with me."

Hannah laughed. "That's gorse, which means love in all seasons. I figured it would take something powerful to get us through the teenaged years." She pointed to the other yellow flower. "This is celandine, which promises joys to come. There will be lots of those in your life." Hannah's voice cracked a little as her emotions welled up.

She'd used all the same flowers for Adam with one addition: a blue starflower for courage. Because he was the bravest man she'd ever known.

Suddenly needing to find him, Hannah looked toward the buffet table and discovered he was already gazing in her direction. He smiled a private smile that went straight to her core. Then he lifted his hand and brushed his fingertips over his boutonniere in a caress. A delicious shiver danced down her spine.

"You must be very flattered." Paul's voice broke through her distraction.

"I'm sorry," Hannah said, flustered as she caught the knowing smile on Julia's face. "What?"

"Matt tells us he wants to follow in your footsteps and become a veterinarian," Paul said.

Hannah felt the same little thrill of pride as when Matt had first announced his new ambition. "I'm both honored and delighted that getting into vet school has given him incentive to do his homework."

Matt was giving her a look of mock long-suffering when the sound of silverware tapping against crystal penetrated the general hum of conversation.

The crowd grew quiet as all eyes turned toward the sound. For a moment, she could hear the more distant sounds of the barn: the clank of water buckets, the thud of hooves, and a soft whinny. Then she focused on where Adam stood in the clear space between the buffet and the dining tables, tapping a fork against his water glass.

"Matt, Hannah, would you join me?" Adam said, with a gesture of invitation. "Lynnie, could you bring Satchmo up too?"

Matt looked at Hannah with a question in his eyes. She shrugged in answer. Adam hadn't told her he was going to make a speech, although it shouldn't have surprised her. He was both proud of and humbled by his new relationship with his son.

As Hannah came up to Adam, he put his arm around her waist and moved her to his left side. Matt stood to his right, having taken Satchmo's lead line from Lynnie. Trace wedged himself between Hannah and Adam, his long pink tongue hanging out as he panted in the spring warmth.

"This party is for you and Matt, not me," Hannah whispered, uncomfortable at being the focus of the guests gathering in front of them.

"Without you, there would be no party," he murmured back into her ear, pressing her against his side for a moment before releasing her.

Shifting his glass to his left hand, he put his other arm around his son's shoulders. Hannah turned slightly so she could see how Adam's face lit up with his newfound awe at being a true father to Matt. The boy's blue eyes blazed with an answering feeling as he looked up at his dad.

Adam swept his gaze across the guests, silencing the last bit of chatter, before he began, his voice vibrating with the power of his emotions. "I wanted to share this celebration with everyone here because you form the community that made it possible for me to be a father to the son I love so much. There is not a single person . . . or animal"—he paused to acknowledge Satchmo and Trace as the crowd chuckled—"under this tent who did not contribute in some way to the journey that brought Matt to me. My gratitude can never be adequately expressed in words. Which is why I cooked for you."

Quiet laughter rose from the gathered guests, but Hannah knew he was only partially joking.

Adam turned to look at Matt and raised his water glass. "I'd like to thank my son for doing me the honor of taking my last name on this happy occasion of his legal adoption. Please drink a toast to Matthew McNally Bosch."

"Dad," Matt muttered under his breath, but he was smiling, one hand buried in Satchmo's mane. "I guess it sounds pretty cool when you say it out loud."

Applause swelled to fill the tent as Adam pulled his son into a hug for a long moment. Hannah felt a happy constriction in her chest while she swiped at the tears spilling down her cheeks.

Adam slid his glass onto the buffet table before snaking his arm back around her waist.

"Don't make a speech about me," she pleaded in an undertone. Her press conference in Chicago had convinced her she wasn't cut out to be in front of an audience.

When she tried to step back, his arm became a steel barrier. "Humor me," he murmured before he raised his voice. "Hannah is the other most important person in my life. She believed in me when I no longer believed in myself, and she had the courage to tell me the truth I didn't want to hear."

Little murmurs of approval rose from the spectators. Hannah felt a blush climb her cheeks. She was torn between the love she felt for the man saying these wonderful things about her and her embarrassment at having everyone else hear them.

He wasn't finished though. "I'm a lucky man to have someone who loves me enough to do that, and I want to make sure I have her forever."

Hannah's nerves gave a jolt and her gaze flew to his face. He was looking down at her with such intensity she forgot about the guests. She thought he was going to kiss her, but then he dropped his arm and went down on his knee in the spring-green grass.

She gasped as he took one of her hands between both of his. "Hannah, I love you with every fiber of my soul. Will you make Matt and me the happiest men alive and stay with us for the rest of our lives?"

She wanted to laugh and weep at the same time. She looked down into the deep pools of his eyes, and what she saw made her rush out her answer. "Yes! Yes! Of course, yes!"

Applause and whistles reverberated through the tent.

Wrapping her other hand around his wrist, she tried to pull him up so she could sink her fingers into his thick, black hair and lean into his strong body.

"I'm not done yet." He freed his hands but remained at her feet, reaching into his pocket and retrieving a black velvet jeweler's box. Pressing the spring that opened it, he took out a ring with a blue stone that caught and threw glints of sunlight like sparkling confetti.

She gasped again as he took her hand and slid the ring onto her finger.

"It's too beautiful!" she breathed.

Finally rising to his feet, he pulled her against him and bent his head to find her mouth. She stopped him with the tips of her fingers against his lips, still not quite believing he had just proposed to her in public. "Did you ever worry I might say no in front of all these people?" she murmured.

"No," he said. "I was afraid you might slug me."

She smiled up at him. "The amazing thing is I'm glad they're all watching us right now because I want everyone in Sanctuary to know how much I love you." With that, she cupped her hand behind his head and met his lips with hers. As her body melted into his, a heat that both scorched and soothed blazed to life inside her. The whistles began again.

"Dad?"

Adam lifted his head and Hannah glanced sideways to find Matt tugging at his father's sleeve with a grin. "I'd like to kiss my mom-to-be too."

Hannah thought she would explode with joy.

Discussion Questions

1) Adam's struggle with his alcoholism is an ongoing fight against a disease that threatens to consume him. The negative aspects are obvious, but does anything positive come from his battle? Is it true that what doesn't kill us makes us stronger? Do you know anyone who is an alcoholic and has overcome it?

2) Hannah and Adam are both running from their past when they meet. Is that why they are initially drawn to each other? Do you think their relationship could have worked if they didn't have the shared understanding of a dark past that affected their present?

3) Food plays a major role in the novel as Adam expresses his feelings towards Hannah, Matt, and the Sanctuary community by cooking for them. Do you think he uses food in lieu of making actual connections with people, or does it enhance his interactions with others? Do you have a nonverbal way of communicating your feelings to other people? What is it?

4) Matt forms a unique relationship with Hannah even though she is not his blood relation. Why is it sometimes easier to open up to a stranger than to a family member?

5) The animals in the book are as much a part of the plot as the human characters. Satchmo and Trace play important roles in getting their human companions to communicate with each other about feelings that otherwise might have remained unspoken. Do you have any experience with animals breaking down barriers? Do you believe Satchmo faked his injury in the climax in order to bring Hannah, Adam, and Matt together?

6) The town of Sanctuary is a character with a personality all its own. How do you think the setting affects the storyline? Would it be possible for the story to have taken place elsewhere, such as a city? How would that have affected the characters and their relationships?

7) Matt is upset when he thinks Adam is going to send him off to live with his distant relatives. Why do you think it was so important to him that he stay with the father he barely knew? Is it that Adam is a connection to Matt's lost mother, or does the fact that Adam is Matt's biological father mean something more than just shared genes?

8) Do you enjoying reading about recurring characters like Julia, Paul, Claire, and Tim, who appear in earlier books in the Whisper Horse series? Which couple is your favorite, and why?

Acknowledgments

WRITING APPEARS TO BE A SOLITARY PURSUIT, YET I could not create my books without the help of a whole battalion of talented, terrific people. Any errors are entirely my own. My heartfelt thanks to:

JoVon Sotak, my brilliant and lovely editor, who guides my work through the complex process of turning a manuscript into a book.

Jessica Poore and the Author Relations team, an incredible group of professionals who provide every kind of support for this lucky author.

Jane Dystel and Miriam Goderich, my extraordinary agents, who are always in my corner. You don't know how much that means to me.

Andrea Hurst, my superb developmental editor and fellow animal lover, who applies both sensitivity and a tough eye to make my books better, faster, and stronger.

Michael Ryder and Tara Doernberg, my copyeditors, who devote their keen and meticulous minds to making sure I get all the details right while not repeating myself.

Heather Mann, my proofreader, who polishes my galleys to a diamond sparkle.

Laura Klynstra, my cover designer, who perfectly captured all the romance and atmosphere of my book with her stunning design. Thank you for the horse on the back!

The staff of Barcelona Wine Bar in Greenwich, Connecticut, where area director Herman Allenson, assistant chef director Adam Greenberg, and sous-chef James Burge allowed me to interrupt them in the middle of their dinner rush to ask my endless questions. Adam and The Aerie owe you a great debt of gratitude.

Rebecca Theodorou, who helped me with all things veterinary and gave my readers the provocative discussion questions at the end of this book.

Lynn Scott, who loaned Adam her black German Shepherd, Trace, and who always believed in my dream.

Jeff, Rebecca, and Loukas, whose support and love keep me sane, even when I'm on deadline. I couldn't do this without you.

About the Author

Phil Cantor, 2003

Although she now lives in the suburbs of New Jersey, Nancy was born and raised in the mountains of West Virginia. A graduate of Princeton University, she majored in English Literature and Creative Writing. Her senior thesis was a volume of original poetry.

Her contemporary romances have won several awards, including the Golden Leaf, the Gayle Wilson Award of Excellence, and the Aspen Gold.

She enjoys vacations to exotic locales (like Niagara Falls and Philadelphia) and shares those with readers on "From the Garret," her own personal blog. She loves animals, having grown up with five dogs, three cats, a pony, and various wild creatures the cats brought home. She has a phobia about driving across bridges and flying.

Nancy lives in a Victorian house with her husband and two mismatched dogs, and cheers loudly for the New Jersey Devils hockey team.

To read excerpts and find out about upcoming releases, please visit Nancy's website: www.NancyHerkness.com. Nancy also loves to connect with fans online:

Facebook: https://www.facebook.com/nancyherkness
Blog: http://fromthegarret.wordpress.com/
Twitter: @NancyHerkness